Praise for...

Tears of Min Brock

Some of the best stories I can remember are those that take me out of my own existence and insert me into a world I have never known. I get to become a part of the story and the adventure and excitement also becomes a part of my own. In *Tears of Min Brock* by J. E. Lowder, I have again found one of those fascinating epic fantasy worlds that are daunting and dangerous, yet broodingly beautiful as well.

- BlogCritics Books

J.E. Lowder has created an intricate fantasy world full of dispair and darkness as well as hope and luminous beauty.

- Examiner.com

Lowder pulls you into a world of chaos and hope. You can almost feel the breeze and smell the foliage as you walk with the main characters through this well written story. I give it far more than the usual five stars!

- Opus 'N' Pen

Tears of Min Brock is going to become a classic right up there with The Lord of the Rings.

- Vic's Media Room

Not too many books can truly be described as epic. *Narnia, Lord of the Rings*, Pullman's *Dark Materials*...and now *Tears of Min Brock*. This is one book that clearly deserves the 'epic' description.

- Book Lovers Paradise

Tears of Min Brock is a heartfelt story of epic proportions with two loveable characters. It is an epic in every sense.

- Sift Book Reviews

Praise for...

Martyr's Moon

Lowder has gilded (his characters) with both strength and flaws, creating a realism that is difficult to deny. His world is dark and deadly, yet holds a sprinkling of hope and light that is beginning to thrust its ways into being. If you are a fan of magic and hope, as well as fierce, epic battles between good and evil, you will love this work.

- Seattle PI

With this novel you find yourself walking through a fantasy world beyond compare. It's astounding. Lowder is a *show, not tell*, type of author. You don't read this story, but rather watch the story unfold before you. He paints a brilliant picture of his scenery.

- Pure Jonel

...the action propelled me forward and I found pages of this book melting away as I read on.

- Literary R&R

Lowder is an amazing storyteller. He demands, simply with action packed words and haunting imagery, that even a dense reader like me pick up his work and keep reading.

- Julie Arduini.com

MARTYR'S
MOON

MARTYR'S MOON

J.E. LOWDER

WordCrafts

To my children.
For allowing me to tell bedtime stories
that birthed books and dreams.

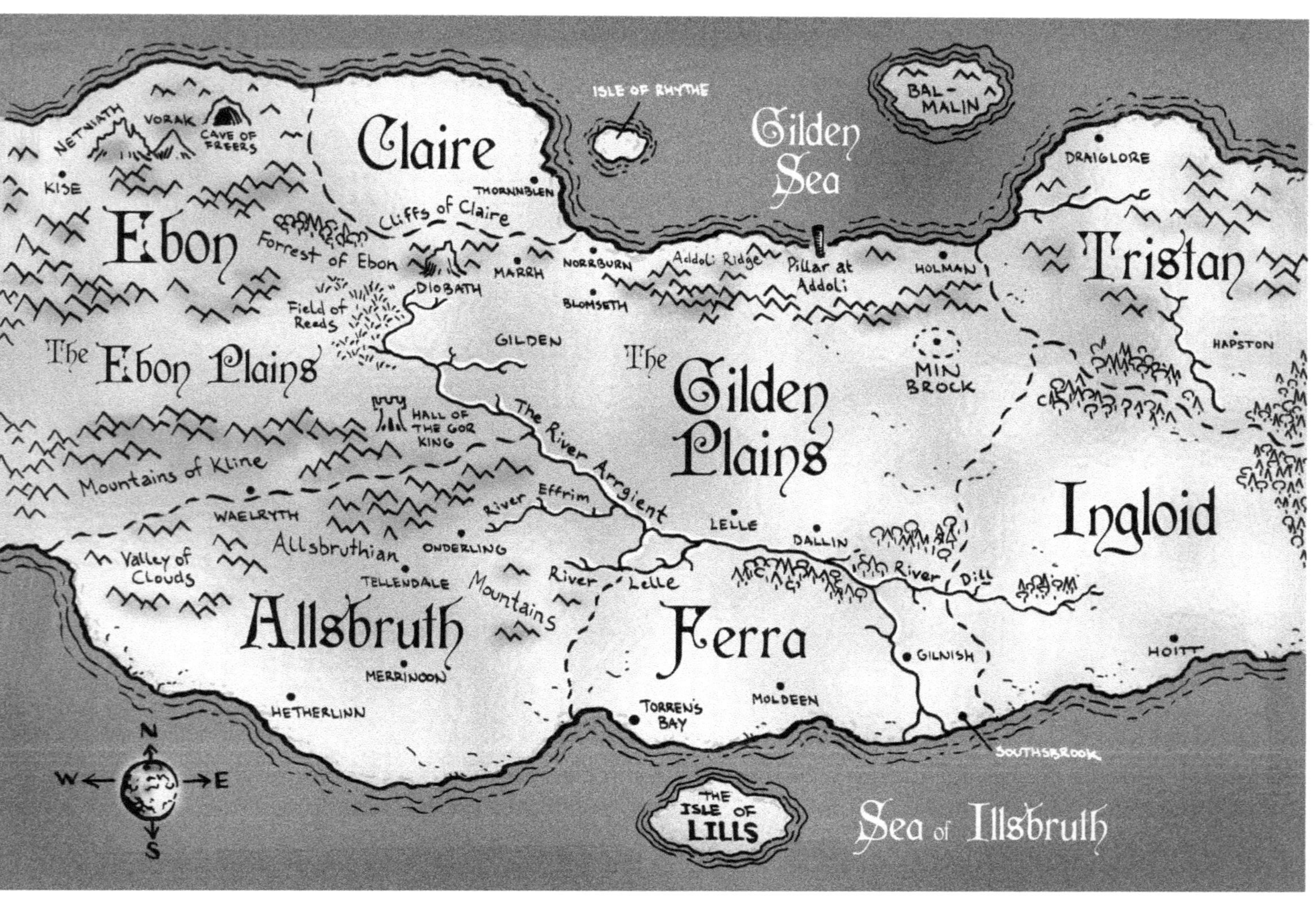

NETNIATH
VORAK
CAVE OF FREERS
KISE
Claire
THORNNBLEN
Cliffs of Claire
Ebon
Forrest of Ebon
MARRH
DIOBATH
NORRBURN
BLOMSETH
Addoli Ridge
Pillar at Addoli
HOLMAN
Field of Reeds
The Ebon Plains
GILDEN
The Gilden Plains
MIN BROCK
ISLE OF RHYTHE
Gilden Sea
BAL-MALIN
DRAIGLORE
Tristan
HAPSTON
HALL OF THE GOR KING
The River Arrgient
Mountains of Kline
WAELRYTH
River Effrim
Allsbruthian
ONDERLING
Valley of Clouds
TELLENDALE
Mountains
River Lelle
LELLE
DALLIN
River Dill
Ingloid
Allsbruth
MERRINOON
Ferra
GILNISH
HOITT
HETHERLINN
TORREN'S BAY
MOLDEEN
SOUTHSBROOK
W
N
E
S
THE ISLE OF LILLS
Sea of Illsbruth

Forgotten Oracle

Whisper sail upon spring's scent and deliver argent tale,
Parchments white, like doves take flight, and soar beyond the veil.
Bell-like tones of Addoli wage war against the drone,
Then return to me, sweet melody, but dare not come alone.

Upon a map blind eyes behold what was becomes no more,
A shimmering veil of fathomless depth becomes a timeless door.
Sage and prophet have reasoned mad, yet slaves are crowned king,
For beyond the veil the lark hails, "Drink from my deepest spring."

Chapter 1

The War of Winds

The Cauldron hurled its fury at Claire in the form of a storm. Icy winds swept a flotilla of gray clouds eastward, and when the squall reached Claire, it attacked. Dark clouds meshed with white and churned like a raging river above the orange sands. Wisps of gray floated below the tempest as if to spy for any sign of counterattack, while dark daggers of mist cut into their enemy's fluffy-white flanks. Billows of black swarmed upward and imprisoned ivory clouds or bowled over strands unable to flee.

The sky darkened and finger-like clouds dropped from the Cauldron's gale. Spinning like tops, the gray blurs dropped to the desert where they wriggled like newborn serpents to be free of their eggs. They danced and jumped and kicked up clouds of orange dust as a taunt to the King of Claire.

Thunder exploded over the noisy winds, and lighting sliced open the blackness.

The silvery flash illuminated Romlin atop a jutting precipice. He braced himself against the warring winds and noted that there were two aromas that battled for him as well: sulfur and swill disoriented him, while a flowering meadow countered to revitalize his senses.

Romlin pulled out his map. The winds tore at it like panthers. He clutched it with both hands and found what he was looking for.

Claire.

"You tricked me," he shouted to the battling winds. "I should have known better than to believe with my heart."

With the map in hand, he struggled to where Elabea sat in his shield. He shoved it in her face.

"I watched the map disappear as we neared the border," he lamented. "I hoped it was a trick of the Cauldron...but it's not. This is all *my* fault."

Elabea scanned the horizon as the winds whip-cracked her hair about her face, but she had also given up hope that Claire existed. She was even beginning to doubt the stories her rusk had told her. Overcome with emotions and loss, her head dropped. She sank back down in the shield, clutched the dead rusk, and rocked back and forth.

A familiar sound averted Romlin's attention and he focused on the drone's dark, sinister pitch. Like the raging winds, it was stronger and louder than anything he had experienced before. He felt as if a coat of iron had been draped over his shoulders. He strained under the weight but felt himself weakening.

Anxious for help, he searched the black clouds for any sign of Manno Vox - nothing. He battled against both the drone and the winds. He drew his sword. He knew that unless the book was open the sword would not glow, but he was desperate. He stared at the silvery blade, wishing and hoping with all his being that it would radiate light. But like his heart it remained cold, dark and lifeless.

Nevertheless, he raised it defiantly into the squall.

"So *this* is our reward?" he barked as he shook his weapon. "You lead us to this place and abandon us to the winds? We deny home and family only to end up alone...on a cliff? You promised so much. If you have the courage, then show yourself. Come face me in battle."

"*How ironic,*" a whisper answered, surprisingly audible despite the storm's raucous squall. "*I recall a summer long ago when you were given another promise that never came to pass. Who spoke such deception?*"

Memories of his childhood flashed and exploded in Romlin's mind.

"*Ah, yes, now I remember: your father.*"

With that the whisper slithered back into the winds.

Romlin's boyhood emotions swirled as tumultuous as the windstorm, and like the serpentine thunderheads kicking up clouds of sand, his anger stirred up his troubled thoughts. He glared at the orange desert and released his storm of rage toward the King of Claire.

"You *are* like my father: A liar!"

Cold winds lapped up his words like a ravenous dog.

"I was starting to believe in you," he shouted. "I was beginning to listen, *really* listen to the stories Elabea told. But now..."

The words trailed off and died. Romlin walked to where the book sat and kicked it. Around and around it spun, stopping just short of the cliff's edge. The cover rose and fell as if disembodied specters battled to turn the pages. Despite his anger, the flapping cover caught his attention. He set aside his fury long enough to study the book with the eyes of a seasoned hunter, and discovered a secret.

The winds are fighting over the book. But why?

The whisper returned.

"*Are you not deserving of so much more? Kick the book off the cliff. End the pain.*"

"If you are truly as powerful as your stories claim, then show yourself and fight me. I don't care what happens to me anymore."

"*Such courage. Such resolve. You will be rewarded greatly.*"

"Lies! You promised so much more."

"*I promised no such thing. You assumed and presumed.*"

"Dare to show yourself."

"To one such as you? You are indeed an image of irony, for you sound as if you are growing mad...just like that certain someone from your past."

Romlin pictured his father in cottage Number 7 babbling about this and that, day after day, season after season. Next, he envisioned Mithe taunting him about the truth to his father's madness brought about by the defeat at Min Brock.

His shame clouded over and his anger billowed like the storm that raged around him on the cliff. Like a thunderclap, his emotions exploded and he swung his blade through the air.

"Yes, I see it is true: You are your father's son. Hopeless. Defeated. Dreamer. Fool."

The drone's weight intensified and the stench of rotting swill filled his nostrils. Anguish met him with every memory of his journey, at every turn of his heart. He recalled his bout with the gor that nearly cost both him and Elabea their lives. He remembered the doubt he felt trying to live up to the new name Manno Vox had given him. He thought of the disappearing map and how he hid the knowledge from Elabea.

Failure was a pit and shame swallowed him whole. As he crept toward the book, he focused on one thought alone: *It is time to end the pain.*

The whisper encouraged him, its tone like a lark in spring.

"I have not come to torment, but to offer hope. You have been deceived by a whisper that imitates my greatness. Would you care to learn more?"

Romlin nodded.

"Then seize the book and step to the edge."

He picked it up and dangled his toes over the cliff.

"Good! I see you hunger for the truth and for freedom. Everyone desires such gifts but few are willing to pay the price to hunt for such treasure. You are a seeker, and so I honor your quest, offering you more than the deceiver ever could. I promise life. The deceiver, as you have discovered, only offers lies. Thus his title: the Only."

Romlin studied the ground far below. Enormous boulders lay scattered at the cliff's base. The thought of falling did not frighten him. It seemed as if the rocks were cheering him on, urging him to jump. He envisioned them as a serene river or a pile of down blankets, offering pleasure...peace...rest.

The drone intensified its weight on Romlin and his shame became unbearable. The whisper continued in soothing tones.

"Do you hear the rocks calling to you? Yes, I believe you do. Their voices confirm that I promise you life, freedom, hope, and joy. Jump."

Romlin looked at Elabea. She hugged herself, rocking back and forth, oblivious to his inner turmoil. Full of self-loathing, he concluded that she no longer needed him, that she would be better off if he were gone. After all, it was his decision to conceal the map from her. He was a part of the monstrous illusion in the war of whispers. His actions were the catalyst for the rusk's death and Elabea's anguish.

With the winds whistling about him, Romlin clutched the book to his chest and prepared to launch himself to the rocks below.

Warm winds exploded against him with such force that he was knocked away from the precipice.

"See?" the whisper pointed out. *The deceiver desires for you to stay and suffer more. You are his puppet. You are merely a game piece he moves here and there in life. Be free. Fight the winds and jump. Claim your independence. Kill the shame and end the pain. Become the man your father never could be."*

Romlin battled back to the ledge as the winds of Ebon and Claire contended for his life. Exhausted, his grip on the book loosed and it dropped from his hand. The cover flew open and its pages flapped like the wings of a bird in desperate flight. Once again, his hunting instincts took over, and he examined the anomaly with patience and logic.

The whisper returned, urgent now.

"Ignore the deceiver's book. Jump. End the pain. Live!"

Romlin's despair waned as he observed the flapping book, and in a brilliant flash of clarity, he realized that the winds, whispers and scents all battled for him, just as they warred for the book.

But who is my ally and who is my enemy?

He cast a glance back at Elabea, but this time he saw her in a different light. She was his friend, perhaps even more. He was responsible for her. Despite his feelings of failure, to leave her now would be worse, infinitely worse. Quick vignettes of treasured times together flashed in his mind: climbing the oak; her wondrous laugh; watching her sleep; her eyes that made him feel weak.

Romlin backed away from the ledge and clinched his fists.

"I don't know who or what you are," he shouted to the whisper. "Nor do I know what's real and true anymore. I may have failed. I may have been foolish to believe. But I will *not* abandon Elabea. Nothing matters anymore except getting her home. At least I can succeed in that."

"So be it," the whisper jeered. Its tone was no longer comforting and gentle, but menacing and dark, *"I have other means at my disposal."*

Fresh noises entered the fray. Romlin instinctively spun around to face whatever neared.

The pursuing Ebonites emerged from the woods.

Chapter 2

Steel Deception

Romlin's heart skipped a beat and his jaw drew tight as he sized up his enemy. Five warriors stood side by side on the cliff, blocking their escape into the woods. Their dark eyes drilled into Romlin's eyes. They stood motionless, as if they too were sizing him up or were waiting for orders to attack. The tallest and most formidable of the warriors had his sword drawn, and based upon his previous encounters with the Ebonites, Romlin concluded he was their commander.

Romlin knew that Ebonites never accepted surrender, so he glanced back at the orange sands and darkening skies, hoping against hope that the Only or Manno Vox would mystically appear to fight.

Nothing but the dancing clouds greeted his gaze.

He faced the warriors. Agitated at being abandoned, he nevertheless set his mind to defending Elabea. He slid his hand over his sword's hilt and vowed in his heart to battle them single-handedly, and if need be, to the death.

"So," the Ebonite commander shouted, his black beard and hair whipping around his helmet. "You're the one who killed our warriors at Waelryth? You're but a boy, and a weak one at that."

"Perhaps. But I'll cut you down as I did your comrades," Romlin replied.

"Really?" the commander sneered. "I read your tracks, *boy*. They tell the story of a child running away; scampering like a dog. Your story is full of fear."

The commander gave his men an order.

"This waif is mine; get the girl."

Romlin turned his attention to Elabea. Her back was to the Ebonites and she continued to rock, oblivious to the danger.

Surely she's heard them, he thought as he edged back toward her. *Why doesn't she run?*

"Look," the commander roared with laughter. "The boy's just like an Allsbruthian: protecting the weak."

"I'm not afraid of you," Romlin declared.

He yanked his blade out of its sheath and gripped it with all his might.

The commander's eyes darted to Romlin's sword and then back to his face. He smirked.

"You hold a blade like a man, but your story from Waelryth says otherwise. Shame and cowardice are your masters."

"Elabea," Romlin shouted without taking his eyes off the warriors. "Run to me. Now's your chance."

Elabea finally stopped rocking and looked up at him. Her face was ashen, but it showed neither alarm nor fear. Rising calmly, she stood beside the shield with the rusk clutched to her bosom.

"Yes, Elabea. Run," the commander taunted in a sing-song mocking voice. "My men need a good game of chase. In fact, retrieve your book, little storyteller, and tell my men a tale."

The warriors chortled.

Romlin gripped the blade's hilt tighter, his muscles taut, his feet set, ready to attack or to defend.

"You see," the commander continued as he swirled his sword. "We do not fear your book, for the stories have been a lie. There is no King of Claire as there is no Claire. We destroyed them long ago in the Dark War. You live in a world full of nothingness. Even a fool can see that from upon this cliff."

"We don't need stories or the Only," Romlin countered. "I'll fight you myself. Then you will see if I am a boy, or a man."

Fueled by the power of the gwyr and Cauldron, the Ebonites' evil laughter echoed all the way down to the desert.

"You are no match for us, *boy*," the commander snapped with a threatening thrust of his weapon. "The Cauldron has filled us with the power of the gwyr. Behold!"

He signaled for one of his men to approach. The warrior carried a dark, canvas bag in his hand and took a step toward Elabea. He opened the top of the bag.

"We bear a gift for you," he sneered. "A rusk."

The animal poked its head out and sniffed the air. Romlin blinked his eyes in disbelief, wondering why an Ebonite would carry such a creature. And then he realized their scheme.

"Elabea," he warned. "Stand fast. It's a trick."

Elabea, who was so overcome with grief, was awestruck. "Look, Romlin," she said dreamily as she stepped forward. "A...rusk."

With his free hand, Romlin drew his dagger and hurled it end-over-end at the bag. The blade sliced the warrior's hand and he dropped the bag, breaking the gwyr's spell. Rolling out onto the cliff was the severed head of the Ebonite from Waelryth.

Shocked at the trickery, Elabea raced through the stormy winds to hide behind Romlin.

"Enough banter," the commander shouted as he marched toward them. "It is time for our metal to talk."

Romlin charged and swung his double-handed blade. Metal struck metal; yellow sparks arched through the air. The commander pushed Romlin's blade away with ease and swung back, just missing his stomach. Romlin counterattacked, but the commander again parried the blow.

"Is that all you have, little man?" he snickered. "I was expecting much more. I've sparred with Ebonite girls who hit harder."

The Ebonite struck like a snake, his quick blow nicking Romlin's left shoulder. Wincing at the pain, Romlin backed away, trying to close the wound with one hand while holding his sword in the other. Warm blood oozed through his fingers.

"Do you smell that?" the commander shouted to his men as he sniffed the air. "First blood!" he roared, raising his sword victoriously into the air.

As the Ebonites celebrated, Romlin spied an opportunity. The commander's raised arm exposed an area unprotected by armor. With lightning reflexes, he charged forward and thrust the tip into the exposed flesh. The commander let out a short cry and stumbled back.

"Smell that, Elabea? *Second* blood!"

"Enough play time, *little boy*," the commander barked, still stunned by the unexpected resistance. He pressed forward. "Now is the time for you to die like the Allsbruthian dog that you are."

He delivered a powerful overhead blow. Romlin raised his sword. Metal collided and a spark singed the warrior's beard. Enraged, the Ebonite started swinging his sword like he was trying to topple a tree: right flank followed by left, then right again. The attacks were so swift and powerful that Romlin's only option was to parry and retreat closer to the cliff's edge. As the rain of steel fell, Romlin weakened from the fight and the loss of blood.

Under the barrage of metal, Romlin watched another Ebonite walking toward his magical shield. Another strike, and Romlin dropped to a knee. He thought about calling out one last time to the King of Claire, but the drone and nauseating smells attacked and ripped apart his last vestige of hope.

"How does it feel fighting a real man," the Ebonite snarled as he slammed his sword down again.

Warding off the blow, Romlin glanced toward Elabea. She was walking toward the cliff's edge.

"No," he cried out in desperation, fearing she would take her own life.

"Better to jump then fall into our hands," the Ebonite commander laughed as his sword descended from overhead.

Elabea stood at the edge of the precipice. The winds pushed and pulled her thin frame with ease. She looked out over the vast desert of Claire. As she clutched the rusk, the drone and scents enveloped her senses.

"Don't do it," Romlin pleaded as more steel fell.

Her lifeless eyes met his and his heart sank. He had seen her look like this before, when Quinn had a night of drink and in the morning, lashed out at her with his rage. She was lost. She was without hope, and he knew there was nothing he could do to help.

Her gaze left his and shifted to the warriors who crept toward her. Despite their threat, her expression remained unchanged, as if she had not seen them or if she did, she no longer cared. Her eyes swept back to stare at Claire.

In spite of the barrage of metal, and despite his tirade toward Claire, Romlin found himself drawn toward the book. He knew that it was their only hope, but when his eyes fell upon the cover, the drone and ghoulish scents intensified their attacks. He looked away to make them stop. As he deflected another blow, he caught the scent of spring and the invisible attackers fled.

The commander hammered Romlin with all of his might, sending him sprawling on his back. Romlin prepared to defend himself, but spared a quick glance at Elabea.

The Ebonites were closer; nearly upon her.

His eyes flickered back to the book, but that summoned the drone and aromas that once more attacked his senses.

The drone and cold winds fear the book. The thought flitted across his consciousness. *But if Claire doesn't exist, and it's useless, then why bother with it? And why do the warriors creep toward Elabea as if she were a wild beast?*

The answer flashed in his mind like sunbeams through a thunderhead. *One only fears what one knows to be true.*

Renewed strength filled his weary muscles as he deflected yet another sword blow.

"Perhaps," the whisper countered. *"But only a moment ago you cursed such tales. How is it possible that you, a traitor, would be helped now?"*

The whisper's accusation sliced open his resolve. He doubted. Shame and guilt once more danced a jig across his passions. Yet, in his desperation, he shouted the truth to Elabea.

"The book. The stories. They're *true.*"

Sensing a shift in the balance of power, the commander paused in the midst of his attack and glanced at his men.

"Seize her! Destroy the book," he roared, his voice suddenly filled with desperation.

"If the Only and Claire don't exist," Romlin challenged, "then why bother with the book?"

"We fear it not," he countered, slamming his sword down in retaliation.

"I never said you feared the book. Yet your confession confirms what I suspected to be true."

The commander struck again. Romlin grimaced as steel met steel, the strain was incredible: fatigue cramped his muscles; sweating palms made the hilt slip in his grip; blood from his shoulder wound pooled at his feet. Time was running out.

"Open it," Romlin shouted to Elabea as he managed to ward off yet another blow. "For the sake of Claire, open the book!"

Elabea glanced at the flapping pages. They called to her, yearning for her to discover their mysteries. She placed the rusk inside an outer pocket and bent down to retrieve it.

As Romlin battled, the scent of flowers reminded him of their miraculous journey: Manno Vox, the flying shield, the glowing sword... Despite the doubts he still had about Claire, the truth he discovered about the book gave him the courage to hope in the impossible once more.

"Hurry," Romlin urged her.

Elabea held the closed book in her palms while the winds battled over its pages. She looked dreamily at Romlin and for the first time, noticed that he was wounded and lying on his back. Blades collided but she heard no report. Romlin's lips moved but the winds snuffed out his words. She felt as if she were in her dreamworld, unable to talk, unable to touch, swimming through tranquil water that soothed her deepest pain.

She looked out at Claire. The black sky and turbulent clouds made the sands appear rust-colored. Despite the horrors around her, she could not find it within herself to open the book. She enjoyed the serenity of her dreamworld. She had found the peace she had longed for.

"Open it," Romlin shouted between blows. "You must *believe*. The book is our only hope."

Hope?

She shook her head. Hope had been wounded when the rusk died. It perished when she beheld the orange sands that had once been the shining kingdom of Claire.

She crept toward the edge and studied with longing the rocks far below. She smelled a repugnant stench, and despite its foul smell, it made the thought of jumping feel, somehow, pleasurable.

As quickly as the stench enveloped her, the strong aroma of flowers made her reminisce about her meadow and oak. Joy flooded her as she recalled the times high in its branches when she dreamt of being anywhere but Allsbruth and being anyone but Elabea. She became elated when the scents reminded her of the night she saw Manno Vox and found his crossbow shaft the next morning. The flowery fragrance reminded her of the whisper that called her name, and the bliss she experienced even in so brief an encounter.

"Elabea." The familiar whisper from Claire snapped her back to reality. *"Tell a tale."*

She took a tiny step away from the edge.

Another whisper came. It sounded identical to the first and it swirled around the other whisper like a bird of prey, fighting for domination.

"I am near," the new whisper encouraged. *"Be still and I will deliver you."*

Her face wrinkled in confusion. This was the first time she had heard both whispers simultaneously. Which was the true whisper? Had she been following the wrong one all along?

The approaching Ebonites abandoned their cautious approach and started to run.

"The book!" Romlin shouted from his deathbed of stone, *"Open it."*

"Do not fear," the first whisper called.

Unexplainable peace soothed Elabea's wounded soul, but her anger and pain were too great. She pushed the first whisper aside.

"Faithful you are," the new whisper encouraged. *"Romlin speaks the truth. I am near."*

She slowly emerged from her dreamworld, rising through the watery depths to once more see and hear all that was in the world around her. She noticed the eerie drone and how its dull numbness covered her like a shroud. She heard Romlin's cries and the clashing swords, and it was in this state of being that the first whisper called to her again.

"Elabea. My delight."

The familiar refrain shooed away the Cauldron's drone, as if it were but a fly buzzing about a teacake. Awakened, she stretched out her hand toward the book's cover, but the winds, drone, and foul scents attacked with redoubled fury. Her hand froze in midair while her mind spiraled in confusion. Despair frothed madly, slashing at her every thought. Worthlessness serenaded her with its dreadful tune. Loneliness tore at her savagely.

All seemed lost when a gentle rush of balmy air chased away her attackers, and her mind became hers once more.

The Ebonites, almost within striking distance, lunged. Elabea opened the book.

Thunder boomed and a bolt of lightning struck the closest warrior dead.

"Seize the book," the commander ordered the others as he continued pummeling Romlin.

Elabea closed her eyes, and just as the other Ebonites dove for her, she shot up into the air. Outstretched arms missed their mark, and the warriors fell headfirst off the cliff, screaming and flaying their arms wildly about.

Hovering above the cliff, Elabea opened her eyes. An odd sensation, like the one she sometimes got in Hetherlinn when someone was spying on her, turned her attention toward Claire. A sunbeam burst through the dark clouds and illuminated a small portion of the orange desert. Visible for the first time were the remnants of two enormous stone columns. White, but weathered by wind and age, they looked like the gateways into a once great city. A faint smile pursed her lips as she relaxed and drew in a deep breath. Shutting her eyes, she recalled the rusk's words to her shortly before his death.

"Elabea. He lives. The King of Claire lives!"

Tears swelled as she remembered his sacrifice.

She began her tale.

Romlin's sword shimmered from dull silver to a fiery orange. Witnessing power return to his blade caused Romlin's tenacity to ignite. The commander swung, but Romlin deflected the blow, then rose to mount his own attack. Romlin's eyes narrowed with determination while the commander's widened in surprise. A powerful downward hack shattered the Ebonite's blade into pieces. Romlin pressed forward and swung again. The commander blocked the blow with the remnant of his weapon but it exploded into fragments. Romlin focused his attack on the Ebonite's armor, hacking it apart, piece by piece.

"You fools," the commander roared to his few remaining men who stood spellbound at the sight of the magic sword. "Attack!"

Romlin's shield floated in the air, longing to travel to its master but an Ebonite restrained it.

"Romlin, go to the cliff and jump," one of the whispers ordered.

No, he replied in his mind, pressing forward his attack. *You tried to trick me into jumping before.*

"That was not me. I promise you. Jump and you will find life. It is the only way."

They have my flying shield. I can't jump. I'll die.

"Stay and you will die. Jump and you will live."

I'm not a fool. You can't deceive me.

The commander managed to disengage from Romlin's fierce attack, and rejoined his men. He seized a sword from one of his warriors and ordered their attack.

Romlin raced against the winds to reach Elabea who had descended back to the cliff.

"Did you hear the whisper," she asked with the book still open in her hands. "It said, *Jump*."

"I know. It is a lie. It's the Cauldron."

"I don't think so. I think it's the King of Claire. Look!"

She pointed to the pearly white columns glowing in the yellow sunbeams.

"Where did *those* come from," he pondered.

"They must be the gateway to Claire. The rusk was right: He *is* alive!"

An Ebonite war cry drew their attention back to their enemy. The commander flew in Romlin's shield while his warriors charged toward them.

Romlin knew he could defeat the warriors with his empowered sword, but would not be able to protect Elabea from the shield's aerial assaults. He glanced back at the white columns and then at the bottom of the cliff.

"We're trapped," he shouted.

"My delights. Jump to life," a whisper hailed.

They looked intently into each other's eyes, communicating without words all they were wondering as only dear friends were capable of doing: *Was this the true whisper? Were the columns the gateway to Claire or a mirage conjured by the Cauldron? Will we live or die?*

They were terrified and desperate, yet despite their fears and doubts, they could not discount the book's mystical powers or the rusk's dying proclamation.

Romlin grasped Elabea's hand. She flashed him a nervous smile and clutched the open book to her chest. Romlin gave her hand a squeeze and she nodded.

Side by side, they darted for the cliff.

"Fools, stand fast!" the other whisper commanded. *"If you jump, you will die. Stand and fight for life. I am coming."*

They ignored the whisper and instead, focused on the white towers. Romlin hoped he would see Manno Vox leading countless warriors to aid their rescue. Elabea longed for the King of Claire to ride through atop a fiery steed.

No one appeared.

Undeterred, they raced onward.

Romlin glanced over his shoulder; the Ebonites were gaining ground. He accelerated their pace. The cliff's edge loomed.

"Are you ready," he asked as he took one last look at the columns.

"Are you?"

Elabea scanned the sands for signs of help. Nothing.

"Here we go!"

Without hesitation, and with fingers intertwined, Romlin and Elabea launched themselves off the cliff.

Chapter 3

Kinmin's Trail

Il-Lilliad followed Kinmin deeper into the Onderling. The passage was pitch black, so Il-Lilliad had to emit a soft, yellow light in order to see. They trudged through unmarked tunnels and passageways, and as TyNorai had predicted, Kinmin was invaluable as a guide. He led with a quick pace. Il-Lilliad, on the other hand, walked with extreme caution, often walking foot-over-foot, pressing his body hard against the damp rock to keep from falling.

The perilous journey increased Il-Lilliad's respect for the SriBrunian. Kinmin did not need Il-Lilliad's light to illuminate his steps; his eyes grew large, gathering any available light and allowing him to see the dark corridors as if it were noon in Allsbruth. Despite his small size, he was strong and tireless, and often waited for Il-Lilliad to catch up. Yet despite his slow pace, Il-Lilliad never felt any frustration from the man.

"So tell me, Kinmin, are all SriBrunian's as patient and as quiet as you?"

Kinmin offered Il-Lilliad his hand to help him up the last part of the grade. He thought long and hard before answering.

"No. Most are quieter and more patient than I."

"Really? That is hard to believe."

"Then you must have faith that what I say is true."

Il-Lilliad chuckled.

"Why do you laugh," Kinmin asked.

"Well, because of the subtle differences between our languages. When I said, 'That is hard to believe,' it was meant in a rhetorical manner; to imply that you *are* a very patient and quiet man."

"So you were lying?"

"No, not at all. You see..."

"If that is what you were truly thinking, then why would you hide it in such a way?"

"That is why I was chuckling, because the differences between our dialects are humorous."

"With all due respect, I find the matter anything but humorous."

"At this point," Il-Lilliad said in a dejected tone, flustered he was unable to explain himself clearly, "so do I. Lead on, Kinmin, lead on."

The companions traveled in silence for a while. Il-Lilliad heard the sound of wind echoing though the darkness. The air grew damp and cool. Kinmin stopped.

"Stay very close. Step only where I step. We will be crossing salu using a very narrow stone bridge."

"Salu?"

"Yes, salu. Can you not hear its rapids far below us?"

"I am not sure what I am hearing."

"You hear salu. It is very dangerous. You must not breathe its vapors from the mist that rises from below."

"Why not?"

"Salu is SriBrunian for 'burning waters.' Even the mists, if left unattended, will eat the flesh off the bone. The vapors themselves will burn your lungs. So hold your breath as we cross."

"Is it a long bridge?"

Il-Lilliad pictured a flimsy bridge that disappeared into forever. He increased his light, ever so slightly, just to be on the safe side.

"For Kinmin, it is not. For Il-Lilliad, I fear it is."

Kinmin rounded the trail's bend. Il-Lilliad's dim light illuminated a thin, stone bridge that jutted out into the empty darkness. Without hesitation, Kinmin crossed at a quick pace and disappeared into the blackness. Il-Lilliad waited, uncertain, until Kinmin's voice echoed from the other side.

"Remember," the SriBrunian commanded. "Hold your breath."

Il-Lilliad looked down at a passage that was no wider than an arm's length. The bridge was without railings.

"I thought you said it was a bridge?" he shouted back.

"Is that not the Allsbruthian word for what I crossed?" Kinmin yelled back. Il-Lilliad's sarcasm was wasted on the little SriBrunian.

"It *is* the correct word," the storyteller replied, and then to himself, "there is just not much of it here."

The roar of the rapids was deafening, and he could feel the cool mist settling on his face. The vapors stung like a sunburn. He pulled back from the edge and quickly wiped off the mist with the sleeve of his tunic. The water ate small holes in his garment before completely evaporating.

"Hurry," Kinmin shouted. "Do not let salu frighten you."

"Frighten?" Il-Lilliad huffed, regaining his composure and resolve. "I have overcome worse obstacles."

He tore off a piece of his tunic and stretched the cloth until it was as thin as gauze. He wrapped the porous cloth around his face then dropped to his hands and knees. He drew in a deep breath, held it in and began to cross. His progress was slow, and he noticed the gauze covering his eyes start to dissolve.

"Faster, Il-Lilliad. Salu will eat you alive if you do not."

Il-Lilliad quickened his pace. The stone cut and bruised his palms and knees while his lungs burned for want of air. A portion of the bridge crumbled, and he dropped to his belly to keep from plummeting over the side.

"Careful, Il-Lilliad. All will be lost if you fall."

I think I know that! the storyteller thought as he scooted forward once more. The gauze protecting his face was all but gone. The mist landing on his back dined on the tunic's fibers like locusts in a field of grain.

"Faster. You are almost here."

Il-Lilliad quickened his pace. When he was close enough, Kinmin grabbed his shoulder and pulled him to safety.

"Quick. Stand and remove the cloth from your face before it eats off your head."

Il-Lilliad ripped off what remained of his gauze and threw it over the edge. His fingers began to burn from the shroud's moisture. He held them up to his face. Within his glow, he watched in horror as his skin turned from pink to red.

"They are burning. I can't wipe it off or it will burn another part of me."

"Lower your hands. Quickly!"

Il-Lilliad obeyed. Kinmin reached into one of his pockets and pulled out a small vile. He pulled the cork and dribbled the liquid onto Il-Lilliad's hands. It was freezing cold and smelled of crushed herbs.

"Wash. Fast."

Il-Lilliad rubbed the fluid all over his hands and breathed a sigh of relief as he felt it soothing his flesh and healing his burns.

"You shouldn't have crawled," Kinmin scolded, for the first time showing frustration with the tall storyteller.

"Had I not crawled, I would have fallen."

"So say you. I say not."

"What did you pour on my hands? It was so cool and invigorating. And my burns," he held his hands up to his face, "they are no longer red and painful."

Kinmin recorked the vile and placed it back into his pocket.

"It is healing water from SriBrune. It is the only thing that will stop the burning waters of salu."

Il-Lilliad studied the short man's face and clothes. Salu's vapors had not affected him at all.

"Did you get burned?"

"No, I walk faster than you crawl. Besides, SriBrunians are immune to the vapors. Over the years, we have built up a tolerance to the mists."

"So we must be getting closer."

"Yes, much closer. When we near SriBrune, we will need to slow down and be very quiet."

"Why," Il-Lilliad asked. An unsettling feeling swept over him.

"To not awaken the dansel lors."

"I'm afraid to ask, but what is a dansel lor?"

"If you are afraid to ask, then why bother asking," Kinmin inquired, perplexed.

Il-Lilliad chuckled. "Simply a silly expression."

Kinmin turned and continued their trek. Il-Lilliad followed, but his imagination worked overtime creating multiple images of the dansel lor. Coming over a crest, Il-Lilliad saw a group of blinking lights off in the distance.

"Dansel lors?" he whispered to Kinmin.

"No," Kinmin snickered. It was the first time Il-Lilliad had heard him laugh. "Those are fingals."

"Fingals?"

"Yes," Kinmin said, still amused that Il-Lilliad was whispering out of fear for such creatures. The fingals' lights fluttered about like miniature stars. Kinmin shook his head. It was obvious he was not impressed by the creatures.

"Do you know what 'fingal' means in SriBrunian?" he asked Il-Lilliad.

"No."

"It means, 'not bright.'"

"But they *are* bright. They are blinking and flashing and..."

"Not that kind of bright. It is better translated to you as perhaps *ignorant* or *stupid*."

"Ah," Il-Lilliad exclaimed. "So, SriBrunians *do* know how to make jokes."

"Jokes," Kinmin asked. "You mean something that is funny?"

"Why, yes, just like these fingals. You see, by saying 'not bright,' you're implying..."

Unimpressed with Il-Lilliad's discourse on languages and humor, Kinmin walked away.

When they were closer, Il-Lilliad studied the fingals erratic swarming. There was no pattern or purpose to their flight; some even flew recklessly into the cavern's wall and fell dazed to their death below.

"See?" Kinmin said. "Very fingal. Not bright."

"Yet they *are* so beautiful."

Kinmin nodded his head in agreement. "Yes, but surely you have people in your world who are bright on the outside but fingal on the inside?"

Il-Lilliad laughed and patted Kinmin on the back. "So we do...so we do!"

After his laughter faded, Il-Lilliad asked the question that troubled him most. "So tell me, what are the dansel lors like?"

Kinmin's enormous eyes blinked quickly. Gone was his jovial expression. In its place was deep concern, and his voice turned solemn.

"The river Correll flows from the great lake, Karajan, and into the land of SriBrune. Karajan is in a large cavern, and Correll flows through a hole in the side of the rock. The only way into SriBrune is by traversing this opening. Deep within the depths of Karajan is where the dansel lors dwell. SriBrune has allowed them to live there for many generations. They protect us from our enemies, but if we are not careful, they will kill us too."

"So it's a fish?"

"No. It is longer than any fish, and faster too. Its long tail propels it swiftly, quietly through the dark waters. Should you walk along the narrow banks of Karajan, it can shoot out of the water and chase you on its small arms and legs. Once you are caught in its mighty jaws, the dansel lor will drag you to the bottom of Karajan. If you are lucky, it eats you whole. If you are not so lucky, you are stuffed between rocks for dinner at a later time."

Kinmin closed his eyes as he focused his thoughts. His head transformed into what Il-Lilliad assumed was that of a dansel lor. A long snout displayed short, sharp teeth that curved back toward its tail. The lower jaw jutted out well beneath the upper and the teeth were exposed, giving it a perpetual snarl. Massive jaws opened and closed with every breath. Opaque eyelids blinked quickly over primal, yellow eyes. Il-Lilliad assumed these protected the creature's eyes while it hunted, killed, or ate.

Its flesh was dark green and appeared wet and slimy, like that of a bullfrog. A thin, short dorsal fin rose from its head and grew in prominence as it ran down its neck. If the head was proportional to the rest of its body, Il-Lilliad estimated that the dansel lor was the length of three Allsbruthian men.

"Are we to swim across Karajan," Il-Lilliad asked as Kinmin's features returned to normal.

"No, that would be foolish. Dansel lors would see, hear and catch. We will use a boat. There is always a boat near the edge of Karajan. It is SriBrunian law. Should one of us stray too far from home, we always have a means to return."

"So who leaves the boat?"

"It is a SriBrunian custom for boys who are about to become men to do this. It is an act of bravery and shows his family that he is ready to be a man in SriBrune."

"This beast could easily pull us to the bottom, even in a boat."

"SriBrunians do not use ordinary boats."

"But…"

"Enough talk. Stay quiet. They are always listening for the sound of footsteps, awakening them to hunt and eat."

Kinmin turned and continued on toward Karajan. Il-Lilliad marveled at how quickly and quietly the little man could move. He tried his best to emulate Kinmin's motions, wanting to do everything possible to keep the dansel lors asleep in the deep, but his efforts never quite equaled Kinmin's.

Kinmin stopped.

"Karajan," he whispered.

Il-Lilliad's light spilled across a large, dark underground lake. The cavern ceiling hovered close to the water and conical rocks jutted downward like a dragon's teeth. Some even pierced the water.

"I will have to lean backwards in the boat to keep from hitting my head on the rocks," he fretted.

Karazan was blacker than the darkest night and eerily placid. It was the most frightening body of water Il-Lilliad had ever seen.

"How will we ever get a boat into such waters?" Il-Lilliad whispered. "The dansel lors will see the ripples."

"Do not worry about ripples, but you should no longer glow. Your light will draw them to the surface."

"It is so dark. I must see a little. I will become just a faint glow."

Kinmin thought the idea over, gave a confirming nod, then walked over to some large rocks and pulled out a long and narrow boat. Extending from its sides were two, short but stocky tree limbs that were attached, but not fixed, to the boat. They looked like they could float and move about freely in the water. Il-Lilliad studied the odd transport, trying to understand the purpose for its length and the four pieces of wood that hung symmetrically on the sides. Kinmin motioned for him to help. It was then that Il-Lilliad began to understand the purpose to its odd design.

"It has the same form and length as a dansel lor," he whispered. "They will think it's one of their own entering the waters."

Kinmin nodded.

Il-Lilliad helped him ease the craft into the eerie waters.

Ripples fanned out over Karajan, announcing their arrival to the lurking dansel lors.

Chapter 4

Beyond the Veil

Elabea clutched Romlin's hand with all her might as they plummeted headfirst over the cliff's edge. Clothes flapped violently as they stared wide-eyed into each other's eyes. Elabea jumped in hope that the King of Claire would race through the white towers to save them. Romlin jumped hoping that Manno Vox would rush to their aid.

A glance at the two columns revealed no help was coming. A sour taste coated their mouths with worry.

In the distance, a whisper laughed. Was it from Claire or the Cauldron?

With death now certain, Romlin and Elabea squeezed their hands to express more than just good-bye. A shared image of their cherished times in the oak's swaying branches flashed through both of their minds.

A rogue gust of wind stole into their pockets and swept their invitations out, but instead of fluttering away, the still pristine parchments flew like birds near Elabea and Romlin's outstretched hands. They beckoned the young people to reach for them. With nothing else to loose, Elabea and Romlin released their grasp on each others hand and grabbed their invitations. The parchments pulled and strained against their fall, slowing their decent.

Elabea glanced down at the rapidly approaching ground.

"We're not going to make it," she shouted to Romlin.

The snickering whisper drowned out her words.

As if with a mind of their own, the invitations pulled with the strength of a hundred eagles and continued to fight to save their owners. Catching another seemingly insignificant breeze, the parchments shifted direction, missed the jutting rocks and flew their passengers away from the cliff and out across the desert.

Elabea and Romlin clutched the parchments in front of them and soared over the orange desert, their toes occasionally brushing the sand. Romlin's face was filled with joy, stunned by the miraculous flight. He was caught up in the incredible adventure. Elabea, felt no such exhilaration. She turned her head sideways to avoid the winds burning her eyes, wishing the flight were over.

She glanced forward, more out of fear than curiosity. The invitations soared toward the towers, but all she could see on the other side was more sand.

Spying their escape, the funnel clouds set a course to intercept them. Howling winds pounded Elabea and Romlin, making their flight bouncy and rough. Sand bit into their faces like shards of glass, and the noise from the cyclonic winds was deafening. Yet, their invitations battled on, darting this way and that, or making a steep banking turn to outmaneuver the swirling clouds.

Sensing danger from behind, Romlin cast a look over his shoulder. The Ebonite commander was in fast pursuit on Romlin's flying shield. Romlin faced forward again and focused on the approaching columns. They were massive, magnificent structures, with tops that disappeared into the storm clouds overhead.

"He's getting closer," Elabea shouted to Romlin.

"Where is Manno Vox or the Only," he asked.

The Cauldron's whisper chortled as the Ebonite hurled curses at their backs. Doubt and fear reasserted themselves in Romlin and Elabea's souls.

"Death begets death," the Ebonite roared as the shield gained ground.

Before the Ebonite's cry finished leaving his lips, the invitations gave a sudden burst of speed and soared with their passengers through the columns.

The sky erupted with a blaze of light that caused Elabea and Romlin to close their eyes against its brightness. Still flash-blinded, they felt confused as their flight slowed down and their parchments settled them down with a gentle landing.

All was quiet. The windstorm, the drone, the counterfeit whisper, the Ebonite - they were all gone.

They blinked their eyes to adjust to the light and gasped. In place of the stormy clouds was the brightest blue sky they had ever seen. The columns - beautifully chiseled by master craftsmen - no longer appeared ancient, but stood untouched by time, stretching up, disappearing into the azure sky. As far as they could see was a translucent, silvery veil that shimmered in the breeze.

"It's as if we're behind an enormous waterfall," Elabea said in a hushed voice.

"I can still see the dark sky on the other side, as well as the orange sand, and the cliff we leapt from," Romlin added. "This glistening curtain makes them look blurred, as if they are not really there."

"So where is the Ebonite and your shield," Elabea asked as she looked all around at her wondrous surroundings.

"For that matter," Romlin added as he took in their lush surroundings, "where is the King of Claire?"

Chapter 5

The Apprentice

Newcomb was awakened by an unfamiliar sound. A quick glance at his rusk made him relax, for the animal merely hovered nearby, its tail and hair relaxed. Then he remembered Draemel. He was relieved to see him still tied to the tree, snoring away the morning.

He stood and rubbed his sleepy eyes while searching about for the source of the noises. Mumbling voices accompanied by strange tones came from the other side of a boulder. He cautiously approached while his rusk flew beside him.

A lute, he concluded as he neared. *That explains the tones I heard, but whose voices are those?*

Peering around the boulder he discovered Lassiter sitting on the ground, holding the instrument, his eyes focused intently on his fingers as they squirmed along the lute's fingerboard. Sitting across from him was his tutor: DeMorley.

"What are you doing," Newcomb asked.

"I'm learning how to play," Lassiter answered without taking his eyes off his fingers.

DeMorley flashed Newcomb a proud smile.

"He's very good. Quick learner."

"Not really," Lassiter added. "I can't seem to make my fingers move like I want."

"Look at him, Newcomb. He'll be playing songs in no time."

"That is what I fear," Newcomb replied to the minstrel. Turning toward Lassiter, he added, "Time to put it down; your music lessons are over. We have a long journey ahead of us"

Lassiter stopped playing.

"I'm not going to Claire."

"We have already been through this. Come, it is time to get ready."

Lassiter began playing the song once more.

Newcomb seethed.

"Lassiter. That was not a request."

"I know what it was," Lassiter cut him off while plucking a few strings. "And here is my answer: *I don't want to go to Claire.* All I want is to learn how to play songs."

"You want to do *what?*" Newcomb exclaimed, flabbergasted.

DeMorley, who was equally shocked by the boy's disclosure of purpose, rose to his feet, his mouth agape. Newcomb turned his fury upon the minstrel.

"I should have known you would poison the boy's mind with your stories."

"I did no such thing," DeMorley countered. "He simply asked if I would show him how to play the lute."

"You can barely tune it, let alone *play* it."

DeMorley waved off the comment with a rubbery arm. Lassiter stopped playing and hopped to his feet.

"This is *my* choice. It has nothing to do with either of you. I simply have no need or desire to go to Claire."

Newcomb looked Lassiter squarely in the face. "What about your invitation?"

"I appreciate what you've done for me on the Isle of Lills, and I understand the promise you made my mother. But don't I have a say in this?"

"A say?"

"Yes, a choice?"

"I suppose, but..."

"Then it's settled. I choose to leave."

"Leave?" both older men said in unison, startled at his rash decision.

"Yes. I'm going to Gilden. It's just over the next hill. DeMorley told me that a minstrel could earn many a golden giln performing there."

"Young Lassiter," DeMorley replied, flashing Newcomb a nervous grin, "what I was *trying* to say was..."

"Didn't you tell me that I had a gift for music?" Lassiter interrupted, knowing the question would not only incriminate DeMorley but would enrage Newcomb.

"Yes, but I was simply trying to encourage you. I never dreamed you were pondering becoming a *minstrel.*"

"Why not? What's wrong with it?"

Newcomb's eyes met DeMorley's. Within the stare, each man reflected his utter contempt for the other.

"Nothing is wrong with it," DeMorley finally replied. "I just don't think you fully comprehend all that it entails."

"I think I do. Your stories are so exciting! The girls, the money, the adventures." Lassiter became giddy with the images he conjured of his future. Letting them fade, his expression grew glum as he considered going to Claire. "While Newcomb's tales are so...so...*boring.*"

"Boring?" Newcomb erupted. "You still think life is to be fun and games?"

"All I know is I don't desire the life *you* have," Lassiter countered. With that, he rose and strutted around the boulder.

"Where are you going?" Newcomb demanded as he followed. He hoped his strong tone of voice would lead Lassiter back from his wayward ways like a shepherding dog herds a stray lamb away from danger. Instead, it was like the wind upon his sails, and drove him further along his chosen course.

"I've already told you," Lassiter shouted as he began mounting his horse. "I'm going to Gilden to be a minstrel."

Lassiter stuffed the lute in his saddlebag, then dug his heals into the animal's flanks.

"Lassiter!" Newcomb cried as he galloped past. Newcomb's voice betrayed his fears of Lassiter being unprotected and worse, that he perhaps no longer needed him anymore.

Awakened by the heated debate, Draemel studied Newcomb as he dashed for his steed.

"Let him go," Draemel instructed in his deep baritone voice.

"Stay out of this," Newcomb fired back as he gathered in his horse's reins.

"What are you going to do when you catch him?" Draemel continued. "Tie him up with me?"

"If that's what it takes."

"Your son is growing up. You cannot bridle him forever."

"He's not my son," Newcomb blurted.

Realizing this revelation should have been kept closely guarded, he hoped both Draemel and DeMorley misunderstood him, or perhaps did not hear because of the wind or the distance between them. DeMorley dashed any such hope.

"Lassiter's not your *son?*" the minstrel said as a mischievous grin covered his face. *"That* explains much."

Draemel's eyebrow arched with curiosity. He had studied the pair closely as any good bounty hunter would. He too had had his doubts and questions about the two. With Newcomb's disclosure, he now knew there was more to their trip to Claire than met the eye.

"So if you're not his father, then who are you to the boy?"

"I am his mentor."

"He's a storyteller, too," DeMorley crowed, casting Newcomb a disparaging look.

A wry smile emerged on Draemel's face as he gestured with his head toward Newcomb's rusk.

"I assumed as much when I first spotted your pet, but thanks to you, DeMorley, you confirmed my suspicions. Last I had heard, all Claire's storytellers were destroyed after the defeat at Min Brock." The bounty hunter cocked his head, waiting for an explanation.

Newcomb pondered his next move. Lassiter needed his protection, but leaving DeMorley and Draemel alone was dangerous, especially now that his identity was known. To a certain degree, Draemel's advice was correct: he couldn't just tie up Lassiter and take him as a prisoner to Claire. Lassiter needed to go to Claire because he chose to. A plan took shape in his mind. He dismounted.

"Your words are true; Lassiter needs to decide for himself. At the same time, he needs to be protected." Newcomb pressed his face uncomfortably close to DeMorley's. "Since you planted these fanciful thoughts of being a minstrel into his zealous mind, *you* will be the one to watch over him."

"I never knew he was pondering such a notion."

"It doesn't matter. He trusts you more than me right now. Follow him and report back to me his whereabouts."

"And should I refuse?" DeMorley said with chin raised and hands on his hips.

Newcomb pressed his nose to DeMorley's, poked a finger into his sternum, and whispered, "I will untie Draemel and watch him tear you to pieces with his gor bone."

DeMorley glanced at Draemel. The bounty hunter's cold eyes made his entire body feel weak. DeMorley huffed, turned, and marched to his horse.

"Fret not," Newcomb called after the minstrel. "We'll be leaving soon, too."

DeMorley mumbled some expletives and mounted his horse. "I'm going only because that boy has my lute, not because you've threatened me. After all, it's a Bellini!" With that, he spurred his horse after the runaway boy.

Newcomb cut Draemel free. As the bounty hunter rose, he massaged his crossbow wound with his tethered hands. It still throbbed whenever he moved.

"Our minstrel has supplied the missing information I needed to figure you out," Draemel said, enjoying this new insight despite the fact that he was still a prisoner.

"And you have supplied the information I needed to figure you out," Newcomb countered.

"How so?"

"You speak with experience in regards to dealing with a boy Lassiter's age."

"Merely a lucky assumption."

"I don't believe in luck."

"If you say so."

"There is more to your story than you let on," Newcomb said.

Draemel gave a respectful nod.

"So tell me your tale."

"Some other time, perhaps."

It was Newcomb's turn to nod respectfully. The storyteller led the bounty hunter to their horses where they mounted, then set out after the minstrel.

As they rode, Newcomb reflected on Draemel's hidden tale. He had seen but a glimpse of the story, but it was enough to convince him that Draemel was vital to their success. Within Draemel, Newcomb could see a deep love for a woman named Merriam and their son. Yet, overshadowing it all was a dreadful sense of despair, a tale so horrific that Newcomb yanked his thoughts free of the story. Despite Draemel's shady character and lack of scruples, Newcomb nevertheless granted the man honor to such secrecies of the grave.

What Newcomb did not know was that their four tales had been woven together many summers before at a place called Min Brock.

Only now were those four tales unfolding as a story.

Chapter 6

Linwith's Dragon

Linwith's travels after his near-deadly crossing of the River Arrgient were uneventful to the point of becoming boring. He grew so relaxed that he grabbed an apple from a barrel and munched on it as he drove, savoring the juicy snack as he listened to the bumps and knocks from the barrels in his wagon. He no longer fretted over the noise he made alerting his enemy, since Rittmar and the nation of Bal-Malin flew overhead.

He wiped tart juice from his chin with the back of his hand, and listened to the barrels' gentle polyrhythm. It reminded him of a song cadence his mother sang to him when he was a boy. He hummed the melody, but try as he might he could not remember the words.

He kicked a boot up onto the wagon's headboard, took another bite, and scanned the horizon. The Allsbruthian Mountains were far behind him. The land before him was gentle in slope and trees were few and far between. He was in the heart of the Gilden Plains.

Far on the horizon stood the Addoli Ridge, a tall mountain line that guarded the Gilden Plains from the Gilden Sea. Like the plains, it was devoid of trees. Wild grass and low-growing bushes were its only covering.

When his wagon rumbled to the top of a small crest, he sat up and pulled back on the reins.

"Whoa."

He gazed across the sloping valley and tore off another bite from his apple. On the horizon was an oddly-shaped hill that looked as if an underground giant had pushed the land skyward. The mound was nearly as tall as the Addoli Ridge, and a road snaked up to the summit, but it was the structure on top that made his shoulders droop. For years, his emotions concerning the citadel laid buried within him, like a dragon asleep in its lair. Seeing the castle stirred the beast. Linwith's breath came in erratic spasms.

Sensing trouble, Rittmar flew down and landed on his right shoulder.

"Min Brock," the creature stated while studying Linwith's face. "Why do you fear it so?"

"I didn't realize I did...until now."

He heaved his half-eaten apple out into the tall grasses of the plain.

"The fortress sits empty," Rittmar observed. "Its once great walls are incapable of stopping the wind let alone an advancing army. Even the Ebonites have abandoned it."

"Yes, but the tales its walls could tell…invisible stories from the dead. I never wanted to see this place again."

Linwith stared spellbound at the desecrated citadel.

"Yet here you are," Rittmar said. "Please, tell me what Min Brock used to be like?"

Linwith reflected for a moment before he spoke. "I'll never forget the first time I saw Min Brock. It was from this very knoll. She was spectacular! White walls glistened like a pearl on a bed of tan sand. Seven towers jutted high like lances and her gates were fiercer than the mouths of lions.

"She was formidable. Six walls sat entrenched on the knoll's summit and stretched skyward beyond our enemy's reach. The east and west walls were the longest and ran perpendicular to the Addoli Ridge. The north and south walls had two walls that jutted out symmetrically and met at an angle. Walkways connected all six walls, allowing soldiers and archers to ward off attacks from any direction. The first time I walked atop that perimeter, I gazed over the Addoli Ridge and caught a glimpse of the Gilden Sea. When the winds were right, the scent of salt air swirled about the castle.

"Six towers were placed at the junction of the walls while the seventh rose from the Great Hall that sat in the middle of the courtyard. From within these towers, archers could stand on the circular stairs and shoot through the thin, long windows.

"At the top of each tower was a platform accessible from the stairs. A protective wall faced outward and a tiled roof kept the rain and arrows out. Within each tower were large gongs that were struck to sound the alarm whenever our enemy approached. Archers and small catapults could be positioned inside the towers as well. If speed was needed to reach the summit, a sophisticated pulley system on the backside could quickly hoist men or weapons to the top.

"What I admired most were the countless families living in Min Brock. At her zenith, Min Brock was more like a city than a fortress. Numerous dwellings surrounded the Great Hall offering housing, vendor shops and barracks for our soldiers and storytellers. The air was rich with the scent of Ingloid fish being smoked, MerriNoon stews simmering and tart pastries from Ferra cooling in the breeze. At night, fires were lit as were pipes, and storytellers told tales of wonderment and adventure. Children laughed and giggled at the storytellers' dazzling lights and stories. Lovers embraced and dreamed of a blissful future. The elderly smiled upon the young, knowing they would leave them a better world."

Linwith turned his gaze away, and in a melancholy tone added, "But that was before we betrayed Claire and all of Allsbruth. Now, Min Brock looks like a shunned harlot. Its white walls are dark and it is fit only as a haven for wild dogs and birds."

"If you fear it so," Rittmar stated, "you must go within to face these feelings."

Linwith's inner dragon thrashed about wildly.

"Never!"

"Then you will be haunted forever."

"Min Brock was destroyed. It haunts me no more."

"You deceive yourself. It hunts you like a beast of prey. Even now I can smell anguish spilling from your pores."

"Look at it. Min Brock is no more. Therefore, I shall pay it no mind. Its towers have crumbled, and its walls have been breached. No one lives there now. No one could live within it again."

"Not even storytellers?"

Linwith's mind flashed back to that fateful day when betrayal ruled Min Brock. He fought against the memories, and shame swept through him like a zephyr.

"No," he answered. "Not even storytellers."

Despite his retort, the dragon ripped apart Linwith's hope and its great wings stirred fear into a great cloud of dust. In a softer but somber voice, Linwith added, "My task is to get these barrels to Tristan. I have no time for Min Brock."

He slapped the reins, harder than was necessary, and the animals lumbered forward.

Rittmar shook his tiny head.

"I have studied the mysteries of many nations and beheld the wisdom in many a creature's tale, but to my last day I will not understand the ways of Allsbruthians. How is it possible to live with such a dragon in your heart?"

Linwith ignored him, and tried his best to ignore the broken citadel of Min Brock.

Chapter 7

A Bed of Tulips

Elabea knelt to the ground.

"It's so *beautiful*," she said as she glided her palm over the blades of grass. They swished at her touch and were cool and wet. She giggled.

Gazing across the great expanse of open land, she saw flowers of every shape and color dancing in the warm breeze like children at a carnival. She stood up, closed her eyes, and breathed deeply. Gone was the stench they had encountered on the cliff. Now, their nostrils drank in the scent of wild flower, spruce, and pine.

The drone was also gone, and for the first time in their lives, they listened with unencumbered ears. At first, the sounds seemed too loud, and they cupped hands over their ears. But as they adjusted to their new aural senses, they lowered their hands and marveled at the nuances of all fresh sounds they could hear; the gentle breeze whisking playfully past their ears, a gurgling patter announcing the presence of a nearby stream, chirping birds and chattering animal calls echoed like merry street vendors.

None of these sounds were new to them; it was just that they now heard them in complete purity, allowing for unfettered depth and clarity, offering them bliss and liberty.

"Look," Romlin exclaimed. "Predator and prey feed together, side by side."

Brightly colored birds flitted from meadow to woods while animals of all varieties grazed leisurely in the meadow. Romlin was awestruck.

"Claire is..."

"Amazing," Elabea finished his sentence as she cast her gaze skyward. "The sky is such a rich shade of blue that I feel I could reach up and touch it." Dropping her eyes, she studied the meadow's perimeter. "Even the nearby woods - I know they are colored green and brown - but those shades are unlike anything I have seen before."

Shielding her eyes, she noticed snow-capped mountains in the distance. She pointed them out to Romlin.

"Those peaks are taller than any range in Allsbruth, and they look so regal."

Romlin was too busy studying the many trails that disappeared into the forest to notice.

"I wonder what adventures await down those paths," he asked.

A low rumble caught their attention and bid them turn. They beheld a distant waterfall whose silver-blue water cascaded over ledge and boulder, cliff and crevice.

"Claire is more beautiful than I dreamed," Elabea declared.

She walked to the shimmering veil that separated this wondrous land from the brown-orange desert beyond, and slowly stretched her hand toward it. Gathering her courage, she let her palm rest on its surface.

Cold as ice.

Ripples from her hand's imprint fanned out like a gentle wave across a calm sea. She stared through the veil at the world beyond. The sky still churned with black clouds, and arbitrary flashes of lightning illuminated the cliff they had leapt from.

"Do you know what frightens me," she asked, her voice tinged with melancholy.

"Sure," Romlin blurted as he joined her gaze at the cliff. "We almost died."

"Yes...I mean no. What frightens me is to think we almost listened to the whisper of the Cauldron and didn't jump." Pausing, she recalled her emotions at the time. "My heart held so much..."

"Anger?"

She looked into his face and nodded.

"Me too," he confessed. "At least you weren't the one shouting and shaking your fist."

"Perhaps, but my anger was yelling inside of me and possibly louder than yours. Isn't that just as horrible?"

"Well, when you put it like that, I guess so."

They turned around to take in Claire's beauty and Elabea gasped.

"I almost forgot *him.*"

She reached gingerly into her pocket and retrieved the rusk. She admired the small animal lying in her open palms; even in death he was stunning to behold. Although his large, prescient eyes were closed, his round face was as handsome as the first day she had met him. His black, human-like paws lay open, as if ready at a moments notice to clasp her tunic and ride fearlessly upon her shoulder. Drooping harmlessly over the side of her hands was his long tail whose poisonous tip dangled. His silky, brown fur was just as soft, and his wings were tucked along his torso.

She stroked the ridgeline of hair that ran from his head down to his tail and recalled how it stood spike-like whenever he sensed danger. The pockets of fleece beside his jaws were still as soft as down feathers. She smiled through her tears as she recalled how much she had loved stroking them while he told her the tales of Claire. They indeed had a special bond.

For a moment, Elabea thought he was just asleep, or that Claire's veil would magically bring him back to life, but his wet nose no longer sniffed her cheek. His body was much too cold, and his whiskers no longer tickled her hand.

One of her tears fell onto a blade of grass, and the sound of its falling pinged like a miniature bell across Claire's landscape. All the birds and animals stopped what they were doing and looked her way, and as if summoned by the teardrop. They approached slowly, reverently as if in honor of an ultimate sacrifice.

Elabea witnessed their approach and quickly wiped her eyes.

"What's wrong?"

Romlin answered by resting his hand upon his sword.

The animals encircled them.

Elabea slid closer to Romlin who quietly unsheathed his sword.

The animals gazed at the rusk still lying in her hands. None emitted even the faintest of bays, howls, screeches or calls. As if cued by an invisible master, as one they bowed to the ground.

Tears rolled down Elabea's cheek.

"They are here to honor him," she whispered.

Romlin sheathed his sword. He too was overcome with emotion, and his eyes misted over. He brushed away a tear, hoping Elabea had not seen.

A large rusk, whose fur was peppered with gray, made his way through the animals, and stood before Elabea and Romlin.

"This rusk was Il-Lilliad's companion," it proclaimed, its voice a unique blend of sadness and joy.

"I can understand you," Romlin exclaimed.

"Yes," the ancient rusk replied. "We all speak with one voice in Claire. But tell me, how did you come to travel with Il-Lilliad's rusk? Did you steal him?"

"No," Elabea replied. "He was a gift."

The elder rusk nodded, sensing the truth of her words. With a deep sigh it said, "Please, finish his story. Tell us how he died."

Elabea swallowed, glanced at Romlin for encouragement, and then told the tale of sacrifice. She starting with the night of Manno Vox's appearing, explained how they received invitations, which in turn, alerted the Cauldron. When an Ebonite warrior chased them in the meadow, she described how fast and fearless the rusk flew to attack. As Elabea's story flowed, dividing into the many stories and adventures they shared together, the animals of Claire leaned closer in anticipation of her next tale. When she came to the part about the rusk's demise, and repeated his final words, a hush settled over the meadow. Even the wind stopped to listen.

"Had it not been for the rusk," Romlin added, his voice choked with emotion, "we would have died, more times than I can count."

The elder rusk searched Elabea's eyes, its whiskers flickering.

"Did you love him," it asked.

The question pierced Elabea's heart like a dagger, for she blamed herself for the rusk's death. Overwhelmed with shame, she dropped to her knees and rocked back and forth with the rusk close to her bosom. Romlin stood frozen, overcome by her sadness, longing to help but not knowing what to do.

Elabea felt a tiny paw upon her shoulder

"Your broken heart tells the tale of truth," the elder rusk told her. "It sings of an undying love."

She wiped away a tear and looked into its eyes.

"Your story brings us great delight," the ancient one added. "Nothing is of greater worth for rusks than to be loved by a storyteller. Aside from his family, no one has loved this rusk as much as you have. I should know. I am his father."

His death is *my* fault," Elabea cried.

"Your fault?"

"Yes," Elabea sniffed, wiping her nose with her sleeve. "Because I took the parchment and didn't listen to reason from my family and neighbors. Had I listened to Romlin, or to the rusk's warning, none of this would have happened."

"You blame yourself because you still think with an Allsbruthian mind, measuring life by your own stories, labeling victories and tragedies with a logic of your own weaving. Look around: you are no longer in Allsbruth; you are in Claire. The *what ifs* and the *why this* of your world cannot, *must* not reside here in Claire. The tragedies of your world are bold victories in ours, and what you hail as triumph in your land we see as nothing more than humdrum. And although you might deny these facts, in time you will see that in Allsbruth, you believed as the Cauldron does: that death begets death. But as I have already said, you are no longer in Allsbruth. Claire is the land where death begets life."

He paused to let his words sink deep into the hardened clay of their beliefs.

"Besides," he continued. "We know this is not your fault. We witnessed the battle ourselves."

Elabea's brow furrowed.

"No," the rusk added as if reading her mind, "we were not there physically; we watched from behind the veil."

"Then why did you ask to hear his story," Romlin asked. "To test us?"

The animal shook his head.

"Until a story passes through the heart of another, it is simply a flow of words, an arrangement of time, an array of matter and consequence of action. By telling his story, Elabea, you have given my son life."

"You know my name?" she whispered, still fearing repercussions from the animals.

The rusk smiled.

"My son did not die for you to be fettered by a shame that is deservedly the Cauldron's. Now rise and honor my son by living. Finish your journey. Become what he longed for you to be, what he died for you to be...a storyteller."

Romlin offered her his hand and gently pulled her to her feet. She in turn handed the father his son.

Reverently the old rusk took the lifeless body in his arms. Without another word, and with its head held high, it turned to leave. The animals parted once more, bowing humbly as the father passed. Elabea, Romlin and the animals watched him disappear down a trail that flowed deep into the woods, forged by the countless footsteps of his ancestors long before.

Had they been able to watch or follow, they would have seen him journey the trail's end to a secluded clearing. Here, he would bury his son beside the other rusks that had fallen in the Dark War. And in time, a bed of red tulips would grow from the grave, blossoming in honor of the one whose story would live on forever in the hearts of a girl and boy from Hetherlinn.

Chapter 8

Dark Prophecy

Escorted by soldiers down Netniath's dark corridor, Brairtok kept his pace brisk and his head held high despite the uncertainty he felt. He knew all too well that the Council only *requested* an audience when there were issues of importance to discuss. Despite being assured of his leadership abilities and his army's progress, a nagging doubt flitted about his mind.

Has the Cauldron uncovered a secret of mine that warrants retribution?

Rounding a corner, Brairtok's entourage marched toward the chamber doors and the sharp reports from their boots echoed up and down the hallway.

Two warriors pushed open the chamber doors and Brairtok strode through, alone. He was greeted by the customary blast of frigid wind. Marching toward the Cauldron, he marveled at the dark flames that lapped the wintry air like tongues of hungry wolves. More importantly, the Council encircled it in adulation; their whispered worship sounded like ice shards scraping stone. He let out a relieved breath he wasn't even aware he had been holding, for if the Council's purpose were to summon him for punishment, then they would have faced him when he entered the room and the purplish flames would have burned black with fury.

Brairtok walked to the appointed place where he was to stand until dismissed by the Council, a spot that was not too close to the Dark Flame, and yet not too far away.

Brairtok snapped to attention and boomed, "My lords, I am here upon your request."

The Council raised their shrouded heads. Shadows hid their grotesque features, and as was routine, only one disclosed a fact at a time.

"Brairtok, a story of horror comes to us."

"Yes. A tale of undeniable disgust."

"The Cauldron has heard whispers from *two* other storytellers."

Brairtok's countenance darkened. Had he misread the Council? Was this to be a hearing after all? He glanced at the flames. Dark purple.

"How can that be when I crushed them *all* during the Dark War?"

"True, but the Only is a charlatan of light and darkness."

Eager to show his allegiance, Brairtok puffed out his chest and fired, "I will find them and enjoy first blood. Where are they?"

"One has slid beneath the soil of this world to the forgotten region of the Onderling."

"Fret not over him, for he is old and a fool. The dansel lors of Karajan shall whisk him to their watery lair."

"As for the other, his name is Newcomb, and he too will be destroyed."

"How," Brairtok asked.

"By a vul jen."

"But there were only four and..."

"Deep within the Cave of Freers, hidden from the Only, are thousands of vul jen eggs. Even now they hatch, soon to fill the sky with their beautiful cries."

"One such vul jen has been ordered to find a demented fool named Paradin..."

"...and will enter his dreamworld..."

"...to become the Gor King and fulfill the oracle of old:

Mothers, guard babes; Fathers, draw steel,
Thunder approaches, soon blood on the fields.
Tempest of war, so black and so vile,
Spreads o'er Allsbruth; lament suckling child.

Orphaned stories, treasures from Claire,
Like buried embers, burst forth and flare.
Hear not a whisper, sweet lark on the wing?
Tales shall crush steel when gors have a king.

"Now go, Brairtok. Prepare for war."

"First blood!"

Brairtok snapped his heels together, sharply spun, and marched out of the ice hall.

"*Tales shall crush steel when gors have a king,*" he mused, his footsteps reverberating sharply off the marble walls. "Now that we have the Gor King, the Cauldron's stories will defeat our foes' armies," he squeezed his hands together as if kneading dough, "even storytellers, should any dare fight."

Leaving Netniath, he breathed deeply.

"Ah, the aroma," he exulted as his lips snarled into a wicked smile. "I can smell war approaching. *Soon blood on the fields.* How delightful a tale."

Chapter 9

Mysterious Map

A small, yellow bird landed on Romlin's shoulder.

"Do you still carry the map?" it chirped.

Romlin stared spellbound at the bird, still mesmerized that animals of Claire talk. At a loss for words, he simply nodded.

"Good," the bird twittered, hopping up and down. "Pull it out. Pull it out!"

Romlin retrieved the map, unfolded it, and held it up with both hands. The bird watched with eager excitement.

"See?" it sang. "The map is alive too."

Claire's border glowed as if on fire.

"Toss it to the ground and observe," the bird ordered.

Romlin dropped the map and watched it flutter to the ground like a leaf from a tree.

Bright flames erupted within the map, outlining the borders of Claire. The flames burned outward, consuming all the other nations, rivers, and cities from the map. Soon all that remained was the outline of Claire.

Romlin and Elabea stared at the map, waiting for some thing else to happen, but nothing did.

"So how is this to help us," Romlin asked bewildered.

"Where are your invitations?" the bird chirped, hopping to Elabea's shoulder and back to Romlin's again.

Elabea, whose focus was solely upon the map, was oblivious to another animal at her feet. It scampered up her clothes and sat on her shoulder holding something in its mouth. Elabea looked over at the young rusk.

"What's this," she said as she removed the items from his mouth.

"Your invitations," the rusk replied. "You left them near the veil. They are necessary in opening the map so that you may go to see the King of Claire. What was once hidden will now be revealed."

The young rusk scampered down her cloak and darted back out into the meadow.

Elabea studied the invitations that had just delivered them from the veil's death as well as their leap from the cliff. They were in perfect condition except for the letters that spelled their names. Instead of gold, they danced with colored lights like that of Manno Vox's face.

"So, bird," Romlin asked, "can you tell us why the King of Claire hasn't come to great us?"

"Simple. Because you must go to him," the bird replied. "Journey to Marsien Vur."

Romlin stared at the map. It lacked any markings to guide their way to this mysterious *Marsien Vur*. His misgivings about the map's tendency to obscure its features returned.

"That is all fine, my little friend," he said, "but how are we to get to Marsien Vur, whatever *that* is, when I don't see it on the map?"

"Place your invitations beside the map then stand back and observe," the bird sang.

Romlin and Elabea laid their invitations on either side of the map, then stepped back. A solitary bolt of light flashed from the sky and struck their parchments. The resulting heat and brightness forced them to cover their faces. They squinted through flexed fingers, hoping to see what was happening, but the light was too brilliant to behold.

As quickly as it had come, the light disappeared. Romlin was the first to lower his hands.

"The map is as big as the Hetherlinn commons," he exclaimed. "And it's alive!"

Romlin knelt to better observe the living map.

"Elabea, look! There is the cliff and the orange sands of the desert. See? The veil with the two columns."

"Amazing," she whispered. She reached out and touched their invitations, which remained unchanged. She picked them up and replaced them in her pocket.

"And look - Claire's landscape that we're in is *in* the map."

Countless mountain ranges, valleys and plains were detailed on the wondrous map. Rivers and streams wriggled across its surfaces, sparkling back at the two young travelers. Elabea marveled at the snow falling on the mountain ranges. And situated atop one of the magnificent peaks was a palace.

"There," the bird pointed out as it landed on Romlin's shoulder. "Do you see? Marsien Vur!"

"Incredible," Elabea said.

She caressed the miniature veil and watched the imprint of her finger travel across its water-like surface.

"It's so...beautiful."

"How can this be," Romlin asked as he continued studying the map from every angle. "It is impossible for this much terrain to fit within the outline of Claire that was on Il-Lilliad's map. That would make Claire larger than all of Allsbruth, Ebon, and Ingloid *combined*."

"As I have said; *what was once hidden is now revealed*," the bird whistled back.

"So this is just a mirage," Elabea asked as doubt oozed back into her heart.

"No!" The bird fluttered, alarmed that she misunderstood his answer. "You are to be a storyteller. Surely you know by now that the Only dances with the impossible."

Elabea nodded her head as she remembered the stories she had learned from the book. The bird continued to explain the mysteries of the map.

"Claire knows no boundaries. The map shows only what is necessary for its master to view. Claire goes on forever. See for yourselves."

Together Romlin and Elabea lowered their faces to the veil's rippling surface. Elabea grabbed Romlin's hand for comfort and he squeezed hers. Remembering that the veil's power probably destroyed the attacking Ebonite on his flying shield, Romlin paused to ask the bird a question that troubled him.

"Will this miniature veil destroy us like the original did the Ebonite?"

"Without your invitations, yes, but since you both carry them, no."

They held their breath and pushed their heads through. The veil was colder than ice and they were thankful it was not too thick. True to the bird's words, they could see forever in any direction they looked. The view was beyond anything they had ever imagined. Filled with a sobering mix of wonder and excitement, they both exited the shroud.

"Now do you believe?" the bird chirped as it darted back and forth overhead.

Elabea was too overcome with emotion to speak. She simply nodded. Romlin was equally affected, but gained his composure more quickly.

"How far away is Marsien Vur," Romlin asked as he studied the castle's location on the map.

"That depends on how one journeys," the bird sang.

"We must journey as before, on foot," Romlin replied as he tried to calculate the distance from where they stood to Marsien Vur.

"Traveling by foot will require several months."

"Months?" Elabea sputtered in frustration.

"But there is another way that would only require a few hours of your time."

"Show us," Elabea shouted before Romlin could even open his mouth.

"Do you see how Claire is divided into regions by its rivers and streams?"

They nodded.

"The wonder of this map is that you can step into any region and be there instantly."

"But once inside the map," Romlin inquired, "how will we get out again into the *real* world? Won't we be trapped inside?"

"You are the owner of the map. It goes wherever its master goes."

"How? The map is too big," Romlin asked.

"Once you step within, the map will return to its normal size until needed. When you arrive, you will find it within your breast pocket. Are you ready?"

Elabea was as eager as she was apprehensive. She grabbed Romlin's hand and tugged him toward the side of the great map nearest Marsien Vur.

"Are you ready, my storyteller," Romlin asked, a twinge of excitement coursing through his words.

"Yes," she exclaimed with a bright smile.

They raised a leg to wade into the cool veil.

"Wait," the bird warned.

The duo stopped, lowered their legs, and looked at the bird.

"I forgot to mention an important detail. Unlike before, when you just took a peek to investigate, this time, since you are traveling to a region, you must jump all the way in. If you do not, well, you could be split in half; part of you here and part of you there."

"I'm glad you remembered to tell us that bit of information," Romlin scolded. "Being divided in half would have been an unpleasant surprise."

Once more Romlin took Elabea's hand. They took a step back, then with two quick strides, they leapt forward and disappeared into the map.

Chapter 10

Karajan Stirred

Kinmin motioned for Il-Lilliad to sit in the middle of the boat. Once Il-Lilliad was settled, Kinmin shoved the craft into the water and hopped quietly into its stern.

He pulled out a wide paddle that was covered in cloth and propelled the craft slowly, silently across the dark passage.

Il-Lilliad leaned back and crossed his arms over his chest to avoid the cave's low ceiling. With his staff resting in the crook of his arms, he tried his best to relax, but the journey was anything but enjoyable. He now understood why no outsider dared enter SriBrune. The passage is too low for anyone larger than SriBrunians, and dansel lors lurked somewhere in the depths.

With his light dimmed to that of a tiny candle, he watched the jagged ceiling roll past, close enough that he could touch the moist rock. Even with his light dimmed, he feared the giants lurking in the lake's dark depths. He peered to his left to try and discern anything in the water, but he saw nothing. Aside from ripples quietly lapping the boat's hull, the only sound was a steady dripping that echoed from the darkness.

Kinmin's paddle strokes were smooth and even, the cloth on the paddle muffling the sound. Il-Lilliad longed to turn and look at Kinmin, to get some sign from him that all was well, but he was afraid his shift in weight would cast abnormal waves and attract the attention of the dansel lors.

Kinmin stopped paddling. Il-Lilliad strained to see Kinmin without shifting his weight. The little man's eyes were wide with panic.

"Your sleeve," Kinmin whispered in alarm. "The hem has been dragging in the water."

Il-Lilliad pulled his arms up and felt the sleeve for moisture. He was about to rebuke the SriBrunian when he felt some dampness.

"I never knew," Il-Lilliad stammered quietly. "Only a little bit touched the waters. Surely that will not alert them. Will it?"

"Just a little bit is all that is needed."

Waves rocked the boat, and both men knew that something large stirred beneath the surface.

Kinmin dug his paddle into the water and pulled with all his strength. "Reach behind you," he ordered as he labored. "Grab the oar. Paddle, quickly!"

Without turning and risking capsizing their craft, Il-Lilliad searched behind him with his hand. He found the oar and drove the blade into the water, doing his best to paddle while lying in his precarious position.

"Where are we going," Il-Lilliad asked while paddling.

"To the entrance into SriBrune."

Il-Lilliad strained into the darkness and saw a small flicker of a light on the horizon.

"It's so far away," he moaned.

"Perhaps, but there is no other way out," Kinmin replied.

Il-Lilliad focused on the distant light and increased his glow in order to better see his surroundings. A sudden bump came from underneath. He looked to his right. A dansel lor's dark, long torso slithered just beneath the surface, its dorsal fin slicing through the black waters. Il-Lilliad's heart raced as more waves rolled their craft.

"They're all around us," he shouted back to Kinmin.

Kinmin did not answer.

"Did you hear? They are everywhere!"

"Yes, I heard. Words are useless now. You must paddle faster. Right now, they are curious. We must hasten, for if they decide to strike, we will be lost."

Il-Lilliad paddled with all of his strength. Drawing the blade back, he hit something solid. A dansel lor shot quickly past and brushed the boat, making it toss uneasily in Karajan.

"They play with us," Kinmin said.

"That's good, isn't it?"

"No. They never play for very long."

Il-Lilliad gazed longingly at the entrance to SriBrune. The dot of light was now the size of a small apple.

"We're closer," Il-Lilliad exclaimed as he pulled his paddle through the waters, thankful the blade did not hit another dansel lor.

Once again Kinmin did not answer. He knew the entrance was still a good ways off and that the dansel lors were growing increasingly agitated. One beast rose out of the water in front of them and arched his neck backwards.

"Watch out!"

The beast lunged, just missed Il-Lilliad's head, and dove back into Karajan. A torrent of water splashed inside the hull.

"They want to knock us out of the boat," Kinmin warned. "Stay low and paddle. Hurry."

A dansel lor shot straight up from the depths and hit the bow with such force that the boat popped out of the water. Il-Lilliad held tight as he slammed into the cave's low ceiling, then cried out in pain as the boat splashed back into Karajan.

Another dansel lor exploded out of the water and sailed over the boat, just missing them both. Il-Lilliad spied a dorsal fin cutting through the black water on a collision course with his side of the boat. Jaws snapped and Il-Lilliad's paddle was gone.

"That was close," he declared.

"Close? They are still playing. He could have bitten you in two had he wanted."

"This is what you call *play*? How do we know when they tire of games and desire to kill?"

"When Karajan gets quiet and still, that is when you should worry."

The light from the entrance was now the size of a man's head.

A dansel lor struck the boat from the left while another attacked from the right. Their craft was tossed back and forth, and Il-Lilliad nearly fell on one of the beasts that swam past. Once the boat righted, Kinmin began paddling, and Il-Lilliad looked this way and that over Karajan.

"They're gone. All is quiet."

Kinmin stopped paddling and looked about. Il-Lilliad was right: the waves subsided, and Karajan became placid. The little man grew pensive.

"They gather at the bottom, watching and waiting," he explained. "Soon, they will shoot for the surface and strike with full force."

Kinmin snapped out of his reverie.

"Paddle," he ordered as he dug frantically through the waters with his oar.

"My paddle is gone."

"Use your hands."

"My hands? They'll bite them off."

"Better to enter life with one hand, than to enter death with two hands. If we do not reach the entrance to Sribrune, you will not have a body for your arms *or* your hands. Paddle!"

Il-Lilliad plunged his arms into Karajan and paddled with wide, sweeping motions. As his arms dug and splashed through the water, his eyes swept the surface, looking for any sign of attack.

Nothing.

He studied the entrance.

We might make it.

Before his hope could crest, the dansel lors attacked.

There was no warning, no brief sighting or dorsal fins announcing their approach. As Kinmin had warned, they struck swiftly and violently.

Though stunned by the strike, Il-Lilliad soon regained his senses, only to find himself being dragged to the Karajan's bottom. Instinctively, he increased his light, but instead of the accustomed yellow glow, he found himself immersed in an eerie green world. He pushed with all his might against the monster's jaws, but his efforts were fruitless. His lungs burned for want of air. His mind spun as if in a deep fog, and his eardrums felt like they would explode due to the water pressure.

Dansel lors swirled and snaked about in a macabre underwater dance of life and death. Il-Lilliad looked for Kinmin, but he was nowhere to be seen. Instead, he saw his staff shoot toward him. Il-Lilliad grabbed it.

If I can just pry open its mouth...

He jammed the staff in and pulled. The jaws would not budge.

I need to breathe...the depths are crushing me...I have but one hope...

He jabbed the staff into the beast's left eye. It's jaws loosened. He pushed himself free and shot for the surface.

As he ascended, his staff pulled to his right. He turned in time to see a beast loom with jaws wide open. He prepared himself for the bite, but another black blur struck the attacking beast's underbelly. Il-Lilliad kicked wildly for the surface as the two dansel lors fought for the rights to consume him.

His head rocketed out of the water and he drank in the cavern's stale air.

The entrance to SriBrune is closer, he observed, once more feeling hope pulse through his veins. *I can make it!*

Something bumped his legs. He gasped. Swirling below in his yellowish light were countless dansel lors. As he watched the snaking death lurking below him, another thought came to mind.

"Kinmin!" he shouted across the waters. "Where are you?"

Kinmin was nowhere to be seen. Il-Lilliad hoped the little man's end had been swift and merciful.

Il-Lilliad held his staff and swam with one arm toward the entrance. His arm pulled wildly while his legs kicked torrents of water into the air. As gallant as his efforts were, his water-logged clothing weighed him down, slowing his progress to a crawl. He silently called to the Only.

Death I do not fear, for fear can never be the master of a storyteller. But failing to accomplish the mission you have assigned me is terrifying. It is a truth I do not wish to behold.

Spurred on by the thought, he swam with renewed determination. He glanced up to get his bearings and his heart sank. Although he was closer, a large group of dansel lors swam toward him from the entrance, blocking his escape.

He treaded water and looked for another avenue of retreat, but he was surrounded. His end was near. When all seemed lost, and his hope was gone, a gentle whisper flitted like a dragonfly across Karajan's surface.

"Swim toward the dansel lors," the whisper instructed.

Recognizing the Only's whisper, Il-Lilliad asked, *Toward certain death?*

"*No, toward certain life.*"

I could tell a story and destroy them.

"*Such would be your right as a storyteller,*" the whisper concurred. *But, even a simple tale would alert the Cauldron to your presence; and the location of SriBrune. The war of whispers would come to the Onderling.*

"*True. And within my tale, the Cauldron would discern my hopes, my longings for Elabea and Galadin's success. This could be used against them, if they're still alive.*

The whisper did not answer.

Il-Lilliad had reached the end of his logic's journey. There was only one solution. He could not succumb to securing his safety with a story; there was too much at stake.

"Death begets life," he whispered to himself.

His staff pulled at him, warning him of an impending attack. Il-Lilliad spun around and scanned the surface for any more dansel lors, but there were none to be seen. Kinmin's words echoed hauntingly within his mind.

"*They gather at the bottom, watching and waiting. Soon, they will shoot for the surface, striking with full force.*"

Panic set in. Il-Lilliad kicked with all his might and even tried using his staff to help aid his escape. A creature from the bottom nicked him and sent him skipping like a rock over the surface. Amazed that he was still alive, he was thankful that the jolt propelled him closer to the entrance and the other dansel lors.

With every stroke and kick, his mind raced. If these were indeed his final moments, he refused to allow the dansel lors to rob him of the joy he had come to know as a storyteller.

He let his memory drift back to when he floated like a cloud on the wind and told stories to smiling children. Visions of Elabea and Galadin emerged, and although he did not know their whereabouts or their condition, a deep contentment flooded over him, confirming that he had lived a full, rich life.

An armada of dansel lors gathered. They were close enough to strike. Il-Lilliad knew his end was near, and he prepared himself for the inevitable.

"Il-Lilliad. We are coming!"

"Kinmin?" Il-Lilliad exclaimed.

What appeared to be dansel lors were a fleet of SriBrunian boats.

Il-Lilliad swam with renewed hope toward the fleet. Between strokes, he saw SriBrunians spring from their crafts and transform into dansel lors to protect him.

A SriBrunian boat sped to his side.

"Take my hand," Kinmin ordered.

Il-Lilliad reached up, but before their hands touched, the storyteller was yanked violently underwater.

"No!" Kinmin screamed as he watched Il-Lilliad sink into the dark, his light fading from yellow to green to finally a dim, drab olive. From an unfathomable depth, Kinmin watched as his light flickered like a candle in the wind, fighting to stay alive.

Kinmin shouted orders to his men but when the emerald glow pulsed no more, and Karajan became black, Kinmin bowed his head in sorrow.

Chapter 11

The Alliance

The sound of growling animals prodded him from his comatose state. Heavy eyelids raised and crazed eyes blinked, trying to make sense of his surroundings. Though still dazed, he realized he was leaning against a tree with his arms tied behind his back. He smelled death thick in the air and searched for the source of the stench.

Shaking the cobwebs from his head, his mind began to clear and he discovered gors sniffing about the Ebonite corpses that lay scattered in the grass. As his thoughts continued to clear, Paradin remembered the events that had led him to his predicament. With a snarl he recalled the names of those responsible.

Draemel. DeMorley.

A bull gor raised its head, sniffed in his direction and approached.

"Leave," Paradin snarled. "Leave! You will never eat me."

The gor reared and peppered the air with grunts as if to hurry death along. Paradin spit at the animal.

"Away. Away. I will not die today."

The gor spied something perched above Paradin that sent him scampering back to the safety of the herd.

A voice from the tree's shadows said, "The Cauldron has chosen wisely."

Paradin twisted his neck to see who, or what, had spoken. Squatting on a limb was a hideous bird-like creature.

"I am a vul jen. The Cauldron has sent me to set you free, so that a stronger alliance may be formed."

"Free me. Free me. Then to Draemel I can go."

"Not so fast, crazy man. There is so much more you can have that you are not even aware of. There is another that I want; one that Brairtok desires as well. Together, we can both satisfy each others'...cravings."

"The minstrel? The minstrel? It is he?"

The vul jen let out a blood-freezing caw.

"No. He is of no significance. It is another whom you have not yet met. A girl whose name is Elabea."

"Draemel and Elabea. Draemel and Elabea. Together they will be our prey."

"Good," the vul jen exclaimed, delighted that the man's madness was working in his favor. "But first things first. Let me bite off those ropes."

The vul jen swooped to the ground and pecked at the ropes with its jagged, sharp beak. Paradin felt the ropes loosen. He pulled, they snapped, and he sprang to his feet.

"Free. Free. I am *free*. Now I can kill Draemel for me."

"Patience, patience. Would you like to have even more power from the Cauldron? Power that would make you invincible to Draemel?"

"Yes. Yes. Power for me, for *me.*"

"Then you need to be a storyteller for the Cauldron. Go fetch a dagger from one of those dead warriors."

Paradin scampered toward the nearest corpse. The gors snarled at him, but he growled, spit and pawed at them like a wild cat. They backed away. Undaunted by the appearance of the half-eaten corpse, he grabbed the dead man's dagger and yanked it from its sheath. He spun around and thrust the blade into the air for the vul jen to approve.

"Excellent, Paradin. You shall be a great storyteller. Now cut off your hair. Cut it to the flesh."

Paradin hacked away at his locks, the long strands falling to the ground in clumps. Once the majority was cut away, he began to carefully shave himself until he was completely bald.

"Excellent. You are looking more and more like a storyteller."

"The Only. The Only. A storyteller he will not let Paradin be."

"My dear Paradin, do not fear what you cannot see... or does not exist. You are to be a storyteller for the Cauldron, telling the tales of glory that made us a great people. You have been born to fulfill the prophecy.

Mothers, guard babes; Fathers, draw steel,
Thunder approaches, soon blood on the fields.
Tempest of war, so black and so vile,
Spreads o'er Allsbruth; lament suckling child.

Orphaned stories, treasures from Claire,
Like buried embers glow, burst forth and flare.
Hear not a whisper, sweet lark on the wing?
Tales shall crush steel when gors have a king.

Paradin became giddy and danced a crazy jig.

"But you need the mark," the vul jen continued, "a sign that you are the chosen Gor King."

Paradin stopped dancing.

"Yes. Yes. A sign. A mark. A kiss from the Cauldron."

"Yes, Paradin, a kiss from the Cauldron. Are you ready?"

Paradin's eyes shuffled in different directions, each absorbed in total madness. He wagged his head eagerly.

"Then lie down and gaze into the sky."

Paradin complied and the vul jen landed and pecked at his forehead. As insane rhymes floated from his lips, tiny drops of his blood rolled into the dry grass. Once finished, the vul jen flew into the air to marvel at his work. Satisfied, he cawed with delight at the sight of a gor's skull. He flew back and roosted on Paradin's chest.

"Now, Paradin, I need you to sleep."

"Sleep? Sleep? Draemel's blood I wish to seep."

"In time. Sleep so I may join you, and we may form an alliance no one can destroy."

Paradin nodded to the plan but continued to rhyme. Eventually, he drifted off to sleep, and the vul jen waited for his dreambreath to come. Even asleep, madness traversed Paradin's face causing facial muscles to flex then relax in a violent manner. When his dreambreath came, the vul jen shrieked, dissolved into a purple mist, and entered into the mad man's dreamworld.

The vul jen flew deep into Paradin's world that was littered with confusion, illusion and despair. He swerved around fantasies and fears to reach his dreamworld where the Cauldron's fumes were already busy at work. Paradin's anger burned with the hottest of flames and was perfect to attack. The vul jen swooped down and sank his bite deep into his rage.

Paradin's eyes popped open, and he shot to a defensive stance. One eye twitched and had a mad tint to it, while the other was darker and blinked like that of a vul jen's. Paradin rolled his head back and emitted a monstrous howl fueled by his madness, the vul jen and the Cauldron's fury.

Frightened by his sinister cry, the pack of gors growled and backed away. Paradin stormed brazenly for them. The bull gors bared their teeth and barked but Paradin showed no fear.

"Are you not tired of eating dead flesh," Paradin asked, his rhyming madness replaced with the calculating thoughts of the vul jen.

Stunned to hear him speaking their tongue, one gor cocked his head to the side and roared.

"Yes, you foul-smelling beast, I am able to speak your language. So I ask again. Are you tired of scavenging for your existence?"

"Yes," the bull replied in his simplistic tongue. "But such are the ways of the gor."

"And who determined such hierarchy," Paradin asked.

"The Only."

"Exactly. But the Only is no more."

The gors turned their heads about in confusion.

"Not true," another bull countered.

"Oh but it is, my friend. He was defeated in the Dark War. Where is he now? Have you seen him? Have you heard him?"

The gors looked at each other dumbfounded. Paradin continued.

"Bow allegiance to me and the Cauldron of Ebon, and I promise you first blood. Fresh kill. Warm flesh."

The eyes of the bull gor narrowed as he studied Paradin. How they had longed for fresh meat, but the stories of the Only forbade it; they were forever to be scavengers. The opportunity for a new start was tantalizing, even if it meant betraying the King of Claire. The gors, being simple animals and not concerned with the deeper truths of life, roared unanimously their decision. They bowed before Paradin.

"Excellent," Paradin said with a crooked smile. "I am your Gor King. And you," he addressed to the bull that spoke last, "shall have the honor of being my mount."

The Gor King let his gaze sweep the faces of the assembled gors.

"Today, we march to the Gilden Plains, not as packs, but as a unified army. There, I shall reap revenge on an old friend and destroy those Claire has sent to obliterate the Dark Flame's Oracles."

The Gor King raised his arms skyward.

"My precious ones, it is time to hunt. Gone are the days when you scavenged for cold blood. From this day forth, gors shall feast upon first blood, warm blood."

The gors roared in approval, eager to unite as an army and forsake their lives as scavengers.

The Gor King mounted his bull gor and emitted his telltale howl. The gor army answered with a deep bark and followed him toward the Gilden Plains.

Chapter 12

Marsien Vur

Elabea and Romlin's jump into the veil took their breath away.

It was as cold as the mountain streams of Allsbruth, yet the scent of spring warmed them as if they had just sipped hot tea.

They landed lightly on their feet and noted that they were in a small meadow that abutted to a dense forest. The mountains that were home to Marsien Vur towered above them. They shielded their eyes for a glimpse of the palace, but the mountains were behemoths that hid the castle from view.

Romlin reached within his tunic, then breathed a sigh of relief.

"I was afraid it wouldn't be there," he said as he pulled out the map. "And look at *this.*"

Elabea stepped closer.

"It's just as the bird said it would be: neatly folded."

Romlin returned the map to his pocket, and they headed toward the woods.

Elabea flashed Romlin a mischievous grin. He knew what she intended, and although he had never beaten her in a race, he loved to try.

She started to jog. Romlin kept pace. In their races to the meadow in Hetherlinn, Elabea would gradually increase her pace from a jog to a full sprint, but they were no longer in Allsbruth. Unable to restrain her zeal at seeing the King of Claire, Elabea took off like a deer, laughing all the way.

She stopped by the edge of the woods and allowed Romlin to catch up with her. His sharp eye discovered a path, and they walked over to a large boulder near the entrance. Romlin pulled out his map and rested it upon the rock to double-check their course. The map became alive, but this time remained much smaller in size, as if discerning that its master wished to only view the region they were in.

"Look at this."

Romlin pointed to translucent blue letters floating above the map.

"This must be the name of the region we're in. I wish I could read."

He touched the shimmering word.

"*Cor len Bluun,*" a whisper announced.

"The map *talks,*" Elabea exclaimed.

Tiny ponds dotted the map, glowing a brilliant shade of green. Rising beyond the ponds were the mountains and Marsien Vur. Romlin and Elabea moved around the map, trying to get a better view of the palace, but they could only get a fleeting glimpse, as if Marsien Vur played a game of hide and seek.

Elabea noted two tiny people near Cor len Bluun.

"Romlin, that's *us* in the map."

They peered at the miniatures that were no taller than the width of their pinky fingers. Every movement they made, their copies duplicated. The scenario grew even more awe inspiring when they discovered a miniature of the map, and within that, yet another set of themselves although tinier, staring into what they presumed to be yet another map.

"If we're staring into *this* map, and they're staring into *their* map, it's as if it goes on forever," Romlin gasped. "I wonder if I can touch..."

Before Elabea could stop him or say anything, Romlin pushed his finger through the map's veil toward the copy of himself. Elabea looked overhead and screamed. Romlin's finger was gigantic and was plummeting toward them at a crushing speed.

"Romlin, stop!"

He stopped, followed Elabea's gaze, and was shocked to see his giant finger looming above them. He yanked his hand out of the veil, and his finger disappeared back up into the sky.

Elabea planted her hands on her hips and flashed him a disparaging look. Romlin's face reddened.

"Well, it looks like we're heading in the right direction," he mumbled as he folded the map and returned it to his pocket.

"Come on," he urged, wanting to forget how his curiosity, and his finger, had nearly crushed them to death. "Cor len Bluun should be just over this ridge."

Romlin led them up a small hill and stopped at its apex. Down below was a wetland full of countless ponds covered with bright green algae. They blazed as if a miniature sun burned beneath their surface.

"Cor len Bluun," Romlin pondered. "I wonder what the name means?"

Elabea shook her head, but realizing an explanation would be in her book, she sat down and pulled it out of her pack. She flipped through the pages and found a story concerning it. Since they were in Claire, she no longer needed the rusk to read it to her; the words spoke of their own accord.

"Since the beginning of all, the Only has whispered stories, sending them far and wide. Whenever a story is denied, a tear from the King of Claire falls. And when it falls, it descends into Cor len Bluun: Pools of Tears."

She looked out at the wetland. "There are so many. Imagine just how many tears had to fall to create so many pools, and the loss involved..."

Romlin viewed the pools differently.

"They look like they would be fun to explore. Maybe there are some big fish swimming in them."

With that, he raced down the hill while Elabea followed slowly behind. Normally she would out race him, but she was still spooked from witnessing his giant sky-finger and wondered what other mysteries awaited.

The pools were similar in size to Allsbruthian farm ponds, which made Romlin feel comfortable in exploring them. As they neared the bank of one, their boots sank into the damp ground. A musky odor filled the air.

With his foot, Romlin lightly tapped the pool's green growth. The pungent scent of stagnant water and algae wafted up to their nostrils.

"It's *so* thick," he pushed the green canopy up and down with his foot, "almost like leather. I wonder…"

Elabea's eyes widened.

"You wonder what?"

Before she could react, and without answering her question, Romlin's curiosity overruled her concerns and he stepped onto the algae. Green ripples fanned outward and he flashed Elabea a smile.

"Oh, no," she said as she covered her mouth with her hand, and then to herself, "*I know what that smile means.*"

Romlin took five long strides to the middle of the pond.

"I don't think that's a good idea," Elabea warned.

"What could happen?" He gave a small bounce. "These are just like our stock ponds back home."

Her hands dropped to her hips, and she resumed the air of a chiding school mistress.

"You can't walk on those!"

"Elabea, stop worrying. I know what I'm doing."

"Really? What about when you hunted that gor and nearly died? What about your massive finger that nearly crushed us? Did you know what you were doing then?"

He waved off her questions with a laugh and jumped all the more. Waves rolled beneath the green canopy and gently lapped the shoreline's grasses. As his confidence soared, he bounced higher, his sword rattling with every leap.

"Elabea, you've *got* to try this."

"I'd rather not."

At the peak of one of his jumps, he caught her eye and said, "You worry too much."

"I do not."

"Prove it."

Angered by his accusation, she trudged through the muck to an adjacent pond and tested the surface. It too was quite thick. Not to be outdone by him, she hopped onto its surface. With six cautious steps, she was at its center.

"Bounce, Elabea. *Bounce.*"

As she jumped, she watched Romlin soar into the air and perform aerial gymnastics. Her fears faded and she started to giggle and applaud, which encouraged him to bounce even higher. At the peak of his bound, he cocked his head to the side and made a funny face. She laughed and applauded all the more. As she watched him perform, she noticed two, large lumps of green on the edge of Romlin's pond.

Were they there before, she wondered, *or did we miss seeing them?*

Romlin continued to jump and twirl and shout with greater vigor. Elabea ignored his comedic antics and instead, studied the surface of her pond and then the others.

Every pool had similar lumps.

Her eyes swept back to Romlin who completed a somersault. The mounds opened.

Those aren't bumps, they're eyes.

"Romlin," she screamed. "Get off. They're alive!"

"Of course they're alive," he laughed as he landed his jump squarely on his feet and launched himself like an arrow into the sky. "Algae grows on our ponds in Allsbruth and..."

"No!" she countered as the pool's eyes focused on Romlin. "They are..."

Before she could finish her sentence, the canopy-creature rose like a giant bird taking wing. Romlin lost his balance and fell. Elabea screamed.

The pond creature was round with a flat body and used the left and right sides as wings. Despite their powerful strokes and enormous size, they only made a gentle swooshing sound.

It glided in graceful circles, occasionally beating its body-wings to maintain altitude. Elabea could not see Romlin, but she could hear him. She could not tell if he was laughing or calling for help.

The creature banked and dove for Elabea. She ducked as it soared overhead, and its white underbelly grazed the top of her head.

Frantic to escape, Elabea made her way over the bouncy surface for the shoreline, but before she was even halfway, the creature beneath her feet took flight.

She plopped down and fought to regain her balance. The creature banked and she felt herself slip. She lay flat to keep from falling and glanced over the creature's side to get her bearings. They were so high that the pools beneath looked like glistening coins, but instead of green they were blue. She turned her attention to her wild flight. The sky was full of the creatures of Cor len Bluun.

"Elabea," Romlin shouted as his creature came alongside hers. "Look at this!"

He rose to his feet and extended his arms into the air. His hair was tossed with wild abandon, his eyes ecstatic.

Elabea, certain the creatures of Cor len Bluun would harm them, cowered on its surface.

"Where are we going?" she shouted over to him.

"I don't know. They fly of their own accord."

A deep voice answered.

"Perhaps a gracious question is in order."

"It talks," they both exclaimed with surprise.

"Naturally. All creatures in Claire are able to communicate, but please, do not refer to us as, *It*. Please address us by our given name: Draiggs, the guardians of Cor len Bluun."

"I might add," Elabea's draigg interjected, "that next time you visit our pools, do not be so rude as to bounce on our backs. We were enjoying a comfortable nap."

"Invitation or not," a third draigg added, "proper manners are essential for draiggs. Perhaps this type of interaction is normal in Allsbruth, but in Claire, it goes against protocol."

"Please forgive us," Elabea begged as she struggled to sit cross-legged. "We are new to Claire and don't know your ways. We are just excited to visit with the King of Claire. If it is not too much trouble, could you please carry us to Marsien Vur?"

"Naturally," answered Romlin's draigg. "After all, that *is* why you are here."

A multitude of draiggs gathered around Romlin and Elabea's draiggs and flew in formation toward the mountain. Elabea peered over the side to get a better view of the region below. The canopy of the woods was close, and occasionally a clearing popped into view where assorted animals gathered to watch their flight.

As they flew higher, the ascent became steeper which made Elabea and Romlin shift their weight to keep from falling off. Cedar and pine scents invigorated their senses, but the chilled air made Elabea pull her cloak tight. She shivered, but whether from the cold air or the excitement of reaching Marsien Vur, she could not tell.

When they reached a higher elevation, Elabea noticed that the woods had changed. Blue-green spruces dotted the landscape of gray boulders, dark, green moss clung to overhangs and multi-colored lichen hung in indiscriminant clumps.

The air was also much thinner and made her feel dizzy, as if she had stood up too fast after blowing on a fire. The alpine temperature and rushing winds made her eyes water and her nose run. In Allsbruth, she would have dotted her nose eloquently, but not wanting to miss one iota of the experience, she wiped her nose with her sleeve.

She glanced at Romlin and flashed him an enormous smile. He returned the grin, marveling at how she rode her draigg fearlessly to the top.

Elabea focused on the summit. The peak was near. The moss, trees, and lichen were gone. In their place were piles of snow that graced the nooks and crevices of the stony mountain. Her eyes strained to see the mountaintop. Outlined against the rich, blue sky was the silhouette of a grand structure.

"*Marsien Vur,*" she shouted to Romlin.

She spotted a weathered staircase of stone that curved up and around the mountain. It was wide enough to ascend side by side. Though covered by a canopy of grapevines, it was without a handrail. She cocked her head to the side in wonderment.

How can grapes grow at this height when no other plants can?

Before she could ask, her draigg gave several strong strokes, zoomed over the summit and leveled his flight. Eager to see the palace and the king, she jumped to her feet and rode standing erect.

"Look at you," Romlin shouted. "Gone are the fears of Elabea."

She drank in his compliment and smiled. Her unbound hair flowed in the wind like a wild pony's; her expression was fiercely joyful. The sight of her made Romlin's mouth go dry, though he could not say why.

Marsien Vur was built from large blocks of white stone in an overlapping fashion. Tiny streams from melting ice and snow trickled down its massive walls. Near the bottom of the palace, moss covered the stones giving Marsien Vur the appearance of growing out of the mountain. Once more she wondered how moss grew at such an elevation and why only on the palace.

Few windows were present and the ones she did see were tall, thin and rectangular. They opened to small, semi-circular terraces made of the same white stone. Black iron railings with matching spindles curved from one side to the other. She peered through a window to get a glimpse of the rooms, or better yet, to wave at a member of royalty, but it was too dark.

On every corner stood round turrets that guarded the palace from any direction. Tapered roofs, shingled with dark gray slate, covered each turret, and snow-white and apple-red flags flapped from their crests.

The summit was flat and wide, and Marsien Vur covered its surface with terraces, gardens and adjacent buildings. They flew over the courtyard and marveled at the well-manicured grass and pebble walkways that meandered through gardens and pools. The waters were placid, iceless and glistened in the sunlight. Elabea imagined that they winked at her, enticing her to land and discover the garden's secrets.

She caught the scent of a fire and turned her attention to a line of gray smoke that floated out of a great chimney.

"A fireplace," she shouted to Romlin.

"Yes, I know, but why isn't anyone down below?"

Elabea had been too excited about Marsien Vur's features to make this keen observation. As she studied the landscape, she fretted over the same fact. Finally, as if to defend the King of Claire, or to help rebuild her own confidence, she shouted, "Perhaps they're all inside waiting for us by the fireplace."

"Then tell me, how can trees and gardens grow on such a high mountain? How can the garden pools not be covered in ice?"

"Let's land and ask. Besides, I could use some hot tea," she added as she sat down and pulled her cloak tight.

Their draiggs banked and used their flat wings to slow their approach. With the gentleness of a mother resting an infant in a crib, they landed atop the lush grass of Marsien Vur.

Chapter 13

Land of Swirling Suns

Il-Lilliad was lost in a world where his senses were fragments of a forgotten time. Eternal blackness enveloped him and swallowed sight, sound and touch. He wondered if he were dead, but dismissed the notion since his mind could reason and even ponder such a thought.

He concluded he was in a nightmare until his sense of hearing stirred to life. From afar came the sound of water lapping against some surface, perhaps a boat or a dock. Men singing an upbeat song. Logic told him the sounds were not conjured by his dreams but came from beyond his darkened world. Passion told him that if he could battle out of the blackness and reach the noises that he would find life once more.

He blinked his eyes. Light flashed. The sounds were louder, clearer. Another blink. His sense of smell was revitalized. The scent of stagnate water and damp wood stirred him from the gloom. Desperate to flee whatever nightmare he was in, he rapidly blinked his eyes and tried to make sense of his environment.

Feeling returned and twinges in his back muscles and bones told him that he was lying on his back in the bottom of a boat. His ears rang, but the ringing was receding. As it faded, the men's song grew in volume.

"Welcome back," a voice from behind him greeted. "I'm glad to see you still in the land of the living."

Il-Lilliad tried to sit up, but a stabbing pain like hundreds of piercing daggers pushed him back down. He looked at the epicenter of the throbbing. Holes, tears, and blood marred his tunic near his stomach.

He propped himself up on his elbows and strained to see who had addressed him from the stern.

"Kinmin," he moaned. "My memory is foggy. What happened?"

"A dansel lor desired to make you a feast in the deep of Karajan."

The memory of the horrific ordeal resurfaced: powerful jaws cut into his flesh; water pressure pounded eardrums; dansel lors swirled in green waters; gloom faded into complete darkness.

"Lucky for you," Kinmin added while paddling, "we reached you in time, but when I saw your light die, I thought you had too."

"Your people...these men," Il-Lilliad said as he observed the nearby boats full of SriBrunians singing, their strokes matching the song's cadence. "They risked their lives for me. Did any perish?"

Kinmin shook his head. "No, but transforming one's self completely as they did is very taxing. It demands all their mental and physical strength. In fact, only select SriBrunians possess such abilities. Some are resting in the hulls."

"Are you able to do that?"

Kinmin shook his head again. "No, like most, I can only alter my face and head."

"After the attack, I looked all about Karajan, but I couldn't find you. I was afraid you were dead...or that you had abandoned me."

Kinmin stopped paddling and his brow wrinkled in bewilderment.

"Abandon you?" His usually calm voice rose in pitch and betrayed his hurt feelings. "You are a friend of a promise. I gave my word to help. In SriBrune, to betray a friend of a promise is worse than death itself."

Kinmin shook his head and drove his paddle back into the water.

"Forgive me," Il-Lilliad said as he reached his hand back and patted Kinmin's knee. "I didn't mean to insult you."

Il-Lilliad better understood why the King of Claire wanted him to venture to the Onderling. If all SriBrunians were as honest, brave and loyal as Kinmin, then they would be invaluable in the ensuing war.

The boat slid through Karajan's opening.

"Welcome to SriBrune," Kinmin announced. "The land of swirling suns."

Il-Lilliad shielded his eyes and stared up at what appeared to be three small suns. They twirled slowly like wagon wheels and cast yellow-brown light across the landscape. The spiraling light flowed in waves and gave SriBrune a magical appearance: images shimmered and twinkled in the light.

"Is the sky always this amber shade," he asked Kinmin.

"Yes, and unlike the stories TyNorai told me of your world, our suns never set."

"So you never have night?"

"If you mean a period of darkness, then no. How do your people see where they are going in such conditions?"

"For starters, we have the moon and the stars."

"Ah, yes, TyNorai mentioned such wonders. How I long to journey above the Onderling to see such things."

Two rocky cliffs of magnificent height, smooth and without vegetation, flanked them. Atop the left overhang was a long, arching bridge of white stone that led to three tall buildings. Constructed of the same white stone, they jutted skyward like lances, and had several small, rectangular windows.

"Are those spires part of the palace," Il-Lilliad asked Kinmin.

"No. Those are watchtowers."

On his right were three more bridges fashioned exactly like the one on his left. One came out of the water and led to a similar watchtower.

The second was halfway up the cliff's side and led to a cluster of similar white structures, though larger than those on the left. The third bridge was nestled near the summit and led to even more buildings.

"Is *that* the palace?"

Kinmin chuckled. "You will find out soon enough, my storytelling friend."

On the bridge to their right were a handful of SriBrunian children. They jumped up and down, waving and calling Kinmin's name. Their jubilant voices echoed across the water.

When their craft was closer, Il-Lilliad noticed they were experimenting with changing their faces. He chuckled. They were not as competent at this skill as the adults and began combining several of his thoughts into one. One child imitated his face perfectly but had added Elabea's hair and eyes. Another discovered his rusk and transformed into a round, furry face but added an apple for the nose.

"They are so small and impressionable," Il-Lilliad chuckled as he decided to join them for some fun. He focused his imagination on the image of a large pumpkin. The children gathered his thoughts and in no time, tiny heads popped into orange gourds.

Il-Lilliad burst out laughing, but this only made his wounds ache all the more.

"Please," he begged Kinmin while laughing and clutching his stomach, "make them stop. They will surely be the death of me."

"Yes, I apologize. They, like all SriBrunians, are very curious."

Kinmin waved to them and gently scolded them. Their heads returned to normal, and they scampered ahead on the white bridge.

"They have great respect for you," Il-Lilliad said.

"Yes, it appears that way."

"You're not the father of so many children, are you Kinmin?"

"No," Kinmin laughed. "I'm too young to marry, and even if I were married, I would not have so many children."

"Yet, of all the SriBrunians in our boats, you are the one they acknowledge."

"They show me respect because one day I shall be king."

Il-Lilliad snapped his head back to Kinmin and nearly capsized their boat.

"King? You mean, you're a *prince?*"

"Yes," Kinmin replied as if it were of no consequence. "In SriBrune, one must be a prince in order to become king. Is that not how it is above the Onderling?"

"Yes, it is the same."

"Then why such alarm?"

"Because you never told me!"

"TyNorai educated me about the ways and customs of storytellers of Claire. I knew that it was your duty to not only serve the Only, but also to serve royalty the world over."

"Yes, but that doesn't explain why you kept this a secret."

Kinmin rested his oar across his lap and looked squarely into Il-Lilliad's face.

"You would have insisted on leading and serving me during our journey through the Onderling," Kinmin explained. "How would you have crossed Salu? Karajan? Such service, although done from a genuine heart, would have killed us both."

Il-Lilliad gave Kinmin a nod of respect.

"I suppose you're correct. I would have led us off a cliff *long* before reaching Karajan."

"Or battled the fingals," Kinmin chuckled and resumed paddling.

The boats followed the river's gentle turn to the right, and once around the bend headed for a large dock at the base of the watchtower. A number of SriBrunians gathered about a regal platform that was taller than the landing. Off to one side was an entourage of musicians. Brass instruments glistened in the magical light and looked to Il-Lilliad like shimmering water. Musicians snapped horns to lips and performed a majestic composition that filled even Il-Lilliad's heart with national pride for Kinmin's country.

Standing on the platform were servants holding long branches with wide leaves. These they used to provide shade over what Il-Lilliad assumed were Kinmin's parents, the King and Queen of SriBrune. Surrounding the royal platform, and standing at attention, were hundreds of warriors with spears to the ready. Several officers stood near the king and queen.

When Kinmin's boat pulled up to the dock, servants grabbed the hull and secured it to the dock with thick ropes.

Kinmin whispered down to Il-Lilliad: "You must exit first."

Il-Lilliad nodded and began to pull himself up onto the dock, being careful not to capsize the prince. His wounds sent dark pain streaking through him. Despite the agony, he kept his emotions at bay and exited the craft.

Once out of the boat, Il-Lilliad offered his hand to assist Kinmin. The prince politely shook his head. Realizing he must have breached a royal protocol, Il-Lilliad bowed and lowered himself to a knee, as was a storyteller's custom when appearing before royalty.

Kinmin, assisted by a servant, gracefully left the boat and walked past Il-Lilliad. Il-Lilliad stood, clutched his injured midsection, and watched the prince approach his mother and father.

The king and queen wore the loose clothing typical of SriBrune, but instead of the earthen colors characteristic of the populace, their attire was trimmed with thick material in rich blues, reds and greens. Their faces were stern; hands were clasped.

Kinmin bowed his upper body until it was perpendicular to the dock. When he had righted himself again, he stood perfectly still. The king and queen's faces remained emotionless. After a long silence, the king spoke, and despite his small frame, he bellowed a deep voice.

"Who stands before me? Who is one such as you?"

"I am Kinmin, the son of King Cameare and Queen Riaa, heir to the throne of SriBrune. I left as a boy but have returned as a man."

King Cameare's face shifted from that of a strict sovereign to that of a father. A smile creased his dark complexion as he welcomed home his son. He descended the stairs and placed both hands on Kinmin's shoulders.

"So it is," he said with eyes that twirled with SriBrune's mystical light. "I have missed you greatly, my son."

He released his grip and stepped aside.

Kinmin turned his gaze up to his mother. Her youthful face was solemn and her chin was slightly raised. A green sash, woven into her hair, draped with regal elegance over her left shoulder. Silvery hair framed her brown features like Allsbruth's forever snow, and sparkled in the magical light.

"Who stands before me?" she asked, her voice smooth and soothing as a spring wind, yet full of grace and strength. "Who is one such as you?"

"I am Kinmin, the son of King Cameare and Queen Riaa, heir to the throne of SriBrune. I left as a boy but have returned as a man."

Queen Riaa's stern facial expression faded to that of a loving mother. Her smile radiated brighter than all three SriBrunian suns. Unable to contain her joy, she ran down the steps and pulled him close.

"So I see," she whispered as her eyes watered with pride. She placed a gentle kiss on his forehead. "So I see."

His parents straddled either side of Kinmin and they returned to the platform. The king put his arm across Kinmin's shoulder while the queen whispered into his ear. Although recognized as a man by SriBrunian custom, he was still their son, and they enjoyed a quiet conversation that only a family could enjoy.

When they reached the top, Kinmin motioned for Il-Lilliad to approach. He lumbered forward and stopped at the base of the stairs. It was then he realized his height might be perceived as irreverent, for his head was even with their thrones. He immediately bowed to one knee and lowered his head.

"Who stands before me? Who is one such as you?" asked King Cameare.

"I am Il-Lilliad," he replied with eyes riveted on the dock's planks. "One of the last storytellers for the King of Claire. He has sent me to SriBrune to tell you his stories and to plead for your assistance."

Il-Lilliad felt the warmth of small hands holding the side of his face. His head was lifted, and he found himself staring into the rich, brown eyes of King Cameare. As the sovereign read the stories in Il-Lilliad's heart, his face changed shape and form to reflect every tale. The process was rapid and the king's features were but a blur. Satisfied, King Cameare let his hands fall. He stepped back and looked intently into Il-Lilliad's eyes.

"Your heart tells of many stories. Some make you dance with joy. Others have caused you great grief. All combined, they have fashioned you into the man you are today. I like what I have read, storyteller for the Only."

It was Queen Riaa's turn. She descended and placed her hands on either side of his face and locked her eyes onto his. As with the king, Il-Lilliad felt her flying through his heart and his memories like an eagle swooping down upon the River Arrgient. Her hands slid off and she also backed away, all the while keeping her eyes riveted on his.

"I saw many wonderful tales, many places of joy and pain. I saw truth and wisdom, but I also saw the faces of two children whom you love very much. Are they yours?"

Il-Lilliad gently shook his head. "You must have seen Elabea and Galadin. They are two children from Allsbruth who have answered the whisper from the Only and are journeying to Claire."

"I saw their faces too, my dear," the king added. "He carries so many feelings, so many dreams for them both."

"And yet," Queen Riaa finished, "so many fears."

Il-Lilliad nodded. *Have they made it to Claire?* he wondered. *Are we stepping toward victory, or have they failed and plummeted us all into despair?*

He abandoned such questions and addressed the King and Queen. "I long to tell you their story and the reason the Only has whispered to them. It is not a short story; it will take some time to tell."

King Cameare looked at his queen and without speaking a word, they agreed on what must be done. It was Queen Riaa who voiced their decision.

"We would find it a great honor to entertain a storyteller of the Only, to learn more of these tales." She let her gaze wonder to his bloodstained tunic. "And what stories they must be, for you nearly lost your life to deliver them. First, we must address your wounds."

With a fluid, graceful gesture of her right hand, she motioned for her maidservant to approach. Queen Riaa whispered into her ear, the servant bowed and retreated from view. She soon returned with a small ivory jar, then scampered down the stairs to Il-Lilliad. With the jar's black top off, she dug her fingers into the creamy, tan lotion and applied it directly to his tunic. She rubbed it around and around until it absorbed not only into the cloth, but into his wounds as well.

Her ministrations were painful. Il-Lilliad winced, gritted his teeth and hoped that this was not some cruel custom but truly was medicinal herb butter. When he thought he could take no more, he felt the pain start to fade and the balm growing warm, reminding him of sunshine on a chilly morning.

As she gathered more of the balm, Il-Lilliad widened the holes in his tunic and peered in at his wounds. The punctures were no longer raw and open but were covered with new skin. Purple bruises were dissolving into a healthy pink hue, and the bloodstains evaporated before his eyes.

Kinmin joined Il-Lilliad on the stairs. "My parents admire you very much," he said.

"I'm so glad," Il-Lilliad replied as the maidservant rubbed in more of the balm. "But tell me, what would have happened if they had disliked me?"

Kinmin smiled. "You would have gone for another swim in Karajan."

Chapter 14

Seas and Worms

Despite nearing Tristan's border, which would signal the end to attacks by lions, Wurmlins and Ebonite patrols, Linwith was troubled. Ever since leaving Hetherlinn, he had contemplated his mission, and no matter how he reasoned, planned or hoped, he kept arriving at the same bothersome conclusion.

"Rittmar," Linwith asked with a gentle slap of the reins, "have you ever been lost?"

"No. The creatures of Bal-Malin never get lost; we are very discerning and calculating and in fact, are excellent mapmakers. Why do you ask; are you lost?"

"No, I know where we are in regards to our location. I was referring to being lost in life. The more I think about my mission, the more I encounter the same conclusion, and it reminds me of a time when I was lost in the woods."

"How so?" Rittmar asked, intrigued by the notion of something he was not capable of experiencing.

"I had been trying to find my way back to Hetherlinn for some time, but I still wasn't sure which way to go. I decided to mark a tree, then I set off in the direction I believed to be true. After awhile, I came upon my marked tree and realized that I had been walking in circles."

Rittmar, being a creature of astute logic and unable to comprehend how this was even doable, simply blinked and continued to politely listen.

"And now, as I ponder my mission, I encounter the same marked tree, as if I'm walking in circles."

"You just said we are not lost," Rittmar said, perplexed. "Yet your story indicates that we have been traversing a circle in the woods, when in fact I know that we have been traveling on a straight course across the Gilden Plains that is without thickets."

Linwith chuckled to himself. "I take it that the creatures of Bal-Malin don't speak with such imagery, using nature or a contrasting circumstance to better explain one's current experience?"

"No," Rittmar replied. "That would be a waste of time. Why not simply state what the problem is, discover the solution, and be finished with the conversation?"

"Very well, then," Linwith shrugged. "Here's my problem: we will not win the war."

"Why not?"

"We don't have enough time."

"But you do. In fact, the war hasn't even begun yet, so how can you predict such an outcome?"

"Simple. How many days has it been since I left Hetherlinn?"

"Six."

"How many more until we reach Draiglore in Tristan to barter for weapons?"

"Two."

"So, to return to Hetherlinn will take us about…?"

"Eight days. However, with a wagon full of steel, your horses will not be able to travel as quickly."

Linwith nodded. "Exactly. Now you understand why we won't win the war."

Flustered by such jumps of logic, Rittmar shook his head.

"No, I do *not*. This simply explains that your trip back is longer, but does *not* explain how you do not have enough time, or for that matter, why you think you'll lose the war."

"Let's continue to examine the facts," Linwith replied. "Based upon your experience trading produce for weapons in Tristan, will we net more or less than what we brought to barter with?"

"Why less, of course. Tristan steel is in higher demand than Allsbruthian vegetables."

"Correct. Now do you see?"

Rittmar was so bamboozled by Linwith's reasoning that he landed on his nose, which in turn made Linwith's eyes cross.

"No, I don't," Rittmar gasped. "The only fact one can clearly see is that you have a longer return trip with only a handful of weapons, but this in no way implies defeat."

Linwith refocused his eyes, trying in vain to see the insect-like creature resting on the tip of his nose. Realizing his proximity was a problem for Linwith, Rittmar hovered just beyond his face.

Linwith continued. "I suppose Allsbruthian reasoning is different than that of Bal-Malin, so here is my point: in order to get enough weapons for our army - which currently doesn't exist - we need more produce, but this will require at least ten to twenty more years of planting and harvesting. By then, we will be too old or Ebon will have found our contraband and destroyed us. Either way, defeat looms. Now do you understand?"

"Yes," Rittmar replied. "We have known such a truth since the day we began escorting you to Tristan."

"You have? Then why haven't you said anything?"

"We did. We told you that you are *Linwith, the Worm Master*, destined to tame the worms of Bal-Malin..."

"Yes, yes, yes," Linwith interrupted. "I know all of that, but that still doesn't help me escape from the woods."

Rittmar, once more confounded by Linwith's imagery, searched for the *woods* Linwith kept referencing. Unable to find even the smallest of thickets, Rittmar opted to clarify for Linwith what he needed to do as the Worm Master.

"Before going to Tristan, you need to visit the lairs of the worms. *Then* you will understand how defeat is not in your future, for the worms of Bal-Malin are ferocious beasts who will serve you faithfully."

Linwith pulled back on the reins, bringing the team of horse to a halt.

"Very well," he said as he began to consider Rittmar's suggestion. "Let's assume I agree to such a redirection, even though I'm still doubtful about these worms. How do you propose we get to your island? Will your people lift me and my wagon in flight like you did when you rescued me at the River Arrgient?"

"No, of course not. The weight is too great and the Gilden Sea is too vast for such an effort. We would need a vessel."

"Exactly. Which leads me to my next problem: I don't own a boat, nor do I know anyone who does."

"If we head north, we will reach the fishing village of Holman. With some of your produce, we can bargain for space on one of their ships and sail to Bal-Malin."

"And how long would this take?"

"One full day."

The thought of being aboard a vessel tossed about by the waves for that length of time made Linwith queasy. He was not adverse to the seas. In fact, he enjoyed sojourns to the coast. When he was a boy, he had visited the Sea of Illsbruth and enjoyed the warm, calm waters. He had even ventured out to depths well over his head despite the fact that the mighty karshe swam out in the deep. But the Gilden Sea? The north winds churned those waters to a white froth, and even during the hottest of summers the waters were cold. He shook his head.

"There must be another solution," he replied, hoping to avoid the perilous sea at all cost.

"If there were," Rittmar answered, "don't you think I would tell you so?"

Linwith gazed toward the Addoli Ridge. Somewhere on the other side was the Gilden Sea whose frigid waters held the truth to the stories told around every campfire: Creatures from deep lairs that consume vessels whole; waves that crest like mountains and crush ships with green and white waters; winds that ambush even the most seasoned of mariners to rip asunder sails, masts and rigging.

He let his troubled thought ponder the isle of Bal-Malin. Was there more to Rittmar's story of the worms than he gave him credit for? Could this obscure island, inhabited by such intriguing creatures like Rittmar, hold the secret to their success in the ensuing war?

Sensing his inner turmoil, Rittmar said, "Perhaps it is simply because I am a creature of Bal-Malin, but to me, I see no other way. However, if I use your way of reasoning, let me add this: what have you got to lose?"

"A lot. I'm not a good swimmer," Linwith replied, his mind still enrapt by the Gilden Sea's tales.

"You won't need to; we will be aboard a ship," Rittmar replied, frustration tinging his tone.

Linwith laughed and shook his head.

"Why are you laughing?" Rittmar asked.

"Because what I was *really* trying to say is that I fear that the boat might sink and I'd perish."

Perplexed by Linwith's linguistics, Rittmar's eyes blinked rapidly. "Why didn't you say so in the first place? Why mask such feelings by omitting words?"

Instead of trying to explain, and knowing such educational discussions were probably a mute point, Linwith knew Rittmar was right. Despite his apprehensions and the tales of the Gilden Sea, he snapped the reins and turned the wagon north for Holman.

Chapter 15

The Guardian of Marsien Vur

Elabea darted off her draigg and raced toward Marsien Vur. Romlin followed, but with much more caution.

"Elabea, slow *down,*" Romlin called as their draiggs joined the others circling overhead. "Must everything be a race?"

As the draiggs disappeared on their journey back to Cor len Bluun, Romlin wondered if being stranded atop the mountain was a blessing or a curse.

Ignoring his pleas, Elabea leapt deer-like, gracefully up the slight incline, but at the summit she stopped. Romlin caught up with her and stared at what had startled her.

A wall of green ivy towered over them and wrapped around the mountain. Romlin pulled away some of the thick vines, but instead of seeing through to the other side, he discovered tan stone. He pulled more of the vines away with the same result. Finally, he stopped and stood perplexed.

"A wall," he said, exasperated. "We travel this far only to encounter *this?*"

"How did we miss seeing it when we flew over," Elabea wondered.

"The ivy must have blended in with the grass," he answered as he took in the formidable wall. "It might be as tall as the trees in Marsien Vur, but our oak was taller. Perhaps we climb over."

Romlin stuck his foot into the thick ivy, grabbed some of the hefty vines, and began to scale the growth.

"This isn't too difficult," he said over his shoulder from a third of the way up. He stopped and looked down at Elabea. "Are you coming?"

She let her hand run over the glossy leaves as she studied the vines. She was not alarmed by its height, for Romlin was correct: their oak *was* much taller. But she feared the unknown. Her experience of Claire so far was not matching up with her expectations. Yes, it was indeed a land of peace and lush beauty, but abiding in all the colors, sights and sounds was a deep mystery. She could feel it grab her heart. It made her feel like she felt when Romlin's eyes beheld her with admiration, or of the times when she was high in her oak during a violent windstorm: frightened, yet exhilarated, at once bold and shy, free and so *alive.*

Tossing caution to the wind, and not wanting Romlin to beat her over the wall, she began to climb. A rustling sound distracted her and she stopped to determine its source. Glancing about, she saw nothing, and was about to continue her ascent when the noise came again from higher on the wall, accompanied by an alarmed cry from Romlin.

A length of the vine had wrapped itself around Romlin's torso like a serpent and yanked him off the wall. It dangled him high over the ground. Romlin tried to kick his way to freedom, and even tried to draw his blade, but the vine was too powerful.

Elabea jumped off the wall to avoid another vine that snaked toward her. She backed away and watched helplessly.

"Elabea," Romlin shouted. "Tell a story!"

She nodded and pulled out her book, flipping through pages looking for a clue to the wall's identity.

"It's tightening," Romlin gasped, "I...can't...breathe."

Through page after page Elabea's eyes raced over fonts and images until she found something that caught her attention.

"Any *time*," Romlin pleaded.

The words on the page spoke, just as they had back at Cor len Bluun.

"Before you is the guardian of Marsien Vur who is neither alive or dead, nor flora or fauna, but is to be addressed as a person and deserving of proper respect. To enter Marsien Vur, stand before the crown of vines with your parchment and declare boldly: 'With our invitations we come.' Do not come mockingly or harbor a desire to vex or taunt, for to do so before such a coronet of green would not only be foolish, but would spell one's demise."

Elabea dropped the book and raced to the wall waving her parchment overhead.

"With our invitations we come," she declared to the ivy.

The vine stopped its defense, but did not relax its hold on Romlin. He drew in what little air he could.

The wall's glossy leaves turned ever so slightly toward the parchment, as if to read and inspect its authenticity, then rustled as if brushed by a gentle wind.

A voice emanated from all around, the Guardian speaking with ancient authority, "Does the boy bear such an invitation?"

"Yes," Elabea cried out. "It's inside his pocket. If you set him down, he'll show you."

The vine lowered Romlin to the ground and released him. Romlin turned in anger and drew his sword.

"Stupid weed!"

"Romlin, no," Elabea warned.

The ivy darted for his boots and wrapped around his ankles. Before Romlin could swing his blade, he was yanked back up and hung upside down like a snared rabbit.

"Dumb ivy," he muttered as he swung his weapon, but all he cut was the cool air. Exhausted, he let the sword drop with a soft *plop* to the grass below.

"He is a feisty one," the vine commented.

"Yes," Elabea agreed as she crossed her arms beneath her breasts in the manner of women who were exasperated by the foolishness of men. "That he is. But he does carry an invitation."

The vine shook Romlin up and down and his parchment inched out of his pocket. The vine pulled the invitation out and began to inspect it. Romlin stared down at Elabea.

"What's it doing?"

She dropped her hands to her hips.

"Romlin, the vine is not an *it*."

"Alright," he shouted back, "then tell me what *he's* doing?"

"He's reading your invitation."

"Reading?" he said. "A vine that reads? Well if it - I mean, if *he* - is reading, then he is taking his own sweet time doing so."

The vine dropped Romlin none too gently on the ground. Rubbing the back of his head where he landed, Romlin retrieved his sword while mumbling to himself about how vines *looked* like weeds, and how was he supposed to know *it* was a *he*, and Elabea *should* have said something sooner.

"Children of Allsbruth," the ivy announced. "As the Guardian of Marsien Vur, let me welcome you to Claire."

"Forgive us," Elabea graciously interjected as Romlin continued to mumble to himself. "We meant no harm in trying to climb you. We are unfamiliar to the ways of Claire."

"My apologies as well, young Elabea. I was unaware you two carried invitations."

"You could have *asked*," Romlin complained.

Elabea jabbed him in the ribs with an elbow.

"Please tell us," she continued, "how do we get to the other side to visit Marsien Vur?"

"There are two entrances somewhere along my wall."

"Somewhere along your wall?" Romlin said, still agitated. "Surely you know their exact locations."

"Yes, but that is not for me to disclose."

"Your wall goes on for a long way, so how will we find these entrances," Elabea asked.

"Actually, my wall encircles the entire mountain top, much like a crown. You each must journey along my wall in the opposite direction. Watch your parchments, for they will alert you to where the entrances are."

Romlin grabbed Elabea's sleeve and pulled her away.

"I don't think we should split up," he whispered. "Aside from the animals, we haven't met anyone from Claire, and now we encounter *this*." He let his eyes wander back to the ivy wall.

"Perhaps we're being tested," she whispered back.

Romlin's brow furrowed. "Tested?"

She nodded. "It's obvious we're to be here. The animals knew our names and had even watched our journey unfold, and the guardian recognized our invitations as well. Besides, if we were to be killed, the draiggs or the wall could have already done so."

"I suppose…"

"I think we should do as the wall commanded."

At the prospect of a new adventure, Romlin abandoned his concerns and nodded in agreement.

"Very well," he announced loudly for the benefit of the guardian of Marsien Vur as he strutted toward the wall, "You go that way and I'll go this way."

Without even pausing to wave good-bye, Romlin held his invitation in front of him and began his trek. Elabea, however, did not move. Instead, her eyes wandered first to her invitation, then to the wall's vast expanse. This was the first time on their journey they had gone separate ways. Although she had encouraged such a parting, the fear of leaving Romlin's side immobilized her. As if reading her mind, he turned and called to her.

"Elabea," he yelled through cupped hands. "If you need me, just shout. My sword is always ready to defend you." He waved once then turned to go, but stopped again and turned back to her. His smile made her knees weak. "Oh, I forgot," he called. "Good luck!"

She flashed him a grateful, nervous smile and was about to reply when he spun on his heels and disappeared into the shadows. With a heavy sigh, she headed in the opposite direction, her steps as timid as her thoughts.

Chapter 16

The Scar

Newcomb rode beside Draemel, thankful for their unhurried pace. It afforded him the opportunity he had waited for: to read more of Draemel's story.

In normal times, he would never venture into such hallowed memories without being invited, but these were not normal times. For Lassiter's sake he had to know the truth.

From the corner of his eye, he watched Draemel lift his tethered hands and scratch the scar on his cheek. His fingers lingered and felt every nuance of the raised flesh, as if to recall the events that led to its appearance as well as the stories that followed thereafter.

This was the chance he had hoped for. Newcomb entered Draemel's stories, and discovered that although the scar had healed many summers ago, pain still lingered. But this was not the agony caused by severed nerves and opened flesh. His was the grief of love destroyed, trust betrayed and hope dashed.

As Draemel stroked the purplish scar, he unwittingly carried Newcomb back to that fateful summer.

Hornlynn fumed as he addressed his men from Min Brock's walkway.

"Our leaders, Quinn and Gundin, have secured a deal with the Ebonites, but I think it is a cunning trick from the Cauldron. In exchange for our storytellers, they will let us return home unscathed, but we must vow to never again follow the tales of Claire. Instead, we're to pay homage to the Oracles of the Council of Ebon."

The men murmured amongst themselves. Hornlynn turned to his faithful commander and confided his deepest concerns.

"As much as I hate the deal Quinn has arranged, I feel we have no more options. The Ebonites surround us and outnumber us."

Draemel digested the words before weighing in with either a comment or retort. Hornlynn waited, knowing his friend's advice would be well-considered. At last Draemel spoke.

"Yes, our enemy is strong, but with the storytellers still in our midst, we can muster up a greater offensive than the Ebonites can withstand."

Hornlynn nodded and patted the white wall as if he were gathering courage from the amassed stones.

"Yes, this is true."

"So why doesn't Quinn call them forth? Why doesn't he unleash tales of destruction from Claire?"

Hornlynn clinched his teeth.

"I fear Quinn has abandoned his belief in the whisper of Claire. Instead, he is confused by the whisper from the Cauldron."

Draemel's eyes widened with horror.

"Can you prove this?"

Hornlynn shook his head.

"If I could, then I would bring such allegations to light and justice would be served."

"Then you must overthrow him," Draemel urged. "Your wife, Anessatia, is King Culdean's daughter. You are closer to being king than anyone else here in Min Brock. Surely the other armies will vow allegiance to you in this uprising."

"We would be fighting against one another; divided as our enemy parades upon the Gilden Plains before us. And when one of us is victor, they will defeat us for sure."

"We must do something," Draemel fired back.

Hornlynn made his decision, and turned to address his men in the courtyard below. Although he did not know them all by name, he knew their stories and the villages they called home. At night, he overheard their campfire tales of hearth, home and hunting. He chuckled when one complained about a nagging wife, yet he knew these men would readily die for their women.

He loved hearing their songs; simple tunes, yet sung with such passion, that Tristan steel would buckle beneath such gusto. Most of all he admired their courage and he vowed to personally shake each man's hand, look him square in the eye, and thank him for his service.

"Faithful army that serves the late great King Culdean," Hornlynn shouted. "Although I do not agree with the surrender terms, it is something we must consider."

Murmurs rumbled below. Hornlynn held up a hand and they quieted.

"We are surrounded. It is only a matter of time before our enemy either starves us into submission or besieges Min Brock. Quinn has abandoned his hope in our great ally, Claire. So we either comply with the terms or…"

He paused, not only to have their full attention but to make sure he could commit to what he was about to propose.

"Or we attack our enemy…one last time."

Draemel nodded to Hornlynn's last declaration. His brown eyes narrowed as he surveyed the army below, curious how they would respond.

One commander stepped forward and peered up at the two men on the walkway.

"If I may, I think I can speak for all of us when I say that none of us wish to die in vain. We'd prefer to go home to our wives than stay here in Min Brock."

Hornlynn gave a somber nod and Draemel's shoulders slumped.

"But answer us this: how are we to live with such shame? Wouldn't we die daily? Wouldn't we reach old age wearing a coat of disgrace? Such a life is not life and in fact, is more horrendous than the death that awaits us beyond Min Brock's walls."

Draemel's shoulders stiffened again.

"I don't know if one death is more glorious or more disgraceful than another," Hornlynn answered. "But I too have reasoned such notions. Like you, I long to pull my wife close and listen to the sound of laughing children, but how could I do so, bowing to Ebon's might and the Cauldron's ways? Peace would be illusionary, the Oracles would be our shackles and life would ebb away.

"So to answer you, commander, if you and your men would honor me one more time in battle, I would consider such companionship as wondrous as that of my wife and child's."

The men erupted in cheers as swords were thrust into the air. Louder and louder they cheered. Hornlynn placed both hands on Draemel's shoulders, pulled him close and embraced him like a brother. Together they descended to their horses and their final mission.

The gates were opened, and as the army galloped out, Draemel glanced back at two men standing on the parapets of Min Brock; the two men who had betrayed their oaths and their armies - Quinn and Gundin of Hetherlinn. He let their faces burn into his mind like a hot brand upon an animal's hide. Come what may, he would carry their images to his death and if possible, return as a ghoul to haunt them to their last days.

Hornlynn's force galloped down the knoll's incline, and when they reached the bottom, the army fanned out into a single rank. The clatter of armor, the thunder of hooves and their shouts of war rumbled across the Gilden Plains.

Draemel focused on the Ebonites. From a distance, they appeared as a dark cloud on the plain that stretched from the Addoli Ridge toward the Allsbruthian Mountains. Never before had he seen so many of their enemy assembled in one place. He fired encouragements off to his commanders who in turn relayed them down the line. Hornlynn signaled the attack. Spurs dug into flanks. Their pace quickened and swords glinted in the bright sunlight.

"For our families," Hornlynn rallied. "For the Only!"

The men cheered and galloped toward their enemy. The Ebonite army was recognizable now, and no longer just an amorphous mass. Draemel could see row upon row of lances, cavalry, archers and foot soldiers. In the moment before the battle began, Hornlynn and Draemel gave each other a parting glance goodbye, then Ebonite archers loosed their volleys and jagged tips pierced man, steel and steed.

Riders were tossed. Horses screamed in agony and crashed to the plain. Still the warriors charged onward, their voices louder than before and their swords eager to strike. Another deadly barrage of arrows fell, and more of Hornlynn's men died.

Hornlynn's force thundered toward their enemy. The Ebonites settled their long lances against the onslaught, piercing warriors and warhorses alike. Warriors flew headfirst onto waiting spears, or landed stunned on the ground. Some were thrust through with swords while others managed to rise to their feet and fight.

Hornlynn and Draemel avoided both lance and spear, and slammed full speed into the unprotected row of Ebonites. Black armor flew in a haphazard dance across the battlefield as warhorses beat a frenzied path for their masters. Blade met blade and lances pressed in, but with amazing skill Draemel and Hornlynn parried the blows and struck down their enemies. They fought gallantly, seeking no quarter, and giving none. They struck first to their left, then defended on their right, but they were vastly outnumbered. It was only a matter of time before Ebonite blades drove deep into their steeds. What was left of Hornlynn's once-proud cavalry found themselves on foot, fighting hand to hand.

Draemel led his men against the swarming Ebonites. Steel crashed against steel and loud reports echoed across the valley. Draemel's courage was no match for Ebon's numbers and his dwindling force was encircled, fighting back-to-back.

Sweat rolled from Draemel's brow as he willed his exhausted arms to continue striking and slicing, thrusting and parrying. He felt a burning sensation across his cheek. Dazed by the cut, he turned to face his attacker when a crashing blow sent him to the ground. Bodies fell on top of him as the Ebonite warriors pressed forward. He labored to suck hot air into his lungs, but the weight on his back made breathing next to impossible.

The sounds of battle faded and an unearthly quiet settled over the battlefield. Draemel knew the end had come. Everything went black.

Draemel wondered if he was dead. He thought he was blinking his eyes, yet all he saw was darkness. His lungs burned for air and he felt a crushing weight upon him, so he reasoned he must be alive. He strained against the weight until the bodies of his dead comrades rolled off.

He clawed his way into the cool night air, drinking in deep breaths as he stared at the carnage all around him. The moonlight washed the battlefield with blue shadows, making the twisted torsos and dismembered limbs all the more eerie. He touched his burning cheek, then examined his fingertips. Blood, still dripping from the gash, glistened black in the moonlight. His mind sharpened and he searched for any sign of the Ebonite army, but it had long since gone, leaving the dead to bury the dead.

A distant roar startled him from his reverie. The lions of the plain had caught the scent of blood and were on the prowl. Their feeding frenzy would be horrible, a bloodbath he was powerless to prevent. He couldn't bury all of his comrades. There were too many. But he couldn't leave Hornlynn's body to the beasts.

Draemel called his friend's name, hoping for the best but fearing the worst, as he stepped over corpses. Desperate, he rolled soldier after soldier over and peered into their ashen faces, looking for his friend.

Another growl echoed from a different direction. The pride was closer. He intensified his efforts and continued to call Hornlynn's name, but when more growls peppered the night, he started to lose hope. He was about to flee for his life when out of the corner of his eye a glint of moonlight on metal flashed. Far from the sea of corpses, alone, lay a warrior. A sword was impaled in the ground beside him and seemed to almost glow in the moon's light. Even from far away, Draemel recognized the warrior's armor and the insignia on his helmet.

Hornlynn.

Draemel raced to the body, rolled him on to his back and began to weep for his friend. The growls grew louder, forcing Draemel to squash his emotions deep within.

He yanked the sword free and slid it back into Hornlynn's scabbard. He draped Hornlynn's body over his right shoulder, struggling beneath the weight, and staggered toward a nearby dry creek bed.

He made his way down the embankment, and rounding a bend, found a perfect burial spot in a sandy cove. He set Hornlynn's body down, unsheathed his friend's sword and drove it deep into the soil to serve as a grave marker. He gathered large stones, worn smooth by the waters of the creek, and stacked them one upon another over Hornlynn's body to prevent desecration by any prying lion or gor.

When he at last set the final stone upon Hornlynn's bier, Draemel's emotions overtook him. He wept and rocked in the moonlight until roars and the sound of tearing bone and flesh shook him from his laments.

The lions had found his fallen brothers.

The sounds of the feeding frenzy reached a fevered pitch. He knew he must flee before he too was discovered by the lions. A glance toward Min Brock told him it was deserted; that Quinn and Gundin were either dead, prisoners of Ebon, or had retreated as cowards back to Hetherlinn.

A growl rolled over the embankment. He reached for his sword but found the scabbard empty. He considered taking Hornlynn's sword but dismissed the idea. Without the marker, how would he find his friend's grave and return him to his homeland for a proper burial?

Dark, primal growls sent chills arcing through him. He stared south across the Gilden Plains toward his home, Hoitt. The distance was great, and the odds were against him surviving in the open plain, but with vengeance as a fire in his gut, he clambered out of the creek bed and put as much distance between himself and the gorging lions as possible.

Throughout the night he trudged; sometimes jogging, sometimes shambling. The stars were his map and the moon his guardian. He identified wild animals by the moonlight reflecting off their eyes, glowing like miniscule lanterns. Green flashes were deer while yellow were gors. When red orbs glowed, he knew he was being watched by lions and steered clear of their path.

As dawn broke he neared the River Arrgient. The river was deep and wide, and its current slow. He walked downstream in search of a shallower crossing, keeping to the higher ground to avoid any Ebonite patrols. When he found a suitable place to ford the river, he hid in the bushes along the shore until he was certain he was alone and then waded with quiet, careful steps out.

The water rose quickly to his knees, but remained at that level all the way to the middle of the river. He paused as a sudden realization broke upon his mind. He was defenseless against a passing patrol, and easy prey. Panic caught in his chest, urging his feet faster. Reason abandoned him, and he rushed forward, oblivious to the noise he created. His feet stumbled over the river bottom's slick rocks and he fell, splashing and thrashing into the water. He regained his feet, righted himself, slipping, sliding, swimming as much as running to gain the far shore.

When he reached the other side, he darted for the safety of a nearby thicket and dove into its shadows. He caught his breath, as the panic receded. He checked his bearings. He knew that if he followed the river that it would lead him to the village of Dallin, in Ferra. He needed supplies. He needed a horse. Without a single coin to barter or a sword to hire himself out as a bodyguard or mercenary, he knew he would have to improvise.

A rumble from his stomach reminded him he had not eaten in more than a day. A quick glance revealed the bushes he was hiding in were wildeberry bushes, and the berries lay thick on the stems. Grabbing a handful, he pressed them into his mouth, and as he ate, he noticed a stand of familiar leafy plants. An old trapper's tale claimed the tuber-like roots of the plant tasted like venison. He knew from experience that while the bitter roots would keep you alive, they tasted nothing like deer meat. A quick yank freed it from the ground. He cleaned off the dirt as best he could and filled his stomach.

Once again able to think clearly, Draemel set out on his journey. By midday, he reached the outskirts of Dallin. Though he had never visited the outpost, he was familiar with its reputation. The nation of Ferra attracted those of a freer spirit and who disliked authority. Dallin was a haven for the worst-of-the-worst.

Though he had lost his sword, he had his dagger. He unsheathed it and proceeded with caution. He avoided the main road, slipping instead from tree to tree, remaining in the shadows. As he neared the outskirts of Dallin he stopped. He expected to hear human voices, animals baying, axes chopping wood - all of the sounds associated with civilization.

All he heard were the sounds of nature; birds and insects.

He ventured forward from a copse of trees. The watchtower of the outpost was burned to the ground. He started walking in the middle of the dirt road that led into Dallin, then started running. He rounded the hilltop overlooking the outpost and froze in his tracks.

Dallin was nothing but ash.

Gors scavenged through cinders that were once homes, searching for food. Crows perched in a nearby tree, cawed at nothing in particular. There was no other sign of life.

Draemel recognized such destruction. It was the handiwork of Ebon. He just hoped they did not get as far east as Hoitt.

He doubled back to the River Arrgient and followed its course until it split in two. The main river turned south to empty out into Southsbrook by the Sea of Illsbruth. The smaller tributary continued eastward into Ingloid.

He followed the eastern tributary. He told himself the Ebonites had not reached his village, that Hoitt was spared their bloodlust, but he wasn't sure he believed it and his fears quickened his steps.

He was almost home when night fell. Finding shelter beneath an outcrop of rocks, he tried to rest, but thoughts of the utter destruction of Dallin and horrors of the battle at Min Brock made for a fitful night's sleep. Morning came early and he trekked onward with only cold river water to fill his belly.

The terrain became hilly and familiar. He reflected on Merriam, his wife, and the many times they hiked the Ingloid countryside. She was a petite woman with an impish grin. Though one of the shyer and more modest girls of Hoitt, she was the one who made him stumble over his words like the town drunk.

They had grown up together in Hoitt, but it was not until she was seventeen summers of age that he noticed her. While loading supplies into his father's wagon, Merriam walked past carrying a jar of water. Entranced by her swaying figure and distracted by her beautiful face, Draemel misjudged what he was doing and dropped a bag of seed in the dirt. Draemel's father chastised him as a clumsy ox, but Draemel was too lost in her gaze to hear.

Her eyes were prisms of green that portaled him off to another world. She blushed and scurried away.

From that day forth, he vowed he would marry her. At the time, he had no idea how much convincing Merriam would need.

When it was the season for hunting, Draemel joined the other men - not just to provide provisions for the town, but to impress Merriam. When the hunters returned, the whole village turned out to view their kills. When Draemel saw Merriam peek through the crowd, he raised an antlered head for her to admire. It was by far the largest buck of the hunt, but instead of running to him desperate for love, or openly praising his hunting prowess, she whispered something to her friend, giggled and disappeared.

When it was time to cut timber for more fishing boats, Draemel chopped, sawed and hacked his way through the largest trees in Ingloid. When Merriam neared, he draped his arm across his stack of lumber and flexed his muscles. She walked on past, unimpressed.

When the hunting season for the fierce sea karshe arrived, Draemel was the first to sign up at the pier for the voyage. As the men prepared to leave, their wives and lovers kissed them good-bye. Draemel stared beyond the embracing crowd and found Merriam standing alone. He gestured for her to run and kiss him, if for nothing more than good luck. She simply shook her head and waved farewell.

Then a dark season came; one that neither Draemel nor any other living person could prepare for. A plague, carried by rats, invaded the village. The very young and the very old were the main victims. Both of Merriam's parents were carried off by the plague. She buried them both on the same day.

Draemel was at a loss of what to do or say. He had never faced death of anyone close to him. He longed to extend his condolences, but as he approached her cottage, his tongue felt as if it had outgrown his mouth. Afraid he would stumble over his words and say something wrong, he walked away.

He tried again, but again lost his nerve at the thought of intruding on a grief he could not consol. He cowered near her home...until he saw Mullins approaching.

Mullins and Draemel had competed against each other since they were five summers of age. When Draemel saw Mullins strutting down the path toward Merriam's with flowers in hand and humming a happy song, something inside him snapped. How dare he think a merry tune and a bouquet of flowers would ease Merriam's heartache.

Draemel darted from his hiding place and planted himself in front of Merriam's door. Mullins stopped in his tracks. The look on Draemel's face threatened physical harm if he took another step. Hurling profanities at Draemel, along with his bouquet, Mullins retreated back down the path.

Draemel was about to walk away himself when the door opened.

Merriam's smile - the one that held him rapt that summer long ago - was gone, and her jade-colored eyes that had beamed eternal light were misty, like the bog.

He gazed into her face and tried to think of some way to rescue her from her sadness, but he knew there was nothing he could do. He searched his thoughts for a sonnet or poem that would make her heart dance, but he was no poet. Even if he were, such words were mortal, and she was dancing with mortality.

He said the only words he could.

"Merriam, I'm so sorry."

Tears misted over her sea-green eyes, and trickled down her cheeks. She reached up and caressed his cheek, then pressed herself against him. He had dreamed of holding her like this, but never under these circumstances. Despite the calamity, he was overwhelmed - no, honored - to be the one she needed.

He wrapped his arms around her and pulled her close. His vision blurred, as if dust had whipped into his eyes and blinded him. He felt something warm rolling down his cheek, and realized he too was weeping.

Draemel brushed off the memory and stroked the cheek lwhere Merriam had first caressed him. It now bore the mark of Ebon.

He ascended the summit that would give him the first view of Hoitt. He had loved bringing Merriam up to this point. They would embrace and dream of life together by the Sea of Illsbruth. When he reached the ridge, his worst fears were realized.

"No," he shouted to the wind. *"No!"*

Draemel dashed down the incline, stumbling, falling, regaining his feet and running faster. As he ran, he remembered how beautiful Merriam looked on their wedding day: her ivory-colored dress glistened, her emerald eyes gazing dreamily into his, her sweet lips echoing, "I do."

He reached the bottom of the knoll and dashed to the main road. He abandoned all reason, all logic, all military training and experience. He ran as a lover, out in the open across the fastest path.

Rounding a bend in the road, he sprinted toward the village. His cheek wound oozed blood and his lungs burned for want of air, but he would not stop. Images of Merriam and their son, Farron, flooded his mind. He pushed himself faster, his heart breaking from the horror he dreaded to discover.

Hoitt was in sight, but instead of seeing the moorings where the men tied up their fishing boats, or the serene array of cottages in the woods, Draemel was greeted by silence and ash.

"Merriam," he screamed as he raced to the pile of ashes where their cottage once stood. Throwing himself into the white cinders, he clawed and dug through the soot, looking for his wife, searching for his son.

"Merriam," he cried as tears fell like rain from his eyes, turning white ash to gray. Down he dug, fingernails breaking and fingertips bleeding. All he found was more dust and ash.

"Merriam," he whimpered as he rocked to and fro, his bloodied hands shielding his face. A sound from behind him squelched his cries and he was instantly a warrior again.

He spun around to see a pack of gors gnawing on a charred carcass.

"No," he shouted as he charged the animals. "Get away from my family!"

The beasts reared and snarled, but Draemel's crazed attack sent them scurrying into the brush. The carcass was only the remains of a cow, but it didn't matter. Draemel from Hoitt had died, and another man was born in his body.

He no longer feared pain or death. Nor did he cherish life. Life was pointless, merely an obstacle course of pain.

He unsheathed his dagger. Brown eyes narrowed to slits of rage. He charged after the gors, dodging trees and leaping over small streams as he followed their path toward the sea. He spotted the herd through the trees.

Draemel charged from the woods, cursing their existence, vowing vengeance and running with the zeal of a man with nothing left to lose.

The smaller female gors scampered down the beach, but the enormous bull stood its ground. Rearing on its hind legs, it towered over Draemel, baring his jagged teeth and grunting in rage. Undeterred by the gor's show of power, Draemel attacked. The gor swatted him with its foreleg and sent him sprawling. The blow cleared Draemel's head. He stood and glared at the bull. He knew that his dagger was useless against its thick hide, so he let his years hunting karshe guide his next steps.

He darted to a wooden box strapped to what was left of a pier post. The lid flew off and he grabbed a metal sphere from within. Spiked and the size of an apple, it was the weapon of choice when killing the karshe. Today, it would serve another purpose.

The gor barked and pawed the rocky beach.

Draemel ripped off his shirt, grabbed both ends, and dropped the steel orb inside. He swirled his makeshift sling overhead. Whizzing sounds meshed with the waves crashing against the rocks.

Memories flashed of his younger days hunting karshe in the sea with his father.

The gor grunted.

Flashes of Hornlynn.

The gor charged.

Merriam…his son…

The beast lunged.

Draemel released the steel ball.

A dull *thud* echoed across the waves as the spiked orb lodged between the animal's eyes. The bull staggered, then crashed to the ground. Draemel leapt upon its back, grabbed a clump of hair on its head and drove his dagger repeatedly into the gor's neck. Satisfied it was dead, he plopped down on the beach and stared with dull, listless eyes across the Sea of Illsbruth.

Draemel didn't know how long he sat there. His eyes had lost the ability to shed tears; his heart was devoid of feeling. Images of the traitors of Min Brock, Hornlynn, his family swirled through his thoughts like seeds caught in a whirlwind. Eventually those seeds planted themselves and sprouted, forming a vision of hunting men for pay, thrusting his anger upon their hapless lives in an attempt to make sense of his.

He did not realize, as his new life mission took shape, that he was skinning the hide off the gor, oblivious to the stench rising from its still-warm flesh. Nor did he remember hacking out bones and whittling them into the most wicked of blades. He was too busy dreaming of the future when his name would conjure fear, his gor weapon would draw blood and his sling would end life.

Chapter 17

The Secret of the Garden

Elabea glanced over her shoulder toward Romlin, but he had already disappeared from sight. She pulled her resolve together and turned to find her way through the wall. As she walked, she studied the ivy, curious as to its purpose and nature.

"Why would someone like the Only need a wall within Claire? Is it to protect or conceal? Besides, if the King of Claire is all powerful, is it even necessary?"

"Perhaps it is neither," the ivy chimed in, its leaves rustling as if touched by a summer's breeze.

Elabea jumped, spooked that the ivy was ever present.

"How are you able to speak here, when the leaves that talked to us are far behind me?"

"I am but one vine with many branches and leaves. Together, we are one, capable of seeing everything encompassing our wall. North, south, east and west…they are but one direction to me."

"You can see Romlin?"

"Yes. He's quite excited."

"Is he able to hear our conversation?"

"No, it does not work like that. I am selective where I direct my speech."

Elabea paused, then asked the question plaguing her heart.

"If you do not protect or conceal, then why are you here?"

"The Only is unlike any other king."

"Yes, I have read his stories," she answered as she continued her search.

"Then you have an idea of what he is like, but this comprehension is only a glimpse, and pales in comparison to all that he is."

"That still does not explain…"

"Your friend, Romlin, stumbled upon the truth."

"I'm being tested?"

"Yes."

"But if the King of Claire is so powerful and all-knowing, can't he simply read my heart?"

"The test is not for him. It is for you."

Elabea pursed her lips, not sure what to make of the vine's explanation.

On she walked, her eyes riveted on her invitation, but nothing extraordinary happened. Her impatience grew. She was about to ask the ivy for help when her parchment flew of its own accord out of her hands. It darted in front of her like a hummingbird. She reached up to grab it, but just as her fingers touched it, the invitation flew away. Excited that perhaps the entrance was near, she raced after it.

The parchment stopped and flapped about in one spot, then submitted to her grasp. As she retrieved it the ivy retreated off the wall, revealing a sealed door of stone with an arch at its top. Etched into the stone, chiseled no doubt by a master mason, was her name, just as it appeared on her invitation. Standing on her tiptoes, she ran her fingers over the grooves that comprised her forename.

"It's so *old.* This must have been chiseled long before I was born. Even before my parents were born. But how? Who would know?"

Curious, she held her invitation up toward the etching. The stone letters began shimmering just like the words on her parchment had in Allsbruth. She heard the sound of heavy stone sliding over wet rock as the stone door opened. She was about to rush through when she remembered Romlin.

"Romlin, hurry," she called out to him. "I have found it!"

There was no reply.

She asked the vine, "Should I wait for him?"

"The archway bears your name only," Ivy leaves rustled. "What do you think?"

Excitement overtook her fears. She nodded, made her decision and walked through the entrance.

Trees swayed in the warm breeze as birds in a dizzying array of sizes and colors chirped and fluttered about. Flowers bloomed in glorious wonder, their scent capturing her senses. She breathed deeply the perfumed air.

I'm near the gardens, she noted. *But how can it be so warm at this height? How can gardens and songbirds live on such a mountain?*

"Romlin," she shouted back to the ivy wall. "I'm inside. Can you hear me?"

She waited for a reply, but none came.

The stone door began to close. For a moment she had the mad urge to run back out, but before she could take a step, it sealed shut. She swallowed her fears, then spun around and continued into the garden.

A tall hedge, trimmed to perfection and twice her height, concealed her view of the other side. In the midst of the hedge stood a tall, black gate that stirred her curiosity. Perched on its crest was an enormous bird.

Brilliantly plumed in feathers of pure white the bird was easily the size of a warhorse. Its face was scooped, like that of an owl, and fierce black eyes nestled on the front, pierced into Elabea's.

"Hello," she called, hoping the bird was like the other creatures in Claire and could answer her questions. Instead, it rustled its great wings and cocked its head to the side to study her. She held her invitation overhead for him to inspect.

"My name is Elabea. I have an invitation from the King of Claire."

The bird blinked its eyes.

"Could you please tell me where I could find him? I do believe he is expecting me."

The bird unfolded its wings and launched itself straight at her. Elabea ducked, marveling at its size as it climbed into the azure sky.

Elabea approached the gate. It was fashioned from ancient, black, iron bars that rose straight and true to an ornate archway. In the middle of the iron crest was a tulip. At first, she thought it was enameled metal, but upon closer inspection, she saw it flutter in the breeze. Silver dewdrops cascaded down its crimson petals. The tulip's ability to grow out of iron was yet another mystery of Marsien Vur.

She grabbed the gate's handle and found it cool and heavy to the touch. She pushed down. It clicked open. She hoped it would open with ease and would do so quietly. Instead, it required much effort, and opened with a metallic screech that announced her entry.

She walked through. She assumed the hedgerow encircled the garden, but since she could not see the garden's far side, she realized it was mere speculation. A stand of tulips grew alongside the hedge and followed its course through the garden. Red petals dripped with dew and swayed in the warm breeze as if to wave greetings to their guest.

Fanning out from the entrance were paths paved with river pebbles that meandered through gardens of gorgeous plants; some she recognized, other were strange to her. A patch on the right side of the path displayed all the flowers that grew in Allsbruth.

She saw a landscaped plot ahead and hurried toward it. Everything she observed was a miniature: ferns, rocks, moss; even the birds zipping about were the size of bees.

With each step her fears lessened and her wonder increased. She rounded a bend and encountered a miniature forest. Grazing in a tiny clearing was a herd of deer the size of field mice. Startled, they turned and leapt into a thicket. She gazed through the treetops and watched them prance through the forest.

Giddy with delight, she skipped further down the path. She encountered a tiny desert, full of white and orange sand, mesas and cacti, but further down the path was a garden that stole her breath.

"Look at *this*," she exclaimed, wishing Romlin were with her to share such beauty as she knelt beside the miniscule mountains.

"They look just like the Allsbruthian Mountains."

She stretched her hand toward the snow-capped peaks and was amazed to feel the temperature drop to that of a wintry day. Tiny brooks trickled down the granite, forming streams in the lush vegetation at the base of the mountains. Within the streams, she saw tiny flashes of light. Leaning closer, she realized it was light reflecting off of trout the size of a grain of sand.

Elabea wanted to linger over the familiar terrain, twinges of homesickness misting her eyes, but she tore herself away and continued her trek. She found herself at a stone bridge, aged and weathered from a myriad of people crossing it for countless summers. It arched over a stream that gurgled across moss-covered rocks, strands of which flowed like hair from a sage-colored goddess.

She crossed, pausing in the middle of the bridge to behold the splendor all about her. Never in her wildest imagination while sitting in her oak had she dreamed of such glory.

She skipped across the last bit of the bridge and followed the path that hugged the meandering stream. Normal sized trees grew along the bank, providing shade for her journey. At the trail's end, she entered a grassy clearing and walked to the water's edge for a drink. She knelt and lowered her hands into the clear, ice-cold water.

She scooped up a handful, then stared into a reflection that did not belong to her.

Chapter 18

Battle at Kiarrey Glen

Romlin traversed along the ivy wall looking for anything marking an entrance - a gap in the ivy; a trail from the woods disappearing into the wall; anything.

Nothing.

He was about to give up and work his way back to Elabea, when he noticed a miniscule bulge in the wall. He pulled back some of the vines - but gently, careful to not irritate the ivy and thus find himself dangling above the ground - and discovered a stone door bearing the same markings on his invitation: his name.

"Elabea, I found it," he shouted.

Then to himself he said, "But how could my name be etched on stone so old? And why isn't Elabea's name here?"

As he waited for Elabea to appear, he pulled out his parchment to compare the writing to the etchings on the stone door. The etchings glowed and the massive door swung open as if pushed aside by a spirit.

He pocketed his invitation, then retrieved his map and got his bearings.

"This must be Kiarrey Glen," he muttered aloud, "but where is Elabea?"

"She has found her own entrance," the ivy replied.

"Why would we be separated," Romlin asked, still not convinced they were safe in Claire.

"She is to become a storyteller; you are not," came the vine's curt reply.

Still en garde, Romlin stepped through the door and entered the glen. Lush grass spread out far and wide from the ivy wall toward a grove of tall, dark trees. Rising out of the dense thicket was Marsien Vur, but no living creature could be seen.

New sounds, metal upon metal, rumbling from the far end of the glen put him on edge. A squadron of mounted cavalry thundered into Kiarrey Glen. Silver armor glinted in the sun. Lances were lowered as they charged.

Romlin turned to run, but the stone door had disappeared. When he turned back to face his foes he discovered he was already surrounded. The warriors pushed their lances inward.

"Wait," Romlin barked, sweat trickling between his shoulder blades. "I have an invitation!"

He yanked the parchment out and held it high. He slowly turned about, keeping his hands clearly visible and away from his sword with the parchment high, so they could each see the validity of his statement.

"My friend and I have journeyed from Allsbruth as ordered by our invitations from the King of Claire."

The circle of warriors remained unwavering for a moment longer. Without a sound, they raised their lances skyward and rested them by their side. Then the ring opened.

Romlin thought they were letting him leave, until he saw a warrior approach from the dark glen. Armored from head to toe and larger than the others, this mysterious combatant sparked fear in Romlin's heart. The knight's horse was obsidian black, like a starless night, and his silver armor flashed with fiery brilliance, like a full moon. This behemoth entered the circle and strode toward Romlin.

"I have an invitation!"

The warrior stopped and leaned forward to read it; his leather saddle creaked beneath his bulk, and Romlin shuddered at his obvious power.

He returned to an upright position and a deep, resonate voice boomed through the vents of his helmet, "Your invitation states your name is Romlin, but I know you by another name, one that perhaps tells of your true heart: *Galadin, boy warrior.*"

"You're correct," Romlin answered, shame at the thought of his old nature coloring his cheeks. "I was once *Galadin*. But Manno Vox gave me this name. I am, *Romlin.*"

The warrior dismounted and unsheathed his great blade. He towered over Romlin.

"What have I done wrong," Romlin asked. He tried to back away, but found himself hemmed in by the circle of knights.

"You have brought illegal contraband into Claire," boomed the reply.

Romlin's brow furrowed.

"Illegal contraband? I don't know what you mean, I only brought what was given to me."

"And what of your heart?"

"My heart?"

"Is there not anger deep within your heart?"

Romlin swallowed, fearful of divulging his inner secrets.

"I don't know what you're talking about," he countered, hoping to stall the interrogation.

With his sword in one hand, the enigmatic warrior removed his helmet with his free hand.

Romlin gasped.

The warrior placed his helmet on the ground.

"The anger in your heart, which is contraband in Claire, is directed at me, is it not?"

Romlin shook his head to clear his thoughts. He hoped the face staring back at him was just a trick of the eyes. Shame and anger percolated through his veins. His breath came in sharp staccato spurts.

"Impossible," he shouted. "You can't be here."

"Impossible. Yet, here I am, staring at you, man-to-man."

"You're not a man," Romlin seethed as his hand slid down to his sword's hilt. "Run back to your day dreams from the Dark War."

"Such anger," the warrior replied, his voice calm and reserved. "What have I done to deserve such rage?"

"Your shame at Min Brock became *mine.*"

Romlin unsheathed his sword.

"So," the warrior noted, his eyes darting from Romlin's face to his weapon, "you truly do desire me dead."

Romlin's heart raced and sweat poured from his pores. He wiped his eyes, hoping to wipe away the apparition standing before him.

"Your eyes do not betray you; I am really here," the warrior replied. "And I *did* fail you...my son."

Romlin's hands shook as he stared at his father.

"How I wish I could change my past," Gundin continued. "But even if you kill me, you will never be free of me. You will forever walk, breathe and live within my shame. You too shall inherit madness, forever to shed the tears of Min Brock."

"*No.* Those will die when *you* die, and I will be a greater man, a greater warrior than you *ever* were."

"You're not listening. Examine your heart, for even as we speak, your anger grows."

Romlin drew back his sword. He glared at his father with rage filled eyes while his father's eyes reflected compassion.

With a deep sigh, Gundin raised his sword.

"So, it has come to this, has it," he whispered. "My son's steel against mine?"

Romlin took a cautionary step forward, knuckles white and eyes glaring red.

"I carry a wound and a pain from Min Brock that is great. Though it is my own, I know it has tarnished you as well. I wish I could reverse my days and remove such shame from your life, but I can't. And since you will not listen to reason, but choose instead to allow your wrath to sweep you to the same madness that consumed me, I see no other option before me."

Gundin raised his sword high over his head, and with both hands, drove its blade deep into the ground. He knelt.

Romlin froze. He expected a fiery display of retaliation, a man ready to defend his honor. Instead, he beheld eyes that were moist, tears staining weathered cheeks. Despite his fury, Romlin knew these were not tears of a coward, nor were they the tears of a man lost in his own self-pity. These were the tears of a father who would willingly die for his son. These were tears of love.

"Do what you must," Gundin said. "But know one thing: I am honored to be the father of Romlin, the future great warrior for the King of Claire."

His father's words were like a torrential rainstorm to his burning rage. Despite the years he had dreamed of such revenge, and as much as he yearned to become a better man than his father, he could not separate himself from the one fact that stood taller than the Mountains of Kline: he loved him, too.

Romlin staggered, his arms suddenly felt weak, not just from the sword's weight, but from the guilt and anger he had carried for so long. For reasons he could not fully explain or comprehend, he drove his blade into the soil next to his father's.

Gundin opened his arms. Romlin sank into his father's embrace. Tears from their eyes washed away the anger in Romlin's heart. His emotions spent, Romlin stood, then took a step back, awestruck, as Gundin's face started to melt like wax near flames.

Horrified, yet fascinated, Romlin could not pull his eyes away from the macabre, beautiful spectacle before him. Where once his father stood, was a man whose face he did not recognize. The stranger's eyes were fierce and powerful, yet there was a tenderness to them that beckoned for him to approach.

"Romlin," the stranger whispered.

Romlin gasped. *THE whisper!*

Chills ran up his spine. Finally, he stammered: "You...you're the King of Claire."

Romlin stood fearfully before the warrior-king. Would his angry barrage upon the cliffs now be questioned? Was severe punishment his lot? He licked his lips and tried to work moisture back into his mouth. He did not know what to say or what to do.

The king rested his hands on his shoulders.

"Romlin, my delight."

The words sank deep into Romlin's marrow where they sparked and flamed into life. The combustion exploded from the alcove of his core and corralled his rage, his shame, and his guilt. Merciless flames burnt them whole, and yet, within such death he found sweet, cool mercy. When the fires were but a flickering flare, they revealed cavernous pools of life. Swirling within the waters were new and wondrous emotions. For the first time in his life, Romlin experienced a sensation most men never do.

Passion.

Chapter 19

Royal Council

Il-Lilliad followed the royal family across the white bridge toward one of the tall buildings. Servants with fans provided shade while soldiers marched at the front and rear of their column.

Il-Lilliad could not help but overhear Kinmin tell his parents about his adventures in the Onderling. King Cameare rested his hand on Kinmin's shoulder, giving an occasional pat as he must have done when Kinmin was a boy. Queen Riaa pressed close, and every now and then fussed with his hair.

Guards stood on either side of the entrance and saluted when their sovereigns passed. The king and queen casually returned their salutes as they continued to enjoy their son's company.

The passageway was well lit by torches that hung on the white, stone walls. Their footsteps and voices echoed down the long twisting hallway. Rounding a bend was the entrance into a great room.

"Magnificent," Il-Lilliad marveled as he walked across the threshold. "The legendary palace of SriBrune."

The large, circular room appeared to be carved from a single, massive piece of white marble, and glistened like fresh snow on a bright winter's day. Il-Lilliad spun about, trying to discern how the room was illuminated, but he could find neither torches nor windows.

The ceiling appeared to be a dome of honey-colored alabaster. Circling below the dome were two levels of balconies. On the highest level stood musicians holding brass instruments. When the royal family entered, horns were raised in unison and majestic music radiated throughout the palace. When the music began, soldiers stationed on the lower balcony snapped to attention.

Near the floor and along the walls were vestibules that contained figurines of intricate detail. Intrigued by their beauty, Il-Lilliad paused for a better look.

"Superb craftsmanship," he muttered to himself. "Life-like representations; carved from onyx, jade, white marble and...what's this?" He leaned closer. "They're moving in place, as if they are...*alive.*"

"Yes," Kinmin explained. "In many ways, these are *our* storytellers. Although they are not alive - at least not as we interpret the word - their theatrics nonetheless tell the tales of our great nation. This one," Kinmin pointed out, "depicts brave battles fought long before the Dark War, while this one shows glorious harvests and celebrations."

"So many," Il-Lilliad marveled, surveying the palace walls. "So much detail crafted into each figurine: emerald chips for eyes; sapphire flakes for water; a shard of ruby to depict a wound; gold and silver threaded garments...*and look*."

He raced ahead to another display.

"I recognize this scene," Il-Lilliad said, his voice pensive. "This is Karajan; the translucent onyx captures the haunting water perfectly. And I recognize those monsters," he said as he pointed to miniscule dansel lors slinking beneath the surface. "Even as models they're frightening."

"Yes, but come. There is much to discuss with my parents."

Kinmin led them to the royal platform that occupied the middle of the room. It was round and covered with a dark, red carpet. A series of ten circular steps led up to two thrones where Kinmin's parents were already seated. The servants with their large fans stood behind them. At its base stood a large number of what Il-Lilliad assumed to be SriBrunian nobility, some dressed in formal military uniforms; others in ornate tunics.

As if reading the question behind Il-Lilliad's eyes, Kinmin whispered, "They are SriBrune's government officials."

Il-Lilliad reached the base of the throne platform, knelt and lowered his head.

"Rise, storyteller of Claire," King Cameare ordered.

Il-Lilliad stood and awaited the king's next words.

"For generations we have been allies to the King of Claire. For just as many generations we have lived in peace. Now, for the first time in our generation, we have a visitor. But you are not just anyone, and you are not just from anywhere. You are a storyteller for the King of Claire. Your presence in SriBrune brings us great joy, yet also great apprehension, for you would not have journeyed so far and have risked your life just to tell us a tale or two. Please indulge us, storyteller: why are you here?"

"I have come by order of the Only to ask for your help."

"Help from SriBrune? We are but a tiny nation full of tiny people. What could we possibly offer ones who walk so tall...and so proud?"

"Brairtok, warlord for Ebon, prepares for war against all the nations above the Onderling. He does the bidding of the Cauldron. Their lust for life immortal will cast a shadow of darkness over our lands the likes of which have never been seen before. The King of Claire has sent me to humbly ask for your assistance in this war."

"We are a peaceful nation and have no desire to involve ourselves with such matters. You have the nations above. Why not rally them to your aid?"

Il-Lilliad shook his head.

"The Cauldron's fumes are too powerful and have numbed the minds of all who used to follow the stories. Its drone, like the jaws of your dansel lors, has crushed the spirit of our freedom and our joy. Ebon destroyed all of our weapons, and worse, the storytellers of the Only are but a mist."

This last bit of news sent a murmur amongst the SriBrunian officials. King Cameare held up his right hand to restore silence.

"How is this possible," the king asked. "How could so many storytellers, full of such power, be gone?"

"They were captured by Brairtok at Min Brock and led away to be destroyed in a marshy grave. I am the only survivor."

King Cameare leaned forward, amazed.

"You are the *last* storyteller?"

"As far as I know."

"Tell me," Queen Riaa asked, "did you return to Claire?"

Il-Lilliad shook his head.

"I longed to journey back, to dine within Marsien Vur with the king, but his whisper led me to a forgotten cave. I knew I was to wait. I was fortunate to find a rusk, a storyteller's best ally, and together, we spent our days scouting Allsbruth for supplies as we studied the effects of the Cauldron after the Dark War.

"I was saddened to watch village after village submit to the Dark Flame's Oracles: Ebonite warriors swabbed black stain above every threshold, numbering every cottage for its census; villagers were forbidden to visit other hamlets for fear of organizing rebellion; weapons were banned. Unable to hunt, most men took up farming; books and parchments filled with the stories of Claire were collected and burned.

"I came upon a smoldering pile of books in a gully. Using my staff, I probed through the ash for any remnants, hoping to salvage a page or two here, or a partial book there. Imagine my joy when I struck what felt to be a solid book. The rusk helped me dig it up. That's when we found many more books that were salvageable. I unearthed such treasures as *Deepest of Tails, Fables, Lore and Myth, Beyond the Veil* and a short book of poems entitled, *Tears of Cor len Bluun.*

"We searched for, and found, more survivors of the flames, and amassed a good number of books. Over the course of many days, I retrieved them and stockpiled them in my cave, hiding them far from the gully, in case Ebonite warriors returned to inspect their incendiary work. My hope? That one day they would be read once more, if only by one person.

"The children you discovered within my mind, Elabea and Galadin, have received invitations to Claire. Even now, they journey to that nation where Elabea will become a great storyteller. Perhaps the stories of Claire will rise up from the ash, in much the same way as I retrieved the burning books."

The king closed his eyes and searched within Il-Lilliad's mind. His face transformed into that of Elabea's. Il-Lilliad stood mesmerized as the mirage appeared, her face rekindling his deep love for her. Then, as quickly as she appeared, she faded and the king's face returned.

"Your heart holds her very dear," the king stated. "Has she reached Claire?"

"I don't know."

"So the balance of your world is held on a razor's edge by these children?"

"Yes. That is why we need your help."

The king whispered into his queen's ear. She nodded. The king leaned back and once more addressed Il-Lilliad.

"Your story of sadness and death has moved us greatly. As one of our great poets has voiced, *Shall your tears not be ours as well?* But you have not come to gain our sympathy, now have you?"

Il-Lilliad smiled. The king continued.

"Claire has been of great assistance to SriBrune. Look about you," he said as he swept his arm about the chamber. "Every white stone used to construct our palace was mined in Claire in distant ages past, and given to us as a gift, yet throughout the vast expanse of summers and winters, Claire has never asked for anything in return...until now. What you ask of SriBrune will require great sacrifice and great courage, but to quote yet another SriBrunian sage, *Even a madman appears sane when dying for a friend.*"

The king paused and gazed into Il-Lilliad's eyes.

"Your heart also tells of great fear and urgency. There is a secret story you have not told us."

Il-Lilliad gave a slow, humble nod.

"I did not do so in order to be deceptive, your majesty."

"Yes, that I also discerned. But please," the king implored, "you must share this with all those gathered here today. SriBrunians honor truth, not secrets."

Il-Lilliad drew in a deep breath. He sensed that all eyes were on him, waiting to hear the news, whether bad or good. Finding his courage, he raised his voice so all could hear.

"Soon, the Cauldron will launch an attack on the Onderling, and eventually SriBrune."

The SriBrunians gasped.

The king looked about at the assembled nobility of SriBrune. Il-Lilliad studied his demeanor.

His eyes, Il-Lilliad thought, *so full of compassion and love for his people; willing to sacrifice his well-being for their benefit.*

The king spoke. "My fellow SriBrunians. It seems war sniffs at our doors. May this dog waddle into Karajan and meet our dansel lors."

The people chuckled, but there was an edge to their laughter.

When they quieted, the king added, "I see only two options: We wait and hope that the Cauldron will not have victories enough to reach our hallowed halls; or we engage in the ensuing war beyond the Onderling with our friends. What do you say, Counselors of SriBrune?"

The government officials gathered at the foot of the dais and discussed the options. Although the debate was passionate, the men kept the matter civil and dignified. At last a consensus was reached, and a spokesman for the people stepped forward. The king summoned him and he nimbly ascended the stairs where he whispered their answer to the royal family. Sovereign heads nodded and the spokesman retreated to the floor.

King Cameare stood and announced their decision.

"It seems that today, SriBrune is of one mind. Sacrifice and devotion are the attributes of our lives, and because of such tenets, we have chosen to assist the nation of Claire."

And then to Il-Lilliad, "What can SriBrune offer?"

"I need at least half of your best soldiers and several of your best military leaders. The remaining officers and soldiers will need to stay behind to guard SriBrune from any counterattacks the Cauldron may muster."

Il-Lilliad studied their eyes.

Have I asked too much?

Queen Riaa whispered into her husband's ear. The king nodded, stood, and while looking squarely at Il-Lilliad, answered, "So be it."

Turning to his queen, he offered her his left hand. She accepted it and rose gracefully from her throne. Together, hand in hand, they descended and stopped on the step where they could look Il-Lilliad face-to-face. Queen Riaa gave Kinmin a smile.

Such beauty, Il-Lilliad noted. *Your smile hides a burden so great, but what is it?*

"You have asked for our greatest leaders," she said. "Therefore, I offer you our son, Kinmin, to lead our forces."

Il-Lilliad's face turned pale as he realized the cause of her troubled heart.

"No," he countered. "That is *not* what I expected from the nation of SriBrune. Your son has only now returned to you. He has sacrificed *more* than enough. He has brought me through the Onderling and has even risked his life to save mine. He *must* stay with you. I insist."

"Il-Lilliad," she replied, her voice like cold iron. "Your need is greater than ours."

"But your majesty..."

"As a storyteller, you should know the tales of sacrifice and love that abound from Claire."

"Of course, but..."

"And as a storyteller, you know that you are obliged to obey royalty, correct?"

Il-Lilliad sighed, but nodded.

"You have asked for SriBrune's best. Kinmin is that. I offer him to you."

With that she turned to address Kinmin.

"Be brave, my son, and serve SriBrune well."

She pulled him close, kissed him lightly on the forehead then turned to join the king. Her eyes glistened with tears but her face was firm and radiant. Il-Lilliad knew her mind was made up and to argue with her would be considered vulgar.

"Kinmin," King Cameare admonished, "your journey prior to today prepared you for this task before you now. Choose your men well, and fight hard for the world above the Onderling. Our future depends on you."

He paused.

"And," he added, his eyes misting over, "I pray and dream of the day when you return to serve by our side."

He gripped Kinmin's shoulders and the two men gazed into each other's eyes. Finally, the king took on the role as father and embraced his son. Kinmin returned the embrace, both men unashamed to express their emotions for all to witness.

King Cameare released his hold and returned to his queen's side where he clasped her hand.

Il-Lilliad stood speechless.

"Is there anything else, storyteller," the king asked.

"No, your majesty," Il-Lilliad answered, a lump rising into his throat. "You have truly given more than enough."

"Then go. Prepare for war against the Cauldron. Long may your stories flow!"

Il-Lilliad bowed low to the ground, then rose and followed Kinmin out of the great palace. As they exited, the brass horns played a glorious fanfare that reverberated not only off the walls but also within the deepest recesses of their hearts.

"Kinmin," Il-Lilliad whispered, "I had no intention of dragging you off to war."

"I know that," Kinmin replied, "I can read minds too, you know."

"If you would rather stay, I will understand and..."

Kinmin stopped and fixed Il-Lilliad with a hard stare.

"Had my parents not offered my services, I would have volunteered. Now come, the decision has been made. We need to prepare."

Il-Lilliad followed him into another section of the palace where Kinmin gathered the best commanders and warriors SriBrune had to offer. As the tiny, dark-skinned warriors, assembled, Il-Lilliad reflected on when he first arrived in SriBrune. He had doubted this nation could be of any help in what would be the bloodiest war the world above would ever know. Now he saw them differently. Never had he met such a passionate and brave people.

"To serve and fight by their side would be perhaps the greatest honor of my life," he thought.

Chapter 20

Lost Lineage

The man's reflection spooked Elabea. She spun around and gasped, "Who are you?" followed quickly with, "Have I done something wrong?"

"No, you've done nothing wrong."

His aged voice reminded her of leaves rustling in the wind. His face was tanned by the sun and wrinkled by time. A few wisps of white hair garnished his round head. Eyes glistened like morning frost and reflected wisdom one would expect to see in the eyes of a scholar or professor. He was about the size of her father, with a little more weight around his middle. His snug, white shirt was tucked into a pair of olive green breeches. Both were worn and weathered, and marked by scattered patches of dust and dirt. A pair of chestnut brown boots ran up to his calves where the breeches disappeared inside. Dried mud caked the boots.

"Forgive me," he said, "I didn't mean to startle you. Please, allow me to help you up."

He offered her his right hand. Elabea studied it, wondering if she could trust him.

"Fear not," he reassured her. "I mean you no harm. Besides, my bones are too old to give chase, and my strength too far gone to restrain you."

A cautious smile creased Elabea's lips as she reached out to take his hand. His grip was stronger than she expected, and instead of being cold, his rough, weathered hand was warm and soothing.

"So, young lady, what do you think of our garden?"

"It is so..." she paused and turned about to take in the surrounding vistas, "stunning. Gorgeous. *Magnificent.*"

The old man flashed a proud grin.

"I'm so glad! As the gardener, I rarely meet guests who journey to Marsien Vur. It is equally rare that I ever get to discuss my life's passion."

"How long have you been gardening?"

"Let's see," he said, tapping a finger on his chin. "To be completely honest, sometimes it feels like forever."

Elabea gave a polite nod, which the gardener repaid with a simple nod. The conversation lagged. Time dragged, and she found herself growing irritable.

"Why isn't he offering a tour of the gardens," she wondered. *"Why doesn't he offer refreshments, and more importantly, why doesn't he escort me to the King of Claire?"*

Unable to endure any more of the friendly face-off, she blurted, "Is he here? I believe he's expecting me."

"Is who here?" the gardener replied.

"The King of Claire," Elabea snapped, wondering if he had any sense at all. "You know, the Only."

Elabea pulled out her invitation and handed it to him. He held it in his weathered hands, his eyes dancing across the white parchment.

"An invitation," he half-whispered. The old man cradled the parchment in his palms and gazed at it like a father admiring his newborn babe. "This is *very* valuable. You know that, don't you?"

"Yes," Elabea said, relieved that the conversation was finally moving along.

The gardener's eyes jumped from the invitation to Elabea then back to the parchment.

"Not that I doubt your word, but tell me, how did such a young lady as you come upon this?"

Elabea eagerly recounted her journey with Romlin as well as the many adventures they shared along the way. The gardener never seemed disinterested, distracted or bored. He became more animated with every nuance and facet of her story. His eyes widened when she described the horde of fea dracas killing the sevritt, and he winced in sympathy when she described her own pain when her rusk died.

"Yours is a wonderful story," his voice glowed with sentimentality. "The King of Claire has spoken of it often, but to hear it from you personally, here in my garden..." he let his voice trail off and handed her parchment back.

While she returned it to her pocket, she scrunched up her lips in confusion.

"If you already knew my story, then why did you wish to hear it again?"

"Because, as the bird near the veil informed you, a story doesn't come alive until it passes through your heart."

"So, you only asked for my benefit?"

"Oh, good gracious, no," he chuckled. "I never tire of hearing your story."

Elabea's brow furrowed as countless questions plagued her thoughts. Sensing her bewilderment, the gardener patted her forearm.

"No doubt you have many questions and wish to meet with him. But first, he wants me to show you something. Please, follow me."

Although he was very old, Elabea was impressed with the gardener's quick gait, sure-footedness and limber legs. Coming to a natural opening in the hedges, he led her into a parcel of the garden she had not seen before.

"This is for you," the gardener announced.

Elabea stood dumbfounded.

"How can this be," she asked as she skipped toward the massive tree in the midst of the meadow. "It looks exactly like my oak from Hetherlinn."

"It is," he grinned.

Stunned, Elabea stopped and stared slack-jawed at the old man.

He nodded to assure her she had heard him correctly, and with animated hand gestures, encouraged her onward.

"Go see for yourself. I believe you'll find some familiar carvings."

She approached the tree apprehensively, still not convinced it was authentic. With her hand on the trunk, she peered up through the long, sweeping branches.

"It sure looks the same," she declared, stroking the bark as if it were the mane of a horse. Then to the oak, "So many times on our journey I longed to be home in your branches, swaying in the breeze, free from all who hunt me."

She circled the tree and let her palm float over the bark until she came to the carvings the gardener had referenced. Tracing the initials with her finger, her thoughts returned to the day they were first carved.

"Romlin, I mean Galadin, cut out my initials here when I was five summers of age. He said it would make the tree my own...forever."

She took a step back and admired the magnificent oak.

"May I climb it?"

"Of course. After all, this *is* your tree."

"How did you get it here from Hetherlinn," she asked.

"Don't be silly," the gardener giggled with a sly wink. "How would an old gardener like me do such a thing as that?"

"Then how..."

"Oh, it's really quite simple: The King of Claire grew this for you many summers before you were born."

"But how...I mean...what I'm trying to say is that, well, that's *impossible.* How could he know about the initials *before* I was born, and how could Galadin carve them here and..."

"So many questions for so young a girl," he laughed, cutting her off. "Are you always this inquisitive?"

Elabea paused, unsure how to answer.

"Please," he encouraged her with a wave of his hand. "Climb away."

That was all the urging Elabea need. With complete abandon she clambered into the arms of the tree. She felt like a little girl, oblivious to the Dark War's savage destruction to her family. When was the last time she had felt such wonderment? She climbed up a few branches, then stopped and looked down at the gardener.

"Go on," he said. "Go as high as you wish. I assure you, the view from the crest is well worth the climb."

Elabea's face wrinkled with confusion.

"You've climbed to the top before?"

"Go," he said with a smile, shooing her upwards with his hands.

She giggled with each branch she mounted, and soon reached the tree's top. Finding the perfect perch, she spanned Claire's panoramic view. The tree swayed in the warm breeze and she felt like her grandmother was coddling her. She breathed deeply, letting the garden's perfumed scents bathe her in luxury. She closed her eyes and basked in the sunlight's warm caress. Her pains and troubles faded away.

"Beautiful, isn't it," the gardener asked.

Startled, Elabea's eyes blinked open. Alarmed to find him sitting nearby, she asked, "How did you climb so fast?"

He ignored her question and instead, gazed at the horizon.

"Is Claire everything you expected?"

"Yes," she answered dreamily, swaying to the rhythm of the tree. "The land, the creatures, the colors and scents. Claire is more than I ever *dreamed.*"

"Did you know that The King of Claire has watched you climb this tree ever since you were a little girl; listened to your dreams, your stories, and longed to wipe away your tears?"

Elabea sat speechless, unable to fathom why someone like the Only would care that much for her.

"In fact," the gardener continued, "the king shares your stories with all the creatures of Claire. That's how I already knew of your journey. But," he smiled as he raised his index finger for emphasis, "we especially liked the story of when you tried to fly."

Elabea's face reddened with embarrassment.

"You mean to tell me that everyone in Claire *knows* that story?"

"Oh, yes. It is a favorite. The king marveled at your determination."

"Determination? It was silliness on my part. I really thought I could fly, but I only landed on my nose, remember?"

His wrinkles formed a joyful smile.

"As wonderful as those tales are," he continued, his tone turning serious, "they fade into a memory, sometimes completely forgotten until a sound or a scent reminds a person that they indeed existed. The tales the King of Claire loves the most are those carried deep inside one's heart: secret dreams and heartfelt passions. Oh, what ageless stories *those* are. If only they could set sail and carry their owners away in bliss. Tragically, they cannot, for they are forced to dwell in darkness, fettered to a ruthless jailer who reigns supreme."

"I'm not sure I understand what you're talking about," she replied.

He faced her and Elabea was struck at how his eyes were so inviting and tender. She thought about her father, and regretted that he was never able to look at her with such love and compassion.

"Merely this," he answered, disrupting her thoughts. "Within you, Elabea, are passions and dreams that will never be free because your anger keeps them locked up."

She pulled away from his eyes.

"If I do have these secrets and passion," she asked, "then how could the King of Claire know about them? I live so far away."

"Stories from the heart," he answered, "have no border, my delight."

Her eyes widened and she snapped her face to his while his last refrain peeled like thunder.

"What did you say," she asked in a half-whisper.

"Elabea," he whispered, the word echoing all about them, *"My delight!"*

"The whisper," she exclaimed as she clung tight to the branch. *"You are the Only?"*

The gardener nodded.

"Are you disappointed?"

"What...what do you mean?" she stammered, suddenly self-conscious of her appearance and wondering if any of her previous words had been misconstrued.

"I'm not what you were expecting, am I?"

"Well," she began, trying to steady her shaking hands and her pounding heart, "I did have a picture of you in my mind that was..."

"A picture?" he interrupted with eyes beaming. "With a picture there is *always* a story. Please tell it to me."

Taking a deep breath to help settle her nerves, she said, "I fancied you being of thirty summers, handsome, and dressed in very expensive clothes."

"Thirty summers?" he repeated with a chuckle. "So you don't find me young or handsome," he asked with a twinkle in his eye.

"Yes...I mean *no*. Well, what I mean is... you see, I thought..."

His jovial laugh washed away her next few words and made the tree sway all the more. At first, Elabea thought he was laughing at her, but when his eyes began to water, and she sensed such joy within his laugh, she felt at ease and joined the merriment.

When their chuckles subsided, he asked her, "Do you know why I sent you the invitation?"

"It said you desired to give me treasures."

He confirmed her answer with a nod.

"Are you ready to receive one?"

She became excited and felt giddy, just like she did when her father would surprise her with small trinkets, but that was long before Min Brock. Despite such mixed emotions, she answered with a resounding, "Yes!"

"Hold on tight," he advised. "This may startle you, and I do not need you to fall."

Elabea wrapped her arms around the trunk, not sure what to expect.

"Close your eyes."

She complied.

"Now open them."

A young boy of approximately six summers sat next to the King of Claire who held an arm around him to steady him.

"Do you know who this is?"

She squinted and studied the boy's face, then shook her head.

"This is your father, Quinn, when he was a boy."

She leaned forward, curious how this could be a treasure and how her father could appear in Claire at such a young age. She was about to disagree when she noticed the birthmark on the boy's neck. It was exactly like her father's.

"Peer into his eyes, Elabea. See how they are filled with such longing and grief?"

She nodded.

"Now look around."

She saw a number of other boys seated on the oak's limbs. All were identical in shape and dress to the boy that was her father.

"Sitting directly across from us is your grandfather. Over there is your great-grandfather, and beside him is his father. Notice how they are identical in every way? Even their secrets are the same, clouding their eyes with an equivalent sadness."

"Yes, I see. But why?"

"Each one expected the older to give him something of great importance. No, not a prized possession, or a shiny brass horn, but the tenets of life - like strength, courage, confidence and most importantly, love. Instead, the older robbed the younger of these treasures, snatched them like a thief picks a pocket. It was not intentional. Some even tried to change, but without my stories to shepherd them, they traversed perilous walkways. On and on the misery traveled, passed down from father to child like a battered, useless toy. And sadly enough, the child could see that the hand-me-down was worthless, while the father basked in his miserly servitude."

"I don't understand," she said, her mind swirling with uncomfortable questions.

"Like the children about you, you too expected your father to deliver great joy and devotion. Instead, he robbed your heart of such worth. That is why you ran to your tree, to find the things of life you lacked: love, purpose and joy."

Buried emotions rose up into her throat and she fought to keep them contained, holding on to the tree with all her might. The Only continued.

"When the invitations came, you journeyed to Claire. Not so much to find me, but to escape from your father's world. You wished to show him you were a treasure worth finding, a treasure worth loving."

"I came because you *asked* me too," she replied, tears welling up in her eyes. "Your invitation promised me treasures."

"I *do* have treasures for you," he answered. "And they are more valuable than you can possibly imagine. Believe it or not, you are beholding the first gift. If you are able to open this present I have for you, you'll be able to fly. Now tell me, what does *Elabea* mean in Allsbruthian?"

"Dreamer of Days," she whispered, her emotions ebbing and flowing like dark tides on a turbulent sea.

"I wish to give you a new name, one that will carry you beyond merely being a *dreamer of days* to someone who soars upon her dreams. The only way it will rightfully be yours is when you are able to love this boy."

With that, the King of Claire vanished, and the boy turned his heartrending eyes upon her. Elabea did not see a boy who needed to be loved. Instead, she saw her father's eyes and her anger flared inside.

"Why are you looking at me so?" she demanded.

"What do you mean," the boy replied.

"Turn away," she commanded. The intensity of her words shocked her. She tried to control her anger and shame but was unable to. The King of Claire's words echoed in her mind.

"It was not intentional, in fact, some even tried to change, but without my stories to shepherd them, they traversed perilous walkways."

She tried harder, but she felt as if she held the reins to a bucking warhorse. Her next volley was even more vehement.

"Why are *you* so sad? *I'm* the one you've hurt."

"I don't understand," the boy whimpered.

"Of course not. You are too absorbed in your own pain, and too *drunk* to love *me.*"

She folded her arms across her chest and scowled at him. The boy's face remained peaceful.

"Your face looks familiar," he said. "As if you were in one of my dreams. Are you my sister," he asked. "I wish you were. Then we could play. Do you like to play in the tree?"

"Yes," she fumed as she loomed forward.

"I do too. I come to the oak because I miss my father. We used to play together in this tree. He said he would come again, but he hasn't. Have you seen him?"

She shook her head then gazed around at all the other boys who were also waiting for a man that would never come.

"Does your father play with you," the boy asked.

Despite her building rage, the emotional vulnerability she heard in his voice softened her heart. For that brief moment, she could empathize with him, wanting to weep for his pain and tell him she understood, that she knew what it was like to have such desires.

The boy's next question crushed her empathy.

"Does he hold you?"

She glared. The countless summers of his neglect rushed back in like a tempest against a dam too small.

"No. He *doesn't.*"

She shoved him.

The boy lost his grip and started to fall.

Elabea, shocked by her own violent reaction, grabbed his hand.

"You're heavier than you look," Elabea exclaimed as he dangled below. "And getting *heavier.*"

Her muscles ached; she could feel herself slipping from her perch. Despite being enraged by him only moments before, she realized she could not skirt around the truth that he was still her father. Angry waves smashed against her feelings of devotion.

"Elabea," the boy said, but in a voice she recognized as her father's. "Let me go."

"No, I can help," she screamed as she slipped further off the branch. "I'll come back home. You'll stop drinking. Our lives will be better."

"No, Elabea, it won't. You can't save me. You were never meant to."

"But I can try," she cried, bitter tears pumping wildly from her eyes as feelings of wrath and love battled within her. "I'll change. You'll see. I'll spend more time with you and not go..."

"You're not to blame."

"I can at least *try.*"

"Farewell."

With that, he let go.

She watched the boy fall and as he plummeted, he transformed into the man she knew.

"*Father,*" she wailed.

Unable to watch anymore, she wrapped her arms about the trunk and began sobbing uncontrollably, mourning not only her grievous mistake brought on by her anger, but by the realization that she truly loved him, despite all of his neglect.

A warm hand caressed the top of her head, consoling her. She opened her eyes and found she was safe on the ground. She was not embracing the tree, but the gardener. He knelt and gently wiped away her tears with a callused finger. As her sobs softened, she looked up and saw silver tears rolling down his own cheeks.

"I never meant to hurt him," she snuffled between tears. "I never realized I was so *angry.*"

"I have known for some time."

His voice offered mercy like water to a parched traveler.

"You have? Then why didn't you stop me?"

"Because you needed to know and see for yourself."

"I tried to stop the anger," she wailed, "but the more I tried, the stronger it became."

"Yes, just like your father tried, and his father before him."

"So how am I to change, when they couldn't?"

"*Without my stories to shepherd them, they traversed perilous walkways.*'"

Her head dropped in discouragement.

"Do not despair," he said, lifting her chin with his hand. "Your anger is the storyteller of your heart, trumpeting the true tale of who you are. As you have seen, such revelation can be haunting. Only my stories can shift your shadows of wrath into dazzling delight."

Elabea blinked as her mind tried to unravel the meaning of his words. Slowly, the truth dawned, like fog lifting off a meadow.

"I think I understand, and I do want to change and have your stories free me. But the boy," she said, her voice trailing off as the memory of his fall sent waves of nausea through her. "I pushed him and he fell. And while he was falling, he turned into my father. Either way, I killed him."

"Really?"

"Yes."

"Then where is the body?"

She looked around, but there was no corpse; not even an imprint in the grass.

"You can't be punished for something that was only a dream."

"But inside of me, I meant to..."

"I know."

"But..."

He quieted her by gently placing a finger to her lips.

"In time," he answered. "In time. For now, let me give you more of this gift."

Taking her hand, he led her to one of the many streams within the garden. Together, they knelt beside the water's edge.

"Look at the water," he instructed. "There you'll find a treasure."

Elabea gazed through the surface to the rocks and moss beneath the stream's clear ripples, but found nothing of value. She scanned the streambed, looking for gold, silver or gems. Unable to see anything of worth, she said, "I'm sorry, but I don't see it."

"I promise you, the treasure is there. Keep searching."

She studied the stream once more but soon shook her head.

"Forgive me, but I don't see anything."

"Can't you? It's right here."

He pointed his finger to the water's surface.

Elabea lowered her eyes once more, but instead of gazing through the water, she focused on its surface. Staring back at her was her own reflection.

"There," the Only whispered, *"My treasure."*

Elabea's brow furrowed.

"Me? A treasure?" She shook her head in disbelief. "I just tried to kill my father. I don't feel like..."

"Elabea, to understand such worth, such treasure, is your first step toward becoming a storyteller. I have fashioned you to soar as never before, to become who you secretly and desperately have dreamed of becoming. So feed your passions with this promise: No matter what you may feel from now on, you are always my treasure, *my delight.*"

"Yes, I do crave this change, but my anger and my emotions...they are so much a part of me. I doubt I will ever..."

"That is why I must give you a new name - to remind you of who you have been, as well as who you are to become. Therefore, you are no longer Elabea, *Dreamer of Days.* You are to forever be known as Ela Claire, *Dreamer of Life."*

The king helped her to her feet and gave her a paternal kiss on the forehead. She closed her eyes and felt his love disperse her shadows of shame.

When she opened her eyes, she found they were no longer in the garden but beside the iron gate where she first entered. She stared at the tulip that grew out of the black iron, and with a furrowed brow asked, "How did we get *here?"*

The King of Claire ignored her question and instead, grabbed her hand and led her away.

"Come. You must be hungry. I have prepared a feast for you within Marsien Vur."

"Wait," she exclaimed as she pulled back on his hand, "I forgot about Romlin."

"I haven't," he said with a smile that betrayed a hint of mischievousness. "He's been here all along."

Chapter 21

Worms of Bal-Malin

Linwith assumed that bartering for a ship in Holman would be comparable to his experience trading produce across the lands: pleasant preamble while examining the wares, followed by congenial negotiations on a fair price. He discovered the fishermen of Holman use a different business model.

"Excuse me," Linwith declared with a raised arm as he marched onto the large dock.

The scent of fish and salt air from sea were heavy on the wind. Fishermen, who appeared as weathered as their vessels, glanced up from their work and scowled at him. Undeterred, Linwith launched into his request.

"I'm seeking passage to Bal-Malin. I travel alone, but will also need transport for my horses and wagon."

A burly fisherman approached. His eyes were dark and cold like the Gilden Sea, and his face was peppered with a wild, unkempt beard. A gray wool hat covered his head but a few strands of greasy hair escaped and drooped about to his shoulders. He carried a loaf of black, crusty bread and was busy hacking off a chunk with a crude looking knife. When he was closer, Linwith gagged; the man reeked of fish, sweat and liquor. The fisherman stuffed the hunk of bread into his mouth while his eyes ran up and down Linwith.

"I'm captain of the *Lady Dorian*," he said while still chewing, bits of wet bread spewing from his mouth. "Tell me something. Why is a fair-skinned man like you bartering for passage to Bal-Malin?"

"That is my business, not yours."

"No, friend," the captain replied, wiping his mouth with the back of his hand. "That's where you're wrong. If I'm to risk life, ship, and crew, then it *is* my business to know if *you*, dear sir, are worth the...*investment*."

He emphasized the last syllable and spittle mixed with bread landed on Linwith's face.

Linwith pulled a kerchief from his pocket and made a show of wiping his face. He took his time folding the kerchief back up and stowing it away.

"So be it," Linwith replied.

Instead of telling him about his mission to acquire illegal arms from Tristan, he settled upon another story, one he personally did not believe wholeheartedly, but that he hoped would satisfy the seaman.

"I wish to seek the counsel of the Worms of Bal-Malin."

The captain's face wrinkled, and his chest heaved with chuckles. He turned to his peers on the dock.

"Did you hear that?" Imitating Linwith's voice, he said, "*I wish to seek the counsel of the Worms of Bal-Malin.*"

The consort of men joined in the captain's revelry. Regaining his breath, the captain once again turned his attention to Linwith.

"Very well," he said. "I suppose you'll only need passage one way."

"Naturally," Linwith replied, trying his best to remain calm and poised. "I'm sure that once there, the worms can assist me further on my journey."

Linwith's words acted like a charm, for the fishermen fell silent. The only sounds were the waves lapping the pier's pylons and the vessels bumping the dock. Linwith stared at their faces, wondering why their barroom expressions had faded to a somber look.

The captain's eyes narrowed and he pressed his face close to Linwith's, studying him.

"Sure they will," he murmured. "Sure they will."

Linwith took a step backward.

"So, I can charter your vessel?"

The captain stared at him for a moment longer, as if he were mad.

"If that's what you want."

Linwith gazed across the Gilden Sea.

Is that what I want? Linwith thought. *No! It's not what I want. I want to be back home. If I have to go to Tristan I want another means of getting there. But what I want is of no consequence. Others are depending on me. I simply have no other option.*

Aloud, with a mournful sigh, Linwith answered, "Yes, that is what I want."

"Very well then, payment for passage for one upon the *Lady Dorian* to the Island of Bal-Malin," the captain pointed toward his ship, "will require all that you carry in your wagon."

Aghast at this unreasonable price, as well as the disarray of the *Lady Dorian*, Linwith's eyes bulged.

"You *can't* be serious!"

The captain scrunched up his lips.

"Perhaps that was a bit rash on my part."

"Indeed," Linwith huffed.

After a quick recalculation, the captain announced, "Aside from your payload, passage will also cost you your wagon and horses."

You call that a better deal?"

"Yes," the captain boomed. "For me!"

"Your fee, sir, is *robbery.*"

"No, *sir*, it is not," the captain poked his finger against Linwith's chest for emphasis. "In times like these, when the Cauldron can hear a man's wayward whisper, and when a man seems to be hiding a secret *deserving* of the Cauldron's attention, I believe my price is fair indeed."

Linwith tried to barter for a better deal, but the captain merely tore off another hunk of bread, folded his arms over his brawny chest and scowled at every offer.

Hearing the squabble, Rittmar flew to assist.

"You will not need your horses, or wagon or produce anymore," Rittmar buzzed into Linwith's ear. "Take his offer."

"And Tristan? How are we to..." He held his last words at bay; the captain was looking at him as if he were mad for talking to the wind.

"You'll have to trust me," Rittmar replied.

Trapped with no other options, Linwith extended his hand.

"Done," he said.

The captain took his hand and shook it, sealing their contract for passage to Bal-Malin.

"Hurry," the captain called to his crew. "We sail immediately. The tide is perfect and the winds are fair."

Linwith shuffled behind the captain with Rittmar hovering nearby. A quick glance overhead at the cloud of Bal-Malinians helped put Linwith at ease, but the reprieve was short-lived.

Before the *Lady Dorian* was out of sight of the shore, Linwith found himself clinging to the ship's railing, white knuckled and green-faced as the ship rolled and lurched over the rolling sea. With each rise and fall of a tall wave, he would toss yet another piece of his last meal into the Gilden Sea.

"How much further," Linwith moaned over his shoulder to Rittmar.

"Not long," Rittmar answered from his perch on the ship's railing. "The coast is on the horizon."

Linwith stared out over the bow. The *Lady Dorian* had just reached the crest of another wave and off in the distance he could just make out the mountainous terrain of Bal-Malin. For a moment, focusing on the land calmed his nausea, but then the vessel plummeted downward, the coastline vanished, and the moment was lost. He turned and emptied what was left of the contents of his stomach into the sea.

"Explain to me again," he slurred, "why these worms are necessary?"

"Because you are Linwith, the Worm Master," Rittmar replied, as if it were the most obvious thing in the world. "With your worms, you can travel wherever you wish, for the worms..."

"I know, I know," Linwith moaned. "They are *the most ferocious creatures one will ever encounter.*"

He wiped his mouth with his sleeve and staggered to the mainmast where he slithered down and plopped on the deck, seasick, and filled with doubts about both the fate of his mission and the power of the worms.

"I just hope you're right," he muttered between dry heaves.

The *Lady Dorian* finally docked and Linwith pushed himself up onto wobbly legs.

"Out of my way," he barked, pushing sailors aside in his rush to the gangplank. "*Move,*" he ordered as he staggered like a drunk across the flimsy planks. Once on the dock, he threw himself to his knees and kissed it, declaring he would never board another sailing vessel as long as he lived.

The crew of the *Lady Dorian* laughed at the plight of the landlubber while the captain added his own jibe.

"Best of luck having counsel with the worms!"

Rittmar landed on Linwith's shoulder.

"Just beyond the dock is a dirt road. It will lead you to the worms' lairs. Only I will be joining you. The others from my nation will wait for our return."

Linwith nodded, his strength starting to return.

He regained his feet, turned his back on the *Lady Dorian* and her crew, and waddled off the dock toward the road. He trudged along, following the road as it wound up the side of the mountain. Thick stands of firs, pines and spruces lined the road, the aroma of evergreens helping to settle his seasick stomach.

"How much further," Linwith asked.

"To the lair? Not much longer. To your future as the Worm Master? That is yet to be determined."

Linwith rounded a bend and stopped in his tracks, perplexed.

"Is this it," he asked, indicating the small clearing that spread out before him.

"No, but we are much closer. See those white trees up the slope in front of you?"

Linwith shielded his eyes for a better look. Half way up the mountain was a grove of large, leafless trees whose bark was pure white.

"Yes."

"The trees are the guardians of their lairs. Let me lead the way," Rittmar said while hovering over a path. "Beyond the white trees is a cliff with seven caves, one is near the ground and the others lie in a row just above the first. You must first enter the lower cave. The Worm King resides within."

"Should I bring him a gift?" Linwith snickered, his natural skepticism returning.

"You're speaking in that manner that is double-sided. Aren't you?"

"What do you mean," Linwith asked, trying to keep pace to Rittmar's harried flight up the slope.

"I've learned that you often say the opposite of what you really mean. You did this recently when you saw Min Brock."

"I suppose I did."

"I find it interesting, yet troubling. Why must your people hide behind their words in such a manner? Wouldn't it be easier to simply state what one is truly feeling or thinking?"

"It's not as simple as that."

Rittmar quickened his flight. There was urgency in the way he flew.

"Linwith, do try and keep pace with me. We must arrive before the sun sets."

"Why? Do worms turn into fuzzy caterpillars at night?"

"I suppose that was meant to be humorous, but I do not understand why you wish to joke when the worms are near. Most men fear them, yet you are nonchalant about this encounter."

"Well, Rittmar," he replied as he puffed his chest out and patted his gut, "it is because *I* am the Worm Master. Besides, I've seen my share of worms in Hetherlinn after a good rain."

Rittmar stopped, dumbfounded, and hovered.

"You have *worms* in Hetherlinn?"

"Yes. Big fat ones. Very good for fishing."

"The worms of Bal-Malin are also large and good at fishing."

"No, not good *at* fishing, good *for* fishing."

"It comforts me to know you are experienced with such beasts."

Rittmar flew ahead while Linwith rolled his eyes and hurried to match his tiny friend's pace.

Onward they ascended, the trees now sparse and scattered. Linwith was about to ask, "How much further?" when Rittmar stopped.

"Over this knoll are the white trees and the lairs of the worms. Are you ready?"

Linwith thought of a snide remark, but knowing this would only confuse Rittmar, he merely nodded.

"Very well," Rittmar said. "I cannot enter the caves before you. This you must do yourself, but do not fear. I will be close behind."

Linwith marched over the knoll. The white trees were huge; much larger than they appeared when he first beheld them; and swayed in the island breeze, their limbs groaned with deep, ominous tones. Even in his upbeat mood, those sounds sent a shiver through him.

True to Rittmar's word, a rock cliff comprised of a tan stone jutted up behind the white trees toward the sky. Near the summit, high above the trees, were six caves.

The caves were larger than he expected, dark and foreboding. Linwith let his eyes descend to the cliff's base. A seventh cave stared back at him.

"There," Rittmar exclaimed, pointing his tiny hand at the black hole. "Behold the Worm King's lair. He has no doubt heard you and sniffed your scent upon the wind. Be bold. Fear not!"

Linwith gathered his resolve and walked to the entrance of the Worm King's lair. The roof of the cave towered over him. Its width was large enough for five wagons to drive through side by side. He shot a quick glance back at Rittmar, then turned and walked into the dark cavern. The floor was coated in wet, sticky mud, and a musky-moldy-fishy aroma permeated the air. Linwith felt his nausea return.

"This is *ridiculous,*" he declared, his voice echoing off the cavern walls. "But if this is what it takes to get weapons for Allsbruth…"

As he walked, he scanned the slimy cave floor. At last he spotted what he was looking for, bent down and picked it up.

"Oh, thou mighty worm," he proclaimed to the slithering worm in his palms. "You are the Worm King. Behold, I am Linwith, the Worm Master."

A low-pitched sound emanated out of the blackness before him.

Linwith straightened.

"Hello?" he called into the abyss.

The noise came again, like leather rubbing against the cave's damp walls; large amounts of leather.

"Whoever you are, I mean no harm," he shouted.

The sound grew louder and whatever it was, Linwith sensed it was closer. Apprehension turned to ice-cold fear. Linwith was about to turn and run when a massive shadow loomed overhead. He quick-stepped backwards, but the shadow rushed forward, blocking what little light managed to penetrate into the cavern.

"Rittmar," Linwith screamed as he stared up at the dark shape. "This is the lair of a *dragon.*"

"No, it is the lair of a *worm,*" Rittmar cried back from the cave's entrance. "You are in the presence of the Worm King."

"No. No. *No. This* is a worm," Linwith declared as he held up the squiggly worm in his palm.

"In Bal-Malin, that is called…"

"Let me guess, *dragon?*"

"No, of course not. That is an *orger.*"

The colossal shadow coalesced into an equally colossal beast that lowered its head to address the leader of the Bal-Malinians.

"This Allsbruthian bears the name," the Worm King declared in a voice deep in tone and rich in intelligence. "Yet he smells of fear and vomit. How can this one be the Worm Master?"

Rittmar landed on Linwith's shoulder and whispered in his ear.

"Tell him a tale you learned as a boy, a tale about worms."

"You mean *dragons*, and I do not know of any such stories."

"No, I most definitely meant *worms*, and you must remember such a tale. Search your mind. Your mother placed the story within you long ago when you were very young. It has remained dormant within your heart like a tulip bulb beneath winter's snow, waiting for spring to bloom."

"And should I not discover such a tale?"

"The Worm King will consume you."

Rittmar flew overhead as Linwith struggled to recall every childhood story, song and game he had ever encounter. Nothing about worms came to mind.

The worm's enormous head neared. More visible in the light, Linwith gasped at how fierce and intimidating this dragon, or worm, really was.

"If you are who you say you are," the Worm King said to Linwith, "then prove it to me, here within my lair."

Linwith stared into the Worm King's glistening black eyes. Deep within were flickering lights that glowed like campfires on a distant ridge. As he stared into the intimidating orbs, his blank mind started to clear, and memories returned in staccato bursts, like heat lightening on a hot summer's day: his mother; a bedtime song; five summers of age.

The song, Linwith thought, the memory from his childhood giving him courage. *I was humming it while crossing the Gilden Plains. At the time, I couldn't recall the words, but now...*

"Perhaps a song from my youth?" he offered, hoping it would appease the worm.

The Worm King scrutinized him.

"Very well. Surprise me, Linwith of Allsbruth."

Linwith closed his eyes. The song was returning in longer succession, but he waited to sing, knowing he had only one opportunity to get it right.

"Are you mocking me?" the Worm King bellowed. "I know when a man is stalling."

Linwith's eyes popped open. The lyrics echoed in his thoughts: sharp, clear and alive. Forgetting the Worm King for a moment, he turned to Rittmar.

"You were right. My Mother *did* place a tale within. I remember; I was only five summers of age. She would put me to bed and caress my back. When I was almost asleep, she would begin to softly sing. It was the most beautiful song, and it carried me to my dreams. I don't remember listening to the words, and yet, here today, they are within my mind as if I recited and memorized them daily."

"Impressive," the Worm King interrupted, feigning zeal. "Now, recite the song you learned at your mother's knee, or perish!"

Linwith took a deep breath, blew it out, then spoke the words from his youth.

Transient arcs of radiant light,
Cross the heavens on a moonless night.
Wings, tails and talons so bold,
Guarding their cache of treasure and gold.

Brothers seven who fly but as one,
Silhouettes grand, traversing the sun.
Bold and strong and mighty of wing,
To do the bidding of their master and king.

The flickering flames in the Worm King's eyes sparked. The worm backed away, closed its eyes, and humbly bowed its head, acknowledging his new liege.

"As you have recited, so shall it be. I am to do your bidding. For you, Linwith, are indeed the Worm Master."

Linwith studied the Worm King without fear or apprehension. His prior trepidation was gone, as if burned away by the worm's deep fires. Now, he felt...*alive* - somehow connected in heart and mind to the magnificent Worm King of Bal-Malin. He approached the creature and patted the side of its colossal head like he would his horse.

Rittmar landed on his shoulder.

"Now what," Linwith asked him as the flames in the worm's eyes glowed red.

"Now, you meet his brothers."

Chapter 22

The Minstrel of Blomseth

Daylight gave way to dusk, and swaths of purple light crisscrossed the village of Blomseth. A rider, with a small animal perched on his shoulder, rounded the bend of the road and approached the hamlet.

Common villagers, unaccustomed to visitors in their town, cowered in shadowed doorways at his approach. One man, who was not intimidated by the stranger, strolled from his home and blocked the road. Barrel-chested and tall, he had red, shabby hair that rolled over his face then off his chin as a beard. He wore a cloak made from a hodge-podge of animal pelts. He raised his thick staff and the rider pulled back on the reins.

"What business do you have in Blomseth," the trapper demanded as he tapped his staff against the palm of his hand.

Newcomb remained calm and replied, "I'm looking for a young minstrel."

The staff continued to thump. The trapper stared at the creature on his shoulder.

"What sort of animal is that?"

"A rusk."

"A *what?*"

"A rusk."

"Never heard of it. I've hunted all my life through every hill and valley the Oracles will allow. I've never seen anything like *that.*"

Newcomb appeared unimpressed by the man's self-proclaimed hunting prowess. The trapper maintained his staff's beat as he assessed the newcomer.

"Judging by your clothes, you're not a soldier or a trapper. What sort of man are you?"

"The dangerous type."

The trapper stopped thumping his staff.

"Is that a threat?"

He stepped toward Newcomb and brought his staff back to swing like an ax.

"No. It's a fact."

"A fact?" The trapper chuckled. "You don't look all that dangerous to me"

"Then tell me, what sort of man rides into a foreign village at night and brazenly defies the Oracles pertaining to travel?"

"A fool!" The trapper pointed his staff at Newcomb for emphasis. "Or perhaps a madman. Whichever you are, I don't fear you. I've battled my share of men - Wurmlins; even Ebonites - and have defeated them all."

He thumped his staff. "So I ask again, why are you a dangerous man?"

Newcomb leaned forward and said loud enough for those listening from their doorways to hear, "Because I'm a storyteller."

Gasps came from the thresholds. The trapper's staff froze mid-cadence.

"Impossible," the trapper blurted. "Storytellers no longer exist. All were killed in the Dark War."

Silence.

The staff resumed its steady *thump, thump, thump*, as if of its own volition.

"So what does a man like you - whatever you are - want with this minstrel? Are you his father?"

Newcomb studied the trapper's eyes and read a portion of his story. He was a simple man, and he truly was a great trapper, but more importantly, he considered himself the protector of the inhabitants of Blomseth. Before Newcomb could ascertain if he knew of Lassiter's whereabouts, the trapper interrupted his search.

"Answer me. Are you his father or not?"

Newcomb yanked his probing thoughts away and decided to tell him the truth.

"No, I'm his mentor. We traveled together once. I have come to find him so we can continue our journey."

The staff's rhythm intensified.

"He never mentioned anyone like *you* before."

"So he *is* here."

The thumps stopped and a petite woman darted from her shadowed cottage.

"Fool of a husband," she shouted. "If your brain were only as big as your hind end."

"I didn't mean to tell," he whined as his shoulders fell and the staff became limp in his grip. "He *tricked* me."

Newcomb smiled, amused that such a tiny woman could antagonize so formidable a fellow.

"Well," she continued, eyeing Newcomb up and down, "he looks harmless enough, but if he really is a storyteller, then you stay nearby in case there's trouble."

The trapper's shoulders righted and he glared at Newcomb, as if his trouble with his wife were all Newcomb's fault.

"Leave your horse and follow me."

Newcomb dismounted and secured his horse to a nearby hitching post. The trapper led him past the cottages to a small clearing where a tavern sat. A fire burned outside and people huddled about it for warmth. Above the tavern door a wooden sign, suspended from chains, swung lazily in the breeze with metallic groans that flitted off into the night.

"The Golden Giln," Newcomb read.

"He's inside," the trapper said.

Newcomb heard a youthful voice singing above the tavern's loud banter. The trapper locked eyes with Newcomb.

"I'm going to stay by the fire. If the boy cries for help, I'll come looking for *you.*"

He pressed his index finger into Newcomb's chest to emphasize the point.

"And I don't care how *dangerous* you are."

A roaring fire emitted the only light within the hall, and its scent barely masked the stench of unwashed bodies, old tobacco and stale ale. The rafters were low and the younger men of Blomseth straddled them, swinging their pewter mugs in time to the song. Scattered about the room were short, rectangular tables where the older patrons sat. A sprinkling of women, both young and old, sat close to the musician and gazed up at him with dreamy eyes.

Lassiter, decked out in bright green trousers tucked inside tall, black leather boots, performed atop a table. His white shirt was hidden beneath a brown minstrel's jacket that was mottled with brightly colored patches. Upon his head sat a red felt hat that formed a point a few inches over his forehead. A large crow's feather stuck out of one side.

He strummed an old lute that was missing the higher pitched string, and when he finished singing his raucous song, the room exploded into applause. He threw open his arms and he received their ovation like a father welcoming home a wayward son. As the applause faded, he leaned down, grabbed a mug full of ale from one of the women and raised it in a toast.

"Men and women of Blomseth; I drink to your good health!"

The crowd roared back its approval as he guzzled the mug's contents then slammed it back down. The young women giggled at his bravado, and one pretty maiden stared at him, with such adoration that Lassiter dropped to a knee and pulled her lips up to his. The tavern erupted with laughter, applause and whistles. He released her, and her face turned red.

You blush, Newcomb observed, *but your eyes reflect a heart that relishes such a kiss. In fact, those lips have been kissed quite a few times and by quite a few men.*

Lassiter was about to start another song when a familiar presence in the room caught his attention. He shielded his eyes for a better glimpse, and a wry smile creased his lips.

"Newcomb? Is that you," he called out in a half-drunken slur.

The tavern grew quiet as all heads turned to look at the newcomer. Had it not been for the shadows concealing his face, they would have seen anger burning in his eyes. Lassiter, oblivious to Newcomb's mood, continued.

"It's been some time since I saw you last. Have you rebelled against the Cauldron's Oracles and journeyed this far for a song?"

"I see you have purchased some new...*clothes,*" Newcomb replied.

"Yes, aren't they exceptional?" Lassiter crowed as he spun around.

"Exceptionally *horrible,*" Newcomb countered.

Unfazed by Newcomb's criticism, Lassiter continued his lively, upbeat dialogue.

"I've performed in Dellin, Gilden and as far north as Marrh. In fact, after DeMorley made me give back his Bellini, he followed me from tavern to tavern!"

"I know," Newcomb declared. "He did so on my instructions."

Lassiter gave Newcomb a bemused look, but whether that look was because he was flabbergasted that Newcomb would go to so much trouble, or because of the ale, even Lassiter did not know.

"And I will have you know," Lassiter slurred, "I have received enough gilns to not only purchase my attire, but this lute as well." He thrust the instrument overhead. "It's old, and missing a string, but I've risen to its challenge and have learned new fingerings to compensate for..."

"You know why I'm here," Newcomb interrupted, unimpressed by his flashy clothes or his professional resume.

"To get a kiss from a lovely lady?" Lassiter joked as he knelt to kiss another girl.

"Stop this nonsense," Newcomb ordered.

Lassiter froze. His once gleeful eyes narrowed to dangerous slits. He stood back up and shouted at Newcomb with a voice that was surprisingly lucid considering his inebriated state and as sharp as a blade.

"I have chosen my path! What more must I do to get this through your stubborn skull?"

"Look at you," Newcomb derided, pointing at Lassiter's attire. "You look like a...a...*drunken peacock.*"

Lassiter's face reddened.

"And you," he paused to select his next volley of words carefully, "are nothing but a useless, old *storyteller.*"

A murmur rose from the crowd. Newcomb could feel their eyes drilling into him. He knew he had to proceed cautiously. If he tried to forcibly drag Lassiter away, these people would rise in his defense. A simple story would render the crowd powerless, but it would also alert the Cauldron to his whereabouts, and reveal Lassiter as heir to the throne.

Newcomb chose another tact.

"What would your mother say if she saw you like this?"

"She would be proud of me."

"Proud of her drunken peacock?"

"*Yes.* That is more than you've ever shown me."

The words were a punch to Newcomb's gut.

"I've often told you how proud I am of you."

"But only when I was living as *you* saw fit."

"That's not *true,*" Newcomb fired back. He could feel their exchange spinning out of control and he fought to manage it. "I have loved you like your..."

"Like my father? That's your problem. You act like you're my father, but you're not. And you never *will* be."

Although Newcomb's face remained stoic, Lassiter's last volley was a flaming arrow that sent wild fires raging through his body.

"Yes, I know," he confessed in lower tones, hoping a calmer disposition would win Lassiter over. "All I'm saying is that you were born for a much greater purpose than to be a minstrel in Blomseth."

Several stout townsmen rose to their feet, eager to defend the honor of their village.

"What's *wrong* with Blomseth?" one raged.

"Let's throw him out," another shouted.

Lassiter held up his hands to quiet the men. They complied, but remained standing. They crossed their arms and mumbled curses at Newcomb.

"I feel," Lassiter explained as he gracefully swept his arm around the hall, "that *this* is my greater purpose. *This* is my life, and *these* are my people."

"I did not mean for my words to be taken in such a disparaging manner," Newcomb apologized.

"Oh, but you *did.*" Lassiter challenged.

Newcomb sighed.

"We've spent too much time together to end our journey like this."

"I'm not the one ending it. *You* are. You keep insisting I become what you want me to be."

"Haven't you pondered your invitation and the possibilities Claire offers you?"

"I threw it away."

"You did what?"

"I said I threw it *away!*"

Newcomb's shoulders drooped. Two blows in one night. The first was Lassiter rejecting the throne. The second was his unwillingness to meet the King of Claire. Newcomb wondered what must happen to make Lassiter change. Although discouraged, Newcomb would not give up. He decided to use logic against Lassiter's folly. He cleared his throat.

"You can't simply throw away an invitation. It has been paid for with the blood of warriors from the Dark War."

"Aren't I allowed a choice?"

"Yes, but..."

"Then our conversation is over. My mind's made up."

Newcomb stepped toward him with arms outstretched as if trying to hem in a wild colt.

"Lassiter, let's step outside, get some fresh air and calmly discuss..."

"Newcomb, *stop*," Lassiter shouted.

The tavern door flew open and the red-haired trapper rushed in.

"I *warned* you." He plowed through the tables and chairs toward the storyteller like a crazed bull. "Now you're *mine.*"

"Be careful," an old patron warned. "He says he's a storyteller."

"Storyteller or not," the trapper huffed, "he's the one that should be afraid now."

He pushed Newcomb toward the exit. The rusk started to attack but Newcomb ordered him to stop. The trapper gave another shove. Newcomb shouted back to Lassiter.

"For the love of all that's good, the Only has whispered for you!"

The patrons taunted, jeered, and spit on Newcomb as he passed. Lassiter crossed his arms and watched him leave.

"*Lassiter,*" Newcomb cried as he clung to the doorframe. "Don't forsake the tales of your youth, or the blood of your father. Remember the Only!"

"The *Only?*" the trapper grunted as he grabbed Newcomb with both hands. "He died in the Dark War. As will you if you don't leave now."

He hurled Newcomb out into the cold night. The door slammed and celebration erupted within *The Golden Giln*, as if the motley crowd had won a great victory.

A mug of ale was shoved up to Lassiter.

"People of Blomseth," he hailed with his mug raised, "I salute you again." Downing the ale, he hurled the mug at the door, where it bounced with a dull clang, then spun to a stop on the floor.

The customers roared their approval and Lassiter prepared to play another song. Before he strummed his lute, he slipped his right hand inside his jacket, and stroked the contents of its inner pocket. His eyes softened, as did his anger toward Newcomb. For a moment, he was five summers of age on the shoreline of the Isle of Lills. He remembered the salty air, the gulls' caws and the presence of someone beside him.

He stroked the invitation again.

Another memory.

Warmth enveloped his small hand - flesh touching flesh - as he and Newcomb watched the sun slide beyond the sea's horizon. With a sigh, Lassiter pushed aside the sentimental memories and stared at the tavern door.

"What are you waitin' for?" a drunken youth slurred from the rafters.

Lassiter kept his eyes locked on the entrance and stroked the parchment while wrestling with conflicting emotions. Although he truly desired to be a minstrel, he could not get over the fact that he hoped Newcomb would charge back in and fight for him.

The door never opened.

"Come on," another cried. "Give us a song!"

It was at that moment that Lassiter realized he had indeed chosen his own path. He was alone and there was no turning back.

"Sing," another voice from the rafters ordered.

Lassiter pulled his hand from his pocket, strummed his instrument and started his song.

Chapter 23

Blessings of Destruction

Brairtok leaned on the window ledge of Castle Vorak, and let his eyes wander up the misty peak rising beyond his window. On the summit was Netniath, home to the Cauldron. In the gloom it looked like a crouching black dragon. Brairtok never tired of gazing at Netniath and reflecting on the Cauldron's power and dominance over all the lands, as well as its promise to give him life immortal.

The Cauldron's recent report infiltrated thoughts and interrupted his adorations, as mist dotted his curly beard. Elabea had reached Claire and would soon be leaving as a storyteller, and a storyteller's whisper had been heard near the Gilden Plains, proof that not all had perished after Min Brock. Although the news was indeed unsettling, he knew the Cauldron had grown to an incredible strength and that no one, not even the King of Claire with his few rag-tag storytellers, could challenge its power.

A knock at his chamber door interrupted his quiet reverie.

"Enter," he ordered.

Boots echoed, armor chimed and leather creaked as two commanders crossed the banquet hall.

"Yes," Brairtok asked, irritated that their arrival cut short such rapture.

"The storyteller, Elabea, is preparing to leave Claire," Commander Hinnmith announced.

"I already know this," Brairtok replied, his gaze still fixated on Netniath. "In fact, it appears she has a new name: Ela Claire. Even though the Cauldron cannot see beyond the veils of Claire, it sensed a stirring within and discovered as much."

Brairtok spun around and delivered his next question to the other officer.

"Commander Kundle, what is your report about Hetherlinn?"

"My men have confirmed your fears about the village."

Brairtok ground his teeth.

"I do not possess...*fears*."

"My pardon, sir," Kundle apologized with a curt bow of his head. "I meant to say, your...*insights.*"

Satisfied with Kundle's revised wording, Brairtok smiled, turned, and leaned once more upon the window ledge.

"Do tell. What are these insights?"

"They are preparing for battle, my lord."

"How? The Oracles forbid men from other villages to travel and join such uprisings, and we have stripped every nation of their weaponry."

"My lord," Kundle replied, his eyes squarely on Brairtok's shoulders should he turn in retaliation, "they are using...sticks."

"Sticks?"

Hinnmith and Kundle flashed each other a nervous glance. They knew first hand how quickly Brairtok's moods could shift from cool ease to hot rage, from congenial conversation to contemptuous dismissal. Since they were the messengers of the report, they prepared themselves for whatever emotion should come their way.

"Sticks," Brairtok chortled. "How desperate."

He patted the window ledge, giddy at the thought of men sparring without sword or lance and how easy it would be to slaughter them.

Hinnmith and Kundle breathed a sigh of relief that, at least for the moment, his mood had not changed.

"Should we ride to Hetherlinn and destroy them," Kundle asked.

Brairtok turned from the window. The commanders immediately noted his changed demeanor: his eyes were black pits of anger and his gloved hands were clinched. They stiffened themselves for his volley.

"Destroy them for playing with sticks in the woods like children?"

"With all due respect," Hinnmith offered, "they have violated the Oracle that forbids training for combat."

Brairtok paced about, adding to the commanders' unease. Much to their relief, he stopped at another window whose view captured his fancy and remained there for a moment.

"You're correct, Hinnmith," Brairtok said at last. "Whether they used sticks or steel, they have violated an Oracle. I suppose your men should ride to Hetherlinn."

Hinnmith's face twisted in confusion.

"So you *do* desire to destroy them?"

"Yes, but with blessings."

The two commanders stared at each other dumbfounded.

Brairtok caught their dismayed expressions and enjoyed feeling that his cunning was superior to theirs.

"You heard correct, gentlemen, I said, *bless them,* and now I shall tell you why."

Brairtok paraded about like a pompous peacock as he elaborated on his order.

"Why do they spar with sticks and knowingly violate an Oracle? Simple. They've started to dream again, and at the core of their newfound hope is a hunger for the weak one's fables. Witnessing the invitations made them doubt he was destroyed in the Dark War, so they wonder if he will return to fight for them, and free them from our rule. Such notions, gentlemen, are far more dangerous than men planning revolution."

Brairtok walked to his dining table and poured himself a goblet of wine. After a long swig, he continued.

"Naturally, a March of Reeds could squash this uprising, but we are in the midst of the trading season. The news would spread to every hamlet from here to Tristan. Whispers of conjecture would swirl as men in every village tried to reason why all-powerful Ebon destroyed men playing with sticks. Naturally, they will argue that it was solely to punish them for violating an Oracle about conspiring to revolt, but news about Hetherlinn's hope in Claire will stir their imaginations. After all, if Claire was destroyed, why should Hetherlinn's revived belief threaten us?

"Before you know it, other hamlets will brave a similar jump of philosophy and believe in the impotent one again, and they too will prepare for war. Without weapons, being vastly outnumbered and isolated, these rebellious factions would never rise to power. However, we would spend the rest of our lives policing our kingdom and crushing these miniscule rebellions."

He continued to sip his wine as he paced. When he reached the dining table, he caressed the mound of food with his gloved hand as if it were an object lesson.

"On the other hand, if we arrive in Hetherlinn and generously give them the bounty they long for, our blessings should squelch their appetite for our foe's stories, and break their will to fight."

Brairtok sauntered over to his commanders to deliver his final edict.

"That is why you must bless them greatly. Let Ebon's bounty satisfy their hunger for peace and comfort, instead of Claire's tales."

Evil smiles pursed Hinnmith and Kundle's lips as they began to comprehend Brairtok's plan. Brairtok spun away and headed for a window.

"When you deliver the barrels of wildeberry wine," he said as he walked past, "be sure to deliver it to cottage Number 17, the home of Quinn. Then go to cottage Number 7 and call out Gundin. Bestow medals upon them both. Say something to the effect of, *Brairtok and the Cauldron would like to recognize your great heroic efforts in the Dark War...* Blah, blah, blah."

"Medals for our enemy?"

The thought made Kundle's blood boil with rage.

Brairtok reached the ledge and turned to address Kundle.

"Commander, these are not medals of honor, but are meant to revive their shame from Min Brock. Such disgrace will rekindle Gundin's madness and Quinn's drunkenness. In time, they will stop visiting that hideous tulip, and the Cauldron can use the very stories they once thrived on to destroy them from within. As you can see, if you satisfy not only their physical hungers but also their secret desires, you ultimately taint the tales of Claire."

The commanders nodded and Brairtok returned to adoring Netniath.

"Provide them with building materials so that the men can construct bigger homes for their wives. They'll be so busy they won't have time to ponder this uprising. Bring them barrels of food to make them fat, so they no longer have to sweat and labor in the fields. Heap our finest fabrics before the women, so they'll fret over whose garments are more fashionable or whose home is more desirable.

"And the children," Brairtok's lips formed a wicked smile. "Toys; bundles and bundles of toys, so the little ones will want for nothing, and thus, no longer need their parents. In short, gentlemen, make them content within their discontentment. *That* is how we will destroy them."

The commanders bowed, saluted with fist to chest and turned to exit.

"And one more thing," Brairtok called out over his shoulder.

The men stopped and turned around.

"I tire of chasing Elabea, or *Ela Claire*, or whoever she is now. Brairtok, the great lion of Ebon, pursuing the pesky rat of Allsbruth like a toothless dog! It is time to end her story. Therefore, I am sending you, Commander Hinnmith, to Hetherlinn. But you, Commander Kundle, I'm sending to the beachhead of Thornnblen. The Cauldron senses that this is where she will emerge. Take one thousand men and drink your fill of first blood. Let our March of Reeds crush their flesh and bone. No mercy. No mercy at all."

The commanders arched their backs and snapped to attention.

"First blood," Hinnmith shouted.

"For the Cauldron," Kundle roared.

"Long live Brairtok," they said in unison.

The two commanders of Ebon spun about and marched out, the reports from their boots beating an evil cadence against the flagstones.

"Yes," Brairtok sighed as he took in Netniath's grandeur. "Long live Brairtok."

Chapter 24

Grand Feast

Ela Claire entered Marsien Vur and gazed about in amazement.

"How can this be," she asked while turning around and around. "This room is larger than the palace and yet fits within."

Her eyes followed a set of walls that disappeared into forever.

"Just one of the mysteries of being who I am," the King of Claire answered from behind her. "Time, shape and matter here are not as they are in Allsbruth."

Elabea faced him and gasped. The gardener was no more; in his place stood a man of regal proportions.

Gone were the weathered, dirty clothes. This man wore garments fashioned from the finest materials: black, polished boots ran up his calves; his trousers were made from a thick cloth dyed black; a crisp, white shirt stood out like snow on a mountaintop beneath his unbuttoned black, velvet jacket; a matching robe - clasped about his neck with a tulip-shaped brooch made of silver and gems - flowed down to the floor; a thin, black leather belt held a silver scabbard covered with ornate etchings reminiscent of drawings she had seen in Il-Lilliad's book.

And not only is he dressed differently, she mused, *but he looks different, too.*

The King of Claire was taller than the gardener. His thick, curly white hair flowed down to his shoulders. Resting atop his wavy hair was a simple, silver crown that, just like the scabbard, was highly polished and contained etchings of the finest detail.

His face was no longer round, but long and lean, with a defined forehead that rose like a granite cliff above his aquiline nose. His jaw lines were sharp and equally defined, giving him an authoritative quality that the gardener had lacked. Yet, despite all the changes in his outward appearance, Ela Claire noticed that his eyes had not changed at all. They still glistened like sapphires in a great light.

"Do you have your invitation?"

His question broke her spellbound mood. She fished out her parchment. It was still as perfect as the day she discovered it wrapped around a crossbow bolt and stuck to her door. Her thoughts carried her back to when she was perched high in her oak and wondered if life had anything more extraordinary to offer. How quickly her days had changed.

She laid the invitation gently in his outstretched hand.

The gold letters that spelled her name glowed brighter than the sun and flew off into the King of Claire. For a moment he radiated with a great light and then returned to normal.

"You won't be needing that anymore," he said as he tucked the parchment inside his jacket. "You're forever welcome in Claire and your invitation is always here."

He pointed to his heart.

She nodded as she continued to take in the great room.

Against the wall closest to the garden was a massive fireplace large enough for several horses to stand in. Constructed of white stone with a black marble mantle, it contained a fire that popped and crackled. Orange and yellow light spilled out onto the hearth where a lion, the size of a small horse, lay. Resting between his front paws was a rusk. The lion looked into Ela Claire's eyes and roared. She pressed closer to the king, afraid that it would first eat the rusk, then rise and attack her. Instead, the lion licked the rusk's head as if he were a cub.

"Such savageness and innocence," she commented. "Living together."

"Correct. The great lion of the Gilden Plains living in peace with a rusk," the king replied. "Yet another mystery of Claire."

Ela Claire took in more of the grand hall. Tall, red candles glowed atop silver stands that stood like soldiers throughout the room. Mounted on the walls and spaced equally apart were black, iron poles that angled toward the ceiling. Torches burned at the ends and filled the great room with warm, inviting light like that of a sunset. A cylinder of white light from overhead followed the Only wherever he went and lit him from head to toe. She strained to discover its source, but just like the walls that went on forever, the light emanated from beyond the ceiling.

The floor was made of what looked liked black marble and glistened as if wet. Ela Claire scrutinized the floor with greater interest, discerning pockets of soft, yellow light deep within its depths.

"The floor," she asked curiously, "has light inside?"

"Yes, it is very deep where you are standing."

"And it shimmers as if..."

Ela Claire froze, trembling in fear.

"This isn't marble. The floor is *water*," she cried out, afraid that she would fall into the dark abyss.

The Only soothed her fears with a soft chuckle.

"You are quite safe," he reassured her. "Touch it. Go ahead, see for yourself."

Without moving her feet for fear of sinking, Ela Claire knelt and touched the shimmering surface. She had expected it to be cool like the veil, but instead was pleasantly surprised by its warmth. Although she knew it was water by the way it felt upon her palm, she was unable to penetrate its surface. Small fish similar in color to the electric green of the draiggs, darted to where her hand rested upon the surface. She giggled as they nibbled at her open palm, amazed they could touch her, but she could not touch them.

"They are so beautiful," she said as more fish gathered beneath her hand, their rich blues, yellows and oranges standing in sharp contrast to the black chasm. Far below in the murky abyss, the silhouette of an enormous fish swam lazily through the pocket of light. Ela Claire screamed, jerked her hand away, and quickly stood up.

"You don't want the dansel lor to nibble at your fingers," the Only asked, an amused smile playing around the corners of his mouth.

Before she could reply, she witnessed a flash of light from far below. Curiosity overcame her initial terror, and she gazed back down into the depths. She beheld a silvery creature slinking through the water. Light danced off its reflective surface and cut through the chasm's darkness. If it swam at the same depth as the dansel lor, it was a behemoth in comparison.

"*That,* Ela Claire," the king explained, "is the great karshe from the Sea of Illsbruth."

"Why would you want such beasts swimming with you in Marsien Vur?" she shuddered.

"Because their beauty lies in their size and power," he said, trying to reassure her. "Fear not. As long as you are mine - and you always are - they will never harm you."

Ela Claire tried to take her mind off the enormous creatures swimming beneath her feet by studying more of the great hall. Wooden chairs with high backs sat near the fire. Built from a light-colored wood that had been sanded smooth, the chairs had arms with rounded ends where one's palms could comfortably rest. Carved into the top of the chairs were tulip icons. Fluffy, cushions of red velvet made the chairs look regal, yet inviting to sit in. Similar chairs sat around small tables that were placed perfectly about the room, forming casual settings where guests could relax, read or dialogue quietly with another.

In the middle of the great room was a long wooden table with legs that were fat and round like tree trunks. Seven silver candleholders were spaced evenly down the length of the table; the candlelight illuminated the varieties of fruits, breads and meats for their meal. The table was elegantly set with fine china and silver that glistened in the golden candlelight.

The ceiling was higher than her great oak and looked as if she was taking in a spring sky. Birds flew across the blue chased by thin, wispy clouds. As she studied the living ceiling, it dissolved into a night sky. The moon and planets blinked back at her while a falling star traced an argent path.

On the wall perpendicular to the fire was a bookcase made of white marble that contained more books than she imagined the whole world contained. Despite the grandeur of the hall, she realized something was amiss.

There were no servants, guards or officials.

But why, she wondered.

As if in search of the answer, her eyes panned to the adjoining wall, where she noticed a balcony high in the shadows. It was shaped like a half-moon, and jutted out over the room. Spindles of black iron supported an ornately, carved railing.

As her eyes adjusted to the dim light, she gasped in surprise, for standing around the balcony was a multitude of men and women. Ela Claire blushed, embarrassed that they had been watching her the entire time. They were richly arrayed in fine apparel, and wore crowns similar to that of the Only's. She heard the echo of their whispered laughter, and felt a familiar sense of hurt and humiliation. She felt like she was back in Hetherlinn, being ridiculed and laughed at by her neighbors.

"Who are they and why don't they like me?" she whispered to the king.

Sensing her uneasiness, he bent low and whispered into her ear.

"These are my storytellers, Ela Claire. They don't dislike you, my dear. They care for you greatly. In fact, you should hear the wonderful things they are saying about you. They are not laughing at you. What you are hearing is joy that you are here with us in Marsien Vur."

"Really?" she whispered in disbelief.

"Yes, really. But tell me something?"

"What?"

"Why are we whispering?"

Ela Claire lowered her eyes. "I'm not used to others talking nicely about me," she said in a quiet voice. She ran her hand over her plain clothes and felt her head void of a crown. "You see, within Marsien Vur, I feel...out of place."

"Oh, I see," the Only answered with a quick nod.

He spun on his heel, and with a determined gate, walked to the middle of the room with his great train swishing gracefully behind him. He stopped and looked up at the gathering. The storytellers leaned forward in great anticipation.

"Our guest, Ela Claire, feels out of place. Would you kindly tell her what her story reveals to you?"

"Brave," an older gentleman shouted out. "We watched her journey from Hetherlinn. A very dangerous trip indeed, and yet...here she is."

"Astonishing," a young woman added. "She will be a *magnificent* storyteller."

"So young and so beautiful," another echoed. "I see the heart of a great woman."

"We have delighted in watching her story unfold," came yet another. "Thus we laughed in celebration of her victory. We applaud you, Ela Claire."

Their accolades showered her like a gentle rain, and her heart - that had been in a desert for so long - drank from their water. At last the Only held up his hand and the storytellers fell silent.

"Now," he said as he returned to her side, "do you still feel...out of place?"

"No, not as much. But to be honest, I still find all they said about me hard to believe."

"I understand," the King of Claire answered. "But you need to remember my words to you back at the stream."

With a wave of his hand, a translucent vignette appeared and floated cloud-like in the air. Within, she saw herself kneeling beside the stream when the gardener told her...

"I have fashioned you to soar as never before, to become who you secretly and desperately have dreamed of becoming. So feed your passions with this promise: No matter what you may feel from now on, you are always my treasure, my delight."

The word, *delight*, pinged around Marsien Vur as the mirage faded away. Ela Claire beamed a smile and faced the storytellers. She humbly bowed to express her gratitude.

"And here is yet another gift, Ela Claire," the king said as he rested his hand on her shoulder. "Anyone can wear a crown, but until you embrace my story and your worth as my treasure, a crown of silver is but a cheap ornament."

"I understand."

The King of Claire turned his gaze to the storytellers.

"They join me in watching the stories all around Claire unfold and meld together. As storytellers, they have a gift: They can read the story within a person's heart. Now that they reside in Claire, they can read stories much faster than when they were alive."

"Alive?" Ela Claire gasped, taking a quick look back up at the balcony. "So, these people...they're all dead?"

"In your world, yes, but here within Marsien Vur, they reside forever, alive with me."

Ela Claire continued to study the storytellers who in turn were admiring her.

"They are very dear to me," the king said with great reverence. "They were butchered by Brairtok in what your people now call the March of Reeds."

"I remember that story from Il-Lilliad's book," Ela Claire said, her respect for the storytellers growing with each passing moment.

Fighting her shyness, she walked to the middle of the room. She searched her mind for words that would convey her thoughts, her respect, for their martyred lives. But she realized no such words existed for so great a sacrifice. Instead, she curtsied. They received her homage, and graciously returned the bow.

"Come," the king said. "Let us eat. I believe I have everything you like."

Ela Claire followed him to the well-laded table. He sat at the head and she chose a chair half way down the table on his right-hand side. A red tulip, its petals still moist with dew, lay across each plate. The handles of the silverware had exquisite etchings, mirroring those of the king's crown.

She set the tulip aside then reached for some bread and fruit, stacking it on her plate. It was then that she noticed that the Only was not taking any food.

"I'm sorry," she said, embarrassed by her breach of manners. "I should have allowed you to choose first."

The Only smiled, shook his head and clasped his hands together.

"My food is in watching you eat these delicacies. Please, enjoy."

He swept his arms outward to showcase the feast.

Ela Claire picked up a fresh roll and pulled it apart. Steam rose like mist off a frosty knoll. She took a bite. The sweetness of the yeast danced on her tongue. She closed her eyes and savored its flavor. She took a bite from an apple, the crunch echoing off the walls of Marsien Vur. The juices were cool and tart, and impossible to contain; they oozed from the corners of her mouth. The Only smiled, delighting in her delight.

She pulled a bowl of steaming soup to her plate as the king raised his right arm in a subtle gesture, which Ela Claire assumed was a signal for more food. She scooped up some of the creamy chowder, but stopped with the silver spoon halfway to her mouth as the wall in front of her transformed into a panoramic view of her meadow.

The sunlight was bright, and lay dappled over the field. Her oak swayed to and fro in a gentle Allsbruthian breeze. Seeing her beloved meadow made her smile. Thoughts of eating evaporated when she saw a young girl come skipping through the tall grass.

"I remember that morning," she blurted as she recognized herself as a little girl. "I felt so alive on that particular day."

The Only smiled. He waved his hand and another scene from her life appeared. This time it displayed her racing a boy to the tree.

"That was when Galadin, I mean Romlin, thought he was so much faster than me. I proved him wrong!"

The Only nodded, then waved his hand again. Vignette after vignette from her life appeared upon the wall as she feasted on the king's bounty. Ela Claire clapped her hands and laughed as she watched the day she tried to fly from the oak's limb, only to crash in the meadow's tall grass. Tears fill her eyes as she watched the villager's chastising her, and when she saw her parents, mixed emotions swelled in her breast. When she could eat no more, the Only allowed the images from Ela Claire's past to dissolve like ripples on the sea. The wall was once again just a stone wall.

The King of Claire pushed himself away from the table and rose.

"It is time," he said as he walked to where she sat. "Would you please come with me?"

He offered her his hand.

"Where are we going," she asked as she took his hand.

"Why, to dance, of course."

Chapter 25

A Warrior's Gifts

Romlin stared at the King of Claire and then at the cordon of cavalry in Kiarrey Glen. His tongue tasted salt on his lips, and at that moment he realized he had been crying. He wiped the tears from his eyes with the back of his hand, and when he opened his eyes again, he was no longer in Kiarrey Glen, but in a massive hall.

"Where am I," he asked as he blinked to adjust his eyes to the dimmer light.

"You're inside my castle, Marsien Vur," the king informed him.

"How did we get here?"

"You're in Claire. Time and matter are not as you know them in Allsbruth."

"And your armor. It's gone."

The Only now appeared before Romlin in the same black attire he wore while entertaining Ela Claire.

"The armor was for your benefit, not for my protection," the king smiled. "It is no longer needed."

"That makes sense," Romlin replied. "After all, this is Claire. Who could hurt you?"

"Or for that matter," the king replied, "who would want to?"

Romlin's eyes swept up the towering walls to the ceiling.

"The ceiling looks alive, as if it's the sky."

"Maybe it is the sky," the king replied with an amused grin.

Romlin tried to reason how the sky could be a part of the ceiling, or how the ceiling could be part of the sky, but his thoughts became too jumbled so he shook off the mystery. He lowered his gaze and discovered a balcony encircling the room. Men and women, who were elegantly dressed and wore crowns, stared down at him. The king followed his gaze.

"I see you have discovered my martyred storytellers from the Dark War. They have enjoyed watching your journey to Claire."

"Really?" Romlin asked as he waved to the crowd.

"Indeed," the king replied as the storytellers returned the greeting. "They especially enjoyed your bout with the gor, and more precisely, the new name Manno Vox gave you."

"Oh yeah," Romlin replied, a spot of crimson staining his cheeks at the memory. "My boyish adventure nearly got us killed."

"True, and yet, it was the dawn of your awakening."

Romlin nodded as the King of Claire continued.

"Now, since I have known you since you were a child, I would presume that you are famished. Am I correct?"

Romlin's brow furrowed.

"Yes, I am hungry. But, forgive me, I've never met you before. How have you known me since I was a child?"

The king didn't answer, and Romlin - who was more interested in satisfying his hunger than his intellect - spied the long table with platters of food and tossed aside the quandary.

He ran to the table, grabbed a piece of smoked boar's meat and was about to take a bite when whispers from the storytellers flitted down on him. Romlin realized his complete lack of manners and quickly returned the meat to the tray.

"Forgive me," he addressed the king who was now sitting at the head of the table. "I should have waited for you to go first."

The Only smiled.

"You need not wait for me. Please, eat your fill."

Romlin reclaimed the meat and began to feast on the smoked delicacy.

"This is fantastic," he managed between bites.

"It is good to see you enjoy yourself, Romlin. You remind me of someone else I love very much."

"Who's that?" He ripped off another bite.

"Your father."

Romlin stopped eating and pondered the notion. Instead of anger or bitterness dominating his thoughts, he was surprised to find that he was proud of his heritage, despite the lingering wounds.

"How *are* you able to eat so much," the king asked.

Romlin shrugged.

"I don't know," he replied as he smacked his lips and grabbed another piece of meat. "I'm just glad it doesn't stay around my stomach, or I'd look like a MerriNoon."

The king's jolly chuckle rumbled up and down the halls of Marsien Vur.

When it faded, the king said, "Let me see your invitation."

Romlin continued to eat with one hand while he fished the parchment out of his pocket with the other. He slid it across the table toward the king. When the king retrieved it, the golden letters glowed like ore from a smith's furnace and then soared into his chest.

"You are forever welcomed in Claire, Romlin."

The king threw the parchment high into the air where it exploded and sent large balls of light careening about the room. The illuminated spheres fell in line, as if by a silent command, and ceremoniously floated before Romlin. Each in turn hovered in front of him, allowing him to gaze within. Romlin witnessed scenes from his youth replayed in minute detail: his first hunting trek, the times he defended Elabea from Mithe's chastisements, countless races with Elabea - and losing them all.

After the final orb paraded past, they all shot up, high overhead, then burst into countless bits that fell like snow, twinkling and glittering until they faded away.

"Rise," the king instructed, "and follow me."

Romlin ripped off a hunk of boar and came along side him as he led the way. They passed through a threshold and proceeded to a circular staircase that disappeared into the depths below.

"Finish eating," the king instructed as they descended the metal stairs. "You'll need both hands for the next part of your journey."

Romlin stuffed his mouth full, wiped his hands on his pants and mumbled, "Where are we going?"

"It's time for you to leave."

"Leave? But I thought..."

"You must help Ela Claire on her journey."

"Ela Claire? Who's that?"

"You will soon find out. First, I have some gifts for you."

The stairs emptied into a room where the ceilings were low enough to touch with one good jump, and the walls and floors were constructed from white stone. Torches fixed along the walls made the room glow orange. Despite the great depth, the air was void of moisture or coolness. The king's face beamed, reflecting the torchlight.

"I promised you rewards for journeying to Claire. It is time for you to receive one."

The Only stepped aside, and Romlin's mouth dropped open in awe. A piece of meat dropped out and fell unnoticed to the floor. Romlin swallowed hard and at last found his tongue.

"This must be the armory of Marsien Vur. Look at all the weapons."

"Choose your weapon and your shield, Romlin. Choose well, for your battles will be great."

Romlin walked past the wall of lances that were varied in length, style and metals. He scrutinized the wall carrying an arsenal of maces and axes. These too were as varied in composition as the lances. When he came to a wall displaying long bows and crossbows, he stopped.

"Manno Vox's crossbow..." he whispered. He touched the massive weapon. "This one?" he asked like a child hoping for candy too large for his mouth.

The Only shook his head.

"Pick *your* weapon. I believe someone else uses that one."

Romlin nodded. He continued down the wall until he came to the display of swords. He admired the weapons that glittered and pulsed in the torchlight. There were ornate weapons for grand ceremonies, the etchings of Claire running up and down the blades. There were swords forged with blue steel, burnished silver and even brightly polished gold. They ranged in size from no bigger than his dagger to larger than any mortal man could carry.

"There must be thousands," he said to no one in particular.

His eyes swept the myriad of swords until he spotted one that caught his attention, and called to him. It was neither fancy or plain, yet he was unable to take his eyes off the blade. He heard, or perhaps sensed, it beckoning him to lift it from the display.

He wrapped his fingers around the hilt's dark brown leather. It was warm to the touch, as if alive, and he wondered if the sword were sacred. He questioned whether it was beyond his ability to wield or to master. He was about to release his grip when the blade warmed even more, and taking this as a sign, Romlin lifted it carefully from its wooden stand. Despite its length, the blade felt comfortable in his hands, as if it were a natural extension of his arms. He touched the blade's edge: sharper than anything he had ever felt. He studied the Clairian etchings near the sword's hilt and wished he could read.

"Such superb craftsmanship," Romlin said as he continued to examine the blade's every facet. "It is unlike anything forged..."

"Forged by the best smith?" the Only concluded, using the exact words Romlin was about to say.

"Yes, but how did you know I'd say?"

"Please," the king encouraged without answering his question. "Try it out."

Romlin traced a pattern in the air with the sword; his movements were fluid and natural. A giant smile creased his face.

"I want this one."

"Good," the king nodded. "I forged that for you before you were born. I have longed to give it to you."

Romlin stopped his sword ballet and studied the Only. The king read his thoughts.

"Yes, Romlin, you picked the one made for you, forged within my fires long before you ever drew breath. It is a man's sword. Gone are the days when you fight as a boy. You *are* Romlin."

"The etchings," he said, drawing the blade close to read the words. "What do they say?"

"Tales will crush steel when gors have a king."

Romlin's brow furrowed.

"What does that mean?"

"It is a glimpse into a tale yet to come."

"Gors don't have a..."

"Now, go pick out your shield."

Romlin shrugged. He assumed the answer to his question was unimportant, so he let it fall from his mind. He ran down the hall toward the next display. Once again, the selection was vast.

"So many, and each so unique. Which one's the best?" he muttered.

"Obviously, the one made for you," the king grinned.

Romlin's eyes criss-crossed the display: looking, studying, admiring, deciding.

There, he thought, focusing not only his eyes on the large shield, but his heart as well. *It was right in front of me all along.*

"Such are most things of worth," the king added.

"You heard my thoughts?"

"You are in Claire. There are no secrets here."

Romlin pulled the huge shield from its fasteners and slid his left arm through the leather straps on the shield's backside. Although quite large, it felt like a natural extension of his torso.

The king looked deep into Romlin's eyes.

"Do you remember Il-Lilliad's challenge to you in his cave?"

Romlin nodded.

"He said that much would be asked of me."

"Are you ready to answer such a question with your life?"

Romlin paused and thought long and hard. As Galadin, he had been accustomed to rushing headlong into a decision. As Romlin, he realized the gravity of his decisions.

The trek to Claire was the most dangerous thing I've done.

True, the Only answered within his thoughts.

And yet, I've never felt so alive, as if I were a part of something greater than life and death.

Yes.

When danger was too great, you always provided help, through Manno Vox or another means.

True again.

Romlin's eyes glowed with excitement but then faded, as if a sudden rain storm had burst upon an open fire.

"There were also times I failed, like when I chased after the gor instead of protecting Elabea."

The king nodded.

"Will I fail again," Romlin asked.

The king gripped Romlin's shoulders, as a father would his son.

"All men fail. The true measure of any one's life isn't whether or not he fails, but if the sum of his days color the landscapes of others with more good than evil."

The Only released his grip.

Romlin swallowed hard.

"I know I have the potential for evil and being foolish. Can you see how my story will end?"

"Yes."

"Will you tell me?"

"No. Besides, would you *really* want to know the ending before you start the journey?"

"I suppose not."

"I can promise you this much. The battles and adventures you faced getting to Claire will be dwarfed in comparison to what lies beyond tomorrow."

"So I *will* be successful?"

"By your definition or mine?"

Romlin squinted, his mind struggling to comprehend the Only's question.

"With all due respect, are you always this confusing?"

The king smiled.

"I don't mean to bewilder, but your measure of greatness and success are not mine. I use a different measuring rod."

Draping an arm across Romlin's shoulders, he asked, "Do you need more time to make your decision?"

Romlin shook his head.

"No. I will go."

The Only's face filled with light and he patted Romlin's shoulders.

"Good! Ela Claire will be coming soon, and she will need you to protect her on her journey."

"Who is Ela Claire, and what happened to Elabea? She had an invitation too and..."

The Only cut him off with the wave of his hand, and in an instant they were standing in Kiarrey Glen. Surrounding them were the crowned storytellers from Marsien Vur.

"Men and women of Marsien Vur," the Only shouted to all that were gathered. "I give you Romlin; warrior for the Only, guardian of Ela Claire!"

The storytellers accolades were drowned out by the sound of galloping horses as the Only's cavalry returned. They formed two rows on either side of the path that led out of Kiarrey Glen, the heads of their warhorses facing inward. The warriors snapped their lances up and crossed them overhead.

Drawn toward their gauntlet of steel, Romlin entered with gallant strides. He felt stronger, as if he had spent a season chopping wood. He knew his muscles had been strengthened, not by exercise, but by the mysteries of Marsien Vur: the king's regalness, the grand feast, and weapons made for him by the king's own hands.

Not only was there a change in his physique, but there was a shift in his emotions as well. Gone was the anger and shame he felt toward his father. In their place was a resolve fortified with invisible steel and oak, while coursing his marrow was a burning drive of liquid fire. He felt lightheaded with zeal as he imagined his future campaigns beyond the veil, battling mightily as a warrior for Claire, championing Ela Claire...whoever she was.

When Romlin reached the gauntlet's end, he turned to say farewell, but Kiarrey Glen was empty. All he saw was an enormous bird gliding down from the sky.

Chapter 26

Blessings of Ebon

"Wagons!" the sentry shouted back to the next post.

"Friend or foe?" came the reply.

"Foe. Ebonites!"

"How many?"

"Ten large wagons and about one hundred soldiers."

"Hurry back. We must alert Hetherlinn."

The sentry joined the other watchman and together, they made a mad dash back to their village and shouted warnings along the way between gasps for air.

Back in Hetherlinn, the citizens were just beginning their day. A few gathered for warmth by the communal fire while most were in their cottages eating breakfast, but when the harried warnings were heard, panic set in.

Mothers scurried to gather their children. Men rambled out their front doors to see what was the matter, while those at the fire scattered for the safety of their homes. Shouts, curses and weeping laments rose from the sleepy hamlet.

Only two remained calm and stood awaiting the sentries: Quinn and Gundin.

The sentries rounded the bend and dashed to their side.

"Ten wagons," the first blurted as he gasped for air.

"And we estimate," the next added with hands on his knees sucking in deep gulps of air, "over…one hundred…warriors."

"One hundred warriors?" Gundin grunted as he studied their makeshift army of old men and young boys. "Our men aren't ready to fight. Look at them. They're as hysterical as old women. We'll be slaughtered."

"I know," Quinn muttered as his mind raced to find a solution. "We have no choice but to enact our escape plan." Addressing the sentries, he said, "Do as we discussed: Take the women and children deep into the woods. With the remaining men, we'll become bait and lead the Ebonites in another direction. If necessary, we'll fight."

The sentries nodded and trotted off to get the hysterical villagers organized. Areall and Daryess, along with some of the other mothers, helped them calm the frenzy. Serenity once more enveloped Hetherlinn, and aside from a few whimpering children, the refugees followed the men quietly across the meadow toward the woods.

As their families fled, the remaining boys and men gathered to hear Quinn's next orders. Before a word was uttered, the sound of thundering hooves and lumbering wagons dashed their hopes.

"It's too late to flee," Gundin declared through gritted teeth. He muttered to himself: "We would have been ready for battle in another month or two. Has this all been for naught?"

Before Gundin's words faded or Quinn could sound an order, the Ebonite caravan rounded the bend. The enormity of the horde did not surprise them, but the manner in which they marched and their attire did. Instead of galloping with swords drawn and lances lowered, their pace was slow and their lances - adorned with flags - were raised as if they were the honor guard at a regal ceremony. The dark green flags fluttered in the breeze revealing the image of Brairtok's seal, a pouncing lion. Even though the cavalry and foot soldiers were adorned in Ebonite armor, there was one noticeable difference: a red satin sash dangled from belts and saddle horns.

"I've never seen them dressed like this before," Gundin muttered beneath his breath.

"Nor I," Quinn replied, equally perplexed.

Entering Hetherlinn, the cavalry encircled the men while foot soldiers fanned out and inspected the cottages.

Commander Hinnmith dismounted and approached the huddled men. He removed his helmet - an act Quinn and Gundin knew went against Ebonite protocol when meeting with the enemy - and curly, peppered gray hair cascaded onto his armored shoulders.

With his helmet tucked beneath his arm, Hinnmith stopped in front of Quinn, snarled and gave a contemptuous military bow.

"So, we meet again."

Quinn's eyes narrowed. Gundin's muscles tightened.

A small voice from within the circle of men shouted, "We're not afraid of you!"

Hinnmith's gaze found the source of the defiant proclamation. He was little more than a boy. Empowered by the gwyr and with the confidence of countless military campaigns to his credit, Hinnmith appraised the boy's metal.

"Yes you are," he said, his cold tone turning the boy's face white with fear.

"Commander Hinnmith," an Ebonite soldier announced as he entered the circle. "Aside from the men gathered here, the village is empty."

Hinnmith's expression remained stoic. He blew out an exasperated breath, annoyed not only at the humility of his mission, but at this bit of news that would no doubt delay his return to Ebon. He addressed Quinn.

"Where are they?"

"Safe," Quinn snapped with shoulders squared and back straight.

"Safe?" Hinnmith snickered. "Where? In the woods? In caves or hollows of trees? Our sevritts will find them."

"As they must have found our children," Quinn countered, a smug smile creasing his lips.

He wasn't certain, but his gut told him that Elabea and Galadin had escaped the sevritts. After all, if they had been captured, the Cauldron would have made a point of displaying their ravaged bodies for all of Hetherlinn to witness.

Hinnmith glared at Quinn, who met his gaze without a hint of the subservience Hinnmith was accustomed to seeing.

Unfazed, Hinnmith continued his rehearsed speech although his biting tone betrayed his disgust for both his task and this hamlet.

"Observe our sashes of grandeur." He swept his arm to point out the crimson cloth adorning his men and warhorses. "These are displayed when we parade the spoils of war before Brairtok and the Cauldron. Never before has such a celebratory procession traveled beyond Kise. Behold, today marks the beginning of a new era. The Cauldron and Brairtok, moved by your sacrifice to the Dark Flame, have ordered such a presentation in order for us to bestow gifts and blessing upon your village."

"Blessings?" Gundin huffed. "Can anything good come from Ebon?"

"Yes," Hinnmith replied without emotion. "Bounty fitting for those of such dedication."

He waved a gloved hand and ordered the lead wagon to draw near.

"Uncover it," he barked to his men. "May the bounty of Ebon bless Hetherlinn forever."

The soldiers threw off the dark, gray tarp revealing a wagon laden with the finest linens one could purchase: silken goods from Ferra, thick wools from Ingloid, multi-colored cloth from MerriNoon. Next to the pile of fabric was a stash of small barrels. The Ebonite wagon-master pried off a barrel's lid with his dagger, dug his hand deep and pulled out a fist full of coins.

"Gifts," Hinnmith announced in a dull, monotone, "and blessings from Brairtok. You will never have to farm again."

"Why," Quinn asked as he crossed his arms.

"The Council of the Cauldron is aware of your loyalty to Ebon and Brairtok. You have sacrificed your children who disobeyed the Oracles, and you did not retrieve any of the invitations delivered by Claire. Such allegiance must be rewarded, for as the Oracles declare,

'Strike the fickle man before death finds you sleeping; bless your enemy's sheathed blade and dine together in peace.'"

Hinnmith ordered the wagon to pass on, then signaled for the next one to approach. The tarp was yanked off to reveal carpentry tools made from the finest Tristan steel.

"With these," Hinnmith muttered, "you can build bigger, better homes for your families. And with these other goods," he signaled the other wagons to move forward, "you can sustain comfortable lives for years to come."

As the wagons paraded past, Hinnmith described the payload in the same passionless tones. The men of Hetherlinn watched as the Ebonites unloaded barrels of smoked meats, fine wines, dried fruits, building supplies, perfumes and lotions, coins, and toys for the children.

"We don't want them," Quinn replied between clinched jaws.

For the first time since his arrival, Hinnmith's face reflected his true emotions. His eyes narrowed to slits of rage and his face contorted with contempt. He pressed his nose to Quinn's.

"I care *not* what you do with them. Burn them if you wish. My orders were to deliver them, and *that* is what I have done."

Hinnmith pulled away, and his boorish expression returned.

"We will now bestow medals to those who fought during the Dark War."

"We battled *against* Ebon," Gundin thundered. "We're your enemy."

"Are we not beyond remembering such trivial events," Hinnmith countered, once more relying on his rehearsed monologue. "Such grudges and misgivings are remembered no more. As you no doubt are aware, the Oracles clearly teach…

'Harbor revenge and it will anchor you in port. Cast off reprisal and sail like the wind.'"

He let the axiom settle within their minds before continuing.

"The Council, as does Brairtok, believes in honoring the brave, even if they were not…"

At this point of his speech, Hinnmith stumbled. Even though he had practiced the entire exchange countless times, and he knew it was empty rhetoric, the last word would require complete humility; a trait he did not possess. Using sheer will power and focusing on the power of the gwyr, he finalized with, "…of Ebonite lineage."

"You have delivered your bounty, commander. Now leave," Quinn demanded.

"My orders are to make sure everyone receives his or her gift. We shall make camp in the meadow until your families return."

With that, Hinnmith donned his helmet, mounted his warhorse and led his men toward the meadow.

"What are they up to," Gundin asked, dumbfounded by the magnificence of Ebon's bounty.

"They're trying to win us with their gifts," Quinn fired as he watched the Ebonites parade past. "The Cauldron and Brairtok must be worried."

"Quinn, these are the spoils we long for from the King of Claire."

Quinn grabbed him by the shoulders and spun him around. Their eyes locked.

"Nothing...*nothing*...good ever comes from Ebon."

He released him and walked away. Gundin studied the cache of treasures and said beneath his breath, "How many summers have I dreamed of giving such blessings to Daryess?"

A whisper graced his ears.

"Is she not deserving of such bounty?"

Gundin studied Quinn as he walked away.

"Yes, but I made a vow. I will be faithful to Quinn and the Only."

With that, Gundin turned his back to the barrels. It was not an easy decision. He yearned for another look, just a peek at the mounds of treasure. The whisper sensed such stirrings, and like a patient fisherman, cast its next line gently upon Gundin's tepid waters.

"Who is doubting such loyalty? Can you not sample a gift and still serve?"

In his imagination, Gundin pictured himself pillaging through the barrels while Daryess giggled in wonder. She called out his name, her voice full of passion and praise, emotions that died upon his return from Min Brock. His pulse quickened.

Perhaps it is possible to enjoy just a little, he pondered.

"Yes," the whisper concurred. *"Just a wee bit will surely be of no harm. Besides, are you not deserving?"*

Chapter 27

Waltz

The King of Claire produced a small book from his jacket's inner pocket, and Ela Claire noticed that it was identical to the one Il-Lilliad had given her. He threw it high into the air, and the pages fluttered and flapped noisily like a flock of doves.

When it reached its zenith, the pages exploded from the binding and glided gracefully about the room. Music emanated from the words on the pages. It was light in tone, and wove from minor to major keys effortlessly. The meter was in three, and the captivating melody transported her to an imaginary place of indescribable peace.

"The music is so beautiful," she exclaimed, enchanted by the melody that moved from a melancholy tone to one of ecstatic celebration.

"I am so glad you like it. It is your song, Ela Claire," said the King of Claire.

"Mine?" she replied, amazed that a composition of such wonderment would be associated with her. The only music she knew were the songs from her childhood sung about the hearth, or the occasional bard who wandered into Hetherlinn. This was the first time she had ever heard music so rich in structure and timbre.

"It's like listening to countless tales, all told at the same time," she added, trying her best to describe to the Only what she was experiencing. "Yet, they don't fight each other or overwhelm my senses. Instead, work together to tell one heroic story."

Unable to ascribe a name to the numerous musical instruments, she nonetheless equated them with images in her mind: the smooth melody she pictured as white silk flowing in a breeze; the reedy counterparts were flower petals opening in spring; the regal tones that accompanied the melodies she equated with a sunrise; the low-pitched notes were her stately oak.

"May I have this dance," the Only asked with a bow.

"Dance?" Ela Claire nervously replied. "I don't know how to dance. Besides, you are a king and I am just..."

He offered her his right hand.

"You are not a *just*. You are my delight. To be a storyteller, you must learn to dance within such joy."

I can't," she countered. Waves of apprehension surged through her at the thought of embarrassing herself before the king and his storytellers.

"But you have," came his gentle reply.

Ela Claire squinted at him in confusion.

"No, your majesty, I am quite confident I have *never* danced."

The Only waved his hand and once more, the wall in front of her transformed into a chapter from her past. She was at the highest point in the oak's branches and it swayed this way and that in the wind.

"See? You are dancing. We have danced together long before your journey to Claire."

"Well," she said with a smile, "if you call *that* dancing, then I suppose I'm a master."

"Simply imagine you are back in your oak."

She gracefully took his hand as the music swelled and the orchestration became more complex. She closed her eyes and let the composition carry her away. She found herself back in Hetherlinn, high in her great oak with a warm breeze gracing her long hair.

Ela Claire opened her eyes to find that they were floating, dancing on air in the midst of the great hall. The pages of the book flew curiously close and the music washed over them like waves from the sea. As they danced, radiant lights of infinite colors sparkled to the shimmering floor. They bounced and hopped across the watery surface and performed a waltz, similar to that being danced by the king and Ela Claire, while the brightly colored fish, and even the mighty karshe, gathered to watch. The candlelight pulsed with the music's meter, the flames brightening to match the passion of the dance.

As the melody's tempo increased and it climbed through different keys to a climax, Ela Claire and the king spun to match the passion of the waltz. A new sense of freedom filled her, and she shut her eyes to enjoy the experience.

Faster and faster she spun, each revolution filling her with confidence of her destiny as a storyteller. She felt capricious yet her thoughts were deeper and stronger than ever. Her shameful childhood dissolved like a forgotten nightmare.

She stopped spinning and opened her eyes just in time to witness the pages magically zip through her. Each one possessed a unique identity, scent and imagery, sometimes in striking contrast. One made her shudder as if icy winds enveloped her while at the same time her thoughts pictured summers in the meadow. Another carried the scent of flowers and mixed feelings of restfulness with urgency. Yet another cast fear over her emotions, but in much the same way she felt when observing a thunderstorm in Hetherlinn: amazed at the storm's power yet not fearing its reprisal.

The music returned to its simple beginnings and slowed to a beautiful conclusion. When the final note faded, she found herself once more on the floor of the magnificent hall.

"I *danced*," she proclaimed.

"Yes, and what a magnificent dancer you are."

"And the pages of the book...I can see, feel, and *hear* them within me."

"You no longer need the book that Il-Lilliad gave you. The pages are forever within you and will never leave. But be careful. The Cauldron desires to turn them into stories that sound true but only serve its fancy. Now come. I wish to show you some things that will interest you greatly."

The King of Claire led her out of the enormous hall and deeper within Marsien Vur. They turned down a corridor and came to a railing overlooking a brightly lit room. It was narrow and the room's longest walls were perpendicular to where they stood. Her eyes raced up these walls in search of the ceiling, but as hard as she looked, she could not see it anywhere. The source of light that illumined the room appeared to be glimmering white ice high above that showered the room with its mystical light.

The walls appear to go on forever, she wondered to herself.

They do, the king replied in her thoughts.

Her eyes bulged with the knowledge that he could hear what she was thinking. He gave her a reassuring smile and pointed out the room's contents.

The floor was white marble, or what she presumed to be marble, but what captured her fancy were the enormous mahogany bookcases lining the walls of perpetual length and height.

"There must be thousands of books," she whispered.

"There are too many to count. But tell me something..."

She looked into his face.

"Why are we whispering again?"

Ela Claire chuckled, thankful that her quirks were not an annoyance to him, but in many ways were appealing.

"Would you care to see them," the king asked.

Knowing her answer before she could think it, let alone say it, he raced down the sweeping, polished wood staircase. She followed after him, her eyes glued on his flapping cape.

Did I just hear his robe challenging me to a race, she wondered.

That you did, the king replied as he continued his harried pace, *for it knows the wonders I'm about to show you and cannot help but urge you to such a run.*

She increased her speed and flew down the steps, but unlike her days in Hetherlinn when she could easily overtake Romlin, this time the victor was the king. He sped to a section of books, then stopped. His face beamed and his eyes danced with light.

"These are the stories of the people you know and love in Hetherlinn. Look," he pointed to a nearby book. "There is your mother's story."

She reached toward it.

"You may touch it," he advised, "but do not remove it from the bookshelf, for I am still writing her story."

Ela Claire nodded and gently ran her fingers over the binding. She could feel her mother combing and braiding her hair and even caught a whiff of her wonderful scent.

"It's like she's right here beside me," Ela Claire exclaimed.

"She misses you dearly."

Ela Claire removed her hand and her mother's presence faded away. She spied another book. Turning her head to the side, she studied the title.

"I wish I could read. Whose book is this?"

"Mithe's"

Ela Claire's face filled with dread.

"The old widow," she uttered disdainfully as she recalled Mithe's hurting words and accusations. "Why do you have *her* book?"

"Because just as I delight in you, I delight in her."

"But she's so *mean.*"

"Yes, she is. I do not overlook the pain she has caused you and others. But I also see Mithe as a mother and wife who suffered horrible losses during the Dark War. In fact, can you think of one person from your village who has not tasted the tears of Min Brock?"

Ela Claire pondered the question, and after a bit muttered reluctantly, "No."

"Am I to only offer my delight to those you find favorable?" he asked her.

She shook her head, although her feelings were still very unsettled on the matter. She continued along the bookcase but stopped when she came upon an inscription she recognized. She reached for Romlin's book but the king intercepted her.

"Why are you stopping me," she asked, afraid she had overstepped some unseen boundary.

"Seeing into the future story of certain people would not be for your well-being."

Ela Claire's face wrinkled up in confusion and wondered how this was even possible. After all, Romlin was her best friend, and if he possessed the same feelings for her as she had for him, then one day he would be her husband. How could knowing the answer to such a dream not be for her good? As doubts and worries started to grow, the Only guided her hand to another volume. The leather was old and tattered, but whether from long periods of hard use or from being abused, she could not tell.

"Whose book is this," she asked.

"Your father's."

She froze.

"Go ahead. Touch it. You might be surprised," he encouraged her.

She brought her index finger short of touching the binding. The Only reassuringly touched her hand. With a deep sigh, she pressed her finger against the book.

She found herself back in Hetherlinn on a warm day perched on the lower branches of her oak. Her eyes wandered across the meadow to a man who turned this way and that as if looking for someone or something. When he spotted her in the tree, his face lit up.

"Elabea," he cried out for joy.

"Father?" she whispered, not only stunned at his sudden appearance, but that his voice sounded so different: his dreary gloominess had been replaced with bliss arcing like a rainbow.

Quinn sprinted through the tall grasses, and when he reached the sweeping branches, he extended his arms to her. Staring into his face, she was taken aback by a smile that made his face glow.

"Elabea," he called up to her, "Jump to me!"

She shook her head and clutched the tree.

"No."

"I'll catch you. I promise."

Despite her apprehensions, and longing for a new beginning, she let go of the tree. Down she floated like a thistle. He caught her and held her close, pressing his cheek to hers. She breathed deeply. Gone was the scent of wildeberry drink. Now, his aroma reminded her of the meadow: clean, vibrant and strong.

The warmth and strength of his embrace made her relax and she leaned into his frame. He rocked her back and forth in his arms like he did before Min Brock, and then he whispered into her ear.

"Ela Claire. My delight."

She yanked her finger off the book and the images and scents vanished. She turned her back to the King of Claire.

"I don't see how that story will ever come to pass," she sniffed.

The king turned her face toward his and gently wiped a tear from her eye.

"Of course not; your wounds are still too deep. Come. I need to show you more."

A great burst of light enveloped her, and Ela Claire found herself outside Marsien Vur.

When she finally got her bearings, she realized she was once more in the garden and that the King of Claire was off gazing beyond the veil. She walked to his side, but he remained fixated as if taking in all the good and evil, truth and deception, whispers and wars beyond Claire.

"The power of the Cauldron is growing," he confided to her. "The vapor and drone are increasing in strength. The distant drums of Ebon pound a cadence that signals war and destruction for all. It will be a war of horrible casualties and terrible consequences."

"I'm not afraid. I'm safe here in Claire with you."

"Yes, for now. But our time is coming to an end."

Her eyes flashed with fear.

"An end? But it's so wonderful here and we've only just met. And I have so many questions. I want to hear more stories. I want to dance!"

"One day you will return, and you will stay," the Only replied tenderly. "But today is not that day."

Stunned by the news, Ela Claire looked away.

The King of Claire put his arm around her shoulder and gazed with her beyond the veil.

"Ela Claire, so many have forgotten my stories or have chosen to listen to the Cauldron's twisted tales. Few even listen for my whisper, either because they rest in the misery the Dark Flame tells them is life, or because the drone's incessant pounding has deafened them. Either way, they are in dire need of a great storyteller, one that will usher in an era of serenity. That is why I am sending you to tell your story; to tell them *our* story."

"Me? Who will believe me? I think it would be best for you to go and tell such tales."

"I wish it were that simple, but it is not. They will believe you more readily than I."

Ela Claire tried to comprehend this assignment, but it was like trying to see the back of her head. After some time, she asked, "Am I going home?"

Lifting her face toward his, he carefully chose the words that would be hardest of all for her to hear.

"My Ela Claire, you can never go home."

She pulled away. Despite the fact that her life at home was littered with heartache, and that she had always dreamed of leaving Hetherlinn, the thought of never returning was suddenly very troubling. His words sounded like a punishment and not a gift.

"Why," she asked. "You just showed me the books of my parents' lives. I even saw my father behaving differently. Why can't I return?"

"Because Elabea no longer lives, and the life you once knew is gone forever."

"But my parents. My home. My life."

The Only squeezed her shoulders and looked deep into her eyes.

"The stories you beheld moments ago are still being written, but they are for Ela Claire to behold, not Elabea. Besides, Hetherlinn has changed since you left. War is coming. Your people are preparing to fight."

"Fight?" she repeated with a glance toward Allsbruth. "Hetherlinn is brave enough to challenge the Oracles of the Cauldron?"

The Only nodded.

"I cannot reveal every aspect of this story, but at this very moment, a man in Hetherlinn is facing impossible odds. He has chosen war over peace, not only to redeem his tears of Min Brock, but for someone he loves very much; someone he has wounded greatly. What frightens him most is not the clash against Ebonite steel, but that this person may never return his love."

Ela Claire gave him a quizzical look.

"I am talking about your father," he continued. "Like the dream you beheld moments ago while touching his book, he is coming for you. When? I cannot tell you, but this much is true: He is willing to fight for you, even to die for you."

"My...father?" she shook her head in disbelief. "The town drunk will rise to fight again? I know the dream of his future showed me a different man, a changed man, but now, out here in the light of day, that seems impossible."

"Remember," he said with a smile, "I dance with the impossible."

She gave a weak nod, still doubtful of such a magical transformation. As she pondered her future as a storyteller, she felt overwhelmed and started to pace.

"I don't know the first thing about being a storyteller. How will I know what to do; what to say? Shouldn't I remain in Claire so you can train me?"

"Normally I would, but the times are not normal. Besides, you now have my tales swirling within you. My whisper will guide you when the time comes."

She stopped pacing and faced him.

"Must I go?"

She asked not in a defiant spirit, but more as one longing for a moment more to enjoy a sunset, or fellowship with a dear friend.

"You may stay if you choose, but I believe it would be too painful for you. You bear the mark of a storyteller, and have the heart of one as well. Remaining in Claire while others are suffering - especially those you know and love in Hetherlinn - would be a burden too great for you to carry."

She pulled away from his mesmerizing eyes and looked at the veil. For a long time she gazed, her mind swirling with questions, fears, hopes and dreams. She sensed the King of Claire's whisper in her thoughts, but never did he press her for an answer. As she wrestled with her decision, one that would no doubt forever mark her life, the music of her waltz hovered in the wind and serenaded her.

Ela Claire drew in a deep breath, and despite her worries and reservations, made her decision.

"Very well. I'll go. But if I'm not to return to Hetherlinn, where do you wish me to travel?"

"I need you to journey to the Isle of Rhythe. There you will find treasures stolen by Brairtok and the Ebonites. You need to deliver them to Min Brock."

"Alone," she asked, fearful once more of what lay beyond the veil. "I cannot. I mean...I'll try, but..."

The Only smiled and with a gentle hand to her shoulder, squelched her fountaining questions.

"How I love your innocence," he admired. "No, not alone. Behold."

He pointed skyward.

A large bird flew toward them. Dangling from its beak was some clothing. The enormous bird circled overhead and dropped the apparel that floated down like a cottonwood seed.

The cape fell gracefully upon her shoulders as if placed there by the Only himself. She rubbed the plush, velvety fabric of midnight blue and marveled at how its color varied, depending on how the light brushed its surface.

"With this cape," the King of Claire explained, "I send you out into a world that has all but forgotten me." He secured the cape about her shoulders with a brooch. "It not only will ward off the cold, the rain and the Cauldron's vapors, but will be a daily reminder that I guide and strengthen you with my whisper."

Ela Claire's fingertips brushed the brooch. It was fashioned out of silver in the form of a tulip. Its stem was composed of green emeralds and rubies formed the petals. Stunned to be the owner of such a beautiful piece of jewelry, she gave the Only a wide grin.

"Remember," he instructed, "the brooch and cape do not make you a storyteller. It is your birthmark and heart that are your true treasure."

She nodded, then stared as all around her, as far as she could see, stood storytellers.

The Only spun around, and with grand gestures and a rumbling voice that carried across all of Claire, he announced, "Gone is Elabea, child of Hetherlinn, *Dreamer of Days*. Behold Ela Claire. Storyteller for Claire! *Dreamer of Life!*"

He waved his arm toward her and a beautiful white dress replaced her simple Allsbruthian tunic. Tied about her waist was a dark red sash.

"They are so beautiful," she exclaimed as she twirled about admiring her attire. "I don't know what to say."

"Your zeal has said it all," the king replied as he signaled the giant bird of prey to land.

The bird obeyed, gliding down and landing beside Ela Claire. She instinctively stepped back from the intimidating creature while at the same time admiring his features.

The bird was pure white, as tall as a man, and stood upon thick, feathered legs. Its feet were tipped with long, deadly talons. Its face was slightly scooped, like that of an owl, and its black, hooked beak sat like ebony amongst his snow-white feathers. Its yellow eyes burned with fiery intelligence. Cocking its head to the side, the bird studied her with great interest.

The King of Claire introduced Ela Claire to the bird.

"This is Previn, the great harrier. I believe you two have met before."

Ela Claire nodded.

"Yes, I met him at the entrance to your garden."

"Actually, you two met before you passed through the veil of Claire."

"No, I think I would remember a powerful bird like this."

The harrier rustled his wings, and to Ela Claire's amazement, spoke.

"My appearance since the time before has changed. It is no wonder you do not recognize me."

Ela Claire's face wrinkled in thought as curiosity drew her closer to Previn.

"Your voice," she murmured as she reached out to stroke its plumes, "reminds me of someone I once knew; someone I loved very much."

Previn pressed against her side like a warhorse coddling his master.

"The sight of you in Claire brings sweetness to my demise by the vul jens."

Her eyes widened and she clasped her hand over her mouth.

"Rusk? It *is* you!"

She threw her arms around the bird's neck and hugged it tight.

The king patted her shoulder.

"It is time. Previn is commissioned to assist and protect you."

Previn lowered himself to allow her to mount, and Ela Claire climbed upon his back as an urgent thought crossed her mind.

"Your majesty, in all the excitement, I forgot all about Romlin."

"Previn will carry you to him."

"Yes, but I want you to meet him."

"I already have."

Her brow furrowed, but before she could ask another question, the Only continued.

"Always be on your guard. Listen to the stories now living within and tell them to all. Beware of the Cauldron, for once beyond the veil it will try to destroy you with its deceptive whisper. Touch your cloak, recall your waltz and know I will always be with you."

Placing a hand over her heart, Ela Claire was astonished to hear her waltz resonating throughout her, the low notes making her body rumble as if wild horses stampeded past. She recalled their dance together and relished the memory. Lost in the moment, she was unaware of the wind blowing through her hair or the warm air becoming chilly. As Previn soared ever higher away from Marsien Vur, carrying Ela Claire away on her journey, she hummed along with her song.

Chapter 28

Together Again

Romlin shielded his eyes and watched the bird as it started its descent. Even from this distance, Romlin could see that the bird was enormous, and that a girl in a white dress with a midnight blue cloak rode its back. He assumed the girl was this Ela Claire the Only had spoken of, but wondered what had happened to Elabea.

The bird landed nearby and Romlin's mouth dropped open with surprise.

"Elabea?" he stammered, "You look so...so *different.*"

"Is different good," she asked, blushing.

Romlin took in her appearance, and liked what he saw. He was entranced not only by her stunning outfit, but her features as well. She still had the same nose, the same mouth and eyes. But there was a glow about her now, a vibrancy that took his breath away.

Unable to find his tongue, he merely nodded.

"You look different too," she added as she slid off Previn's back.

Although they had only been apart for a short time, Romlin appeared larger, stronger, even more masculine than she remembered, if that were possible. His eyes were full of fire, but not the ones she had seen in Hetherlinn, burning for vengeance against all the wrongs from Min Brock. The fire in Romlin's eyes was now full of purpose, resolve and confidence.

"How," Romlin asked. "I'm wearing the same clothes you saw just moments ago at the wall. So how am I different?"

Ela Claire sighed, unsure of sharing her deepest feelings for him, when a movement in the glen averted her thoughts and attention.

"Whose horse is *that?*"

Romlin spun around to face the stallion. The horse was black as a moonless night, while its saddle was a rich, chestnut brown. Its flanks were covered with silver armor and a variety of weaponry hung near the saddlebags.

"Mine, I presume," he replied.

The stallion whinnied in recognition of his master's voice. Eyes locked: warrior to warhorse, warhorse to warrior.

"Come," Romlin commanded.

The stallion reared up on its hind legs and boxed the air. Dropping to the ground, it frisked to Romlin's side and nudged him playfully with his snout.

"What a magnificent warhorse," he said, running his hand over the animal's armored flanks. He fastened his shield to the side of the saddle.

"You're much stronger than anything the Ebonites have," he said to the stallion. "I shall call you, Devron."

"No, you shall not," the stallion curtly replied.

Instead of falling back in surprise, Romlin merely nodded.

"Oh, I forgot," he said. "Animals of Claire can talk. Do you have a name?"

"Bar-Treb."

Romlin patted the stallion's neck.

"Then Bar-Treb it is."

He grabbed the reins and launched himself into the saddle as the animal pranced about, eager for a new adventure.

"Guess what," Romlin said to Ela Claire as he maneuvered alongside Previn. "I met the King of Claire. He was incredible. I've never seen a warrior as strong."

"What are you talking about," Ela Claire raised an eyebrow. "I just left him, and he was a gentle, wise king."

Romlin smirked.

"That's impossible, I was just with him moments ago, deep within the castle's armory."

"You *must* be mistaken," she countered. "*I* just left him at Marsien Vur, and I never saw you."

"And I never saw *you*," Romlin challenged. "We can't *both* be right."

"If I may assist," Previn interjected, "You should remember that time and matter are not as they are in Allsbruth. It is very possible, in fact probable, that you both met the King of Claire at the same time in Marsien Vur and yet, never saw each other."

Romlin, unable to grasp such a complexity, shook his head.

"I suppose it's not *that* important. What *is i*mportant is this: where is Ela Claire?"

"Why," she asked, feeling pensive about her new appearance and role as a storyteller.

"Because, the King of Claire has assigned me to escort her on her journey. I am to be her protector."

"Romlin," she whispered, "the King of Claire gave me a new name."

"Really," he asked, feigning interest while he continued to search for his new charge.

"Yes. My name is Ela Claire."

He stared at her in disbelief.

"*You're* Ela Claire?"

"Yes. Is that a problem?"

"No, it's just, well no offence, but I was expecting someone...else."

Romlin's voice trailed off into embarrassed silence. They stared at each other and searched for words to break through the moment of confusion. They both yearned to be vulnerable, yet feared rejection and hurt. Ela Claire turned away from the awkward moment.

"I'm sorry to disappoint you," she said as she stroked Previn's feathers.

Romlin sat speechless and stone faced. Bar-Treb turned his head back toward him and whispered low enough to reach only his ears.

"This would be a good time to say something."

Romlin gave the horse a sideways glance, then cleared his throat.

"Elabea, I mean Ela Claire, I'm not disappointed. It's just that, well, you look so...so..."

"Choose your next words carefully," Bar-Treb warned with a whisper.

Romlin gathered his courage then finally said, "Beautiful."

Ela Claire gasped and looked into his face. When Romlin witnessed her eyes dancing in pools of light, and felt his heart beat as if he sprinted up a hill, he realized he had perhaps revealed too much of his feelings. Embarrassed, he pulled away from her stare and focused on patting Bar-Treb's neck.

"My mission," he said with a shy peek in her direction, "is to escort you on your journey. So, where are we going?"

"To the Isle of Rythe," she answered. She desperately wanted to see his face and read his expression.

"Do you know where it is," Romlin asked.

"No," she sighed, afraid his interest in her was waning.

"Did the Only give you a map?"

She shook her head. The moment was gone.

Oblivious to her feelings, Romlin focused on the problem at hand.

"How am I supposed to get you there if we don't know where we are going?"

Bar-Treb whinnied.

"Look inside my saddlebag."

Romlin dug through the bag's contents.

"Well, what do you know," he exclaimed, "a map."

Unfolding it across his lap, he noted that like the previous map, it showed multi-dimensional aspects of the terrain as well as floating words over regions for identification. Since he could not read, he ran his fingers over each one to hear them speak. He stroked the one for the Isle of Rythe, and saw how far away it was.

"We have quite a journey ahead of us."

"Good," she answered, "the longer we stay in Claire the better."

"Maybe," Romlin offered, "we can jump into it, like we did the other map and get there today."

Ela Claire shook her head.

"Even if we could, I'd prefer to take our time. I have a lot to think through as a storyteller."

Romlin was about to argue when Bar-Treb whinnied in an effort to silence his master's tongue. Romlin sensed as much, and swallowed his word.

"We still need to hurry. Come on, I'll race you to the veil."

"Why must you make everything a race," she asked. The thought of passing through the veil and relinquishing Claire left her unsettled.

"Me? You've been racing me all my life," he replied as he slapped his reins and galloped off.

As she watched his cloud of dust rise into the wind, she wondered what lay ahead of them, outside the veil. Fear nibbled at her confidence. She placed her hand over her heart and closed her eyes. The gentle strands of her waltz washed over her and she relaxed.

"Did you hear what Romlin said," she asked Previn while mounting.

"Of course; the Isle of Rhythe is far and we must hurry."

"Yes, but he also said that I'm beautiful," she murmured.

"But Ela Claire," Previn replied as his wings beat the air. "You say this as if it is a surprise. I have known you were beautiful even when I was your rusk and told you as much."

"Yes, but this..."

She paused to relish Romlin's word and cupped it with her feelings like she would a gem. The facets twinkled.

"This is different."

Chapter 29

Brothers Seven

Linwith marched out of the cave's darkness with Rittmar flying close by his side. Following behind them was the Worm King, whose long tail dragged in the dirt like a royal train. Once in the light, Linwith was able to admire the towering creature in greater detail.

The worm's upper scales were spruce green, while its underbelly - made up of scales larger than those on top - was pale-blue and ran from his chin all the way down to his tail.

Four oak-like legs supported the worm. His rear appendages were bigger and stronger than those near his chest. Ivory talons curled like scythe blades; four protruded forward from his feet while one projected backward, enabling the worm to snatch, grab or perch like a bird of prey.

The Worm King arched his long, thick neck and Linwith saw the worm's ridge of spikes. Beginning at the base of his head, they jutted skyward like small mountain peaks and diminished in size down the ridge of his neck before disappearing altogether well short of his torso.

Staccato barks that boomed like boulders colliding, echoed up toward the six caves, and when the Worm King opened his long snout, Linwith saw rows of sharp teeth. The worm's head was wider than his neck, but unlike dragons, he did not have any horns, yet his face was formidable, with almond-shaped eyes capable of instilling fear into any who gazed into them. Larger than a dragon's eyes, the glossy orbs of indigo held mystical flames that glowed as if from another realm. Linwith watched the flames burn from yellow to orange, then red to white, as if to match the worm's passions and moods.

The Worm King unfurled his enormous wings and extended them over Linwith and Rittmar. They arched back toward his tail and were covered with a taut, thin membrane of green flesh. Linwith reached up to touch them.

Soft as down yet strong as leather, he marveled as sunlight filtered through and bathed them in emerald light.

The most captivating feature was the worm's tail. It was a shade of blue reminiscent of the Sea of Illsbruth's deepest depths, and although not metallic, reflected the sunlight as if it were blue armor. The shimmering sapphire color ran from the tail's tip toward the body and faded into the spruce green and light blue shades.

"I never should have doubted, you, Rittmar," Linwith declared. "The worms are indeed fierce and powerful creatures."

The Worm King faced the cliff caves where six worms, summoned by his barks, perched.

"My brothers," he hailed. "We have resided within our lairs for over five hundred summers, patiently awaiting the day when our new master would arrive. That day is now. The stories of Claire flow once more. We will soon soar through the skies and do battle for the King of Claire. My brothers, it is with great honor that I present to you, Linwith of Allsbruth - Worm Master!"

The six worms spread their wings, the vast expanse blocking out the sun and casting a dim shadow on those below. Identical in color and size to their brother, the Worm King, each worm had a distinguishing tail: crimson, gold, mandarin, emerald, amber and pearl. And like the Worm King's blue, their colors glistened like polished metal in the sunlight.

The brothers seven arched their heads skyward. Together, they emitted a call, like a massive horn, deep, rich and majestic.

The Worm King lowered his head and addressed Linwith.

"It is time."

"Time? Time for what," Linwith asked, dumbfounded.

"Time for your inaugural flight to commemorate this momentous day."

With that, the Worm King flew to the opposite end of the glen. With his front talons, he removed the pine saplings stacked against the side of a round hill. He stepped aside to reveal a set of stone doors that led into the knoll.

"Behold, your armory," the Worm King advised. "Enter, and retrieve all you will need. We shall wait for you here."

Linwith approached the doors. Chiseled into the stone panels were the likeness of seven worms with wings poised for flight. Above them were words in a tongue Linwith could not read.

"It is Clairian," Rittmar offered as he hovered beside him, "and says, *Ride again upon the winds of Claire.*"

Linwith looked for a handle or latch with which to open the doors. Nothing. He pushed. They did not budge. He turned and looked a question at the Worm King.

"Am I supposed to know how to enter?"

"Remember your song."

Linwith faced the stone doors.

"Transient arcs of radiant light,
Cross the heavens on a moonless night.
Wings, tails and talons so bold,
Guarding their cache of treasure and gold."

The sound of grinding stone filled the glen. Cool air rushed out, along with the scent of damp earth. Linwith peeked into the darkness within. A set of stone stairs led deeper into the knoll and disappeared into the blackness. He found an unlit torch by the entrance and with steel and flint, ignited it. With the orange glow from his torch casting shadows into the depths, he and Rittmar began to descend.

As was his habit when climbing or descending stairs, Linwith began to count.

"...twenty-nine...thirty...thirty-one...thirty-two...thirty-three..."

He was at the bottom.

"Thirty-three steps," he announced to Rittmar.

"I am sorry, Linwith, but I do not see the importance."

"Perhaps nothing, but I am thirty-three summers of age."

"Ah. Another confirmation."

The landing opened into a large, dark room. Linwith saw rows of unlit torches hanging on the wall and began to light them. Their combined light bathed the chamber in a golden glow. Linwith stared in amazement at the contents of the room, and nearly dropped his torch.

"*...Guarding their cache of treasure and gold,*" he breathed aloud.

In the center of the room was a stone platform holding a large wooden chair of regal proportions. On either side were chests overflowing with gold and silver coins. Opposite the chair was a long bench, and resting on the bench was a silver helmet. Linwith walked over and picked it up. Turning it over in his hands, he noted master-craftsmanship. It was lightweight, and designed to cover one's entire head and face. The two, long eye openings were covered with thin, tinted alabaster.

"Try it on," Rittmar encouraged.

Linwith lifted it up. Two thin leather straps dropped out.

"What are those for," he asked as he lowered the helmet.

"To secure it on your head when you command your worms to dive or twist in flight."

Linwith looked out through the alabaster lenses. The room took on a subtle orange shade.

"And this," he asked, tapping the transparent eye covering with his fingernail.

"You do not fly, do you?" Rittmar answered with a chuckle. "When you soar through a swarm of flies you will be thankful those are there."

Linwith took off the helmet and picked up a pair of the strangest looking riding gloves he had seen. He slipped his hand in and wiggled his fingers to settle them into the soft, taut fingertips. They were a perfect fit. Around the wrist was a thick band of leather that did not touch his flesh. It ran up to his elbow and was wide enough that it did not touch his forearm. Fastened to the outside of the thick leather were thin sheets of silver armor.

Hanging above the bench was chest armor and several jackets. The armor was silver, completely smooth in appearance and would even completely cover his back. He pulled it off the wall.

"Extremely light," he noted.

"Yes, but stronger than any metals forged from Tristan," Rittmar informed him.

Placing the armor next to the helmet, he scrutinized the jackets. As if reading his mind, Rittmar explained.

"These you wear beneath your armor. The thinner one is for spring and summer. The bulkier one is lined with fleece. It will keep you warm during your winter flights."

Linwith nodded while walking to another stand adjacent to the bench. A set of wooden stairs consisting of four steps sat nearby.

Once more, Rittmar served as instructor to the Worm Master.

"You will use the steps to mount the Worm King."

Perched on top of the stand was a magnificent leather saddle and leather skirt. The saddle's horn was made of silver and arched back toward the seat. Around the crown of the horn were seven gems, each the size of his thumbnail and each a different color. The brown leather was soft, smooth and polished to a gentle lustre. The cinch straps were long and thick, but it was the stirrups that caught his attention.

Constructed of thick leather and covered with a thin layer of silver, they looked like boots that were already in place. The backs of the stirrup-boots were open, enabling the rider to slip his leg in and yet be completely shielded from the front.

Next to the saddle was the bridle. It too was made of silver, was of enormous size, and had long, brown leather reins.

"I'm to place *this* in his mouth? Have you seen his teeth?"

"You *are* his master."

"Yes, I just hope his teeth remember that."

Linwith spotted a small, arched entry-way and led into an adjacent room. He thrust his torch inside and was blinded by the reflection from the amassed piles of coins and exotic gems.

"Rittmar," he exclaimed. "Do you realize how much treasure is here?"

The chancellor flew to him and hovered in front of his face.

"Of course. Why wouldn't I?" Rittmar replied, unable to comprehend Linwith's irony.

"Imagine," Linwith said as he paced about the room, "bartering a small amount of these treasures for Tristan weapons. We would be able to accumulate enough weapons in one trip to supply all of Allsbruth."

"Of course," Rittmar said. "That is why trading your wagon for passage..."

Linwith cut Rittmar off mid-sentence.

"How soon can we fly to Tristan?" he exclaimed as he understood how important his role was to be in the ensuing war.

"First, you must fly with the worms."

"But there isn't time..."

"You are the Worm Master. There is time."

Linwith nodded. With the energy of a young boy, he grabbed the saddle, which though large and cumbersome, it was not as heavy as he had expected. Partially carrying and dragging it, he left the armory then quickly returned to retrieve his jacket, armor, the bridle and the stairs.

"Are you ready," the Worm King asked.

"Yes, but I will need your help. I have never ridden a dragon before."

The fires deep within the worm's eyes burned red-hot.

Linwith took a cautious step back and shot a questioning look at Rittmar. Rittmar darted to his ear.

"*Never* call them dragons. It is an insult of the highest proportion to them. Even as their master, you must not dishonor them. Dragons are simpletons, mere lizards of puffed proportions with the aptitude of mules. These are the Worms of Bal-Malin. Behold them! Dragons pale in comparison. And if their glistening tails are not enough to dazzle your imagination, then their unique gifts and deep intellects will. From now on, you must always refer to them as *worms*."

"I'm *so* sorry," Linwith apologized to the Worm King with a sincere bow. "I am an uneducated man. Now that I know, I will never utter that word again."

Convinced of Linwith's genuineness, the fire in the worm's eyes returned to a glimmer of yellow.

Lowering himself to the ground, the Worm King folded his wings to his side.

"Toss the skirt across my back," he instructed. "Next, place the saddle on top. Do not worry about the cinch straps; you will tighten those when I rise. Lastly, place the bridle in my mouth."

Linwith hurried about his tasks, but when it was time to insert the bridle into the worm's mouth he paused. He looked at the long snout where rows of spiked teeth lay hidden within. As if reading his mind, the sapphire worm encouraged him.

"Linwith, you are the Worm Master. I am your Worm King. Don't worry. I won't bite you. Had I wished to destroy you, I would have done so long before now."

Linwith nodded. He approached and gazed into the worm's shiny eye. Deep within, he saw the fires flicker and dance as if in anticipation of a grand feast or celebration.

"Yes, Linwith," the worm said, "I am as excited as you are with the tasks before us. My brothers and I have waited patiently for this day for five hundred summers. Now hurry. Let us cast our fate to the winds!"

The colossal creature opened his mouth, and Linwith placed the bit inside with tender care. The worm tasted the metal and flicked his black and orange tongue to settle the bit in place. Satisfied, the worm rose.

"Now," he ordered as his tongue darted about as if sensing the dawn of a new era, "tighten the cinch straps, then don your jacket and armor. When you are ready, you may mount me."

Linwith did as ordered. He placed the wooden stairs on the animal's left side. Ascending to the top step, he placed his left foot into the stirrup and grabbed the leather handles dangling from the saddle. With a push and a pull, he swung his right leg up and over the saddle.

"Strap yourself in," the worm instructed.

Linwith found the two leather straps on either side of his saddle and fastened them tightly around his waist and upper thighs. He retrieved the reins from the horn of the saddle and gazed up at the six worms on the cliff. The alabaster lenses of his helmet made them appear darker and even more formidable than before. Their tongues flickered in and out of their fearsome mouths and their wings quivered in anticipation of the upcoming flight.

Within his mind, he heard them call to him, each with a unique voice, and oddly enough he knew who each one was.

"Hail the Worm Master," cried the crimson worm.

"Victory to his worms," came the reply from the amber one.

"Long live Linwith," shouted the golden.

"Death begets life," roared the emerald worm.

"All hail the King of Claire," the pearl brother announced.

"Long live the stories of Claire," the mandarin worm exclaimed.

The Worm King extended his long wings, and beat the wind with long, hard strokes. Linwith felt the animal lurch into the air and his heart raced with excitement. As the worm's wings increased in speed, so did their altitude. They cleared the leafless white trees and sailed up into the sky.

Linwith looked over his shoulder. The six brothers launched themselves off the cliff and ascended toward them, single file. Down below, the Gilden Sea glistened like an emerald, and the white crests of the waves rolled and pounded the rocky shoreline of Bal-Malin.

The six brothers joined their flight and flew three on either flank while their wing cadence matched the Worm King's beat-for-beat.

"Place your thumb over the sapphire gem on the horn," Linwith heard the Worm King's voice in his mind.

Linwith looked down at the jewels on the saddlehorn. Arcing around the left side, from bottom to top, were pearl, mandarin and emerald. The right side held the amber, gold and ruby. In the middle sat the sapphire. He placed his thumb over the blue jewel and heard the Worm King in his mind.

Each gem represents one of my brothers, the worm instructed in the silent tongue of worms. *To communicate with that worm in our silent tongue, place one of your fingers over the corresponding gem. Cover them all with your palm, and we all will hear you simultaneously.*

Linwith studied the jewels and quickly associated each with a worm brother. He placed his index finger over the ruby. Another presence entered his mind. It was powerful, and yet seemed subservient to his will. He felt a great heat within the worm and was able to see through its eyes as it flew. Linwith moved his finger to the emerald and experienced similar results, only instead of a great heat, this worm had a mysterious quality that he could not quite discern.

He covered all the gems with his palm. Immediately, all seven brothers were within his mind, awaiting his command. He focused upon a thought. In answer, they pulled in their wings and dove for the Gilden Sea. Linwith leaned forward, pressing his head close to the Worm King's neck to be as streamlined as possible. With his eyes focused straightaway, and the wind howling around his helmet, he focused on another thought. The worms spun as they dove. Another thought. They pulled out of the dive and soared above the greenish sea as talons crashed through rogue waves.

Back on the island, the creatures of Bal-Malin gathered around Rittmar and watched the aerial display of power, grace and might. Throughout the dusk the Worms of Bal-Malin soared as one, swooping, twirling and diving about the sky. Into the night they flew, the tails of each worm glowing in its unique hue. Soon, the evening sky was filled with an incredible light display.

Awestruck, Rittmar recited from the Worm Master's song:

"Transient arcs of radiant light,
Cross the heavens on a moonless night..."

C h a p t e r 3 0

SriBrune's Gifts

Il-Lilliad followed Kinmin and his entourage, which included commanders and a trumpeter, through the maze of passageways within the royal palace. All were well lit, by what Il-Lilliad could not deduce, and were constructed of the same glistening white stone he had seen elsewhere in the palace. As he passed wonderful works of art and windows with grand views, he yearned to stop and investigate, but Kinmin's brisk pace and serious demeanor told Il-Lilliad this was not a sightseeing trip.

They rounded a corner and the corridor stopped at a double door. Doormen pulled the doors wide and the group stepped out into a large expanse of land. Unlike the landscape near the river and surrounding the palace, this area was void of children and women. Instead, scores of men, most shirtless and gleaming with sweat, practiced archery, swordsmanship or strengthening exercises. A group on horseback galloped through an obstacle course, no doubt intent on improving their skills as horsemen. Armored cavalry partook in sparring events and javelin throwing exercises.

"Welcome to our training ground," Kinmin announced with a sweep of his arm. "We may be small, and there may not be many of us, but we are fierce."

"That I do not doubt," Il-Lilliad said as he took in the vast field and reflected on how Kinmin's warriors had saved his life from the dansel lors. "But if you never go to war, why amass such an army?"

"To not have an army is to assume one's enemy doesn't either. We would rather be prepared than suffer such consequences."

Il-Lilliad nodded as arrows pierced targets and javelins arced the air. He could tell they were experts in the craft of war, but since SriBrune had never been attacked, he pondered a troubling notion.

"So, these men have never seen combat."

Kinmin searched Il-Lilliad's face.

"I've read your thoughts, my friend, and let me reassure you that SriBrune will not falter when it is our time to fight."

Il-Lilliad gave him an apologetic nod and turned his attention back to the cavalry. This time, he noted that the horses appeared to be the size of an Allsbruthian colt. Despite their small size, he was impressed with their speed and agility. Kinmin followed his gaze.

"I see you've noted our stallions."

"Yes, they're little but quite agile."

"And yet I read apprehension within you."

Il-Lilliad bit his lip and looked deep into Kinmin's eyes.

"Please don't misunderstand such feelings; they're not born out of doubt or misgiving but come from my deep concern for your men and warhorses. Since SriBrune has never seen an Ebonite warhorse or experienced a March of Reeds, I fear your cavalry will be overwhelmed by the sheer size of Ebon's forces."

"Ah," Kinmin replied with a raised index, "but you are forgetting that these are SriBrunian horses."

Kinmin stared at Il-Lilliad with a broad smile as if he expected the storyteller to comprehend the deeper meaning of his comment. Instead, Il-Lilliad's brow twisted with confusion.

"You see," Kinmin explained as he turned his eyes toward the cavalry, "in SriBrune, the horse and horseman must be of the same spirit. When a boy first walks, his father takes him to the stable where, with the help of the stable master, he is matched with a colt of the same temperament. Once introduced, the two grow up together as if they were brothers, learning how the other thinks, feels, moves and behaves under various circumstances. Unlike your world, where I understand one finds any mount that suits his purpose or price, this union is of great importance, as both animal and master must be of one mind, one notion, one will."

Il-Lilliad nodded as if he understood, but his scrunched lips revealed lingering confusion.

"Allow us to give you a demonstration."

Kinmin signaled the trumpeter who stood off to his right. The SriBrunian nodded and then snapped his brass horn to his lips. Staccato notes pierced the calm and blasted orders to the cavalry.

"Do you remember when you were in the boat," Kinmin asked as the cavalry formed into a single row, "when our men altered themselves and became dansel lors?"

"How could I forget? You said it was exhausting work, and dangerous."

"Correct. Unless you are blessed with a gift...*this* gift."

Before Il-Lilliad could ask for an explanation, the cavalry charged toward them.

Although a good distance off and being small animals, their charge nonetheless stirred up a cloud of brown dust and the sound of their hooves on the ground boomed like thunder. Il-Lilliad watched, impressed with their power and might.

"They are indeed extraordinary," he shouted to Kinmin.

"Not yet, but soon they will be."

Once more, Il-Lilliad's face clouded with confusion until he noticed that both rider and horse were altering their shape. Before his eyes, the SriBrunian cavalry transformed into the larger Aggellon cavalry, and with their increased size came an increase in speed. Hooves tore open the ground, silver and gold armor blazed beneath the three suns, and lances loomed.

So sudden was the change, and so much faster the pace that Il-Lilliad found himself retreating backwards. At the last possible moment, the cavalry reined in, showering the storyteller in a cloud of dust.

Il-Lilliad coughed, brushed the debris off his tunic and peered through the grime for a better look at this formidable cavalry, but all he saw were the tiny SriBrunians, once again at their normal size.

"As you can see," Kinmin said as he patted the nose of a nearby warhorse, "not only can the rider completely alter his appearance, but so can his horse. Both can do so for a considerable amount of time without the exhaustion that is common to my people."

The trumpeter sounded another signal and the cavalry unit turned as one and galloped back to their exercises.

"Remarkable," Il-Lilliad said as he cleared his lungs one more time. "But how do you transport an army beyond SriBrune? Karajan doesn't seem a likely option, and I've yet to see any other avenues that lead up into my world."

The prince pointed toward a distant vista.

"Over that rise is a stream that flows from the Allsbruthian Mountains. You know it as the River Effrim, and it meets the River Arrgient near the Gilden Plains, but this is just the edge of the Onderling, for it stretches as far north as the Gilden Sea and as far west as the Forest of Ebon. At the headwaters of the River Arrgient, where the rapids churn and froth, there is an enormous waterfall. Hidden behind the mists of the fall is a massive cave, called *Caace*. From this cavern, Aggellon and SriBrune can enter your world."

Il-Lilliad looked doubtful.

"You've been to the world above through this...Caace?"

"Of course not," Kinmin replied. "No one still living in SriBrune or Aggellon has journeyed through Caace."

"Then, how do you know it is there? With all due respect, Kinmin, this Caace would have been noted by a trapper or explorer, not to mention the Cauldron or the King of Claire. I've never heard of it, and...well...I must confess, I find your story hard to believe."

"You will have to trust me when I tell you that it is there and is hidden from your world. Should someone search behind the fall, they would encounter nothing but a stone wall."

"Such illusions could never deceive the Only."

"You are right, my friend. The King of Claire would not be fooled, for the King of Claire not only knows of Caace's existence, but fashioned its barrier himself. And apparently," he added with a wry smile, "such a secret he even concealed from his most trusted storytellers."

Il-Lilliad smiled and then stared off into the distance.

"This cave...this Caace...must be a good distance away."

"Which is why we must leave as soon as possible."

Kinmin shouted an order to the trumpeter. The brass horn snapped to his lips and a lively melody danced across the training ground. For a brief moment, the warriors stared in disbelief to make certain the trumpet call was not merely a drill. Witnessing the serious expressions worn by their commanders, the army of SriBrune went into action as if awakened from a spell: cavalry gathered as a whole; warriors gathered their weapons; leaders herded their regiments together.

All this was done without panic or excess noise. Their steps were purposeful and although they were not seasoned veterans, their expressions were determined. Il-Lilliad's confidence soared.

SriBrune was ready for war.

Chapter 31

A Force of Six

Fear.

It loomed before Ela Claire in the form of a shimmering veil. A towering sheet of glistening silver, the veil stretched up into the clouds and swooped left and right as far as she could see. The sight of it made her grip Previn's feathers tighter and her breaths came quicker, and more erratic. Her mouth went dry, and her tongue grew parched.

Once beyond the veil, she would be hunted again.

A glance over Previn's side at the terrain below revealed Romlin keeping pace on Bar-Treb. Despite his calm demeanor and his promise to protect her, the veil was a stark reminder of the reality they were soon to enter: a world dominated by the Cauldron whose sole purpose seemed to be to track her down and kill her. Would Romlin be able to defend her from Ebon's might? Would she have the courage to press through to the other side and face the battles that lay in wait for her?

She wondered if it was wrong to want to stay in Claire. After all, everywhere she looked there was beauty unlike anything in her world. And the creatures of Claire greeted them with such admiration and love, whereas life beyond the veil was filled with the Cauldron's drone and Ebon's cruelty.

Previn sensed her dire mood.

"Fear not, my storyteller," he encouraged. "I will protect you, as will Romlin."

"I don't doubt your abilities, or Romlin's," she sighed. "I doubt mine."

The veil before her looked like a magical waterfall. The wind made it shimmer, and light danced off its surface with a dazzling display of multi-colored hues.

Previn cawed in alarm.

"What is it," she asked, straining to see beyond the glistening curtain.

"Ebonites are camped just on the other side."

"Where?" Her eyes swept back and forth across the horizon. "I don't see anything?"

"My eyes can see where yours cannot."

"Then we'll go a different way."

"You cannot elude the inevitable."

"Maybe I can't stop the inevitable, but I can at least delay it. Previn, land in front of Romlin."

Previn obeyed and plummeted toward the ground. He extended his talons to land, forcing Romlin to yank hard on Bar-Treb's reins to avoid crashing into them.

"What are you doing?" he chastised as he came to an abrupt stop. "We almost ran into you."

"We'll camp here," she answered, as if that settled the matter.

"Camp?" Romlin pressed back. "But the veil is in sight. We can't camp *now.*"

"I said, we camp here," she snapped. "Previn saw Ebonites on the beach beyond the veil."

"So?" he argued. "We've faced Ebonites before."

"This time's different."

Romlin shook his head in disbelief and maneuvered Bar-Treb closer to Previn. "Are you *sure* you saw Ebonites," he asked the harrier.

Previn just blinked, offended Romlin would even ask such a question.

"He sees things we can't," Ela Claire interjected as she plopped down onto a mound of grass and sat cross-legged.

"Very well," Romlin said. "How many are there?"

Previn did not answer. Instead he looked to Ela Claire as did Romlin. Realizing they were all staring at her, she glared back.

"What?"

"Previn won't answer my question," Romlin replied as he dismounted. "I guess only *you* may ask."

She closed her eyes and leaned her head back. *I wish I was back in Marsien Vur, or sitting in the garden, trailing my fingers through the cool waters...*

"Ela Claire," Romlin pressed. *"Please* ask him."

She never opened her eyes. Instead, she released a deep sigh that Previn rightly discerned was filled with irritation.

"Tell him," she softly ordered as she continued to dream of her time in Claire.

Previn faced Romlin.

"There are at least three hundred cavalry and about four hundred on foot. I also estimate that there are approximately two hundred archers."

Romlin's eyes widened.

"That's not a few Ebonites," he whistled. "That's an *army."*

His eyes found Ela Claire. Her head and shoulders drooped, as if under a great weight. He sympathized. He was battling his own doubts. Despite battling fea dracas, ryators, bangaleers, Wurmlins and Ebonite patrols, they never had to face so formidable a foe in such large numbers.

"Perhaps she's right," he said more to himself than to Previn or Bar-Treb. "We can camp here. We need to make a plan. Or better yet, find another way through the veil."

"There is no other way," Previn said.

"Then we wait," Romlin fired as he stared at the silvery curtain.

Albeit diffused, he found he could make out their enemy's numerous tents beyond the veil. Flags snapped in the strong sea breeze. The tents extended beyond his sight. Romlin gulped.

"Can they see us," Ela Claire asked as she joined his side.

"No," Previn stated. "Nor can they hear us, so we do have the element of surprise on our side."

"Surprise," Romlin chortled. "Us against them? I don't care how much *surprise* you have, that's an army." He rested his palm on his sword's pommel. "I'm but one warrior. How could I win a contest against so many?"

"Count again, Romlin," Previn countered. "There are three of us."

Romlin looked at the harrier who rustled his wings as if to to display his might.

"I don't doubt your heart, Previn," Romlin replied, "But I think I would prefer five hundred warriors over a warrior, a bird and a storyteller."

Bar-Treb snorted and pawed the ground.

"But you are forgetting me," he whinnied. "That now gives you *four.* Much better odds."

Romlin rolled his eyes, but felt a wry smile creep across his face.

"I'm not afraid of a fight, but to attack with only four..."

"Count again," a deep voice thundered from above.

Romlin squinted into the bright sky and found Manno Vox and his steed hovering overhead.

"Now there are five," the colossal warrior boomed.

"Manno Vox," Romlin noted, respect bordering on awe tinging his voice. "You are indeed a great warrior, but what I need are five *hundred...*"

"You're forgetting your battle at the watchtower," Manno Vox interrupted.

"No, but that was more like 12-to-one, not 1,000-to-one."

"1,000-to-*five*," Bar-Treb corrected.

"Very well. *Five!* However you add it up, we are still out-manned. It's impossible."

"Nothing is impossible," Previn countered. "And I believe the count is six, not five. You are forgetting the Only. He promised to go with us."

"The King of Claire delights in the impossible," Manno Vox ventured. "This is his battle, not yours. Previn is correct: there are six of us."

Romlin studied the amassed Ebonite army.

"But they are so many." His voice fell as if being flung from a cliff.

"Didn't you learn anything in Claire," Manno Vox reasoned. "Hasn't the Only always been with you in your battles?"

"Yes, but the numbers were not so incredible."

Romlin spun around and took in Ela Claire. She stared at the encampment beyond the silvery wall. Her face was solemn.

Romlin wrapped his fingers around his sword's hilt, more in an effort to find strength than to draw it. He made his decision.

"My orders are to serve and protect Ela Claire," he announced to them all. "I will do whatever the storyteller wishes."

Ela Claire placed her trembling hand over her heart, hoping to still the anxious beating within. The warm refrains from her waltz gushed over her like a spring wind. She closed her eyes, recalling her dance with the King of Claire in Marsien Vur. Rejuvenated by the memory and the music, she opened her eyes.

"There are so many Ebonites," she observed, her voice heavy with dread, yet full of wisdom beyond her summers, evidence that Claire's tales were taking root in her heart. "And how I wish there was another path, but I know there isn't."

She looked over her shoulders and let her eyes drift across Claire's beauty: the distant mountains, the pristine blue sky, the woods teaming with life.

"It's painful thinking about leaving such a wondrous land as this, but the Only was correct: it's not right for me to bask in such luxury knowing those I love beyond the veil are being hunted by the Cauldron."

She once more faced the shimmering wall. After a lengthy pause, she said, "Together, and with the help of the Only, it might be possible."

Romlin's jaw dropped to his chest. Ela Claire fixed him with a glance, and he closed his mouth again.

"Possible," he mumbled, flabbergasted by her sudden change of heart. He took her shoulders and half-whispered, "You don't have to do this."

She looked into his face and saw concern mingled with affection. With a subtle sigh, she said, "Could you stay in Claire knowing that everyone we care for will be destroyed by Ebon's army and the Cauldron's power?"

He glanced out at the massive army then back at Claire.

"No. Of course not."

"Perhaps this is madness, but I'd rather risk an attempt to help than live within such sanctuary knowing I never tried. Does that make sense?"

He nodded, squeezed her shoulders and for a moment, thought about kissing her cheek. Instead, he brushed a stray lock of hair away from her face and settled it behind her ear. With nothing more to say, and her mind made up, Romlin turned and mounted Bar-Treb.

"Romlin," the King of Claire whispered, *"Become who I have invited you to be. Be my warrior. Protect Ela Claire."*

"Yes, I promise, but aren't we fools to attack so many?"

"Only if you fight without me."

Romlin twisted about in his saddle. His hunting instincts took in the ensuing battleground and screamed at him to retreat. The whisper from Claire wooed him to defy such logic. Romlin stiffened in his saddle. Bar-Treb shuffled about, sensing his master's decision.

"Battle we will," he roared as he unsheathed his blade and thrust it toward their enemy's encampment. His heels dug into Bar-Treb's flanks and he galloped wildly toward the veil. Manno Vox swept down and blocked his advance.

"I admire your zeal," he said. "But we *do* need a plan."

Manno Vox floated over to Ela Claire and directed his next words to her.

"Look how they are camped: One thousand men lounging about the beach of Thornnblen, waiting. If they knew the power you both possess, they would be battle ready. Instead, they camp in leisure, openly displaying their contempt for the stories of Claire. That is why you, Ela Claire, must go first and tell a story. It will spread like a fire across all the lands, announcing that the Only is returning to fight again. You, Ela Claire, are to be the usher of war."

Usher of war, she mused.

She swallowed hard and bit her lip. Her new title stole her breath away as if she'd just stepped outside into an arctic storm. In an effort to escape the terror before her, and her new title, she fingered her brooch. She traced its silver outline and let the smoothness of the ruby and emerald gems transport her mind back to Marsien Vur. She could hear the music, feel the king's hand in hers, and sense she was dancing upon air in his castle.

The wind brushed her cheek and her memories dropped as if they'd been bumped from her hand by a clumsy passer-by. The arctic blast was back, but it was not from the weather. It was brought on by Manno Vox's charge.

"You, Ela Claire, are to be the usher of war."

She pulled her midnight blue cloak tight and was about to question her qualifications for such a role, when the reality of her mission came into focus. Instead of returning to Allsbruth to be hunted, the King of Claire was asking her to be the huntress.

Her eyes wandered to the veil. No longer focusing on the beauty of its sparkling surface, she studied her enemy's tents and flags. Shadowed images milled about; Ebonites ready to strike her with steel to draw first blood or to trample her to death in a March of Reeds. Their numbers were staggering and brought even more chills crashing over her like waves from a glacial sea.

Ela Claire closed her eyes. She loved being in Claire, free from the Cauldron's power and whisper, free to love and live as she had always dreamed. As she reveled in such memories, a familiar whisper spoke in her thoughts, like a lark's song in spring, and a smile creased her worried face.

I wish I could return to Marsien Vur and dance some more, she replied in her thoughts to the whisper.

As do I, but now is not the season for such liberty.

Why must I be the usher of war? Why can't Romlin do it? He's a warrior.

He has his role. Your task is unique, in that a story, not steel, will be the spearhead in this war of whispers.

But I don't know what to say, and I'm new to being a storyteller and...

Fear not, Ela Claire. I have not selected you for this mission to simply abandon you in your hour of need.

Can you at least show me how the battle will end?

You must step out boldly despite what you see, feel, smell and hear. In much the same way that you and Romlin leapt from the cliff to find Claire, so you will have to march through the veil to find life as a storyteller.

The whisper left her thoughts and the coldness she had felt was gone. She still had her reservations, but something pulsed through her veins and her emotions that had not been there before.

Courage.

Ela Claire's eyes flew open.

"I'm ready."

Unaware of Ela Claire's internal conversation, confusion masked Romlin's face as he cast a glance at Manno Vox.

"If she's to be the usher of war, how am I to protect her," he asked.

"You will, just not now," Manno Vox encouraged. "Now here's how we will attack: Ela Claire will confront them head on and you will follow soon afterwards. I will take the far right flank. Previn, will take the far left."

"Shouldn't Previn carry Ela Claire," Romlin asked.

"This time, she must journey alone, on foot."

"Why," Romlin asked, not out of fear or disrespect for the order, but birthed out of his evolving feelings for Ela Claire.

Manno Vox offered no answer. Instead, he continued outlining the battle plan.

"Romlin, you will attack directly behind Ela Claire. You will charge toward the heart of the enemy. Wait until the Only has given the sign."

"The sign," Romlin said. "What sign?"

"You will know it when you see it. It will be something only the King of Claire can accomplish. Watch. Be alert. When you see it, do not delay. When you cross the veil, beware of the Cauldron's power. Prepare for the drone's attacks and the Cauldron's whisper. Ignore them. Listen intently to the Only's commands. The sands will slow down both horse and man so use your flying shield. The Gilden Sea blocks their backside from a retreat. There is only one avenue for them to escape and that is down the beach back toward Ebon. In essence, they are trapped."

"Escape. Trapped?" Romlin snickered. "You talk as if we have them outnumbered."

"We do. And one last thing."

Romlin's eyes danced across Manno Vox's fiery face.

"Draw first blood," the warrior encouraged.

Manno Vox turned and raced to the far right flank while Previn flew to the far left. Romlin rode up next to Ela Claire.

"Are you *sure* about this," he asked.

Ela Claire raised her somber eyes to meet his, and nodded.

He leaned down toward her so only she could hear him.

"If you need me," he said as he drank in her doe-like eyes. "Simply call. I'll be there in a flash. Okay?"

She graced him with a half-smile, that was at once pensive and determined.

"I'll be fine. All I ask is that you come when it is time."

"I promise," he confirmed with a nod and a fist to his heart.

Romlin righted himself, dismounted and untied his massive shield. Bar-Treb boxed the air, anticipating the battle that was approaching like a hurricane far out at sea.

Far away, in the halls of Marsien Vur, the storytellers watched Ela Claire walk to the veil. They admired her courage and sang a song that was simple yet beautiful in form and melody. The Only leaned on his balcony and marveled at the village girl who had followed his whisper all the way to Claire. Closing his eyes, he began the battle with a whisper.

"Are you afraid," he asked her.

"Yes," she replied in the silent tongue.

"If you weren't then you would not be ready to be a storyteller."

Ela Claire stopped just one step short of passing through the veil and entering into the battleground. She raised her hand and moved it in a measured fashion toward the veil. Her flesh brushed its surface; it was cool to the touch, as she remembered from when they first arrived. Despite the diffused affect of the veil, she could discern the long, deep beach of Thornnblen. It was void of any dunes to hide behind. The tan sand rolled gently down to the sea where the gray-green waves lapped the shoreline. The sky was a sapphire blue and the sea breeze tugged at the Ebonite banners with ease.

She heard a familiar sound resonating all about her, and turned back toward Marsien Vur.

"Do you hear that," the whisper asked her.

"Yes," she answered within in the quiet of her mind. *"It's my waltz."*

"All the creatures of Claire are singing the song in your honor. It is your battle-song. Remember, beyond the veil the vapors of the Cauldron will once again be listening to your words. It will tell you its stories and try and turn mine upon you. You will also hear the drone, so focus your heart and thoughts on your song. Let it live deep within you. Are you ready?"

"Yes," she said aloud and with a confidence that even surprised her.

Without a second thought, she stepped through the shroud and entered the battlefield.

Chapter 32

Usher of War

The Ebonite watchman leaned on his lance and scanned Claire's orange desert for the young girl and boy from Allsbruth. He had been at his post all night, watching for their arrival, an assignment he considered demeaning. The sun had risen over the Gilden Sea, his shift was nearly over, and lack of sleep tugged heavily upon his eyes. The boredom of this mission dulled his senses, as it did all the warriors camped on Thornnblen.

He tried to control his thoughts, knowing full well that the Cauldron could hear the faintest of whispers or the dullest of reflections. But as hard as he tried, they sparked like flint on steel.

"One thousand Ebonites to destroy two children is a waste of time, an insult to our power."

Yet he was well-trained, and took his duty seriously. He continued to stare at the desert, unable to see the veil and those preparing to attack.

As he watched, a form emerged from the desert, as if out of thin air. His lethargic mind found it hard to believe what his eyes witnessed. Walking toward him was a girl dressed in white with a crimson sash and wearing a dark blue velvet robe. At first, he thought he was seeing a mirage, but then his military training took over.

"Alert," he shouted down the line. "She's here."

Drums thumped Ebon's odd-metered cadence to summon the Ebonites to arms. Soldiers scrambled from tents, their frantic feet spraying sand everywhere. Commanders shouted orders; warhorses were mounted. The cavalry formed two lines while the foot soldiers fell in four rows behind them. To the rear were the archers, their backs against the sea.

Ela Claire strode toward them, undaunted by their show of power and strength, the stories of Claire enveloping her within her own inner veil.

This was her first time to the sea, and she thought how ironic the experience was. There was the beauty of it all: tan sand flowed like a long blanket down to the waves; the salt air invigorated her senses; seagulls cawed overhead in the clear blue sky. Yet amidst such natural splendor was an unnatural wall of one thousand Ebonites ready to kill her.

As the whisper of Claire had warned, the Cauldron's drone became audible again. Dull at first, it rose to a heightened pitch, and the monotone bass note began to smother her waltz. She focused her will, as the Only had ordered, but it was much more difficult than she had anticipated. She wanted to cry aloud to him, but knew the Cauldron could hear every word she uttered, possibly even turning her cry for help into a destructive force.

She stopped.

So many warriors, she thought.

"*What did you expect,*" the cauldron whispered into her mind. "*We've been expecting you. Welcome back, little storyteller.*"

She closed her eyes and clung to the distant remnants of her waltz, but she felt it slipping away, growing fainter by the moment. As her waltz diminished, another emotion grew stronger.

"*Do you know what that feeling is?*" the whisper taunted. "*Fear. Unbridled, pure fear. You can't hide behind your veil now. Welcome to my world, you weak, homely girl.*"

Ela Claire thought about turning around and running back to the other side of the veil until she noticed the cawing gulls. Their voices were uniformed, orchestrated, singing out a familiar melody.

"*They're singing a song,*" she said to herself.

"*Yes,*" came the whisper from Claire. "*It's your waltz.*"

"*Waltz,*" the Cauldron chided. "*It will be her dirge.*"

"*I will not abandon you,*" the Only replied to Ela Claire.

"*But you already have,*" the dark whisper challenged. "*Why don't you show yourself, and fight your own battles, rather than sending an untrained girl to do your dirty work.*"

"*Let me tell you a story,*" the whisper from Claire offered Ela Claire.

Despite the looming army, and the Cauldron's threatening whisper, she closed her eyes.

"*No. No!*" the Cauldron screamed, but its echo faded away as the tale unfurled within Ela Claire's mind.

"There was a young boy lost in the wilderness: alone, afraid, and desperate. Coming upon the River Arrgient, he knelt beside the rushing rapids to drink the cool waters. With each tiny handful, he felt the water sooth, quench and calm his troubled spirit. He scooped up handful after handful and enjoyed the river's mystical effects. Wanting to gather even more of the precious liquid, he waded out into its depths and splashed about. He soon forgot his fears of being lost and instead, grew joyful, laughing as he played in the water.

"The boy heard a noise nearby, something fearsome, prowling in the woods. He turned to see who or what was there. A dark figure stood in the

shadows of the woods. Frightened, the boy waded back to shore to run away, but when the form stepped forward, he recognized his father. The boy ran to his father's outstretched arms.

"'How did you find me,' the boy asked.

"'I looked everywhere for you,' the father replied, 'and feared I had lost you forever. But I was drawn to the river by the most curious of sounds: That of a boy laughing, playing and splashing amidst such great danger.'"

Ela Claire pictured herself as the frightened boy and much in the same way, drank from the story's waters and the whisper's tale. Her eyes flashed open, invigorated with courage as if the King of Claire had embraced her like the father in the story embraced the boy.

The drone and the Cauldron renewed their attack, but her mind was seared with the tale. Despite her fears, she faced her enemy, and like the boy in the story, did so with a playful spirit.

The drums changed cadence and thumped out a slower, more ominous tempo. Commander Kundle ordered the cavalry to split into two. One line galloped toward Ela Claire's right flank while the other situated itself on her left.

It's the March of Reeds, she acknowledged.

The cavalry lines turned toward her. Hooves tore up the sand as the two lines marched in and encircled her. The drum cadence stopped, as did the March of Reeds. The foot soldiers formed two circles around the outside of the cavalry. Ela Claire peered through the wall of warhorses at the warriors' hardened faces. Their eyes radiated hate.

A chill raced down Ela Claire's spine as fear wrapped cold fingers around her heart. The refrain from her song floated away like a flower petal caught on on autumn wind. She tried to recapture it but she could only hear the Cauldron's drone. She panicked. Sensing her anguish, the King of Claire whispered.

"Fear not, my delight."

The drone from the Cauldron faded from her mind, chased away by the whisper from Claire. Purpose enveloped her, steadfastness upheld her and her waltz danced about her again, smothering her anxieties with its sweet melody.

The Ebonite circles opened to allow Commander Kundle to ride through. He stopped in front of her.

"So *this* is Elabea, the little girl who has caused such consternation in the hearts of all Ebon," he muttered as he leaned out over his horse to get a better view of her. "Where is the boy? We know you don't travel alone."

"Ignore him," the Only spoke into her mind. *"Listen to my whisper. Let your song make your heart dance."*

"I suppose he was wiser than you," Kundle snickered. "He chose the coward's path, like all Allsbruthians. Your friend desires to live, and not follow a dead king and a dead cause. You should have followed his example."

"Be still. Know that I Am."

"And where is the great Manno Vox? The Only?" Kundle shielded his eyes and made a show of looking about for the entertainment of his assembled troops.

"Be ready."

"It's as I thought," Kundle continued. "They're dead. And look at you, too frightened to even beg for mercy."

"Listen to the story I'm about to whisper to you and repeat it to the Ebonites."

She closed her eyes.

"Lances," Commander Kundle ordered. The foot soldiers handed the long spears up to the cavalry. They in turn aimed them down at Ela Claire and awaited further commands.

"Now. Tell the tale."

Ela Claire's eyes flew open and she spoke in a voice of power and authority as she delivered her story.

"The girl known as *Elabea* no longer lives. I am Ela Claire, storyteller for the Only. I have journeyed from Claire by order of the Only to tell you a story."

Kundle folded his arms across his armored chest and sneered.

"A story," he repeated as he turned about in his saddle to look at his men while chuckling at her naivety. "Did you hear her, warriors of Ebon," he boomed. "She desires to tell us a...*story.*"

The army burst into laughter.

Kundle returned his attention to her.

"By all means, tell us a story before we *crush* you into the sands of Thornnblen."

With her head held high, she began the tale from the Only.

"Gaze back at the years when your youth was but a stirring ember on the fire of life. Remember the whisper of Claire, banished by the Cauldron, whose hushed breath told you tales that sparked your cinder to flame, enabling your heart to dance across the plains, hopping over the desserts, soaring above the crags of life's empty realms.

"Return your gaze to this moment. Behold the whisper is speaking again, a summons from the King of Claire, who this day is graciously offering mercy. But mercy only if you return to the stories of Claire and forsake the Cauldron's. For the tales of Claire bear great light and truth, and will crush the lies and darkness of the Cauldron.

"But this moment of mercy is not without end. How you respond to such generosity will determine how your story continues...or how it ends."

The Ebonites stood in stunned silence. Most had never heard a storyteller tell a tale, and her words pierced them to the core like flaming arrows. Many considered her offer and wrestled with turning their allegiance from the Cauldron back to Claire. Even Kundle, who participated in the March of Reeds that supposedly exterminated all the world's storytellers, found her words weighty and they smashed his convictions like rocks against dry weeds.

The Cauldron also heard her story and refused to yield such an easy victory. It intensified its drone and smothered the remnants of her words to recapture the hearts of its warriors. As evidence of their returned allegiance to the Dark Flame, several warriors snickered. This enflamed others with renewed convictions and they cackled, which spread from warrior-to-warrior until the entire army was laughing uncontrollably at her story of mercy.

"Such arrogance," Kundle shouted down to her. "*You* are the one who will bow down in defeat and surrender."

Ela Claire raised her eyes to meet his stare. Her eyes danced with light, and color, and fire, much like Manno Vox's face. Unable to maintain his gaze, Kundle moved his steed away from her.

"Enough banter," he exclaimed. "You have chosen the ending to your story. *Death begets death.*"

He exited the circle and the drums struck up their haunting cadence. The March of Reeds commenced.

Ela Claire watched the circle shrink with every drumbeat and watched their lance tips moving closer and closer. She glanced in the direction of the invisible veil.

Can Romlin see me, she wondered. *Is he ready?*

She looked to the skies searching for Manno Vox, but the sky was empty.

"*Fear not, Ela Claire,*" the Only whispered. "*I am here with you. Drink from my waters. Drink your fill.*"

She acknowledged the whisper with a nod, then noticed the breeze had stopped and the seagulls had flown away. Had something alarmed them? Had their senses discovered a hidden danger the Ebonites could not see?

The sky that only a moment before had been a brilliant, clear blue was now deep red. Thornnblen was transformed into a ghoulish seaside of crimson shadows.

The Ebonites saw the sudden change too. The drummers ceased their pounding; the cavalry stopped in mid-stride. Every Ebonite warrior stared up at the blood-red sky, desperate to see who, or what, had caused such a drastic change. Before an order could sound, or a question be asked, the sands beneath Ela Claire rumbled.

"Pull your robe tight about you and twirl around."

Although the king's order sounded ridiculous in her mind, Ela Claire had learned to trust his word. Grabbing her cloak, she wrapped it around her and started to spin. After a few revolutions, the sand beneath her feet rose into the air and encircled her to form an impenetrable chrysalis of sand.

Romlin watched from the other side of the veil as his childhood friend, who was now something more than a friend, crossed over into the battlefield. When the March of Reeds closed in on her, he started to rush to her side.

"Romlin," Manno Vox ordered from afar in the silent tongue. *"Wait. Be strong."*

He continued to watch. The circle of death stopped and Ela Claire spoke.

"I can't hear her. What's she saying," he asked.

"She is giving them the terms of surrender," Manno Vox replied.

Romlin's face contorted with many questions.

"Surrender? Ebonites never surrender, he gritted his teeth.*"*

When the circle of death began to shrink about her once more, he asked, *"Am I to rush in now?"*

There was no answer so he waited, albeit not peacefully.

The Only stilled the veil and it became as smooth as the sea on a still night, allowing Romlin to see clearly. He watched horrified as the Ebonite lance tips pressed toward Ela Claire.

"We need to act," Romlin demanded of Manno Vox.

"We need to listen."

"But I promised her..."

"And you will honor such a promise. Watch. Listen."

Romlin complied, but he wasn't happy about it. As he watched, the seagulls darted away and the blue sky bled into crimson.

Mesmerized by the sudden change, and taking it for the expected sign from Claire, Romlin asked, *"Now?"*

But Manno Vox remained silent. Romlin felt the ground rumble and watched Ela Claire pull her cloak tight and spin about. A swirling column of sand rose up and concealed her.

"Is that the sign?"

Again, Manno Vox did not answer.

Without warning, the ground beneath Ela Claire's column fell away, as if being sucked down by an enormous monster lying deep beneath the beach. A black pit formed where the sand had been, and it spiraled outward from Ela Claire toward the encircling Ebonite warhorses. The cavalry turned to flee the approaching death but the black abyss pulled at them like a riptide of earth, dragging them backwards against their will.

Although Romlin could not hear, he could see the horses thrashing and men crying out in fear. The swirling sands were too powerful to escape. Down into the void horses fell along with their riders. Some desperately spurred their warhorses to climb out of the dungeon of death. Others leaped from their horses and tried to scamper up the walls of the collapsing sand. All efforts were futile. As quickly as it appeared, the hungry sands sealed back up. In the blink of an eye the entire Ebonite cavalry lay encased deep beneath Thornnblen's beach.

"Now," the Only whispered.

Romlin shot through the veil on his flying shield, his sword at the ready. Bar-Treb galloped faithfully by his side. A quick glance at Ela Claire confirmed she was still surrounded by the spiraling sand.

Kundle ordered his archers to take aim at her, but when their arrows hit the spinning column, they glanced off and flew erratically across Thornnblen.

Romlin, convinced she was safe, glanced to his right and saw Manno Vox zoom over the sands to attack the Ebonites' left flank. Kundle's archers refocused their aim in his direction and fired a barrage of arrows, but they flew harmlessly through his incorporeal body and mortally wounded Ebonite warriors on the other side.

On Romlin's left, Previn swooped down from the reddened sky upon the unsuspecting archers. With his talons, he grabbed a handful of Ebonites and used them as battering rams as he flew down the beach, knocking over archers, foot soldiers, cavalrymen and warhorses.

Commander Kundle spotted Romlin heading straight into the heart of his formation and ordered his archers to fire in his direction.

"Kneel in the shield," the King of Claire ordered. *"Grab the handles. Hold tight."*

Romlin obeyed. The shield flipped upside down, and he zigzagged across the beach like a bat on a night hunt. Arrows rained down on his shield, making loud *pings* and *dings*, but doing no harm. When the noise subsided, and he was safe from the first barrage, the shield righted itself again.

My senses are so alert, Romlin noted. *It's as if I can see danger before it happens...even more than when I fought the ryators in the Valley of Clouds.*

He stood up in his flying shield and slid his feet beneath the leather handles to brace himself. He clutched his sword in front of him, and using his extraordinary new awareness, swatted away stray arrows or javelins that coursed his way.

"Death begets life," the King of Claire whispered.

"Death begets life," Romlin cried across Thornnblen.

"Long live Ela Claire," the whisper urged.

"Long live Ela Claire," Romlin hailed as he smacked a heaved javelin and watched it explode into splinters that littered the sands below.

The Ebonite foot soldiers were stunned by the destruction of their cavalry, and routed by the onslaught of Manno Vox, Previn and Romlin. Some stood their ground, awaiting commands, but could not hear their generals' orders above the chaos. Most turned and ran, casting shields and weapons aside in their haste to escape.

Romlin spied a group of Ebonites standing unsure and unguided. He charged them; his sword glowed deep orange like the sands of Claire. As he swung his weapon toward them a blast of orange light flung from his blade and decimated the lot. He swerved the shield and directed his attack on another group of warriors. He struck again, and the orange glow flew far and wide like lightning bolts, burning men to a crisp or severing them in two. Energized by his sword's magical abilities, his confidence soared and Romlin pressed his shield forward into the heart of the Ebonite formation.

His shield acted as if it had a will of its own, banking and swerving to avoid swords, javelins, and arrows. At times, it would swoop down on a hapless warrior like an eagle upon a fish, and send him crashing to the sands.

Bar-Treb galloped alongside, matching every turn and change the shield made, creating a choreographed dance of grace, power and utter destruction amidst a battlefield of disarray. Bar-Treb plowed down any warrior unlucky enough to cross his path, subjecting them to his own March of Reeds.

Previn dove from great heights, snatching groups of Ebonites in his talons, then rising high into the red sky. From his aerial perch, he dropped them to their deaths on the cold sands of Thornnblen, then zoomed down to repeat the process over again.

As Manno Vox had predicted, many tried to escape down the beach, but he blocked their way and destroyed swaths of men with his massive sword.

Commander Kundle sat in the rear and watched the battle from high atop his warhorse. He was in shock. His once highly disciplined army was no more. In its place was a horde of frightened, disorganized individuals fleeing and fighting only to survive. Some ran in circles looking for a place to hide from the blood-red sky and the warriors from Claire, but Thornnblen offered no such sanctuary.

Disgusted, he barked out orders to rally his troops.

"Warriors of Ebon," he thundered with his sword thrust high overhead, "turn and fight. We outnumber them."

His charge went unheeded.

Desperate to gain control over his forces, he positioned his warhorse to stop the retreat of several of his warriors.

"In the name of the Cauldron and Brairtok," he shouted with a threatening thrust of his blade. "I order you to turn and fight."

"Fight?" one countered, heedless of Kundle's sword or of being court martialed for cowardice. "How do you battle sands that eat cavalry? How do you fight blood-red skies or a glowing giant? *You* fight!

They skirted around Kundle's steed and sprinted with a gathering cohort of Ebonite deserters toward the Gilden Sea.

When they reached the shoreline, many were so frightened by the ordeal that they forgot that they were fully armored and waded out into the choppy surf like men possessed. Once they reached deeper water, they dove and tried to swim, but their actions were futile. Their armor became anchors and they sank to the bottom.

Witnessing their mistake, the others stripped off their armor and ran wildly into the dark sea. Had they been able to hear the Only whisper to the lairs of the deep, they would have fled back to shore. Rising from their lairs in the Gilden Sea came the la-zeer: predators of the sea.

On and on the Ebonites swam, fleeing the Battle of Thornnblen, kicking and clawing their way out into deeper waters. Once they were far from shore, they huddled together and rode the gray waves. They bobbed on the rising surf, occasionally catching a distant glimpse of Romlin's flashing sword, Ela Claire's swirling sand cloud, or Manno Vox's surreal form.

They believed themselves safe, until one of the men let out a blood-curdling scream. Heads turned his direction in time to catch a glimpse of his flaying arms before he was yanked down into the depths.

Alarmed, the Ebonites scanned the waters for the predator. On the sea's horizon was a cresting wave, and within its murky water were countless dark shapes. Sleek, large and terrifying, they dove for the Ebonites. Hundreds of dorsal fins cut the frothing surf like an armada of death.

La-zeers.

The men spun about, hoping to find a means of escape, but were uncertain which direction offered hope. One la-zeer bumped unsuspecting legs. Men shrieked in horror. The la-zeers' dorsal fins circled the men, and then as quickly as they had appeared, they submerged, one by one. A gut-wrenching cry from an Ebonite rose into the air followed by another, and another. The gray-green sea became a churning froth of foam. When the screams and thrashing stopped, the only evidence the warriors ever existed was a crimson stain floating across the cresting waves.

Romlin pressed his attack. With shield and steed and glowing orange blade he battled, his mind so focused on the minutia of war that when he found himself in front of Manno Vox, sitting calm and poised on his mount, he was bewildered. Romlin stopped and surveyed the battlefield. Thornnblen was littered with the dead while the Gilden Sea washed Ebonite blood up on the beach.

The Ebonite army was no more.

Previn flew toward the duo with a captive dangling from his talons while Ela Claire allowed her swirling sands to diminish and at last die out.

Previn swooped down and dropped his prisoner with a dull thud onto the beach at their feet. Commander Kundle regained his feet, and brushed sand off his armor with as much dignity as he could muster. Even with his army defeated and his own life hanging in the balance, Kundle remained insolent.

Romlin, still in the grip of the rage of war, drew his blade to kill him but Manno Vox raised his hand to stop him.

"I fear no man," Kundle sneered. "Especially not this *boy* and his deformed accomplice. Death begets death!"

He spat at them.

Manno Vox's face glowed liked a stoked furnace.

"I do not doubt that death is what you wish for," he replied. "Unfortunately for you, death is not what we offer."

Kundle's defiant expression dropped from his face, replaced by confusion.

Manno Vox leaned out over the head of his steed and stared down at the commander.

"By command of the King of Claire, I order you to return to Ebon."

Color ran out of Kundle's face.

"Never," he barked. "I choose to die here with my men. I will *never* obey the orders of an impotent king like your...*Only*."

"You forfeited the opportunity to negotiate when you defied Ela Claire's terms of surrender," Manno Vox boomed. "Now, as your conquerors, we order you to return or Previn will personally deliver you to Kise."

Kundle's nostril flared with rage. His chest rose and fell with each breath. In a last ditch effort to die with Ebonite honor, he yanked out his dagger, but Previn had anticipated as much. Before Kundle could attack them or slice his own throat, Previn snatched the weapon out of Kundle's grip with his beak. Furious, Kundle arched his back and screamed at the top of his lungs into the blood-red sky.

Romlin, Manno Vox and Previn merely stared at him, neither impressed or moved by his expression of grief and rage.

Once his tirade was over, Kundle lowered his face and stared at the trio with snarled lips. But he said no more.

"Return to Kise and tell Brairtok your story and the tale from Ela Claire," Manno Vox further instructed. "Shout from Netniath these words: *The Only lives and is coming for first blood.*"

Kundle's eyes narrowed to slits of rage.

"I'm the master of my own destiny," he said, his hands planted on his hips. "You can't control what I say or where I go."

"Perhaps, I can't," Manno Vox replied. "After all, I am but a warrior for the King of Claire. Ela Claire, on the other hand, is a storyteller. And she certainly can compel your actions."

He pointed over Kundle's shoulder. He turned to see a young girl in a white dress with a dark blue cloak walking across the beach's battlefield.

"Her?" he huffed back up at Manno Vox. "What can a girl do to one of Ebon's finest commanders?"

"As a girl, nothing. As a storyteller, everything."

Kundle's narrowed eyes opened in horror. As a battle hardened warrior from the Dark War, he was all too familiar with the capabilities of Claire's storytellers. His head snapped about as he contemplated running to the sea to drown or be eaten by a la-zeer, or diving for a sword that littered the ground to fight to the death. Before he could decide, he heard a whisper.

Lilting like a lark, he recognized the whisper as not coming from the Cauldron, but from the King of Claire. He fought against it with all his might and will, but he was no match for such an adversary. His knees buckled. He dropped to the sand finding it difficult to breathe. He was unable to speak and the scent of flowers made him double over with nausea and retch into the sand.

When he was able to right himself again, Kundle found himself looking up into Ela Claire's face. He tried to look away but felt his muscles tighten and freeze in place. He attempted to close his eyes, but felt them being pried open as if by invisible fingers. He fought to maintain control of his thoughts, but they were no longer his own. He stood as a helpless child, submissive to the will of the storyteller standing before him.

Ela Claire spoke in the silent tongue and repeated the words the King of Claire had given her to speak.

"Young pyres of anguish, lost hearts black as night,
Shall bloom like a tulip, shall stand tall and strong.
Justice we call forth, ride moon's bluest light,
And rescue such treasure, who sing their lost song.
"So fly, shattered hearts, upon the winds of Claire,
Gird loin and arms amidst the Cauldron's gales.
Castaways of darkness, young hearts don't despair,
For whispers birth stories, and lore begets tales."

"Arise, bended knees beside crimson cup.
Breathe deeply of sweet flora's mystic scent.
Lo, a whisper hailing, 'Wake up! Wake up!
Fear not for victory's birthed in your dire lament.'"

"We will not cower beneath darkest of flame,
For justice comes upon moon's bluest light.
'To battle!' we shout, with stories none can tame,
For 'Death begets life!' shall rally our fight."
"Flee from this land, dire tone from lifeless flame.
Hear not our hearts trumpeting our eternal refrain?
Such melodious wonders from the Only's name,
Sweetest of songs from Claire's royal domain."

"We shall not listen to tone that dements,
That shepherds by fear, that cordons by might.
We whisper Claire's stories of succulent scent,
And cast you back to your land of perpetual night."

When she was finished, she backed away and Kundle's strength returned. He wiped his mouth of traces of vomit and staggered down the beach like a drunk. His legs moved of their own volition, and he found himself heading toward Ebon to fulfill his mission for Claire and his destiny - no doubt execution for cowardice - as an Ebonite commander.

"*Run,*" Manno Vox ordered.

Kundle sprinted.

Once Kundle disappeared from sight, the crimson sky surrendered to blue and the sea breeze once more caressed the sands. The gulls returned and began feasting on the macabre remains of the Ebonite army.

Romlin sheathed his weapon, then leapt off his hovering shield.

"Ela Claire, you were incredible," he praised her as he fastened the shield to Bar-Treb's side.

"I simply repeated to the commander what the King of Claire told me to say."

"Yes, that was amazing too, but I'm talking about how you fought. Don't you remember?"

She shook her head.

"All I remember is telling the army a story, hearing Claire's whisper, and seeing the sands twirl about me. Other than that, I don't remember anything else. I suppose I fell asleep."

Romlin shook his head, chuckling in amazement.

"How could you sleep when all of *this* was happening," he asked as he swept his arm about the carnage littering Thornnblen.

Ela Claire took in the bloody battlefield, and merely shrugged.

Romlin strode up to her, grabbed her shoulders and declared, "Your twirling sands devoured their cavalry. The beach opened up like a pit and swallowed them whole. You, Ela Claire, were the Usher of War."

She pulled her eyes away from his, awestruck that she was responsible for so much death and destruction. Even though she knew these men desired nothing so much as her death, pity washed over her at the massive loss of life.

Romlin, still elated by their victory, draped his arm over her shoulder, not in an affectionate manner, but more as an expression of camaraderie from one warrior to another.

"Come on. It's time I got you to the Isle of Rythe."

With a playful swat on her backside, which she did not appreciate, he remounted Bar-Treb and led the way.

Previn bowed low to the sands and allowed Ela Claire to climb upon his back. The harrier gently lifted into the air and followed Romlin's galloping steed. As they soared above Thornnblen, her heart swelled with a symphonic song of victory yet still ached for the dead below, even if they were her enemy.

"Well done, Ela Claire," the Only whispered. *"The nation of Claire celebrates this great day."*

Amidst the triumphal victory music was a stark, countermelody that was simple in composition and range. A woman sang the melancholic theme that floated atop the victory march like a funeral barge on a rising sea.

"Why is her song so sad?" she asked as they circled Thornnblen.

"As a storyteller, you will not only know all my tales, but you will also experience all that I feel. Look below."

She gazed down at Thornnblen. Normally a seaside of majesty and beauty, it was now a wasteland matted with Ebonite blood. Taking in this intermixing of splendor and horror, she began to understand the meaning of the woman's song: it was a dirge mourning Ebon's refusal to return to the Only's stories. As this realization moved from observation to reason, Ela Claire felt the king's deep feeling of loss.

"Now close your eyes."

Her eyelids shut and she found herself soaring above Claire as if in a dream. Below her was a draigg circling Cor len Bluun, and riding atop was the King of Claire. Silver and white tears fell from his eyes and created a pond in memory of the fallen Ebonites. They sparkled like the facets of many jewels until a draigg glided down to cover the surface. When the last flicker of light disappeared from the pond, she realized the tremendous responsibility she carried as a storyteller: Her words in the war of whispers would mesh joy with sorrow, victory with loss.

She shuddered under the weight of such duty.

Chapter 33

The Wages of Life

As instructed by Quinn and Gundin, the young sentries led the women and children away from Hetherlinn and deep into the woods. Their pace was swift and quiet as they navigated through the shadowed forest. The younger children sensed the urgency of their escape and kept their voices quiet while the older ones encouraged those who were frightened.

When the sentries reached the predetermined rendezvous point, they huddled the group together on higher ground to wait until Quinn sent for them. The men signaled for them to sit on the forest floor, and with a finger to their lips, indicated that no one was to talk. The group complied and the women and children nestled together on dried leaves. Aside from an occasional whimper from a child or an elderly woman's labored breaths, not a sound was heard from the refugees.

Time and boredom took their toll, and the villagers began to relax and feel safe from Ebon's threat. That all changed when they heard a whisper.

"Gifts. Bounty. Blessings from Ebon for you."

The women murmured amongst themselves. The Cauldron's whisper was not unfamiliar to them, but it usually came with chastisements or new regulations. Never had it offered blessings before. Could the whisper be trusted? The women of Hetherlinn soon began to ponder the possibility, and question among themselves what types of gifts and bounty might await them back in Hetherlinn.

"Gifts from Ebon?" Areall asked Daryess with a worried frown.

"They are trying to lure us from our safety," Daryess replied while shaking her head.

But the others would not listen to reason. They rose to their feet, their murmurs evolving into chatter before exploding into frantic talk of returning home.

The sentries waved their arms in a vain attempt to restore quiet and order.

"Women and children of Hetherlinn," one of the men declared as the women's' voices quieted. "These are dangerous times. We can't trust such news from a whisper. Besides, when has Ebon ever given us anything but Oracles and taxation?"

"I agree," Areall confirmed. "Even if these gifts exist, can the nation of Ebon be trusted?"

"Quiet," Mithe hissed. She wobbled forward on her cane while the remaining women of Hetherlinn stood behind her and glared at Areall with arms crossed. "You speak from a heart that has lost a child, thus you desire us to suffer as well. You're simply jealous, ashamed that your man was unable to provide us with such bounty."

"No," Areall replied with quick, firm shakes of her head. "This has nothing to do with Elabea and Quinn."

"Ah, but it does," Mithe declared as she wagged her bony finger in front of Areall's face. "Your man took life from us at Min Brock. He delivered tears to all of us. We're deserving of such treasures."

"Yes, you are," Daryess chimed in as she joined Areall's side. "But is it wise to receive them from the Ebonites? Remember, it was only a few days ago they tried to crush us in a March of Reeds."

A few of the women nodded in agreement to Daryess' logic while others merely scowled.

"Perhaps this is a sign of the peace we have all longed for," one woman reasoned.

"Ladies, please," the one sentry implored. "Do you really believe that the Cauldron desires to give us peace and prosperity?"

"Maybe not to *all*," Mithe answered with a cutting look at Areall and Daryess, before turning to address the others. "We're the faithful ones who scorned the invitations, were we not?"

Heads nodded.

"Did I not assist the Ebonites in finding these rebellious children by giving them their clothing to be tracked," Mithe asked them.

Firm nods once more came from the group.

"Then perhaps the Cauldron is rewarding us for our devotion and dedication," Mithe offered.

"I'm tired of wearing this," one mother whimpered with a tug at her common tunic. "Imagine being given fine dresses to wear."

"Or expensive cloth for us to sew our own attire," another added.

"Do you think they'd give us building materials for new homes?" a young mother chimed in.

"What about toys," one of the older children added. "I'm tired of make-believe games."

In no time, their imaginations exploded like fire on dry kindling, and despite the sentries' best efforts to quiet them and have them sit back down, the group charged down the hill eager to bask in the blessings of Ebon.

Their fear of an Ebonite reprisal had been replaced with a zeal for new lives and gifts beyond their wildest dreams. Areall, Daryess and the sentries followed their hurried pace homeward, but at a slower clip.

Commander Hinnmith looked up from his fire in the meadow. He had heard the excited squeals of women and children coming from the woods. A feral smile crept over his face while several warriors, who had also heard the refugee's noisy approach, ran to mount warhorses. Hinnmith stood and halted his zealous warriors. A quick glance into the thicket's shades revealed the silhouettes of the women and children. They hovered at the meadow's edge like a herd of wild deer, contemplating whether it was safe to cross or not.

"Let them pass in peace," Hinnmith ordered his men, loud enough for the women to hear. He turned toward them and recited more of his rehearsed speech. "Women and children of Hetherlinn. Come taste of the blessings of Ebon and feast upon the Cauldron's bounty."

Hinnmith swept his arm toward the wagons of goods.

Mithe followed his gesture. Despite being a good distance off, and partially blocked from view by the thicket that lay between the meadow and the village, she spotted the stacks of barrels and the spoils lying about in the village.

"Look," she pointed out to her followers, "The whisper *spoke truth. The Cauldron has blessed us.*"

The women and children abandoned any fears they may have harbored and burst into the meadow, pushing and squealing like a pack of boars. Even Mithe attempted a faster gait, resulting in a hop-hobble, hop-hobble movement. Some ran so fast that they lost their footing and fell which ignited ridicule among the Ebonite warriors.

Areall and Daryess, along with the sentries, refused to join the frantic race and instead, walked boldly past Hinnmith without giving him the satisfaction of glancing his way.

Reaching Hetherlinn, the women and children were met by their husbands and sons. The throng proceeded to dance and sing about the bounty with more gusto than during any of the other festivals Hetherlinn celebrates.

All except for one. He stood apart from the others and glared across the meadow at Hinnmith. Areall made her way past the revelry to where Quinn stood. She took his hand.

"Look at them," he fumed. "Over one hundred Ebonites lounging about in our meadow as if we were allies. But I'm no fool. I can see that they mock us."

"While our friends," Areall sighed as her neighbors tore into the gifts, drunk with excitement, "celebrate as if today were a grand festival."

Gundin and Daryess joined the couple.

"Can you blame them," Gundin asked with a hint of jealousy in his voice. "Are we not deserving of such rewards?"

"Of course; even I long for such bounty," Quinn fired back. "But can't you see what the Cauldron's doing? Our resolve to fight is gone. The men we've been training are now uncommitted."

"Not necessarily. We can still fight," Gundin muttered as his eyes swept over the barrels of wealth. "In fact, we can use the coins to purchase weapons from Tristan and Ingloid."

Quinn grabbed him by his lapels and stared into his face. "Listen to you," Quinn yelled with a firm shake of his friend. "You sound as if you desire to join them."

"Never," Gundin snapped, unable to look Quinn eye-to-eye as he remembered the taunting whisper's charge to him. "I will fight."

"But they won't," Quinn replied as he let go of Gundin. "They love the bounty and the prospect of comfort over true freedom…and life."

Areall tugged on Quinn's arm.

"What does *he* want," she asked as she pointed to Hinnmith and some of his men riding into the village. Hinnmith raised his arm and the small entourage stopped in the middle of the town.

"Citizens of Hetherlinn," Hinnmith belted over the hoopla, once more feigning zeal while his heart lusted for first blood. "It gives me great joy to see you enjoy such blessings."

Quinn marched to his side.

"You have delivered your goods. Now leave us."

"After I complete my mission," Hinnmith countered with a smug smile.

"Mission?" Gundin gripped his quarterstaff firmly in his hands. "You'd better not try a March of Reeds on us," he said with a firm thump of his staff in his palm.

"March of Reeds," Hinnmith repeated as if offended and even held up his hands to repel Gundin's verbal assault. "My dear man, we have more gifts."

Hinnmith signaled and one of his men rode up beside him. He promptly handed the commander a small, wooden box. Hinnmith held it up for all to see. The villagers encircled them and their eyes danced over the box, dreaming of what wonders lay within. Convinced he had everyone's attention, Hinnmith rattled off more of his speech.

"Brairtok wishes to bestow medals of valor and honor upon those who fought bravely in the Dark War."

He lowered the box to his lap, opened it, and turned it so all could see its contents. A unison gasp went up as they marveled at the bright silver and gold medals nestled on a bed of silky, black cloth.

"I now call forth the following warriors of Allsbruth: Gundin and Quinn."

Gundin's eyes got as big as a harvest moon.

"A medal, for me," he asked with a curious step forward.

A whisper flitted to his ear.

"Are you not deserving of such glory? Such honor?"

"Gundin," Quinn yelled. "Stand fast."

Hinnmith ordered one of his men to dismount. The soldier retrieved the box of medals then marched ceremoniously toward the two men. He saluted Gundin then pulled out one of the medals.

Quinn's face flushed with anger. He turned toward his friend.

"Gundin, don't accept it."

"But am I not deserving of such glory? Such honor?" he replied, reciting the whisper word for word.

"Gundin, warrior of Hetherlinn," Hinnmith boomed as he began his presentation speech. "Brairtok recognizes you for your bravery and sacrifice in the Dark War and at the battle of Min Brock. Long may you live!"

The medal was pinned. Quinn's head dropped.

The soldier marched over to Quinn and removed a medal. Quinn backed away, but as he did, the drone pounded his senses like a battle-ax against armor. Gritting his teeth as if straining against a powerful foe, Quinn focused his entire strength upon the tulip's scent and his morning's kneeling beside the flower.

"Why fight us?" the Cauldron whispered into his ear.

Quinn grimaced and continued to concentrate on the crimson petal.

"We are too great and your forces no longer desire war. And look..." The whisper and drone forced Quinn's eyes toward his cottage. *"We have brought you your favorite drink: wildeberry wine. Are you not deserving of but a sip...just a respite from this war of whispers?"*

Quinn yanked his sight from the casks and shouted, "Never."

Seeing his resistance, Hinnmith spurred his horse forward. He stopped near Quinn and leaned down and whispered.

"You and I, Quinn, are men of action. Let there be no misunderstanding between us. If you don't receive this medal, I will take your beautiful wife to my camp as a prize for my men."

Quinn glanced at Areall. Her eyes were filled with distress. Snapping his head back, he glared at Hinnmith and roared, "Pin it if you must, then leave this place. But hear this: although it rests upon my chest, it comes no where near my heart."

Hinnmith smiled and sat upright. The medal was pinned.

"Wonderful citizens of Hetherlinn," Hinnmith shouted, his voice overly sweet. "Enjoy the fruits of your labor," he swept his arm toward barrels of cloth. "Drink your fill of wine," he swept his arm toward Quinn's cottage. "Build fine homes. Live long and prosper."

With that, he and his entourage galloped back to their camp.

Quinn studied Gundin, hoping to see him ready to fight and train for war. Instead, Gundin stared at his medal and mumbled, "I *am* deserving, yes, I am…" His fingers stroked it like a lover caressing his beloved.

"Gundin," Quinn shouted but the warrior was lost within his own world.

"Fight it," he yelled again.

But Gundin continued caressing the gold.

Quinn slapped him hard across the face. Their eyes met. Instead of witnessing his desire to fight, Quinn saw a man delighting in the minuscule victories from the past, and ignoring the challenging battles of tomorrow.

"No," Quinn stammered as he backed away. "Not you, too."

Quinn spun toward his neighbors. Unimpressed with the medal ceremony because it did not involve them, they were once more relishing the spoils of Ebon.

Areall gently put her arm around her husband and he pulled her close.

"*Where is Elabea?*" the Cauldron's whisper asked them. "*Where is young Galadin?*"

"Leave us," Areall demanded while Quinn's head hung in defeat.

"*Can you not see? You can never change what you did at Min Brock. Forever will you eat its rotten fruit. More tears, more tears, all for naught, all for naught.*"

The drone peppered Quinn with memory after memory of his failures, reminding him of vows gone unmet, of promises he would never keep. Areall could feel his body weakening. Not wanting him to retreat to his days of drinking and brooding, she pressed her body closer to his. She thought he was about to buckle to the ground in defeat when another whisper entered the fray.

"*Min Brock does not seal your fate,*" the whisper from Claire ordered them. "*One step forward can transform such bitter memories into the sweetest of wines.*"

"*Oh, yes,*" the Cauldron chided, "*trust in yet another empty promise, just…*"

Before the Cauldron could finish, the strong scent of tulips enveloped the couple. The drone faded while the Cauldron's whisper slinked off into the shades.

Quinn clasped Areall's hand. He pulled her close and she leaned into him, enjoying the comfort of his arms. She looked up into his face, relieved to see his eyes filled with a fiery determination.

"Brairtok will pay for this," Quinn vowed as he led her toward cottage Number 17. "He will pay dearly. I will not stop fighting, Areall, even if it means we fight alone. I will not fail Elabea again. I hope you know that."

Areall nodded and rested her head on his shoulder.

Inside, they gathered about their fire and stared into its embers. Every now and then, doubt would slip into their thoughts like a frosty draft, bringing with it the echoes of their neighbors celebrating their newfound lives.

Quinn turned toward Areall. Did she want to run and join them? Would she have the strength to endure another war? Did she believe he could champion them as a husband and father?

He found her eyes. They burned like brown fire and reminded him of Elabea's eyes when she gazed upon him with such adoration. But that was before Min Brock. He reflected on what the whisper had promised:

"One step forward can transform such bitter memories into the sweetest of wines."

"One step forward," he said with a smile as he gently kissed Areall's lips.

Chapter 34

Brairtok's Reprisal

Two warriors entered Brairtok's citadel, Vorak, and proceeded down the hall toward their warlord's main chamber. The younger of the two, an officer, glanced over at the commander he was escorting. Kundle was a decorated hero during the Dark War, and was reputed to be one of Ebon's most brilliant military minds. But as they rounded a hallway corner, the young officer was struck by Kundle's odd demeanor: His shoulders drooped, his boots shuffled, and eyes were glossed over as if he walked in a dream.

The gait of a dead man, the young officer concluded.

Although he did not know the reason behind Kundle's lack of military decorum, the officer knew he had returned from battle without his men and unarmed.

He's disgraced Kise with his cowardice, the officer judged. *Why didn't he kill himself and die with honor?*

They reached Brairtok's chamber and the officer pounded on the massive door.

"Enter," a muffled voice ordered from the other side.

The door creaked open and the officer led Kundle to the large dining table where Brairtok was slicing a piece of meat.

"Commander Kundle," Brairtok said without looking up, "back from your campaign at Thornnblen already. Good. I'm sure your report will be more delicious than this tough meat."

Frustrated with the grisly beef, Brairtok tossed his knife onto the table, pushed away from the table, rose and strode forward to meet one of his best commanders.

"So tell me, was first blood as sweet as wine?"

Kundle held his tongue and stared into nothingness.

Brairtok's jaw muscles tightened. He pushed his face close and hissed, "I'll have your report, Commander. That is an order."

Kundle's bemused eyes merely blinked. He knew he had breached military protocol by not delivering his report when first asked, yet he did not fear Brairtok's reprisals. He welcomed death; had longed for it since his defeat and dishonor at Thornnblen.

From the moment Manno Vox forced him to flee back to Kise, he knew that such a retreat would be his death sentence. After all, Ebonites do not retreat. Yet, Kundle, a decorated war hero, had been utterly humiliated in combat.

And by children, he mused with self-loathing.

When he jogged away from the victors after the Battle of Thornnblen, he hatched a plan. He would do the honorable thing and kill himself. But every time he jumped from a cliff, or threw himself into a river, or tied a noose around his neck, Manno Vox rushed in and saved his life. As a last resort, he tried to change direction to avoid returning to Ebon, but Ela Claire's story was on the prowl in his mind and thwarted any attempt to step away from his destiny.

So it was that with each step closer to home, his once proud gait took on the slothful pace of a traitor. Even his mind was no longer his, as he relived the battle over and over as well as her tale. Images from the battle haunted him like ghouls. No matter how many new scenarios, or stratagems, or tactics he fashioned in his imagination, the outcome was always the same.

Defeat.

Brairtok shook Kundle's shoulders.

"Answer me."

"They're all dead," Kundle half-mumbled as Ela Claire's story rattled in the background of his thoughts.

Brairtok's flushed face became tranquil once more and he released his hold.

"Excellent," he gloated as he stepped away. "The pesky girl and boy from Hetherlinn shall torment me no more."

"No. Sir. You don't understand," Kundle replied, his voice flat and emotionless.

"What don't I understand," Brairtok snapped, the veins in his neck bulging.

Kundle's next words were forced out of him by Ela Claire's tale.

"Our men. They are all dead. I'm the only survivor of the Battle of Thornnblen. It was a massacre."

"Massacre?" Brairtok snickered. "It is a fine joke, Commander, but I'm in no mood for such stories..."

"I'm telling the truth," Kundle heard himself mutter. "All my men were destroyed."

"Destroyed?" Brairtok paced about. "How? By...by...Allsbruthian *children?"*

"Yes, but they did not attack us alone," Kundle answered, something akin to awe shepherding his voice. He could feel Ela Claire's story pressing the truth from his lips, like fingers forcing diseased pus from an old wound. "His name was Manno Vox."

Brairtok froze, but his eyes burned with rage. The story forced Kundle to continue.

"He allowed me...no, he *forced* me, to live. And the girl, Ela Claire, told me a story of such terrible beauty, that I was compelled to come back to tell you about the massacre and..."

Brairtok's eyes narrowed. He crept toward Kundle.

"And to tell you that the Only lives..." Kundle finished his report, his voice devoid of emotion, "and is coming to end your story."

The rage Brairtok had held at bay exploded through his fist as he struck Kundle hard across the face. Kundle absorbed the blow as if it were a buzzing gnat or bothersome fly, as if it were of no consequence. Yet had Brairtok been watching his glazed eyes, he would have seen a quick shift, as if Kundle had awakened from a nightmare and was pleading for Brairtok to end his suffering with a coup de grace.

"The girl has a new name," Kundle continued. "Ela Claire. She told a tale of mercy and surrender to my army, and I watched my world crumble." Tears streamed down his face. "Sinking sands consumed my cavalry. The Gilden Sea turned to blood. The sky looked...bruised and angry. There was a glowing warrior on a flying shield with a magic sword and..."

Brairtok waved his hand to silence him. Kundle complied. He was spent.

"These are bedtime stories mothers tell their children, not a battle report. One thousand warriors could never..."

"He truly lives," Kundle interrupted.

Brairtok brought his hand back to strike him again, but restrained himself. He turned away for a moment to regain control. When he turned back to address Kundle, his tone was calm, his demeanor, father-like.

"So, the Awakening has happened," Brairtok soothed draping his arm over Kundle's shoulder as if he were an unfortunate sailor, saved alone from a shipwreck. "No matter, no matter at all."

Brairtok guided Kundle back to the door, and with paternal kindness said, "You need rest from your ordeal and strenuous trek back to Kise. You must be famished. Fear not, Commander Kundle; you have served Ebon and the Cauldron faithfully against this Awakening, a feat most difficult, most difficult indeed."

Brairtok allowed his voice to fade, patted Kundle on the back and dismissed him. Kundle, indifferent to either kind or harsh words, turned to go without the customary fist to heart. Brairtok watched him shuffle through the threshold, then turned to the young officer who still stood at attention.

"Give him anything he desires," Brairtok ordered.

The officer, confused by Brairtok's mercy and gentle words to Kundle, glanced a question at his warlord, but dared not put the question into words. Nor did he have the need. Brairtok spun away and the officer watched his face darken like a thundercloud.

"Yes, give him anything he wants," he seethed. "Rich foods, and plenty of it. Get him fat. Get him as fat as a sow. Then stake him in our parade grounds and let our sevritts have their way with him. He has shamed us all, and so it is that *all* shall witness this act of retribution."

The officer's eyes bugged out in horror as he imagined the gruesome death prescribed for Kundle. Not wanting a similar fate, he swallowed down his worries, snapped a sharp salute, and marched out.

Alone once more, Brairtok walked to his dinner table as if nothing of importance had transpired. He sat back down, and for a long moment, stared at the meal, trying not to be disturbed by Kundle's story of blood-red skies, beasts of the sea devouring men and Manno Vox returned from the dead and riding into battle.

As hard as he tried, he could not restrain his rage that gushed and brewed like a tar pit. He grabbed his platter of beef and hurled it into the fireplace.

Chapter 35

Gold, Steel and Worms

Linwith flew with the Worms of Bal-Malin throughout the night, soaring with wild abandon across the starry sky. As dawn approached, Linwith grabbed the saddlehorn gems and silently commanded them all to return to Bal-Malin. Diving for the sea's surface, they skimmed the frothing waves and spray misted his alabaster lenses. He watched as one worm snatched a large fish near the surface and dined upon the delicacy from the sea.

As was their custom, the worms circled Bal-Malin several times before landing. Rittmar and all the creatures from Bal-Malin were waiting for their return.

"How was your flight," Rittmar asked Linwith as he slid off the Worm King.

"Invigorating," Linwith exclaimed as he took off his helmet. "Flying is the way to travel over land and sea. *Especially* sea. I'll never set foot on a ship again, that I can promise. Not once did I feel sick to my stomach, and although I've been awake all evening, I'm not the least bit tired."

As his zeal waned, Linwith remembered his quest.

"But now we need to plan our mission to Tristan to acquire weapons."

The sapphire worm lowered his head and joined the conversation.

"My brothers and I can carry the gold to barter with, and then carry the weapons back to your brother's army."

"Army?" Linwith chuckled. "The men of Hetherlinn, the ones that can still fight, struggle to be brave and are too few in number to be called an army."

"Perhaps," Rittmar chimed in. "But you have been gone for some time. Things change. Perhaps others have joined them."

"I hope so," Linwith pondered, still doubtful such a change in his brother, let alone the men of Hetherlinn, was even possible. "But in the mean time, I have a quandary: how do the worms carry the gold? I know they could grasp a handful with their talons and fly across the Gilden Sea, but that would require too many trips."

"Allow me to show you," the sapphire worm said as he glided to another mound hidden from view by a grove of trees.

Hovering overtop, he bayed for his brothers to join him. Once assembled, the seven worms lowered their talons onto something hidden from Linwith's view. In one motion, they ascended slowly into the sky. In their grip was what Linwith presumed to be the knoll's roof. It was flat, square, and appeared to be constructed from baked clay.

They set the roof gently on the ground then returned to the knoll. One-by-one they disappeared into the mound, then emerged carrying what appeared to be enormous shields and chains. They dropped their load before Linwith.

"Six silver shields and three chains? What does this have to do with transporting gold?"

"These are not shields, for we have no such need," the Worm King replied as his sapphire tail flicked in the grass. "Our thick scales provide enough protection."

"Then what are these," Linwith asked as he examined the six shield-like objects.

"They are carriers to transport weapons or personnel to a battlefield."

Linwith walked around the massive pieces of metal, studying their craftsmanship.

"How do they work?" he asked as he ran his hand over the glossy surface of one.

"They are designed to conform to our chests and the leather straps attach to our saddles," the Worm King explained. "Because they are long and smooth, they enable us to fly unencumbered and with less resistance from the wind. Notice the latch on the back end."

Linwith walked to the transporter's opposite end where it was the widest and had the most depth. Large hinges with latches were on either side.

"These," he asked, pointing to the hinges.

"Yes. When you wish for us to unload, simply give the command. We land and release the latch with our talons to open them."

"Can you do this while flying?"

"Naturally," the Worm King replied, the black orbs of his eyes dancing with fire. "Although the process is a bit more challenging."

"How so?"

"In flight, once the latch is released, the wind will pop them open and whatever is inside will immediately tumble out. This requires perfect timing with my brothers in order to drop the contents on target. We must also prepare for the blast of wind striking the container like a sail and affecting our flight."

"This sounds difficult," Linwith noted as he opened the container. "Are you sure you and your brothers can do this?"

The Worm King turned and stared into Linwith's eyes; the fires within his black orbs glowed bright as if stoked by a sudden wind.

"The ability to perform such a maneuver is not our responsibility. It is yours."

Linwith dropped the lid and it clanged loudly across the glen.

"Oh, I see." He tore his gaze away from the worm's piercing eyes. "Well, I suppose I will need to practice. Yes, lots and lots of practice."

"But of course."

Linwith knelt and studied the carriers from the side angle.

"Several men could lie side by side in these."

"Yes, if that is what you wish," the Worm King answered. "Or you could use them to carry weapons, provisions or gold."

Linwith nodded as his mind began to comprehend the transporters many options. He stood and walked over to the pile of chains.

"And what of these?"

"Grasped within our talons, these chains are a formidable weapon."

"How?"

"Feel how strong and lightweight they are."

Linwith picked up one end of the lengthy chain. The links were as large as a man's head, but were as light as driftwood. He pulled and grunted and strained to bend it out of shape but to no avail.

"Imagine," the Worm King said, "that length of chain held taut in the talons of two of my brothers."

Linwith envisioned it stretched between two worms flying side by side.

"Now," the Worm King continued, "imagine them swooping down upon an advancing cavalry or army."

Linwith's eyes widened as he grasped the chain's capabilities as a weapon. The images were gruesome.

"But right now," the sapphire worm continued, "we do not face such an enemy. Our first mission is to transport gold to Tristan so you can barter for weapons."

"You're correct," Linwith said as he marched toward his armory. "I will begin retrieving the treasure. Rittmar, can you gather some of your people to assist?"

"There is a much faster way," the Worm King interjected. "With the Worm Master's permission, may we show you?"

Linwith nodded.

The Worm King called to his brothers and all seven worms took to wing. Once over the armory, they descended and removed its clay roof to expose the treasury. Each worm grabbed as much of the gold as their talons could carry, then flew back to the silver carriers and dropped the treasure inside.

"Will that suffice," the Worm King asked Linwith.

Linwith's face radiated, not so much by the incredible display of riches, but from the sunlight reflecting off the mounds of gold and silver. "Yes," he mumbled, then finding his voice, added, "That was so much faster than any plan I could have devised."

The worms replaced the roof on the knoll then landed beside their carriers and closed the lids with their snouts. Linwith and Rittmar latched them in place and secured the treasure inside.

"Next," the Worm King instructed, "you will need to attach the six carriers to my brothers. They will kneel and lay their chests upon the carrier. Simply toss the leather harnesses over their neck and midsection and fasten them tightly."

The worms lowered themselves upon the silver carriers, and Linwith scampered about, fastening them securely in place. Soon, all six worms stood erect.

The Worm King inspected each to make sure they were properly attached. Satisfied, he swung his head around and said to Linwith, "We are ready, my master."

Linwith donned his helmet, climbed the stairs and remounted the sapphire worm.

"Their loads are heavy," he said as he strapped himself into his saddle. "Will they be able to fly above the surrounding trees?"

"It has been many summers since we have flown on such a mission. Nevertheless, I am confident their strength is still vibrant and fresh."

Linwith nodded and then turned to address Rittmar who fluttered near the ground.

"Rittmar, are you joining us," Linwith asked.

"My role is done, Worm Master. We were simply to escort you to the Worms of Bal-Malin. How sweet is our success!"

"Yes, but there is still so much I need to learn about the worms."

"The Worm King is your new instructor. He is a patient teacher."

Linwith gave a solemn nod.

Placing his gloved hand over all the gems of the saddlehorn, Linwith gave the silent order to fly. The worms began to beat their wings, each flap perfectly synchronized. While flapping, they began to walk and then trot until they were running to gain speed for their ascent. The six worms strained against the wind, their wings beating great strokes to lift their heavy loads into the sky. Linwith stared ahead at the white trees, fearing the worms would crash into them, but with several strong efforts, all six sailed over the treetops.

Rittmar led his people up into the sky for a better view of Linwith's departure. They watched the Worm Master and his seven worms fly east over the Gilden Sea, out toward Tristan. Radiating in the bright sky, and clearly seen by Rittmar and his people, were shimmering tails of sapphire, ruby, gold, silver, amber, mandarin and emerald.

Chapter 36

Caace

Over the course of several days, Il-Lilliad assisted Kinmin's men with packing the necessary gear for their march: Tents were rolled up and stashed in wagons; water, dried goods and smoked fish were sealed in barrels; armor was inspected and polished; swords, lances and arrows sharpened.

When the last article was either strapped to their small horses or secured to a wagon, Kinmin mounted his steed and made his way to Il-Lilliad. There, he gave a signal to one of his officers and a frisky mount was led to Il-Lilliad.

"I'm sorry we do not have a larger animal," Kinmin apologized, as Il-Lilliad looked the SriBrunian horse over. "But despite his size, he is very capable of carrying you on this long journey."

Il-Lilliad patted the animal's head. The horse whinnied and shook its mane.

"He is indeed a fiery steed, but with all due respect, Kinmin, he is comparable in size to a large Allsbruthian dog. My feet will drag the ground."

"Suit yourself," Kinmin answered. "But the journey ahead of us is long and I fear walking such a distance would be too strenuous for a man of your age."

Il-Lilliad stiffened his back and trained his eyes onto Kinmin's face.

"Of my age?" he countered. "I'll have you know that during the Dark War, storytellers marched for days without rest. The trek before us now will be more like a stroll through a meadow."

Kinmin's eyes blinked, baffled why Il-Lilliad should be so upset over what he perceived to be simply keen observation and facts.

"I detect resentment from you. Did I offend you in some way?"

Il-Lilliad started to defend his outburst, but realized it was only his pride that had been wounded. Reason bridled his tongue, and wisdom, the type that only comes with age, he admitted to himself, steered his answer in a different direction.

"Forgive me, Kinmin. I suppose it is hard for a man of...my age...to be willing to accept the truth of his own limitations." Il-Lilliad let his eyes drift away from Kinmin and out across the land before them. "You're correct: I'm much older than I was during the Dark War, a season in which I bore the legs of a young man and the passion of one as well. But now?" He lightly patted his thighs. "These muscles lack the vigor they once possessed, although my heart - my passion - burns like never before. If only it could make up for my weakened physique."

Acknowledging his age with a deep sigh, Il-Lilliad placed his left palm on the horse's head to steady himself, then swung his right leg over the animal. Once he was settled in the saddle, as he had predicted, his feet touched the ground.

Kinmin's eyes sparkled, and a mischievous smile - rare among the SriBrunians - arced across his face. The smile blossomed into a chuckle that flew like a spark to the other leaders and warriors and lit them into laughter. Soon, the entire army was laughing, and it was at this point that Il-Lilliad realized that he was not only sitting atop a tiny horse, but was sitting in the middle of a joke.

Kinmin waved an arm to silence his men and wiped away a tear from laughing so hard.

"Please," he said between his final laughs, "it is now you who must forgive me. You see, you are mounted atop a SriBrunian warhorse."

Il-Lilliad's brow wrinkled in confusion.

I'll never comprehend SriBrunian humor, he mused.

Then he remembered the demonstration Kinmin had given him. As enlightenment dawned, his wrinkled brow smoothed and he too began to smile.

With a gracious nod to Kinmin to acknowledge his craft at fashioning a practical joke, he dismounted.

"You're telling me that, like your men, this horse can transform."

Kinmin nodded, his smile so infectious, that Il-Lilliad began to snicker, then to chuckle, then to laugh so hard that he was doubled over.

"I must have appeared quite foolish; a giant riding a dwarf horse," he gasped, when he finally caught his breath.

"And your feet," Kinmin added, "would have dug trenches had you rode in such a manner."

The laughter faded as Kinmin turned his attention to Il-Lilliad's mount. The animal morphed until it attained the stature of an Ebonite warhorse.

"That's more like it," Il-Lilliad said as he stuck a foot into the enlarged stirrup and sprung into the saddle.

With the joke over, Kinmin's serious demeanor returned, and he signaled for the army to leave. Riding at the head of the column with Kinmin, Il-Lilliad glanced over his shoulder at the warriors of SriBrune. They acknowledged him with a determined smile or a head nod. Gone were the suspicious expressions when he first arrived as an outsider, a giant whose skin was paler than theirs and who bore the reputation of a mysterious and powerful storyteller. Now, they viewed him as simply, Il-Lilliad; their peer, comrade and brother.

Turning back around, Il-Lilliad smiled, thankful for Kinmin's gag.

"Nothing prepares an army for war," he said to Kinmin, "like stories, ale and jokes."

Kinmin flashed him a smile.

"Yes, and better on you than on me."

The army trudged along and the SriBrunian landscape seemed to roll on forever. Il-Lilliad often wondered where they were in the Onderling in proportion to the world above.

"Tell me," he asked Kinmin, "how much further until we reach the waterfall...what was it called?"

"The entrance you reference is called Caace, but please tell me you are not going to constantly ask, *are we there yet?* We have only been riding for half a day."

"True," Il-Lilliad answered, "and I don't want to sound like a whining child, but if I had some bearings, some sense of distance, then I would feel more at peace."

Kinmin was unable to grasp Il-Lilliad's dilemma, but he realized that because Il-Lilliad was not SriBrunian, the storyteller's needs were different than his own. SriBrunian logic would only waste time and hurt feelings. He chose another means of communication. Pointing to a dark cloud line on the far horizon, Kinmin spoke like a teacher to a pupil.

"Do you see the line of gray clouds off in the distance that looks like a river?"

Il-Lilliad nodded.

"At that point, high above in your world, is the River Arrgient. If memory serves me correctly, I'd say it is approximately near the village of Gilden."

Il-Lilliad's shoulders righted and he relaxed in his saddle, relieved to know his prospective in the Onderling in relation to the world above.

"Based upon this," Il-Lilliad said as he imagined looking at a map of his world and calculating travel time from Gilden to Caace, "by my estimation, when we reach that location you just pointed out, we'll be just over half way there."

"Correct."

"Good," Il-Lilliad exclaimed with a smile and with an energized tap of his hand on his saddle horn. "It's comforting to have a sense of where I am and where I'm going."

"So I take it that being in the Onderling is disconcerting for you?"

"Yes. Aggellon's world was too perfect while SriBrune's has three suns, lacks nights, stars or moon. Not to mention that I glance up regularly to make sure our world isn't falling down into yours. The Onderling is *very* perplexing."

As the army plodded along, Il-Lilliad correlated their trek with that of marching north from Gilden. When they turned northwest, he knew they were following the River Arrgient's course and were nearing its headwaters. Soon, they would reach the waterfall and Caace.

"Notice the incline," Kinmin advised as he pointed to the horizon. "See how subtle it is?"

Il-Lilliad followed Kinmin's line of sight, and had it not been for him pointing out the change in elevation, he would have missed it completely. Onward they trudged, the ground becoming rockier and the trail winding about boulders and pockets of shrubs. As they climbed, the light dimmed as if they were entering a cave. The air also changed from that of an arid region to that of being in the mountains: crisp air intermixed with the scent of spruce.

"We're very close," Kinmin said over his shoulder back to Il-Lilliad. "Listen for the sound of water."

Il-Lilliad strained his ears for the bubbling, churning or thundering sounds he knew existed at this portion of the River Arrgient. But all he heard were the sharp reports from the hooves of the SriBrunian cavalry, clopping against the rocky ground. And then…

"A rush of wind," Il-Lilliad exclaimed, "and what sounds like drums."

"Those aren't drums you're hearing. We're nearing the waterfall," Kinmin explained as he led his mount around a sharp turn. When Il-Lilliad rounded the bend, the sounds intensified, taking on the cadence of stampeding horses, but as Kinmin had explained, no drums or horses created the raucous noise.

A blast of cold air took Il-Lilliad's breath away as did the sight of a tiny circle of blue glowing on the horizon. Kinmin stopped and pointed at the shimmering pinhole of light.

"Behold; Caace. Soon, we will be in your world, my friend."

Il-Lilliad nodded, but Caace reminded him of his ordeal in Karajan when he had to swim toward the portal of SriBrune as dansel lors swirled beneath his feet. He cast off that memory and ignored the chill wind, and instead, focused on better days beyond Caace.

Kinmin spurred his mount and the army advanced. Caace grew in size with each step they took. When they reached the watery portal, Il-Lilliad dismounted and stared through the wall of water.

"Stunning," he shouted above the roar of the falls on the other side of the Onderling. "The power and might of those falls is deafening, and if my eyes aren't deceiving me, guarding this entrance is exactly what I expected to find."

He marched forward, but stopped well short of the waterfall and extended his palm toward the flow. Flesh touched what felt like ice and he watched ripples fan out in all directions like a spider web.

Caace is shrouded by a veil, he concluded to himself. *Much like the one encircling Claire. No wonder the secret of this entrance has remained intact.*

He spun on his heel and strode to Kinmin's side.

"Do you know if the veil, I mean *Caace*, will let us return?"

Kinmin shrugged his shoulders.

"No one knows. This will be the first time anyone from the Onderling has passed through."

They turned their gaze to Caace. The veil was once more perfectly taut and smooth.

"Well," Il-Lilliad said, a lilt in his voice, "it beats swimming across Karajan."

Kinmin flashed him a smile, and then declared, "Since we are about to enter your world, it is only fitting that you should lead the way."

Il-Lilliad gave a solemn nod. His thoughts became preoccupied with passing through the veil. He knew that to enter Claire's veil, one needed an invitation. Was the same true for Caace? And should they need to return, would Caace allow them entry or would it bar their way? He cast a concerned glance at the army of SriBrune. Would they be able to pass through the veil unscathed? And if so, would they truly be ready to battle the Cauldron and Brairtok's warriors and beasts?

"Il-Lilliad," Kinmin shouted over the thundering fall, "I've once more sampled your thoughts. Do not be afraid. We will be fine. Now please, lead us to your world."

Il-Lilliad returned to his warhorse, mounted and without another thought or even a hesitation, led the army of SriBrune through Caace.

As they passed through the shimmering veil, Il-Lilliad was struck by how bitter cold it was - much like the veil encircling Claire - and the chill cut deep into the warmth of his core. Once on the other side, he turned to see what Caace looked like. True to Kinmin's account, it was nothing more than a rock wall with the waterfall thundering and splashing off to one side.

Except that now, the entire army of SriBrune was magically passing through the stone on its way to war.

Chapter 37

Newcomb's Tale

DeMorley squatted by the fire and warmed his hands over its small flames. Night had fallen and the surrounding woods were dark and quiet, which set his nerves on edge. He dared a glance at Draemel, who sat with his back against a tree, still tied fast to the trunk. His head hung limp and rode his rising chest as he breathed the cool nocturnal air. Even asleep, Draemel intimidated DeMorley. He yanked his eyes off the dozing bounty hunter and found comfort in the glowing embers.

A branch snapped. DeMorley spun toward the sound. Out in the gloom, leaves rustled as someone - or something - approached his fire. He hopped to his feet and for a brief moment considered running to hide behind Draemel. He knew it was a crazy plan, as he was sure whatever crept toward them had already seen him. But if he could lure the monster, or the rogue assassin, toward Draemel, he might have enough time to flee into the woods. Or, he reasoned, he would untie Draemel in hopes he would rise and fight off the looming threat.

Before he had the chance to decide, Newcomb's silhouette on horseback emerged from the darkness. DeMorley released a breath he wasn't even aware he was holding, and placed his hand over his heart as if to help stop it from beating out of his chest.

Newcomb had been gone for most of the day and DeMorley had fretted constantly. Not because he was concerned for Newcomb's attempt to try and convince Lassiter to rejoin them on their quest to Claire. His anxiety was rooted in self-preservation, and specifically in the fear that Draemel would somehow slip free and slit his throat.

"Well," DeMorley asked as Newcomb dismounted. "Is Lassiter returning?"

"Tonight was like all the other nights you have reported," Newcomb replied as he tethered his horse beside the other animals. "Only this time, I fear he has made his true choice."

He joined DeMorley by the fire and allowed his thoughts to drift as he gazed into the glowing orange coals. A moment from many summers ago on the Isle of Lills unexpectedly flashed in his thoughts. He stood on his terrace watching the sunset. The waning light painted the horizon with pastels while the salty air and cawing gulls invigorated his senses. He was so awestruck by the glory of the sea and sunset's grandeur that he was oblivious to a boy of eight summers taking his hand.

With a glance, Newcomb recognized Lassiter, and he smiled. Hand-in-hand, they watched the tangerine sun slide beyond the sea's purple horizon.

No words were spoken.

No words were needed.

Newcomb savored the memory from long ago, and more importantly, the feelings he had at the time of not only being the boy's mentor, but of connecting with his heart like he would if he were the boy's father.

The sweet recollection was chased away by the events at *The Golden Giln.* After being tossed outside, Newcomb stared at the slammed door in hope that it would burst open and Lassiter would emerge to join him once again. But when Lassiter's voice rose up in song, and the throng received him with raucous applause, his vision faded like a wisp of smoke.

The pain of Lassiter's rejection was unlike anything Newcomb had experienced before; the cut of an enemy's blade or the sting of a friend's death. Newcomb's pain for Lassiter was a deep, hollow darkness that, like a shroud being drawn over a corpse, shadowed his hope and robbed him of purpose and life.

Newcomb shook the dread, as best he could, from his thoughts and stared into the glowing coals.

"And yet," he said more to encourage himself than for DeMorley's sake, "despite what I have witnessed with my senses, I believe the Only will help Lassiter. A minstrel's life is not what the Only has invited him to become."

Draemel's eyes flew open.

"Why not?" he asked.

"I thought you were asleep?" DeMorley quipped with a nervous flutter in his voice.

"A bounty hunter learns how to sleep and listen at the same time," Draemel replied as he zeroed his steely eyes onto DeMorley's quivering frame.

The minstrel pulled away from his gaze, and Draemel's eyes jumped over to Newcomb.

"You didn't answer my question, old man. Why is being a minstrel something the Only would want to alter? Why should the Only even care?"

Newcomb picked up a stick and stirred the coals of the fire.

"His lineage calls for him to be...someone else."

"Stop talking in riddles," Draemel grunted. "Why are you so set on not allowing the boy to pursue this dream?"

"Because," Newcomb countered with a jab of the stick into the flames, "he doesn't understand what his dream really *is*."

"And you do?" Draemel argued.

Newcomb spun toward the bounty hunter.

"Yes!"

A wry smile unfurled across Draemel's face.

"You've done well to conceal your secret from me, but tonight, you've blundered and let your true feelings whisper revelation."

Newcomb's eyes narrowed and he spun back around to poke the fire.

"You see," Draemel continued, "the only reason a storyteller like you would risk his life for a boy that is not his own is this: Lassiter is more than you present him to be. The question yet to be discovered is, what is his greater worth?"

The three men sat in silence as the fire's cracks and pops echoed into the darkness.

Newcomb heaved his stick into the flames and plopped down on the ground. He stroked the rusk's soft fur in an effort to comfort his woes, and wondered if all was lost.

With his identity as a storyteller discovered by Draemel and DeMorley, surely the Cauldron was aware as well. A plan, albeit desperate, came to his mind. He would form an alliance with Draemel. When he read the bounty hunter's deepest tale, Newcomb knew that it was no accident that Draemel had found them.

Draemel had known Lassiter's father, Hornlynn. If Draemel learned that Lassiter was his former commander's son, and that his destiny was to sit on the throne, perhaps he would desire to have an influence on Lassiter's future.

Newcomb stole a look at Draemel and DeMorley. But in order to reveal as much to Draemel, he would not only be giving DeMorley such insight, but the Cauldron as well. The risk was great, even dangerous, but time was running out and he saw no other way.

Newcomb drew in a deep breath, gathered his courage, and spoke.

"Lassiter is destined to be King of Allsbruth."

DeMorley fell off his perch and landed on his rear end.

"A king," he snickered. "Lassiter is to be *king*?"

"You don't get to be a king just because you want to," Draemel countered, his interest suddenly piqued. "Or in Lassiter's case, because *you* desire this for him. You have to be born into the royal family."

"Lassiter comes from the royal line," Newcomb answered.

"You're certain of the boy's lineage?" Draemel asked.

"Yes. His mother, Anessatia, was the daughter of King Culdean. She married Hornlynn and shortly thereafter, Lassiter was conceived."

"Hornlynn?" Draemel repeated.

The bounty hunter's countenance shifted. Newcomb took note of his change and liked what he saw.

"You're certain Hornlynn was the boy's father?"

"Positive. And since Anessatia was next in line to rule the throne, I was commissioned by the King of Claire to take her to the Isle of Lills, along with Lassiter, to protect her during the Dark War. I was charged to mentor Lassiter."

"But if Anessatia is to rule next," Draemel asked, "then how could Lassiter be king?"

"Hornlynn died during the Dark War and Anessatia shortly thereafter," Newcomb explained, as he watched Draemel's eyes turn to stone. "Therefore, according to Allsbruthian law, the next in line to rule is the first grandson: Lassiter."

"Royalty," DeMorley gloated while leaning back on his hands. "And I thought fate had dealt me a bad hand. Not only will I get a treasure from Claire, but now I will be able to - how should I put it - earn my way into the services of the King of Allsbruth."

Newcomb was about to upbraid the minstrel when a foreign sound deep in the woods caught their attention.

The sound came again.

"It's a young man's voice," DeMorley noted.

"Calling for Newcomb," Draemel added.

Newcomb recognized the voice and hopped to his feet.

"Lassiter," he gasped as he raced to his horse. "He's changed his mind and has come to join us. Reason has redeemed madness."

Newcomb swung his leg up and over his saddle as his rusk flitted nearby.

"I must hurry to him," he said as he gathered in his horse's reins. "Danger lurks in these woods. The Cauldron hunts for his blood."

"Untie me and let me help," Draemel urged as he squirmed to free his bonds.

Newcomb shook his head.

"There's no time. Besides, now that my identity is known, I can freely fight with stories and my rusk. We'll be back soon."

Without another word, Newcomb galloped off as the dawn's purplish light seeped into the black night's sky.

Chapter 38

Hetherlinn's Life

A lone figure leaned against the threshold of cottage Number 17. With arms crossed, Quinn scrutinized the activities of his neighbors.

Hinnmith and his men marched out of Hetherlinn days before, and took with them his men's passion for war. Now their energy was spent building new lives with the *blessings* of Ebon. Day and night they labored to build larger homes while the women gathered around the communal fire to sew, knit and gossip about who would have the biggest home or finest clothes.

Quinn took note of an adventurous young boy as he climbed into an empty barrel that lay on its side.

Children laugh and play with the myriad of toys...

The boy's friends rolled the barrel down the hill where it crashed into a tree.

And when they bore or one breaks...

The rider of the barrel emerged, laughing and wobbling about from the dizzying ride.

They toss it aside and run to fetch new ones.

The children ran to scoop up toys from a freshly opened barrel.

Areall joined him in the doorway.

"It's so good to hear children laughing again," she said as she rested her hands on his shoulders.

"If you say so," he grumbled.

She let her hands fall.

"Why are you so disgruntled," she asked.

"Just look at them," he scoffed with a wave of his hand their way. "They're oblivious to Ebon's threats of war."

Areall took note of their neighbors, but saw them in a different light than Quinn.

"What's wrong with a little happiness flowing through Hetherlinn?"

Quinn snapped his eyes toward her.

"Is that how you see this? As just, *a little happiness*?"

"Yes," she replied as she crossed her arms beneath her breasts. "Let them build and play and dream. What harm could come?"

"There is treachery in these gifts," Quinn sneered. "That's why I haven't taken the tiniest of spoils. I'm still their leader, and I must continue to lead by example."

Areall nodded and sighed. She had chosen to support his decision and also did not partake in any of the treasures, but as the larger homes were built, and clothes were fashioned from exotic material, envy stirred in her bosom.

"Quinn," she coaxed, hoping her honesty would not awaken his sleeping anger, "we deserve some bliss too, my love. What harm would there be if we partook...of just a little?"

"That's the problem," he chided. "You can't partake of *just a little*. A tiny bit of their spoils poisons one to the core."

Areall bit her lip.

"I'm trying to understand, but I don't see how..."

Quinn grabbed her shoulders.

"Areall, please. Don't tempt me with this talk."

Areall's eyes widened in fear as his anger gushed out over her and she squirmed to be free from his hands that held her too tight. Realizing, he not only had frightened his wife, but bruised her as well, Quinn released his grip.

"I'm sorry, Areall. I never meant to harm you."

She nodded while rubbing her sore shoulders.

Quinn regained control over his emotions and with a gentle finger to her chin, lifted her face up to his.

"Areall, you *know* I wish to bless you with a better life, but I will not do so with such spoils. I need you to trust me...believe in me. Without you, I'm all alone."

She took in his face, relieved to see it placid once more.

"And I would be lost without you, too," she answered as she took his hand in hers. "But lately, all you do is brood and grunt your displeasure at our neighbors' new lives; at our *friends'* new lives. You've separated yourself from every one, *including* me."

He sighed and let her hand fall.

"You're right," he apologized as he turned his attention once more to his neighbors. "I never meant to harm you, but seeing them live in denial angers me. Don't they know that war is imminent?"

"How do you know war is on the march?"

"War doesn't march," he answered. He put his arm around her and she leaned into his frame. "It creeps through the night, hiding within the shadows, watching and waiting until we suspect it no more. That is why Ebon has bestowed us with such bounty, so we become numb to their attack. The Cauldron is fattening us for the slaughter."

Across the way, Daryess stepped out of cottage Number 7 and shook out a dusty tapestry. Gundin sat in a chair and leaned back against their home. He was too engrossed in admiring his medals to notice she was even there.

"I suppose," Quinn said as he watched dust from the drapery engulf his friend, "that my anger began when *he* accepted the Ebonite decorations. Look," he growled as he pointed to Gundin. "There he sits, day and night, twiddling his medal."

As though Daryess could hear Quinn's charge over the hoopla from the children and parents, she turned her head to find Quinn and Areall staring. Expressions of mistrust replaced their former friendly waves. Daryess's eyes narrowed. She snapped her head away and stormed back inside. The door slammed shut while Gundin continued to mumble and play with his medal.

"She's to blame for Gundin's slip back into madness," Quinn accused.

Areall pushed herself away, and planted her fists on her hips.

"Why is this Daryess' fault?"

"She's his wife, isn't she?" Quinn muttered. "She could say something to him, or at least throw away that cursed medal."

"And just what have *you* done to help?"

"I've talked to him. I've tried to reason with him," he defended himself.

Areall folded her arms across her chest, tapped her foot and glowered at Quinn.

"Since he hasn't changed like you want him to, you've quit trying to help. You're as much to blame as anyone."

Quinn slowly turned his face toward hers. It glowed red with with anger. Areall gasped and backed away from him. She knew this expression all too well. She had experienced his drunken rages in the aftermath of the Dark War. Although his visits to the tulip had changed him - a softening she welcomed wholeheartedly - seeing how quickly his anger returned not only made her fear his hand, but his retreat back to his former ways.

Seeing the fear in is wife's eyes brought Quinn back to his senses. He drew back, ashamed that his anger had once more threatened the love of his life. He let his gaze wonder over the dusty ground to the lone tulip growing near his home, and recalled the countless mornings of drawing in its sweet aroma, focusing on the richness of those respites and a distant whisper wooing him with soft delight.

He sighed. Would he become the man he dreamed of being, or remain a captive of his failures at Min Brock?

Unable to look Areall in the eyes, he simply gave her a solemn nod.

"You're right," he said, his voice at once penitent and pensive. "I've *not* been a very good friend."

Quinn stepped across the threshold of his home, and sauntered toward the barrels of wine stacked nearby.

Areall covered her mouth with her hand and watched helplessly as he placed both hands upon the highest barrel. When his head dropped, so did her tears. Unable to find her voice, wishing she could save him but knowing she could not, she fell back against the door and gasped for air.

Quinn's head snapped upright; he had made a decision.

"Death begets life!" he boomed.

He pushed with all his might.

The barrels toppled to the ground and split open like melons upon a rock.

Mithe sat with the other women at the communal fire and spun tales of leisure while they all sewed new clothes for their families. Their voices were joyous and full of laughter until the sound of splintering wood from cottage Number 17 silenced them all.

Mithe snapped her head toward Quinn's cottage.

"Look," she exclaimed with a crooked finger wagging at Quinn. "He's so drunk that he's destroying his precious wine."

The women turned to look. Broken barrels lay everywhere while rivers of wine snaked across the dusty ground. Quinn turned and marched their way.

"He's gone mad," Mithe chattered as she fumbled for her cane in order to flee. It fell out of her reach. Spooked, she focused back on Quinn whose gait was swift and purposeful.

"Stay away from us, you drunken fool," she cried out in a last ditch effort to avert his attack.

The women clutched their cloth so he would not snatch it away from them and cowered in fear. Quinn stormed past them without a word, his eyes focused instead on cottage Number 7. He stopped in front of Gundin who still leaned against the wall of his cottage.

"Good day, friend," Quinn announced, but Gundin continued mumbling and fumbling with his decorations, oblivious to his presence.

Undeterred by Gundin's lack of response and focusing instead on the hope the tulip offered him as a man, Quinn continued.

"I see you've been awarded a medal by Ebon."

"Yes," Gundin cooed as he fondled the gold medallion through half-glazed eyes. "And rightly so. I am honored above *all* warriors."

Gundin wrapped his fingers around his medal, suddenly fearful that Quinn might try to snatch it from him. His voice trailed off as he slowly raised his foggy eyes to meet Quinn's stare.

"I am honored above all warriors," he repeated."Even you."

Quinn nodded, unfazed by his friend's demeanor.

"Yes, Gundin was indeed the greatest warrior to ever walk Allsbruth. Such a pity he died."

Gundin cocked his head to the side.

"Dead? I live, or are you too drunk to tell."

Quinn shook his head.

"No, I am quite sober, and I can see that *you* live, but Gundin is not alive. That, my friend, is where we disagree."

Quinn's gaze fell to the medal.

"It is indeed beautiful."

The medal was forged of gold and silver and flashed dazzling light onto its red satin ribbon.

"You must be proud," Quinn added.

"Very proud," Gundin sighed. "You were a great warrior too. That's why you got a medal as well." Gundin's eyes searched Quinn's neck for the crimson sash. "Where's your medal?"

Quinn chuckled as he reflected on the answer. Although forced to receive the commendation from Hinnmith, when the last Ebonite rounded the bend out of Hetherlinn, Quinn struck out for the cabbage fields. He marched up to the compost mound, unpinned the medal and heaved it into a pile of manure.

"I've merely put it where it belongs," Quinn replied as his eyes narrowed.

Without warning, Quinn lunged and grabbed the ribbon. Startled, Gundin fell to his knees and Quinn jumped behind him and pulled with all his might.

The satin ribbon cut into Gundin's throat and he started to choke. Gundin wrestled to free himself, but Quinn held the advantage, and when Gundin tried to rise, Quinn kicked his legs out from under him.

"Stop," Gundin gurgled between gasping coughs. His arms flayed about as he tried to grab Quinn, "you're killing me."

"I'm not the one killing you," Quinn fired as he dodged Gundin's swirling arms. "Your medal is."

Alarmed by the noise, Daryess charged out of the cottage.

"Stop," she shouted at Quinn as she beat on his back. "You're choking him, you drunken fool."

By this time, Mithe had found her cane. She stood and pointed a bony finger at Quinn.

"Men and women of Hetherlinn," she shouted, "Behold the murderer. He will never change. *Never.*"

Quinn gave a hard yank. Gundin's face matched the color of his ribbon.

"Throw it away and live," Quinn commanded.

"Never," Gundin choked as his strength waned. "I deserve it."

"Then it shall be your demise," Quinn declared between gritted teeth.

Areall, who had also heard the commotion, raced to the cottage and pulled Daryess off her husband. Areall held her friend against her will and took in Quinn's face. It was not filled with rage or madness, and although she didn't understand why he was attacking Gundin, she chose to trust that his motives were for Gundin's good.

Quinn put his right foot between Gundin's shoulder blades and pulled back with all his might.

"Gundin, warrior for the Only," Quinn challenged. "throw it away and live."

"No," Gundin gagged as he twisted his enormous frame in an attempt to throw Quinn off, "I'm deserving."

Quinn gave a sharp yank.

Gundin coughed and gagged.

"Fight the Cauldron's whisper," Quinn urged. "Join me in this fight and you will gain medals of honor beyond your wildest dreams."

"Useless," Gundin coughed and then between gags, "The whisper...the drone...are...too *strong*."

"Remember our times by the flower. Remember Galadin. Let those inspire you to fight...to live."

"But my medal..."

Gundin felt light-headed, and in this dizzy state, he saw Areall comforting Daryess who wept. His eyes darted out to the tulip's red pedals outlined against Hetherlinn's gray landscape. As he wrestled Quinn, he pondered his challenge to fight for what he truly treasured. He heard a whisper from Claire. He sensed the tulip's aroma filling him with strength, and more than anything else, he wanted to become the man he dreamed of being.

"*Enough*," Gundin roared.

Empowered by the whisper and the flower, he rose and tossed Quinn off his back as if he were a rag doll. He bent over and put hands on his knees and drew in labored breaths. The medal dangled from his neck and swung like a pendulum as sweat from the battle beaded on his forehead and dripped to the ground. Gundin stared at the gold and silver that swung lazily back and forth, back and forth.

He stood upright and wiped the sweat from his brow.

The citizens of Hetherlinn, whether standing by the communal fire or spying out their cottage windows, watched to see what Gundin would do. Would he take off the medal and join Quinn, or hold Ebon's medal dear and abandon Quinn to his own fate?

Gundin wrapped his hand around the medal. A corporate gasp arose from Hetherlinn's onlookers. Gundin looked into Daryess' face.

"If I remove this medal," he said, his voice still raspy from the attack, "the peace and happiness we have recently enjoyed will end. Difficult days will come."

Daryess wiped her eyes and stepped toward her husband. She looked up into his eyes.

"Gundin, my tears are not because I fear difficulty. I weep because we've been living within a nightmare disguised as a wondrous dream. Peace and happiness under the hand of Ebon?" she said as she reached up and touched his cheek. "Without our son? Without you?"

She let her hand drift from his face to his dagger. She unsheathed it, and raised it before her. Staring at its sharp edge, she pondered whether she had the courage to face the unknown. Finding her answer, she offered it to her husband.

Gundin reached for the dagger and a whisper was heard.

"So," the Cauldron snarled. "*You desire a fight for honor? Try battling this.*"

The drone fell oppressively upon the two men.

"*Honor? Fight? Glory? Such days are but vapors, lost at Min Brock, never to be recouped.*"

The men groaned against the drone's weight and the whisper's taunts. Areall ran to Daryess and they clung to each other, alarmed to see their husbands attacked in such a manner, and horrified that they could not help.

Quinn dropped to one knee and stared up into Gundin's eyes, wondering if he'd see the fog of retreat or the fire of fight.

"Do it," Quinn shouted between gritted teeth as he battled the invisible forces of Ebon.

"*Do it? Yes, you fat fool, go ahead and slice the ribbon. But who will stand by your side?*"

Sweat streamed down Gundin's face as he strained against both the drone and the decision before him. The dagger quivered in his hand. He glanced at Quinn, who was now down on both knees.

"No matter what," Quinn shouted up to Gundin. "I will stand by your side. I will stand by your *side.*"

Gundin's eyes narrowed.

With a swift yank, and a war cry he had not shouted since the Dark War, he sliced the ribbon. The medal landed with a soft *thud* in the dirt.

"*So be it,*" the whisper said. "*Death begets death!*"

And with that, the whisper retreated and the drone returned to its normal pitch and volume.

Gundin sheathed his weapon and stared down at the medal. Quinn regained his feet and put his arm around Gundin's wide shoulders. Together, they walked toward the town fire.

The women huddled about the communal fire and clutched their precious cloth close to their bosoms, fearing the worst.

"Men and women of Hetherlinn," Quinn announced as he turned about, making sure he had everyone's attention. "Ebon has not blessed us. It has dulled our senses, lulling us toward an unnoticeable death. War is coming. The Cauldron desires to crush us."

"You talk babble, like the meadow's brook," a man shouted from the doorway of his new home. "Why would Brairtok bless us only to attack us later."

"In order to fatten us like a prize calf before it is butchered," Quinn countered.

"Words from a jealous fool," Mithe hissed. "You envy our fine homes and clothes. You're resentful that Elabea has abandoned you while our children remain. But all of this is your own doing. Your actions at Min Brock brought such shame upon you."

"True," Quinn answered with a slight nod. "But I've never blamed Hetherlinn for my mistakes, nor am I jealous of your new possessions. I challenge you because I'm concerned for your well-being. Can't you see that these gifts are trickery and bribery to rob you of your passions? I urge you to return to the stories of Claire. It is time to fight for our freedom."

"The tales of Claire are but bedtime stories of delusion," another man shouted from his large porch. "If what you say is true, then why hasn't Claire blessed us in such a manner? Where is the Only? He either doesn't exist or sits on his throne and does nothing."

"What about the invitations," Areall interjected as she joined her husband. "We all received one and yet the only ones brave enough to accept them were Elabea and Galadin. Aren't we all to blame for lacking such courage?"

"Courage," Mithe spat as she hobbled toward Areall. "It is because of their *courage* that Ebonite warriors with their sevritts descended upon our tiny village. Did the army of Claire intervene? Was even a whisper of hope heard? No. The evidence is clear: Claire is no more."

Mithe turned to address the men, women and children of Hetherlinn.

"I say follow what we can see with our own eyes. As the Oracles declare, *'Give honor to those that honor you!'*"

Enthusiastic cheers arose from the masses.

Areall clinched her fists, but Quinn gently restrained her.

Facing the group, Quinn asked, "Is this the consensus of all?"

Some nodded. Others simply looked away from his fiery eyes.

"So be it," Quinn replied. Only Areall noted the tinge of sadness in his voice. "Our paths will divide. We will pack up our belongings and leave Hetherlinn as soon as possible. We will bother you no more, and wish everyone the best of luck."

"Let me have some time with them *alone,*" Gundin challenged as he patted his rotund midsection. "I can persuade them to see the truth."

"Muscle and brawn might sway the will, but not the heart, my friend," Quinn replied as he clasped Areall's hand. "Their decision has been made; there is nothing more we can do or say."

Turning away from the communal fire, Quinn and Areall walked hand-in-hand back to their cottage while Gundin led Daryess back to theirs.

When they were far away from the others, Areall glanced up into Quinn's face. It was as cloudy as the sky above.

"You look troubled, my husband."

"I suppose I am," he answered with eyes focused straight ahead. "Leaving Hetherlinn will be very painful, not only for us, but for them as well."

Areall glanced over her shoulder back at their neighbors. Despite the oppression of the Oracles, despite the suffering and pain they had experienced together as a family through the Dark War, she loved Hetherlinn's simple beauty and the potential it had to once more be the village of wonder from her childhood.

"Emblaze what you see in your memory," Quinn advised as he opened their cottage door. "This is the last time you'll see them alive. For that matter, this is the last time you'll ever see Hetherlinn."

Areall took in the children playing with their new toys, and then the men who gathered with pipes to discuss their latest projects. Lastly, her eyes wandered to the communal fire where the women had once more taken up their cloth and their jovial conversations. Areall imagined mortality pressing through the outlying woods like a fog, gray and ominous, shrouding Hetherlinn with its mists. As she pictured all her neighbors succumbing to death, even old Mithe, she shivered with dread and shook her head in a vain attempt to cast the gruesome vision from her thoughts.

Areall wanted to argue with Quinn, to ridicule his doubt and his gloomy prophecy of war and destruction. But her intuition told her that this time he was right. Tears welled up into her eyes and Hetherlinn took on a diffused, mystical glow. Her gaze fell away and she followed Quinn inside to pack.

Chapter 39

Dark Deceptions

Newcomb's rusk darted through the dark woods toward Lassiter's voice. As dawn's light burned away the wood's eerie blackness, and they got closer, Newcomb could discern what Lassiter was saying.

He's calling for help!

Newcomb leaned forward in his saddle and dug his heels into his horse's flanks. As the terrain descended and the foliage thinned Lassiter's cry grew louder. They jumped a stream, and Newcomb spied a large meadow through the trees. Out in the middle, tied to a post, was Lassiter.

Odd, Newcomb mused as he cast his eyes about looking for any sign of an enemy. *There is no one else in the meadow. Is this a trap? And what happened to his minstrel clothes? He's wearing just a simple tunic.*

Newcomb glanced at his rusk flying just in front of him, its fur standing up on end.

What do you see, little one?

Newcomb scanned the meadow again but saw nothing. He stopped at the meadow's edge, pondering his decision. Did he race in to rescue the boy and possibly enter a trap, or wait and see what had alarmed the rusk?

"Newcomb," Lassiter cried out in desperation, his voice racked in pain, "make them stop." The boy writhed in agony. "Please, make them stop."

Newcomb cast logic and strategy to the wind and followed his heart. He galloped into the meadow and thundered across the field.

His rusk still led the way with fur up on end, but Newcomb saw no sign of danger. When he was close enough to Lassiter to dismount, he witnessed a bizarre scene and immediately pulled back on the reins. Lassiter's body began to change in shape and dimension, as if invisible forces were stretching his flesh and bone in unholy contortions.

Lassiter was gone. In his place was a man with a familiar face, mounted upon a bull gor. His hair was cleanly shaved off and he bore a scar on his forehead in the shape of a gor. But it was his eyes that made him recognizable. They were filled with madness and each operated independently of the other.

"Paradin," Newcomb stammered, horrified at his mistake.

Paradin flashed a wicked smile.

"I remember you. You're a storyteller - as am I. Behold, I am now the Gor King."

"You are no more a storyteller than your beast can talk," Newcomb fired as his rusk hovered and awaited the command to attack.

"Tsk, tsk, tsk," the Gor King replied with the clicking of his tongue. "Time will tell, but you do have someone I need to meet, a boy by the name of Lassiter."

"Never," Newcomb shouted as he signaled the rusk to attack.

The rusk zoomed forward in a streak of brown, but the Gor King shot up his hand with speed no human could match, and snatched him in flight. The Gor King cocked his head to the side. With his vul jen eye he studied the rusk; with his Paradin eye he glared back at Newcomb.

"Tsk, tsk, tsk. What's this, this *this*," the Gor King boomed in Paradin's sing-song, mad form of communication. "A rusk, a rusk, to poison me, to poison me. But death, you'll find, will set you free."

The Gor King dangled the squirming rusk out over his gor's salivating mouth. The bull gor roared and opened its jaws. Paradin tossed the rusk within and the gor slammed his mouth shut.

"*First Blood*" the Gor King exclaimed triumphantly with arms raised in the air. "Fresh meat, my pet, just as I promised. Is it not better than dead, maggot-covered flesh?"

The gor roared its approval and glared at Newcomb. In a primitive form of man-talk, he declared: "Long live Cauldron. Brairtok. Death to Only."

Newcomb was dumbfounded not only by his rusk's demise but by the fact that the gor talked.

"Impossible," he stammered. "Gors don't eat fresh meat. It is forbidden. And gors can't talk."

"And yet he *does,* and he *did,*" the Gor King stated as he patted his animal's massive neck. "As a storyteller, surely you know the oracle. *Tales shall crush steel when gors have a king.* And to steal from one of your familiar quotes, *The Cauldron dances with the impossible.*"

Realizing the nemesis he faced was far more powerful than he, Newcomb turned his steed toward the woods and dug his spurs into its flanks.

I must warn the others and find Lassiter before this Gor King does. I've never seen a power like his, even during the Dark War.

Newcomb focused all of his attention on reaching the edge of the forest. Shadowed forms stepped out of the darkness and entered the meadow.

Hundreds of gors, amassed as one. How can this be?

The Gor King barked out orders that, carried by the gwyr, overpowered any and all sounds in the meadow.

"Come to battle, my faithful army. No longer do the stories of Claire reign. May the tales of the Cauldron rule forever. Death to the Only."

The gor army rose as one onto their hind legs.

"Death to Only!" they roared back in simple man-talk. Dropping to all fours, they charged Newcomb.

Dark, primal barks echoed through the woods.

"What was that?" DeMorley squeaked.

"Sounded like a gor," Draemel replied, "but something's different about it."

"I *know* what a gor sounds like," DeMorley shot back at Draemel. "That was too deep in tone to be..."

"Something's wrong," Draemel interrupted. "Something's very, very wrong."

He tried to fathom how a gor could bark so loudly and what could make them sound almost...human. Unable to find an answer to the mystery, Draemel's warrior instincts told him that Newcomb and Lassiter were in grave danger.

"Cut me loose," he ordered DeMorley as he strained against his bindings. "I need to go help them."

DeMorley snickered at him.

"Do you think I'm that stupid?"

Draemel stopped wrestling with the ropes and glared at DeMorley.

"Newcomb and Lassiter are in trouble. Cut me loose, you fool."

"Cut you loose so that you can kill me, get Lassiter and receive all the bounty," DeMorley said with a cocky grin. "No, I don't think so. Besides, how do *you* know they're in trouble?"

Draemel's jaw tightened.

"You don't," DeMorley said, his grin widening. He spun away from Draemel and fired back over his shoulder, "You've finally met your match. Fate has smiled upon me today. You're tied to a tree unable to give chase, while Newcomb is rescuing Lassiter, from what, I have no idea."

He stopped to ponder the matter but then quickly waved a rubbery hand to dismiss it.

"I suppose what's out there isn't important. Whatever it is, Newcomb can defeat it with his rusk and a story. What *is* important is that I journey to Claire to receive my reward and..."

DeMorley's reverie was interrupted as more harsh barks peppered the woods, only this time there was more than just a pack bellowing. DeMorley froze in his tracks with his back to Draemel.

"Odd," he pondered aloud. "That sounded like a large number of gors. But gors don't travel in large groups."

"*Exactly,*" Draemel confirmed as he squirmed to loosen his knots. "Newcomb is in serious trouble."

"Well, if he is," DeMorley replied, "what am I supposed to do about it? Besides, he's never appreciated me anyway..."

"Shut up you fool, and cut me loose."

"...and besides, should he die, that leaves more treasure in Claire for me when..."

Dark ominous voices from afar cut off DeMorley's next words.

"Did you hear *that?*"

DeMorley stared flabbergasted into the woods.

"It sounded like all the gors said..."

"'Death to Only,'" Draemel replied, gritting his teeth as he pulled against his restraints.

DeMorley tapped a contemplative finger against his pointy chin.

"But gors can't talk."

"You *idiot,*" Draemel shouted. "Whatever's out there isn't just after Newcomb and Lassiter. They want *us* as well."

"Perhaps," DeMorley rebutted, flashing Draemel a condescending smile. "But I'm more cunning than you give me credit for. After all, you're the one who is tied to a tree."

"For *once* in your life, think about someone other than *yourself.*"

"*Please,*" DeMorley chortled as he wagged his head at Draemel. "Don't flatter yourself. Our hearts beat with the same purpose: self-preservation. The only difference between us is that my weapon has strings."

"Yes, yes, *yes,*" Draemel offered with firm head nods. "Guilty as charged, but if Lassiter is to be King of Allsbruth, even a cold-blooded killer like me can comprehend his importance."

DeMorley gathered what little courage he had and stared into Draemel's eyes.

"As can I. It means I'm to live a regal life - and you're to die."

Draemel's eyes narrowed.

DeMorley flashed an arrogant smile, turned on his heel and marched toward his horse. He gathered in the reins and then stiffened as if spooked by an unresolved question that niggled the back of his mind.

"Now, how is that possible?" DeMorley pondered aloud. "Lassiter's cry came from far over there..."

DeMorley faced in the direction Newcomb had galloped toward.

"While Blomseth is back over there."

He spun around and faced the opposite direction.

"So how did Lassiter travel so far in so little time?"

DeMorley's eyes filled with panic. He dropped the reins and faced Draemel.

"That wasn't Lassiter crying for help."

The color drained from Draemel's face as he too realized how they had all been deceived.

"Someone or something imitated his voice," he muttered. "Newcomb's walked into a trap."

"And Lassiter," DeMorley said as he faced in the direction of Blomseth, "is in more danger than I imagined."

Despite the urgency of the moment, both men pondered the situation. Whatever was beyond the woods, DeMorley feared it more than Draemel's gor weapon. He quickly deduced that setting Draemel free offered him the best chance of survival. Draemel, on the other hand, considered himself connected with Lassiter because he served the boy's father in the Dark War, and longed to fight for the boy's life.

DeMorley spoke up first.

"If I cut you free, do you promise not to harm me."

"Yes," Draemel snapped. "Now please, *hurry.*"

DeMorley sprinted to the tree and pulled out his dagger. Draemel felt the ropes loosen, and in an effort to get to the battle sooner than later, pulled with all his might and broke the final strands. DeMorley, fearing retaliation, cowered on the ground, but the bounty hunter hopped over him without a backward glance and darted for his horse. Draemel leapt into the saddle.

"Go to Blomseth," he ordered DeMorley. "Find Lassiter and protect him. Do you understand? I'll be there shortly."

"Yes, of course," DeMorley replied, shocked to not only hear himself comply to an order but to also put his life in harm's way, "but why do you suddenly care so much about the boy?"

Draemel spurred his horse and flew past the minstrel.

"Because I knew his father."

Chapter 40

The Battle of the Storytellers

When the gors emerged from the woods, Newcomb pulled back so hard on his reins that his horse nearly sat back on its haunches. Newcomb stared spellbound at the army of gors advancing toward him.

Gors don't attack or gather as a unified force. This defies logic and the teachings of Claire.

He glanced over his shoulder at the Gor King, who continued to watch from atop his bull gor in the middle of the clearing. It was the creature's demeanor that had Newcomb on edge. His shoulders were slumped forward, as if he were relaxing after a long trek, and the only motion was his head that occasionally snapped from side to side, like a scavenging bird, to take in the whole ordeal.

And this ghoul, Newcomb reasoned, *has no doubt formed an alliance with the Cauldron. But why is he so calm? Doesn't he realize I could tell a story and end this game right now?*

As if in answer to Newcomb's thoughts, the Gor King righted his shoulders and shouted to his charging horde.

"Chase. Eat. Fresh meat."

Newcomb roused from his daze and dug his heels into his horse's flanks. He galloped across the clearing toward the woods on his left and the gor army gave chase. Their thundering paws and rhythmic snorts increased in volume, and Newcomb knew they were gaining ground. Horses did not have the stamina of gors, and his poor mount would run itself to death if he didn't do something.

He pushed aside his fears and focused instead on the thicket up ahead, but when more gors emerged from that region, he once more pulled back on the reins. The gors formed a line along the meadow's edge, rose up on their hind legs, and roared. Then in unison, they dropped to the ground and charged.

The Gor King snickered as he watched the two units closing in on Newcomb like giant pincers, one from the rear and the other from the front. Filled with the power of the gwyr, the Gor King shouted to both groups.

"My faithful ones. Encircle him. Bring him to me."

The two columns fanned outward until their edges connected around Newcomb in a giant circle. The gors slowed the pace to a walk and squeezed Newcomb toward the epicenter where the Gor King sat.

Newcomb galloped within the corral of gors in search of a gap, but finding none, came to a halt. The gors also stopped. Despite their massive numbers, the Gor King's command and the promise of fresh meat, they could not dismiss Newcomb's scent. This was a storyteller, and one of immense power. Their fear kept them at bay. At least for the moment.

The meadow grew unusually quiet. Even the insects and animals of the meadow and woods were hushed, like the calm before a storm.

The gors' stench washed over Newcomb and his mount. The horse pranced about in fear while Newcomb gagged and fought back the urge to vomit.

"Ah," the Gor King declared as he sniffed Ebon's cold wind. "How I love the scent of gors. It purges my senses, do you not agree?"

Newcomb regained control of his whinnying horse, swallowed his nausea and glowered at his nemesis.

"Since you know who, and what, I am, you know I won't fall prey to your trickery or your twisted tales," he countered.

The Gor King raised an arm and swept it around his circle of gors.

"I beg to differ, storyteller from Claire, I beg to differ."

Newcomb's silvery hair blew in the breeze as his jade green eyes burned into the face of the Gor King. The Paradin eye hopped from Newcomb to his army, then back again, while the vul jen eye narrowed to a thin slit of rage. Despite the mystique of the gathering of the gors, and Paradin's display of power as the Gor King, Newcomb did not panic. Although he had not been in combat for some time, his fighting instincts were as sharp as ever. Instead of waiting for the Gor King's next move, he decided to begin the battle.

He called out to Claire for a story.

"My king," Newcomb bellowed in the direction of Claire. "Hear my cry and whisper a story against this foe."

The Gor King cupped a hand to his ear, as if listening for a reply.

"Tsk, tsk tsk," he chided in Paradin's singsong voice. "What's this, this, this?"

He goaded his mount closer to Newcomb.

"A call to Claire, a call to Claire, but such a cry can't leave my snare."

In a smooth relaxed motion, he removed his hand from his ear and pointed to his twitching eyes.

"You'll see, I say."

He pointed to the scar on his bald head.

"You'll know, I know."

His hand dropped and once again grabbed a clump of his bull gor's fur. He glowered at Newcomb.

"The Cauldron's drone, the Cauldron's drone rules this day; you're all alone, you're all alone. What will you say, what will you say?"

Newcomb dismissed the threat and continued to call for help as a shadow crossed over the meadow. Newcomb squinted up into the bright sky in hope that Manno Vox or some other ally had created such a shade. Instead, he gasped in horror at the sight.

"You see, you see," the Gor King crowed. "So marvelous a sight. So great is their might. Vul jens, vul jens, too many to count. Circle the sky, ready to fight, ready to fight."

Newcomb lowered his gaze and stared into the face of the Gor King.

"I am a storyteller from Claire who can, and who will, annihilate your forces with a story."

The Gor King bowed his head in mock humility and extended his arms with palms raised.

"Then please," he answered in the vul jen's voice.

Unlike Paradin's mad rhymes, the vul jen delivered each word in a calm, monotone, devoid of emotional rises and falls. The voice made Newcomb's skin crawl and his anger boil.

"Tell us such a tale, storyteller from Claire. My faithful ones would...enjoy...a good story before they feast on your flesh."

Newcomb's jade green eyes burned red with anger. He snapped his gaze away from the Gor King and turned his attention to the encircling gor army.

"Remember the days of promise," Newcomb shouted to the gors. "Remember the days of old when goodness flowed like the River Arrgient."

The gors turned their heads about as they pondered his words. Some grunted as if in response, or perhaps in an effort to reply. Newcomb was encouraged, and continued his tale.

"The Only gave you so much. You were never without food. There was peace amongst your herds."

The Gor King nodded his head as if to confirm the validity of Newcomb's tale, and using his vul jen voice, he addressed his army.

"Yes, indeed, you remember this story, don't you, my faithful ones? Dead meat; rotten spoils from another's hunt; filth; and disrespected by all." The Gor King snapped his head back around toward Newcomb. "Yes, storyteller of Claire. Those days we *do* remember. We remember them well. And we are determined to never see them again."

The gwyr pulsed through the Gor King, and his hatred for the stories of Claire flowed like a flooded river against a dam too small. Rage gushed out of his mouth like an earthquake.

"Attack him," he ordered his gors.

The beasts broke out of their trance and roared in unison. The circle of death pressed inward. The Gor King smiled at Newcomb, and much like his eyes, one half of his mouth twitched while the other half barely moved at all.

"So be it," Newcomb declared as he prepared to fight. "Death begets life."

He closed his eyes and a waterfall of colorful light gushed out from him and spilled out onto the meadow.

"I am Newcomb," he thundered as he rose off his horse and hovered above the field, his lights now a dazzling display of amazing hues no human could put a name to. "I am a storyteller for the King of Claire. A teller of tales that bring life."

The ground shook and rumbled. Spooked by the quaking sod, the gor army stopped their attack and looked to the Gor King for guidance or protection.

The Gor King remained calm. If he were the least bit concerned by Newcomb's story or the lights that bounced off the ground like sparks from a smith hammering red-hot metals, he did not show it.

"Lies, lies, *lies*," the Gor King chimed out to Newcomb. "Your king may indeed live, but his power is no more. Behold Ebon's might." He placed three fingers over the gor scar on his forehead to salute the Dark Flame and bellowed: "I am the Gor King; storyteller for the Cauldron. You are powerless before me."

He removed his fingers and pointed up at Newcomb floating overhead. The lights of Newcomb's power blinked off and the Only's storyteller tumbled from the air and crashed to the ground.

Newcomb rose to his feet as Ebon's fierce winds slammed into him. He staggered about to regain his balance. Though dazed by the fury of the Gor King's attack, he continued shouting out his story with gusto. But the Gor King's tale started to overpower his thoughts, and Newcomb's words flew away as if they were bits of paper he could no longer clutch in his hand.

Weakened by the ordeal, Newcomb dropped to his knees. Stunned by how powerful the Cauldron had made Paradin, Newcomb nevertheless rallied his thoughts and tired muscles to continue to battle. Once more, he slowly stood to enter the fray of tales.

The Gor King urged his mount to where Newcomb wobbled about against the winds. The gor army, their confidence revived by their leader's tale, crept closer and salivated, wondering who would be blessed to taste first blood and fresh meat.

"Where is the boy," the Gor King asked Newcomb.

"I travel alone," Newcomb spat out.

"More lies," the Gor King shouted with an accusing finger aimed at Newcomb. And then to his bull gor: "Show him what we do with liars."

The gor struck Newcomb with his front appendage and catapulted him through the air where he landed with a *thud* in the grass. Newcomb sat up and felt the side of his head where he had been struck. Blood oozed onto his hand. His head pounded from the blow, and the pressure from the drone threatened to crush his skull. Still Newcomb pushed himself up to stand and face his adversary. He glanced skyward for any sign of help.

The Gor King followed his line of sight.

"Tsk, tsk, tsk. What's this, this, this," he taunted. "Claire's blue sky is graying with mist. Ironic, horrific or a strange fateful twist. Those you love and promised to not fail will be crushed by my gors, what a heartbreaking tale."

"You disgust me," Newcomb hurled as he spat blood from his mouth.

The Gor King spurred his bull gor closer to Newcomb and leaned out over him.

"I am a storyteller for the Dark Flame, and have powers you can only dream of."

Newcomb's eyes narrowed.

"*Behold,*" the Gor King bellowed.

In a manner that mocked Newcomb's abilities as a storyteller, he lifted his arms skyward and rose off his bull gor. He hovered above Newcomb as glistening black and grey droplets of darkness splattered the ground below.

"As a storyteller for the Dark Flame, I can read the boy's story in your heart. And look! I see how it serpentines around your tale of gladness. Lassiter is his name. How precious. A king he is to be. How delusional. That, my pitiful storyteller, will never be. Now, tell me where he is and I will be merciful to you as well as the boy. You will die, but you will die quickly."

Newcomb mustered all his inner strength to shield his story from the Gor King, but as hard as he battled, he could not restrain him from pressing in.

"Tsk, tsk, tsk, what's this, this this," the Gor King sang. "Fear, fear, fear. How dear, dear, dear."

Newcomb lifted his heavy head and growled up at the shimmering shape: "Return to your pit of pain."

"A fighter you are," the Gor King observed as his vul jen eye widened with joy. "And yet, your story *oozes* with horror. It is so prominent within you, that I can smell it even at this height."

Newcomb shook his head.

"I don't fear death, for death begets life. To be with the Only is..."

"Blah, blah, blah," the Gor King interrupted with the wave of his hands as if to disperse Newcomb's words. "I know all that storyteller *gibberish*. And yet, despite such banter you worry that your life has been a tragic waste; a mound of gor dung. You wonder if you have failed the ones you love, and if great harm will come to them. These are good things to fret over, storyteller, for I have come to give life to your deepest reservations. Perhaps I will allow you to live so that you may die twice. First, as you watch your suspicions become reality and consume your loved ones. Second, by a physical death as my faithful ones consume you alive. What a quandary," the Gor King chirped in a happy tone as he tapped a finger on his chin. "Which ending shall I choose?"

Newcomb battled against the winds and the Gor King's might and slowly raised his face to the sky. His body was racked with pain, but his will was firm.

"My name is Newcomb," he muttered with eyes fixed on the hovering Gor King. "I am a storyteller for the Only. I have been commissioned to protect the future King of Allsbruth who will..."

"Who will forsake his throne in order to become a *minstrel.*"

Newcomb gasped.

"Don't look so surprised. I see it all within your thoughts. I see him dressed like a jester...and what's this?" the Gor King stared down into Newcomb's face. "You even made a pet name for him: *Lassiter the drunk peacock.* How delightful," he said with his twisted smile. "Another tragedy to add to your tale, a story of incredible waste - Sir Newcomb, the *Dung Master.*"

Newcomb regained his composure and refocused his will and his strength on the fight at hand.

"I am Newcomb, a storyteller for the Only..."

"Either way," the Gor King blasted, "I will find out where he is, whether by reading your thoughts or in following his scent. Now, tell me where Lassiter is and I will allow you both to serve the Cauldron with power and glory the likes you have never seen. The boy will become king and great will be his reign. You will serve him faithfully as you have always dreamed, and your story will have a beautiful ending. Join us and taste the sweetness of life. All you need to do is leave the tales of the impotent one of Claire. I implore you once more, as one storyteller to another; where is the boy, the one you call Lassiter, the future King of Allsbruth?"

Newcomb staggered about, not only because of the winds and the Gor King's might, but because the offer was tempting. The Gor King had read his inner emotions accurately: he longed to be guaranteed that all he sacrificed and strived to accomplish for Lassiter would come to pass.

Alone, isolated from Claire and surrounded by his enemy, Newcomb's resolve began to melt like butter over a hot flame. His tongue pressed against his bloodied teeth, ready to shout surrender and offer up Lassiter's location.

What else can I do? What other option do I have? At least the boy will live.

He glanced up at the hovering Gor King and then scanned the faces of the encircling gors. Something deep within him stirred and grabbed hold of his remaining hope. Visions of Anessatia and Hornlynn flooded his battered mind and he found himself disgusted with himself that he had abandoned Lassiter so quickly. He shook his head as if to cast out the destiny of being branded a traitor and instead, once again aligned himself with his sole purpose of protecting Lassiter...

...no matter what.

Newcomb drew in a deep gulp of air and stared into the twitching eyes of the hovering Gor King.

"I am Newcomb," he delivered through clinched teeth. "I am a storyteller for the Only. I have been commissioned to..."

"Silence him," the Gor King ordered down to his bull gor.

The blow was swift and Newcomb tumbled across the ground like a doll thrown by an irate child. Dazed and tasting blood again on his tongue, Newcomb slowly stood up and wobbled about as he regained his senses and strength. He lifted his head and stared once more into the Gor King's face.

"I am Newcomb. I am a storyteller for the Only..."

"Shut up," the Gor King spat at him. "This is the last time I'll ask. Where is he?"

A smile creased Newcomb's face, as something akin to joy lit his eyes.

"I have been commissioned to protect the future King of..."

The third strike came from overhead and sent Newcomb crashing to the ground. Waves of searing pain rocketed through his body. He couldn't move his shoulder. His ears rang. Clumps of his silvery hair, matted in blood, hung down in his face. Yet despite the physical agony, it was the horror of possibly failing to accomplish what he was born to do as a storyteller, and as Lassiter's mentor, that were the most crushing of all pains.

The Cauldron caught wind of Newcomb's dark apprehensions and whispered.

"Turn to me. End the pain. Are you not deserving of so much more?"

Ebon's drone pounded his weakened mind with relentless fury as the whisper of the Dark Flame continued to tempt. Newcomb tried to rise to his knees, but he was too injured. He fell back to the ground. Broken within and without, he cast a silent whisper to the King of Claire.

"Death stalks me. My strength is all but gone. Grant me enough might to die well. Forgive me for failing Lassiter. Help him become who he was born to be."

"I heard that," the Gor King barked from his floating perch. "Here is the truth that you will carry to your grave: The boy will die by my own hands. My gor army will tear him to pieces. There will be nothing left to bury."

The Gor King floated back down to remount his bull gor while his army pawed the ground and growled for first blood and fresh meat. The Gor King jerked his head around to address his impatient army.

"I am the Gor King," he yelled at them with a fist to his chest in a salute to Ebon. "I will say who gets *what* and *when.*"

It was during this lapse that a whisper came upon the wind, like a lark's call in spring.

"Newcomb. My delight!"

The Gor King spun his head around to find the whisper that emanated all about. Unable to find the source, the Gor King addressed his legion of gors with a glee-filled voice.

"Listen, my faithful ones. The Only speaks from afar. He is afraid to face us. How pathetically *weak* he is. He won't even come to aid one of his storytellers."

The Gor King's smile faded, and his vul jen eye darkened. He glowered down at Newcomb.

"How does that make you feel, *Dung Master*? You have dedicated your life to selflessly serve this *king*, and where is he now?" the Gor King mocked.

Pouting like a spoiled child, the Gor King looked this way and that for the King of Claire. With a dramatic shrug he offered, "He's not here."

His clownish expression faded and was replaced by the Gor King's evil countenance.

"No, he's not here. He watches from Marsien Vur," he hissed down to Newcomb. "From the comfort of his palace while you suffer...alone...at my hand."

Newcomb ignored the rant, and focused instead on the whisper's message. Renewed strength flowed through his battered body.

"You have done well," the whisper from Claire announced. *"Victory is yours."*

The Gor King chortled.

"Victory," he fired in the direction of Claire. "Victory in death?"

He turned his attention back to Newcomb lying in the brown grass matted with his own blood.

"You failed to protect the future King of Allsbruth. Your time is up. Death begets death. First blood. Fresh meat."

"Look up," the Only's whisper ordered Newcomb.

Newcomb rolled his head to the side and gazed skyward. Not sure if he was witnessing a vision or reality, he pushed himself to his knees for a better view. He squinted through the blood that burned his eyes and marveled at the vision that filled the sky. It showed a great battle being led by a young leader adorned in armor. He raised his visor.

"Behold," Newcomb declared as pointed up into the sky. "I see the future. Lassiter. The King of Allsbruth."

The Gor King turned his head skyward, but all he could see were the clouds and the vul jens circling about.

"You're deranged," he chided.

Newcomb, his eyes fixed on the vision, staggered to his feet and the whisper spoke again.

"Newcomb, rest in this: Your life was of great purpose. Lassiter will do well. Death begets life!"

"Long live the stories of Claire," Newcomb declared, knowing that his life would soon end. "The Army of the Only will be victorious."

"Shut up," the Gor King roared as he fidgeted in his saddle. For the first time since their battle began, he was spooked. He believed he had quarantined Newcomb from Claire by his might. How was it possible for the whisper to break through his stronghold? As the Gor King's confidence turned to panic, he envisioned Manno Vox racing through the sky to join the fight.

"Strike him down. Hard," he ordered his bull gor. *"Hurry."*

Claws ripped open Newcomb's back. He screamed in agony before crashing to the ground. The gor army, stimulated by the sight and scent of fresh blood, pawed and grunted, eager to charge in for fresh meat.

Newcomb's eyes blinked open. His mind reeled from the blow, yet, despite the attack his body was free of pain. He sucked in labored breaths, but realized that his fears of living a failed life were also gone. Blood flowed into his eyes, but now he did not feel the sting. In this dreamlike, pain free state, he heard another sound emanating from Claire.

A beautiful waltz.

He had never heard the music before, yet he knew it was the inaugural song for a young storyteller. The music's tone and meter fashioned visions of a girl of fourteen summers, dazzlingly arrayed in a white dress and wearing a midnight blue cape.

The gor army also heard Ela Claire's waltz and it had a mystical effect on the beasts, soothing their primal instincts for first blood. Some were even lulled to a peaceful state and reclined on their back haunches to listen and enjoy the melody. Others rolled their heads from side to side, keeping time with the meter of three.

The waltz attempted to woo the Gor King away from his allegiance with the Cauldron, but his heart and will were too seared with the Dark Flame's purposes. Instead, he drank a deep draught of the gwyr to rally his forces back to their mission.

"Ignore the song. Rise. Prepare for first blood."

The Gor King's voice shook off the waltz's mystical effect. Once more, the army fell into formation. They bared teeth and waited for the order to attack.

Satisfied he had control of his army again, the Gor King ordered his bull gor to raise his right front leg. It dangled above Newcomb, ready to crush him to death.

"I know of this *Ela Claire*, too," the Gor King hissed down to Newcomb. "My faithful ones have a special day planned for her as well."

Newcomb turned away from the gor's hovering leg and resigned himself to his fate. Within his thoughts the whisper from Claire merged with Ela Claire's waltz. Newcomb had the strange sensation of being lifted off the grass by the music as if each note was an invisible hand. As the music pulsed and grew in orchestration, he found himself free of pain and worry. He floated above the meadow. In his dreamlike state, he glanced down. The circle of gors continued to prance, and the Gor King continued to hurl insults, and the bull gor still hovered over his own body that lay in a pool of blood.

The whisper and waltz directed Newcomb's gaze to the distant woods on the meadow's edge. Hiding behind a large tree was the silhouette of a man aiming a crossbow at the Gor King. His reddish hair fell about his shoulders and covered a wicked scar on his left cheek.

After being freed by DeMorley, Draemel galloped off in the direction of the gor grunts. The early morning light was dissolving the forest's deep shadows and he strained into the dimness with the eyes of a seasoned warrior and bounty hunter. The last thing he needed to do was to race blindly into a trap. All the while, his thoughts were obsessed with two anomalies: the gathering of gors and Hornlynn's son - Lassiter.

He urged his mount down an incline, and as his horse hopped a small creek, he tried to imagine how it was possible for gors to assemble in so large a group. They were scavengers, usually timid creatures that prowled about in small herds feeding on the carcasses of dead animals. Yet he was confident he had heard hundreds barking, possibly even *talking*, if that was possible. And there was nothing timid in the way they sounded. The only explanation Draemel could come up with to explain such behavior was the Cauldron.

Draemel ducked beneath a low-lying tree limb as flashbacks of his days with Hornlynn at Min Brock blazed across his mind. Each memory dredged up feelings he had suppressed since the fall of Min Brock...since Merriam's death. Since his son's death. Like alternating blasts from fiery furnaces and icy winds they came: joy and agony; love and loss.

Merriam... he mused as he steered his mount around a tall oak.

His throat tightened with grief and his breathing became erratic as wave after wave of dormant emotions crashed against him. He allowed himself to envision her face once again, something he had denied himself since her death, and he relished her impish grin and jewel-like eyes. For a brief moment, he basked in her love. He inhaled her wondrous scent and could feel her warm body pressing into his.

The moment passed, and Draemel shook off the sensations and focused on the task at hand.

Until Lassiter's face popped into his thoughts.

Draemel knew Hornlynn had a son, so Newcomb's revelation did not catch him completely off guard. The surprise was that Hornlynn had never mentioned his son or wife by name. At the time, Draemel did not think anything of it. Now, he realized Hornlynn had done so to protect their identities, and their connection to the throne of Allsbruth, from the Cauldron. Draemel's admiration for his fallen commander grew to new heights.

Farron...

He envisioned his young son toddling to his outstretched arms.

If you were still alive, you'd be Lassiter's age.

Once more, he shook the memories with their accompanying emotions from his mind, but they had done their work. His passion to fight for a cause larger than himself had been resurrected.

He galloped through the woods like a man possessed, toward uncertain danger, much like he had on his return to Hoitt to champion Merriam and Farron. He only hoped that this time he was not too late.

As the woods thinned, Draemel caught the strong pungent scent of gors. He pressed on, and up ahead, he saw the clearing full of gors...hundreds of them. The sight was staggering. The largest herd he had ever seen was not more than five cows and a single bull.

The stench from this massed army of gors was overpowering, but Draemel did not flinch or gag. He had smelled worse on the battlefield of Min Brock. His mind was focused on the task at hand. He drew upon all his skills and experiences fighting in the Dark War or hunting men for pay. He was just thankful the wind was in his favor and did not carry his scent to the gors.

Faces of those he loved, and who he felt he failed - Merriam, Farron and Hornlynn - drove him onward to face so great a foe. He vowed he would not fail to rescue Newcomb and Lassiter; that he would sacrifice his life if necessary. In fact, he welcomed the notion of death as he realized how tired he was of seeking revenge.

He pulled back on the reins to settle his horse, then he jumped off and tethered the animal to a bush. He retrieved his crossbow and a quiver of bolts. He cocked and loaded the weapon.

Once armed, he swung the quiver over his shoulder and worked his way on silent feet toward the army of gors. He stepping lightly to avoid cracking twigs or rustling leaves, a skill he learned as a warrior, and that had paid off handsomely when hunting men for pay. When he was as close to the meadow as the available cover allowed, he crouched behind a large tree for a better view.

The gor army shuffled about, eager to charge forward and attack whoever, or whatever, was in the epicenter. The jostling gors parted long enough to give Draemel a clear view into the center. Sitting atop a bull gor was Paradin.

Draemel flinched, unnerved by the appearance of his former partner.

Although Paradin's features appeared unchanged, there was something different about him. He carried himself with a greater purpose, or power, as if someone else ruled his thoughts and body.

Paradin's gor had one leg raised above someone lying on the ground, but the surrounding grass was too tall for him to see who it was. Draemel did not need his sense of sight to know the person's identity. Instinct told him it was Newcomb. He remembered his vow. He pictured Merriam, Farron, and Hornlynn.

Gritting his teeth, he raised his crossbow and aimed at Paradin's head. He had a clear shot. He knew he would not miss, but what kept his finger frozen in place were the countless scenarios racing through his mind of what would happen after the kill.

Would he be able to rescue Newcomb from all the gors?

Would the army of gors chase after him?

And what about Hornlynn's son, Lassiter? Would he be able to protect him, or would he fail him as he felt he had failed Hornlynn at Min Brock?

As he wrestled with what to do, he heard a whisper. It did not resonate from the woods but instead, sounded within his mind.

"Draemel, don't shoot. There are too many gors for you to attack single-handedly, and you must live."

Draemel, stunned to hear Newcomb's voice within his head, lowered the crossbow.

"I must do something," he replied in his mind.

"And you will, but not with a wasteful act of bravery."

Although Draemel centered his vision on the body in the field, Newcomb's words originated from where his spirit floated above the meadow. And although the bounty hunter could not hear the waltz, Newcomb knew that the music shielded their conversation from the Gor King's probing thoughts.

"Then what am I to do," Draemel asked.

"I have read your story. You fought with Lassiter's father, Hornlynn, at Min Brock. It was no accident that you were sent to find us."

"But I was sent to find DeMorley not..."

"I have seen the story of things to come. Be strong, Draemel. Lassiter needs you now more than ever. Teach him well."

"No. I can't. I'm not a teacher or a storyteller. I'm a cold-blooded..."

"The boy no longer needs one such as I. He needs a man like you. He must learn from a great warrior..."

"Warrior? I kill men for a few gilns. My deeds shadow me with darkness...

"Perhaps, but I've read of your love for Merriam, and your son, Farron. No man should suffer such loss. You cannot rewrite those stories, but you can Lassiter's."

Draemel searched the clearing for any sign of the boy who would be king.

"Is he here in the meadow?"

"No. Your conjecture with DeMorley was correct: Lassiter is still in Blomseth. Now hurry, for the Gor King will soon learn this as well. Leave me. Go save the king."

Draemel shook Newcomb's whisper from his head. The request was too much. He was a cold-blooded killer, not a nursemaid to a rebellious youth. His life's work had been to seek revenge for Hornlynn's death at Min Brock; to avenge the senseless slaughter of his wife and child. Besides, what could he possibly offer Lassiter in regards to becoming king - or for that matter, in becoming a man?

"Draemel," Newcomb whispered again, jolting Draemel from his introspection. *"There is nothing more you can do for me. Honor my last request. Tell Lassiter I love him. He was always like a son to me. Tell him that I am proud of him, and that he will be a great king. Tell him..."*

Newcomb stared down at his body, the gors and Draemel. Flashes of memory with Lassiter on the Isle of Lills flooded his senses. The vignettes were so rich, so full of life and hope. He could hear the gulls, smell the surf, and feel Lassiter's hand in his.

"Tell him...he was my greatest delight."

Draemel swallowed in an attempt to keep his emotions from overflowing from his eyes as he watched the Gor King lean out over the head of his bull gor. He stared down at Newcomb lying on the ground and shouted.

"Tales shall crush steel when gors have a king!"

The raised gor leg fell.

Draemel cursed beneath his breath as the gor army charged in to ravage Newcomb's body.

"Stop, stop, *stop*," the Gor King ordered his army with arms raised to press them back. "I shall decide who gets this honor."

Grunts and barks of dissatisfaction peppered the air.

"Back away," the Gor King commanded.

The gors complied and returned to their former position. Before the Gor King could address them further, the wind shifted and delivered a fresh scent to the army. The gors jerked their heads in the direction of the wind. Sauntering out into the meadow, unaware of the crazed gors hunger for fresh meat, was a herd of deer.

The sight not only turned the gor army's thoughts away from Newcomb's body, but from their Gor King's commands as well. The entire unit spun around and charged after the unsuspecting herd.

"Come back," the Gor King demanded, but even with the power of the Cauldron, he was unable to stop his beasts' primal lust for first blood. As a final act to disgrace Newcomb, the Gor King spat on his body before chasing after his army.

The deer, spooked by the stampeding gors, leapt back into the safety of the woods. The army of gors, along with the Gor King who continued to try and regain control of his army, gave chase while the vul jens flew escort overhead.

Draemel, desperate to rescue Newcomb's body and give him a proper burial, waited until he was convinced the gors and vul jens would not return. Once the natural sounds of birds and insects returned, he breathed a sigh of relief, shouldered his crossbow, and entered the meadow.

Before he had taken two steps, a fantastic horse with a rider that glowed blue like ice landed beside Newcomb. Draemel was so stunned by his appearance and sudden arrival that he froze in place.

The warrior, who had a face that danced with the colors from a rainbow, dismounted and knelt beside the martyred storyteller. Manno Vox removed Newcomb's cape and dagger and placed them in a pile off to the side. He lifted Newcomb's lifeless body into his arms and carried him back to his mighty steed. Once mounted, Manno Vox draped Newcomb across his broad lap.

"Who are you," Draemel asked, too stunned by the appearance of this apparition to even reach for his crossbow.

Manno Vox stared at Draemel. Instead of answering his question, he gave the bounty hunter his next orders.

"Prepare for war," he boomed in a voice that made the ground beneath his feet rumble. "Protect the King of Allsbruth at all costs. Train him to be a warrior-king. Prepare him well, Draemel of Hoitt."

Countless questions flew into Draemel's thoughts, but before he could ask a single one, Manno Vox spurred his horse and retreated into the sky with a flash of light.

"Why did Newcomb have to die," Draemel shouted after the wisp of light. And remembering the demise of Hornlynn, Merriam and Farron, his rage boiled and with clinched fists, he added: "Why did *they* have to die?"

The arcing light was gone.

Draemel shook his head in frustration. His eyes fell from the sky and he stared at Newcomb's cloak and dagger. He found himself drawn to them. Were they the keys to unlocking his unanswered questions? Would they give him a reason to live again?

With his eyes sweeping the area for any sign of returning gors, he strode over to the blood-matted grass and retrieved the cloak and dagger. As he turned them over in his hands, his mind turned over his unanswered question - why those he loved had died such cruel deaths.

Outraged at finding no answer, he wadded the cloak and dagger up into a ball and prepared to hurl them across the meadow. As he brought his arm back, he was stopped by the sound of a song.

He was not an expert in music, but thought it sounded like a waltz. As his arm muscles flexed to throw the cloak and dagger away, Ela Claire's waltz serenaded and massaged his tortured emotions. Visions of Newcomb flashed in his mind. He saw Hornlynn, Merriam and Farron. Although their faces only added more questions to his already clouded thoughts, he sensed that they were championing him to accept his new role as Lassiter's mentor.

His muscles relaxed, and he lowered his arm. As if in a dream, he found himself staring at Newcomb's cloak and dagger lying in his open palms. His jaw line tightened, his brown eyes narrowed in determination. He made his choice.

Clutching the cloak and dagger tight in his fist, he raced for his tethered steed.

Lassiter needed him.

And he needed Lassiter.

Chapter 41

The Martyr's Moon

Once the army from SriBrune had passed through Caace, Il-Lilliad led them eastward toward the Gilden Plains. Their pace was slower than he would have liked, not because they were warding off Ebonite attacks, nor due to inclement weather, but because every SriBrunian, including Kinmin, was awestruck with the world beyond the Onderling. Il-Lilliad found himself bombarded by a firestorm of questions.

"I knew your world only had one sun," Kinmin said as he shielded his eyes to marvel at the morning sunrise, "but I never dreamed it would be so bright, or so large."

"Perhaps that is because our terminology is misrepresented."

Kinmin flashed Il-Lilliad a puzzled look.

Il-Lilliad explained. "In your world, as with that of the Aggellon's, your suns are not really *suns* as we define the word. As you can see, our sun arcs a sky that goes into forever, while your three suns are much smaller and dangle in a sky that has a measurable end. In other words, it is impossible for a sun like ours to be contained in the Onderling. In fact, as best as any storyteller can ascertain, our sun is a behemoth and is too far away to be reached by any flying creature. Some even suggest that the sun is actually much larger than our vast world, despite it appearing smaller overhead."

He swept his arm across the horizon to accentuate his point.

"I understand," Kinmin replied with a nod, "but why does it rise and move about?"

As Il-Lilliad formed his answer, he noticed that Kinmin's leaders positioned their horses closer to listen in.

"There are two theories to this phenomenon," Il-Lilliad answered. "One is that the sun is orbiting our world, which is why you see it arcing the sky. The second premise is that the sun is stationary and our world circles it."

The leaders immediately began to debate, some amongst themselves and others directly with Il-Lilliad.

"The sun must be the one circling," one commander challenged him. "If we were the ones moving, then we would feel the motion and be unable to walk."

Before Il-Lilliad could answer, the debate became even more heated and branched off into different topics.

"How can you prove your sun is larger?"

"Why is your sky blue and not brown like ours?"

"Are there dansel lors in your rivers?"

The dispute became so intense that the SriBrunians halted their advance to debate the matter in more detail. Il-Lilliad, who typically was a man of great patience when explaining such stories, fidgeted in his saddle and turned his head this way and that, observing arguments among the warriors that looked like they might come to blows.

They were near the border of Ebon and he knew the Cauldron would soon sniff out their existence. Time was of the essence. In an effort to get the army's attention, he waved his staff over his head and shouted above their din.

"I applaud your desire for knowledge, but we are near our enemy's territory. We must keep moving and you must remain quiet. I'll do my best to answer your questions, but please remember that we are going to war - not to school."

Il-Lilliad felt them probe his thoughts like the fingers of curious children in search of hidden presents.

"*Stop* that," he scolded, his gruff tone of voice startling them out of his mind. "You may not do *that* either."

Their faces fell, for their intention to read his stories was not driven by selfishness, but by their zeal for knowledge. Kinmin offered a suggestion.

"I shall be my army's emissary. In that way, you will only have to dialogue with one SriBrunian. I can then relay the answer back to my men."

Il-Lilliad pondered the idea for a moment, then gave Kinmin a confirming nod.

So their pace continued, as did the question and answer sessions. At night, when Il-Lilliad was ready to rest beside his campfire, their queries increased all the more and were focused solely on nocturnal wonders.

"Where does your sun go?"

"Do the stars only come out at night?"

"Could stars be miniscule suns?"

"Why isn't the moon as bright as the sun?"

After several days of traveling in such a manner, Il-Lilliad was not surprised to hear their excited voices one night when he was in his tent trying to fall asleep. He turned over in an attempt to distance himself from their raucous discussions, but to no avail. He pulled his blanket up over his head to muffle their voices. Still he could hear their chatter.

With a loud huff, he threw off his covers and pushed himself up off his mat to see what the fuss was about. He hoped a quick answer would appease their curiosity so he could get a decent night of sleep for a change. He threw open his tent flap and with staff in hand, made his way to where Kinmin and his leaders pointed up through the trees.

"What do you see now?"

Kinmin pointed. Il-Lilliad yawned as he followed Kinmin's line of site. Blankets of clouds raced across the night sky.

"Your moon," Kinmin answered, "does it ever change color?"

"That depends," Il-Lilliad replied as his eyes found the faint glow marking the moon's hiding place behind the cloud cover. "Why do you ask?"

"Because moments ago, before the clouds came, it wasn't silver-blue like we witnessed the night before. It was a different color."

As if on cue, the clouds parted. As one, the SriBrunian army gasped.

Gazing down, like a one-eyed monster, was a full moon of extraordinary size. And just as Kinmin had explained, it was a new shade, the sight of which made Il-Lilliad's heart sink.

"This can't be," he stammered as he rubbed his eyes, more in an attempt to wipe the image from his vision than to clear the sleep from his eyes. He staggered backwards as if struck by an invisible assailant, and caught his balance with the help of a tree trunk.

"So this red color is not normal," Kinmin asked with eyes focused on the crimson moon.

Il-Lilliad stared up at the blood-red orb.

"No," he answered in a melancholic voice. "This isn't good, and yet, I'm equally perplexed by its appearance."

"So this is a sign, an omen," Kinmin noted, still unable to grasp the disparity in Il-Lilliad's voice.

Il-Lilliad let his eyes fall.

"The last time I witnessed such a moon was after the massacre of the storytellers in the field of reeds."

The chittering SriBrunians fell reverently silent. They were familiar with the tragic account and were suddenly filled with the same dread that had taken Il-Lilliad.

Il-Lilliad recited the tale that explained the nocturnal phenomenon, but his voice was not cheerful as it normally was when telling a story from Claire. His words shivered and quaked and were carried by a mere wisp of a breath.

"When the moon stares back like a dragon's eye, red with rage for all to behold, know that one of my delights has perished. As their blood flows, so does the Martyr's Moon glow.'"

"Your story still does not help me understand the pain I can see covering your face," Kinmin said.

Il-Lilliad looked into his eyes.

"A storyteller has been killed."

Kinmin quickly read Il-Lilliad's thoughts.

"Elabea, the girl you carry in your inner world with such grace, the one journeying to Claire to become a storyteller. You believe this Martyr's Moon is for her?"

"Who else could it be for?"

Il-Lilliad started to pace while his staff's figurine hummed a sad melody. He shook his head as he tried to fathom how such a catastrophe could have occurred.

"Aside from me, there were no other storytellers. Therefore, I have to conclude that Elabea reached Claire and became a storyteller, only to be hunted down and butchered."

And with a heavy sigh filled with lament, he added: "She was so young...so impressionable. I was certain she would be the one to turn the tide in this upcoming war of whispers."

His eyes wandered back up to the Martyr's Moon.

"How could this have happened? Why didn't the Only stop such a tragedy?"

As Il-Lilliad wiped away a tear, a whisper was heard.

"Return to SriBrune. Stay. Wait."

Spooked by the whisper, the SriBrunians looked about for its source. Kinmin's brow furrowed. He turned to Il-Lilliad for answers.

"The whisper was from the King of Claire. Evidently, he needs us to return to SriBrune. We must regroup."

"But this makes no sense," Kinmin replied as a buzz arose from his commanders who were equally perplexed by the news. "We've come so far. Does the King of Claire find us unfit allies? How have we failed?"

"Kinmin, I am as confused as you. But this much I've learned in my many summers serving the Only: a retreat is merely a temporary delay to victory."

Il-Lilliad rested his hand reassuringly on Kinmin's tiny shoulder. "SriBrune has not failed, and there is no shame in this. Pass the news quietly to your men. We head back tonight."

Kinmin nodded as more questions swirled around in his mind.

"And I hope Caace allows us reentry."

"As do I," Il-Lilliad replied with a heavy sigh as he gazed up at the Martyr's Moon. "As do I."

Brairtok sat by the fire in his great chamber sipping dark wine. Lying beside his chair on the large rug was an Ebonite tiger whose deep purrs rolled through the hall. Brairtok stared into the flames with one arm dangling beside the chair rubbing the tiger behind his ear.

Someone pounded on his chamber doors.

He did not reply. Instead, he took another sip and continued to let his fingers stroke the animal's short fur.

Fists continued to hammer his doors.

"Lord Brairtok," a male voice shouted on the other side, "please allow us to enter. We bear great news!"

"Great news?" he murmured as he patted the tiger's head. "It had better be *great* to interrupt the leisure time of your *great one*. Enter!"

The doors flew open and several commanders charged in and exclaimed, "My lord, come to the window!"

Brairtok fixed the men with a glare and took another sip of wine. His voice was deadly calm, but his words dripped with rage.

"What do you *mean* breaking protocol by storming past me like I'm a waif in the street, and then speaking before bowing?"

The men froze and passed nervous expressions amongst themselves as they realized their mistake. But instead of begging for mercy or even offering a belated bow, one commander blurted: "Forgive us, my lord, but you *must* see the moon!"

Instead of waiting for Brairtok to lead the way, as was customary of their military etiquette, they raced to the nearest window like excited schoolchildren and pulled back the long, dark drapes. Crimson moonlight flooded Brairtok's chamber, its eerie hue making his eyes appear all the more wicked.

"My, my," he said as he rose from his chair and waded through the red pool of light pouring into his chamber. His pet tiger raised his head, licked its chops and watched its master's every move.

"What have we here," Brairtok asked as he made his way to the window, knowing the answer to his own question.

"A Martyr's Moon, my lord!" one commander answered, hoping the sight would burn away Brairtok's wrath for their misconduct.

"Yes, I know." Brairtok's voice was serene which put the commanders on edge.

Brairtok leaned on the ledge and caressed the red orb with his eyes like a lover.

"The last time I witnessed this was after the March of Reeds in the Dark War. And now I see it again. You are correct, gentlemen: this is a *great sign*. For a storyteller's blood has been spilt."

Brairtok turned away from the moon and faced his leaders. His expression was childlike; a countenance they had never seen before. They exchanged nervous glances and swallowed down their rising fears. Before either one could react or respond, Brairtok spoke, his tone coy, even playful.

"Could it be for the one who entered the Onderling?" Brairtok tapped his bearded chin with his index finger. "Perhaps it was for the other, what was his name, Newtron, Nubrum, Newbottom…” He waved off the question with his hand. “No matter. What’s in a storyteller’s name anyway?”

He paced about the hall and his tiger rose from the rug and matched his gait. The commanders stared at one another, not sure if the questions were to be answered or were to be left untouched. Brairtok stopped with his back to the men and raised his hand. The leaders trembled. Brairtok turned slowly around.

“But my hope,” he chimed with a smile that put the men at ease, “is that this moon burns brightly for that urchin, Ela Claire. Her new name was no doubt given to her by…” he let his voice trail, unwilling to utter the King of Claire’s title.

“Either way,” he said, his voice once more dark and malevolent, “the Martyr’s Moon is a great portent for Ebon.”

“Victory for Ebon,” the commanders shouted in unison with arched backs and stiff salutes, relieved that they would be spared retribution for breaking military protocol. “Long live Brairtok!”

“Yes, yes,” he replied with a flippant wave of a hand and in a tone as silky smooth as his tiger’s fur.

Brairtok sauntered to the open window and leaned on the ledge. His tiger also rested its paws on the windowsill, and together, they basked in the blood-red moonlight.

“Yes. Long live Brairtok,” Ebon’s warlord repeated as he stroked his tiger’s neck.

Crimson moonbeams sliced open the dark woods beyond their fire’s glow. Only Previn saw the abnormality, for his vision was much sharper than the others. Knowing the story behind the anomaly, he knew he needed to show Ela Claire and Romlin the moon, but the woods were too dense. He would have to find a clearing.

“Follow me,” Previn said to them both. “There is something you need to see.”

“Right now,” Ela Claire yawned as she pulled her cloak tight about her to ward off the cool night air. “Can’t it wait until the morning?”

“No,” Previn answered. “Now. Tonight. There is no time to waste.”

Ela Claire gave him a quizzical look. She was familiar with that tone of voice, even when Previn had been a rusk, and tonight there was urgency in his voice.

Romlin, who was not as insightful, tossed another stick into the fire.

“Go on, Ela Claire.” He leaned back on his elbows and wiggled his feet near the flames to warm them. “I’ll keep the fire hot until you return.”

"You're coming too," Previn snapped. "Mount Bar-Treb and follow me. Now."

Romlin sat up.

"At this time of night," he whined. "We're exhausted and..."

"Now!" Previn snapped with a flutter of his wings that stirred the fire and made the flames leap higher. Within the brighter light, Ela Claire flashed Romlin a worried look. He merely shrugged.

"Okay," she answered as she urged Romlin to rise with the flick of her head. "Show us whatever it is that has you so worried."

While she climbed upon Previn's back, Romlin tugged his boots on, then pushed himself up off the ground and mounted Bar-Treb. Previn glided up through the trees while Romlin followed their flight through the woods.

Previn cleared the last limb. Ela Claire gasped in awe of the crimson sky.

"What's wrong with the moon," she whispered.

Previn did not answer. Instead, he beat a frantic pace toward a nearby rocky precipice.

"Did you hear me," she asked.

He ignored her and focused on gliding down to the cliff.

Something's really wrong, she thought. *Previn has never behaved like this before.*

She found her eyes drawn to the blood-red moon, not as one observing a rare and beautiful astronomical occurrence, but as one witnessing a tragic event; horrified to be watching a disaster unfold, yet unable to turn away.

The crimson beams washing over Ela Claire filled her with an unfathomable feeling of dread. As a storyteller, she sensed that there was a horrible explanation for the moon's unnatural appearance. With an effort she pulled her gaze away.

Previn landed on the cliff as Bar-Treb crested the final ascent and carried Romlin to their side. As Romlin hopped off, Previn fixed his site on the blood-red orb.

"It's a Martyr's Moon," Previn declared.

"A Martyr's Moon," Romlin muttered. "You dragged us away from a nice warm fire in the middle of the night to look at the moon, just because it's a different color?"

"The last time the moon appeared thus was after the massacre of the storytellers in the Dark War," Previn explained, awe mingled with mourning tinging his voice.

"When the moon stares back like a dragon's eye, red with rage for all to behold, know that one of my delights has perished. As their blood flows, so does the Martyr's Moon glow."

"I still don't understand," Romlin replied with a yawn.

Ela Claire's mouth hung open in shock.

"I do," she stammered. "The moon is a sign; a lament." She looked into Romlin's face. "This means that a storyteller has been killed."

Romlin searched her face but still was unable to grasp the deeper meaning.

"That's absurd. The only storyteller that still exists is you...and..."

Romlin's voice trailed off and as the face of Il-Lilliad floated through his thoughts. His eyes widened in horror and the message of the Martyr's Moon sunk in.

"So this moon means that Il-Lilliad is...dead?"

"I am unaware of any other storyteller, so it is the only conclusion I can make," Previn answered. His eyes blinked rapidly, as he gathered in his emotions at the thought of losing his former master when he was a rusk. "I suppose there is the possibility that another storyteller existed that neither of us were aware of. No matter, tonight is the darkest of nights, for a storyteller has perished, and with that death, the Cauldron grows that much stronger."

The full weight of the tragedy fell on Ela Claire and she dropped to her knees, overwhelmed at the loss of Il-Lilliad. With his death, she was the last storyteller. The Cauldron would focus solely on her demise. Horrified by her new reality, she let her head fall to her chest.

Romlin was unable to comprehend everything she was feeling, but could tell by her slumped body that she was not only heartbroken, but very afraid. Kneeling beside her, he draped his arm over her shoulder while Previn extended his wings to protect them from the night.

They spent most of the evening bowed in sorrow, mourning the loss of a great storyteller, and hoping against hope that all was not lost.

C h a p t e r   4 2

The Price to be King

In the hamlet of Norrburn, by the Gilden Sea, *The Twisted Spur's* door flew open. Frigid nocturnal winds swept inside the timbered walls and stirred the scents of stale ale, wood smoke, tobacco and sweat.

Patrons turned to see who had entered. No one was there.

Before one of the locals could close the door, a whisper entered and delivered a message to the tavern's unsuspecting minstrel.

"Death begets life!"

"Who said that," Lassiter asked.

"Who said *what?*" the owner answered as he slammed the door. "All I heard was the sound of the wind."

Lassiter pondered the words.

Where did I hear that saying before?

The door flew open yet again, though no one other than the minstrel and the tavern keeper turned to investigate. This time there was someone there.

Standing in the threshold was a formidable man with flowing red hair and a scar across his cheek. He held a dagger in one hand and a wicked-looking weapon made from animal bones in the other. Standing behind him was a thin man who stood in stark contrast to his companion. No one would call his appearance *formidable*.

"Who dares to barge into our hallowed hall?" a slightly inebriated man challenged from inside the tavern.

All eyes of *The Twisted Spur* turned toward the strangers.

"Sit down and shut up, you drunken fool," Draemel ordered as they entered and shut the door. "Our business is not with you."

"When you crash into *my* tavern, " the owner countered, stepping into the light, "your business *is* with me!"

Draemel addressed the skinny man behind him.

"Take this," he calmly ordered. He passed his dagger back to DeMorley and pulled another from his belt for himself. "Keep your eyes and dagger on *that* one over there," Draemel said with a nod toward the tavern keeper.

DeMorley thrust the dagger at the man who in turn, studied the minstrel's extended arm. It shook, but not from lack of warmth.

The owner roared with laughter.

"He's shaking with fear! You expect *him* to stop the likes of me," he blurted between laughs while wringing his fists.

"No," Draemel replied, his tone as dark as the night. "I only expect him to detain you. Once I get what I've come for, I'll slit you open myself."

The owner stopped laughing. As his eyes ran over Draemel's larger frame and his arsenal of weapons, his smile faded and his fists fell harmlessly to his side.

From the shadows of *The Twisted Spur*, a voice called out.

"So what is it you have come for?"

Draemel recognized Lassiter's voice.

"I'm looking for a minstrel," he said as he scanned the darkness for the boy. "We lost track of him in Blomseth where he performed at *The Golden Giln*."

"And what will you do to him when you find him," the voice inquired.

"That business is between us."

"Well, whatever business you have is now with his family."

"Family?" Draemel asked as his eyebrow arched.

"Yes," the voice replied as he stepped into the smoky light. Lassiter continued his diatribe. "I no longer recognize you, Draemel, or the one that sent you - Newcomb."

Lassiter hopped atop a table, pulled his lute from behind his back and began strumming some chords.

"These people are my family now," he declared, "and this tavern my home."

The men of *The Twisted Spur* lifted up mugs and loud cheers.

When the raucous chatter diminished, Draemel addressed the boy.

"This is *not* your home and these are *not* your people."

"You're entitled to your opinion," Lassiter said as he fingered a different chord. "All I'm telling you is that I'm not leaving."

"So you'll let these people decide your fate?"

Lassiter stopped strumming and glared at Draemel.

"Yes."

"So be it," Draemel muttered between clinched teeth.

In one swift motion, Draemel cocked his arm and whipped his dagger at Lassiter. The blade struck the lute's neck. Strings snapped one-by-one and made funny pinging sounds.

A hush fell over the tavern.

Lassiter stared at the blade that had just missed his fingers.

"You could have *killed* me," he screamed, his voice high-pitched like a frightened little girl.

"If that were my intention," Draemel replied as he gripped his gor weapon tighter, "you would be dead."

"You don't frighten me," Lassiter scoffed, though his high pitched squeal suggested otherwise.

"I don't care if I frighten you," Draemel answered in the cold hard tones of a man who was accustomed to hunting men for pay. "I don't care if you want to stay or if you believe these drunken fools to be your *family*. I have only one purpose here: to escort you away."

"So Newcomb resorts to threats and having you destroy my instrument to get his way. How petty of him," Lassiter replied as he set the lute down on the table. Rising back up, the boy planted his hands on his hips, and asked, "So how much has he paid you? I'll double it for you to leave me alone."

Draemel held his answer and let his eyes burn into Lassiter's.

"Will you really, boy? Do you have the courage to hear how much Newcomb paid for your return?"

The darkness in Draemel's voice quality commanded absolute silence in the tavern. No one even dared to breathe.

"I *knew* it," Lassiter managed at last to work some moisture back into his mouth. He pointed an accusing finger at Draemel. "Newcomb will stoop to nothing to get his way."

Lassiter crossed his arms over his chest, and as if to prove he was brave enough to take Draemel's challenge asked: "So how many gilns did he pay you?"

"First you answer me, man-to-man: do you have the courage to hear the truth?"

Lassiter dropped his arms and smirked as if appeasing a petulant child.

"Yes, I have the courage, now *tell* me!"

"It was an unfathomable amount."

"How much? Ten gilns? Twenty? *One hundred?*"

Draemel stepped forward. The regulars scooted out of his path.

"More," Draemel answered.

"More?"

"Much more," Draemel whispered.

Lassiter gleefully retorted, "How nice to know that I'm worth..."

"Do you have the courage?"

"Yes. *Yes,*" Lassiter waved his arms to accentuate each retort. "I have the courage to hear, so tell me."

Cold, brown eyes locked onto Lassiter's.

"Newcomb paid with his life."

Silence.

Lassiter's cocky expression dissolved like snow on a hot hearth. "What are you talking about?" he stammered.

"Newcomb's dead. And so, *boy*, are you really ready to pay double?"

Lassiter's face maintained an arrogant mask, but his shoulders slumped at the thought. When another thought came to mind he quickly stiffened his back and shoulders again.

"You lie! Newcomb is trying to trick me, and he sent you to do his dirty work."

"Did he?" Draemel stood calm, unflinching. "Step outside, *boy*, and witness for yourself. Or are you no longer...*brave*?"

"Witness what?" Lassiter fired back. "I'm no coward, but I'm not stupid. Once I set foot outside that door you'll jump me and cart me away to Newcomb."

Draemel retreated from Lassiter while the patrons - none of whom wanted any part of their argument - scooted chairs and tables to clear a path.

DeMorley watched the whole ordeal from his post by the door with panic-filled eyes. In an effort to appear threatening, he waved his dagger to and fro, but it looked more like a kitten boxing the air with a paw than a man threatening to attack.

Draemel chose a table far away from the door, sat down and began twirling his gor weapon in a playful manner.

"I will sit here, where your...family...can keep an eye on me. Now, go look at the moon."

"The moon?" Lassiter scoffed.

"Yes. The moon," Draemel repeated. "I believe it is called a Martyr's Moon. Surely Newcomb told you tales about such a phenomenon."

Lassiter scowled, but curiosity was one of his stronger attributes, so hopping down, he marched to the door while keeping a sharp eye on Draemel. He opened the door and glanced outside.

An enormous red moon hung above the trees of Norrburn. The crimson orb filled him with dread.

"Death begets life!" he muttered to himself, recalling the whisper he had heard only moments before. "The whisper...the words...a Martyr's Moon..."

Lassiter's heart felt heavy, as if great stones had been heaped upon it. As the red lunar beams shrouded his face with a macabre glow, Lassiter remembered the story Newcomb had told him many summers ago on the Isle of Lills when he was still just a lad. After the storytellers were massacred, the King of Claire cast the moon in red for all to witness; a sign that their blood would not go unjustified; a sign that death begets life.

Newcomb was the only storyteller left.

Newcomb?

Lassiter bowed his head.

Newcomb was like a father to me, he lamented. *He was the only person, aside from my mother, that knew me completely.*

He felt tears leaking down his cheeks.

But how do I know for certain this moon is his? What proof is there? Yes, that's it!

Lassiter spun around and challenged Draemel.

"This moon is *not* for Newcomb. Newcomb's *not* dead. It's for someone else."

"No boy, it's not," Draemel answered as he leaned his chair back against the tavern wall and continued fidgeting with his gor weapon.

"What proof do you have?"

"Inspect the dagger," Draemel said, and then, in a more condescending tone, "if you have the courage."

Lassiter shut the door and strutted back to the table where his damaged lute lay. He stared at the dagger jutting out of the neck and could feel the eyes of every patron in the tavern burning into his back. In his imagination, he pictured Draemel smirking at him. All the while, he wondered if indeed he had the courage to learn the truth.

He pushed aside his apprehensions and dragged the lute across the table. A dull, hollow tone arose from the wounded instrument. Cautiously, as if it were a viper, Lassiter picked up the lute and ran his finger along the dagger's black leather handle. He recognized Newcomb's personalized inscription on the blade.

The truth of Draemel's words shot through him like a crossbow bolt. He dropped the lute to the table where it bounced and clanged.

"This proves nothing," Lassiter denied the evidence hotly and stared at the lute wobbling on the table. "There's another explanation. There's another reason the moon is red and you have Newcomb's blade."

Another possibility came to mind and Lassiter spun around to face Draemel.

"I know. Newcomb gave the dagger to you so you could trick me into coming with you."

Draemel pulled a wad of cloth from his pack and threw it across the room. It landed on Lassiter's shoulder. He pulled the fabric close and inspected it.

Newcomb's cloak, he mused as he rubbed the cloth between his fingers. *But this can be explained. Can't it? This is simply another trick to get me to go to Claire.*

"Listen to your heart," Draemel said as he kicked one leg up onto the table and continued to lean back in his chair. "Would the Newcomb you know part with his dagger *and* his cloak?"

Lassiter knew the answer to such a question, and despite his best efforts to explain it away, he felt his heart embrace the truth of Draemel's story. Lassiter sank into a chair.

"Newcomb's really dead? But how?" he mumbled. Suddenly, he snapped his head up and shot up out of the chair that toppled over.

"You *murdered* him?"

The patrons of *The Twisted Spur* had sat idle in rapt silence, observing the squabble without getting involved in it. But now that murder was the subject, they began to murmur to themselves.

Draemel let his chair drop back down and rested his elbows on the table.

"You think I murdered him," he repeated with a chuckle as he pointed his gor bone incriminatingly at his chest.

"Yes!"

Lassiter grabbed the dagger-pierced lute and pointed it at the bounty hunter.

"It explains everything. You have Newcomb's cloak and dagger. The Martyr's Moon proclaims his death. You killed him because you wanted all the treasure from Claire!"

"Brilliant reasoning, young master," Draemel clapped his hands in mock admiration. "So explain to me; why did I bring *him* along?"

Draemel gestured with his gor weapon toward the wiry DeMorley. Lassiter searched for an answer, but nothing seemed plausible. Finally, he came across an idea.

"Because you need him to enter Claire; you don't have an invitation. Without DeMorley, you can't get your treasure."

"Perhaps," Draemel said as his eyes narrowed, "But then, why have I come for you?"

"Because..."

But there was no reasonable answer. Lassiter lowered his head.

As Lassiter sat and continued to wrestle with his emotions, Draemel took in the patron's darting glances and their hushed whispers. As a masterful bounty hunter, he could read such behavior to determine how they would react as a whole and as individuals. Most were either too old or too inebriated to pose a threat. There was the tavern owner, but even his prior disposition had changed. He now leaned against his bar and watched the events unfold while sipping a mug of ale.

A table of younger men eyed Draemel with looks he had seen too many times before: youthful zeal fueled by feelings of immortality. The last thing Draemel wanted was a fight. He had no qualms about shedding innocent blood, but it was an unnecessary interference with his purpose and mission.

Draemel shifted his attention for a moment on this table of young men. He selected his words like an archer chooses an arrow. He would use their own fickleness to his advantage and let them cast Lassiter away from Norrburn.

Draemel kept his eyes glued on their faces, but directed his words to Lassiter.

"Have you told *them* your tale?"

Lassiter raised his head.

"What are you talking about?"

"That your former mentor served the King of Claire as," Draemel paused until he had every eye in *The Twisted Spur* focused his way, "a storyteller."

A corporate gasp arose, and like reeds blown by a sudden wind, every head turned toward the boy, even the table of young men.

"A storyteller," one of the men asked as his hand slipped over the edge of the table to find his dagger. "You never told us the old man was a *storyteller.*"

Lassiter stared at them speechless.

"Impossible," another added. "All the storytellers were destroyed in the Dark War."

"Not all," Draemel interjected, setting his words like well placed sparks to tender, inflaming their fear into panic. "At least one remained. Isn't that right, Lassiter?"

"If that's true," the tavern owner added as he stepped away from the counter toward Lassiter, "then you've violated the Oracles by listening to his words. You've cursed my tavern by your very presence here."

"No, wait. I..." Lassiter stammered, stunned to see how quickly the crowd turned from praising his songs to murmuring for his blood.

"I knew it," another man shouted as he glared at Lassiter. "Your songs were *too* good. They're proof that you were trained by a storyteller."

Lassiter waved his hands in front of him in an attempt to avert their accusations.

"No, I'm anything but..."

"That explains everything, "another fired, cutting Lassiter off mid-sentence.

"I want nothing to do with those old tales," Lassiter argued as he turned about, searching for an ally.

"He has brought death to us," came the shout from the shadows.

"The legions of Ebon will destroy our peaceful village because of him," another warned.

"The Cauldron surely has heard his songs," shouted a heavyset woman near the fire.

"He's violated the Oracles. The Council will destroy us all!"

As the crowd became unified in their mistrust, Lassiter's face grew white with fear. He looked to Draemel for help, but the bounty hunter simply cocked his eyebrow and smiled.

"Kill him," one of the young men shouted as he stood up. "His death will prove our allegiance to the Oracles!"

The Twisted Spur erupted with cries for Lassiter's blood.

The table of young men stood and rushed Lassiter. They grabbed him and gruffly hauled him toward the door. Lassiter fought to get free and even tried to dig his boot heels into the wood floor to stop from being carried off. Lassiter screamed to Draemel for help. He simply leaned back and twirled his gor bone weapon. The mob dragged Lassiter outside kicking and screaming, and slammed the door shut behind him.

The tavern was empty except for two men.

"Aren't you going to do anything?" DeMorley asked, still holding the dagger in his shaking hand.

"As in your business, minstrel," Draemel replied, "timing is everything."

Outside, Lassiter was heaved to the ground. Stunned not only by the impact, but by how quickly his fortune had changed, Lassiter pushed himself up from the dirt. Someone hurled Newcomb's cloak at his feet while the mob spat curses on him.

"Kill him," the barmaid shouted. "Let us draw first blood and show the Cauldron that our allegiance is still true."

"Yes," another agreed. "He deceived us. We knew *nothing* of his storytelling associations."

Lassiter studied the villagers that encircled him like a pack of rabid wolves. Some held rocks, others gripped daggers. As the circle closed, he heard a commotion and saw men being jerked away or pushed aside as if by a force of nature.

Draemel tossed a young tough aside with ease and entered the circle to stand beside Lassiter. He raised his ghoulish gor blade and let the people in the crowd get a good look at it.

"Men and women of Norrburn," he addressed the mob. "The Cauldron salutes your allegiance. You have demonstrated your faithfulness. Now return to your pipes and your drinks and the warmth of your fire."

"How can we?" the owner demanded. "He's a storyteller."

"Storytellers must die," another added.

The mob resumed their chant for Lassiter's death.

Draemel raised his arms to settle them back down again, then raised his voice.

"Look at him. Does this *boy* really look like a storyteller?"

The patrons looked Lassiter over. Since they were only familiar with tales, and had never seen a storyteller in person, they were dumbfounded.

"Is it not said," Draemel inquired while spinning Lassiter around as if showing off a young colt at a fair, "that storytellers were powerful men and women? Friends, I know you are not fools. Tell me: does *this* look like a great storyteller from Claire? And if this *is* a storyteller, would he ever be seen in public dressed like *this?*"

Draemel swatted off Lassiter's comical hat then pulled at his multi-colored jacket. Chuckles arose from the crowd.

"Besides," Draemel added, "It's my understanding that storytellers tell stories from..." Draemel held his last word until he was certain everyone was watching and listening. The pack instinctively leaned closer. Draemel whispered, "Claire."

Eyes widened with fear at hearing the forbidden land uttered aloud. Before they could regroup to claim first blood, Draemel added: "All this fool is guilty of is singing trite songs and dressing like a..."

Draemel looked square into Lassiter's eyes, "Like a drunken peacock!"

Hearing Draemel quote Newcomb, Lassiter's face reddened with rage as the mob exploded with laughter. And like an unexpected rainstorm upon the Gilden Plains, their laughter quenched their thirst for death. One by one, they returned to *The Twisted Spur* to light up a fresh pipe and down a cold mug of ale.

DeMorley, who had stood far away from the mob during the whole ordeal, watched as the last man entered and the door slammed behind him, then stormed over to Draemel.

"They were going to *kill* him and then *us,*" he chastised.

"But they didn't." Draemel replied. "Now fetch our horses. We need to hurry before the Gor King finds us."

DeMorley huffed, but he marched off in the direction of their horses to obey.

The tavern door flew open, and Lassiter's lute was hurled out like an unruly cat. It bounced and splintered, then rolled across the ground like a burst melon to rest at Lassiter's feet. He stared down at the demolished instrument, and at Newcomb's dagger, as the light from the Martyr's Moon bathed him in its blood-red glow.

"I don't understand," Lassiter said more to himself than to Draemel. "How could my life change so quickly and so dramatically?"

Draemel scooped up the broken lute and pulled the dagger free. With a firm hand upon Lassiter's back, he pushed him after DeMorley.

"Now is not the time to answer such questions," Draemel replied.

"Will there ever be a time," Lassiter asked.

Draemel thought about the question. He could see Hornlynn's dead body on the Gilden Plains. He smelled the burned remains of his home where Merriam and Farron had perished. He felt his anger rise around his own unanswered questions.

"No," he choked between clinched teeth.

Chapter 43

Hunter, Minstrel, King

Spears of red moonlight cut an eerie pathway through the blackened woods for Draemel as he led DeMorley and Lassiter away from *The Twisted Spur.* They cantered single-file without saying a word and once they were far away from the tavern, Draemel slowed their pace.

"Trouble?" DeMorley squeaked after riding up to Draemel's side.

"No," Draemel replied with a glance back at Lassiter.

The boy's head and shoulders drooped as if he were asleep in the saddle, but Draemel knew that was not the case.

"Lassiter has been through a lot tonight. I'm sure he has many questions."

"Can't they wait until morning," DeMorley chirped as the hoot of an owl made him jump.

"No. Look at him. He's too distracted by the events of the night," Draemel noted. "Should we have to fight, he would be useless and perhaps even endanger our own lives. Stay here. I'll have a talk with him."

"Well, hurry," DeMorley half-whispered as his eyes darted from shadow to crimson moonbeam. "There's no telling what could be hiding in these woods."

Draemel dropped back beside Lassiter.

"You alright?"

Lassiter lifted his head and turned his face to Draemel's.

"So he's really dead?"

Draemel nodded.

"How?"

"Now's not the time to discuss the details, but it was Paradin. He's...different, stronger. It's as if the power of the Cauldron flows through his blood. He calls himself the Gor King."

"Gor King," Lassiter repeated with a furrowed brow. "But Newcomb's a storyteller. Why didn't he destroy him with a tale?"

Draemel shook his head.

"I don't know. I wondered the same thing. Perhaps he was unable to do so. Perhaps he was unwilling to do so."

Lassiter turned his eyes away and stared off into the dark woods.

"Did he say anything, you know, before he died?"

Draemel refrained from answering.

Lassiter spun back around to look into Draemel's face.

"Did you hear me?"

They stared at each other for a long moment, their faces awash with the glow from the Martyr's Moon.

"Yes," Draemel finally answered. "I heard you. And *yes,* he said something before dying."

"And?"

Draemel shuffled in his saddle and found that Newcomb's sentimental words sere difficult for him to rearticulate.

"He said…" His voice became unnaturally dry and soft. "…that you were like a son to him. That you were his greatest…delight."

Overcome with emotions, Lassiter pulled away from his gaze. In the quiet of his mind, Lassiter reflected on his life with Newcomb and hoped such thoughts would somehow find his mentor and honor him.

He remembered Newcomb's laugh. It was not frequent, but it resonated with such joy and wonderment, that it made anyone within earshot chuckle as well.

He recalled the large rock that jutted out of the Sea of Illsbruth like a fortress. Together, side-by-side, they would sit on its summit for hours while Newcomb told him tales of Claire. It was upon this rock, with the surf crashing about them, that Newcomb taught him of Hornlynn, his father, and how he had fought valiantly for the Only.

Even as a child, Lassiter sensed in Newcomb's voice that he respected and revered Hornlynn. As Lassiter continued to reflect and lament, he realized just how much he respected and admired Newcomb.

He only wished he had told him so.

Draemel watched Lassiter cover his face with his hands to muffle his cries. Moved by his loss, and remembering his own son, Draemel reached out to console him, but quickly stopped. Unwilling to feel his own pain, or that of another, Draemel retracted his hand and once more resumed his emotionless gaze into nothing.

Lassiter wiped his nose.

"Did you bury him?"

"No," Draemel answered with a sigh. "A warrior upon a flying horse that glowed like the moon swept him away. All he left behind were his cloak and dagger."

"Did this warrior's face look like fire in a wintry night sky?"

Draemel's curiosity was piqued, and he stared into Lassiter's wet eyes.

"You've seen him before," he asked.

"His name is Manno Vox," Lassiter nodded as he remembered that fateful night long ago. "It was back when I lived with Newcomb on the Isle of Lills. I couldn't sleep, so I went to my window to watch the waves crest in the moonlight. That's when I saw him flying - floating actually - on his horse. He fired a crossbow shaft into my door. The next day, Newcomb told me I'd seen Manno Vox: one of the Only's greatest warriors."

When Lassiter uttered his mentor's name, he grew maudlin again and more memories of their time together swept through him.

Most impressionable were the times when Newcomb entered Lassiter's chamber at night to check on him. Lassiter, who was half asleep, felt the cool sea breeze flowing through his window and sensed Newcomb kneeling beside his bed, rubbing his back and quietly reciting stories over him until he fell asleep.

Lassiter turned away as tears leaked down his cheeks. It was unmanly, he knew, and he didn't want Draemel to see. Draemel, who was not certain what to say or do, merely shifted about in his saddle.

Regaining control, Lassiter asked, "I still don't understand how Paradin could kill him. I thought Paradin would be dead by now, since you and DeMorley left him tied up."

"As did I, but evidently that's not the case. And to make matters worse, Paradin now commands an army of gors."

Lassiter wiped his eyes and flashed Draemel a confused look.

"So you witnessed this battle?"

Draemel gave a firm nod.

Lassiter's eyes drilled into Draemel.

"Then why didn't you help him?"

Draemel did not like what Lassiter was insinuating. Pride swelled and his chest rose, but instead of retaliating with an angry word or the back of his hand, he kept his feelings in check. In as calm a voice as he could muster, he replied.

"Because Newcomb ordered me *not* to."

Lassiter shook his head as if to free himself of the gruesome death scene his imagination conjured. His feelings shifted and Lassiter started to blame himself.

"This is my fault," he muttered between clinched teeth. "I should have listened to him when he visited me in *The Golden Giln.*"

"This is *not* your fault," Draemel fired back. "Newcomb was butchered by the Gor King."

Lassiter shook his head and continued to blame himself for Newcomb's death.

"Listen to me," Draemel ordered. "Newcomb told me that you would be a great king, and that I'm to train you."

"Train me? For what?"

"War."

"War?" Lassiter repeated, befuddled. "I can't lead an army of men. Newcomb was right. Just look at me. I'm nothing but a drunken peacock."

While Lassiter wrestled with the difficult truth of what he was, what he was not, of what he might never become and what he could never change, the whisper from the Cauldron flitted amongst his thoughts.

"Peacock of anguish, why trouble yourself with the unattainable? Release your heart to me and I shall ease your pain."

Although still mounted on his steed, Lassiter felt the sensation of being shoved from a cliff and falling into a black pit. He spiraled down into the abyss, his agony increasing with his dizzying descent. In desperation, he cried for help, but no sounds came from his mouth.

And just when he felt his fall would end in disaster, another whisper joined the battleground of his mind.

"Death begets life!"

Gentle and soothing was this whisper, and yet the words cut through his confusion like the sharpest battle-ax ever forged. With his last bit of will-power and determination, Lassiter reached longingly toward the new whisper.

But the Cauldron countered...

"Lies," it boomed. *"Deception!"* it rumbled. *"Look what happened to Newcomb when he obeyed the impotent whisper."*

Despite these accusations, Lassiter clawed toward the whisper of Claire as if he were digging his way out of a fresh grave.

"Are you not to blame for Newcomb's death, you drunken peacock?" the Cauldron accused. *"Had you listened to him, would he not still be alive?"*

Lassiter once more felt himself sinking deeper into the black pit, and as he descended, he heaped more blame upon himself.

The whisper from Claire would not abandon him. From deepest delight the whisper asked Lassiter, *"Why does the Cauldron fear you?"*

"I fear no mortal," the dark whisper retorted.

"Is it possible that the Cauldron sees your future, just as I do?" the Clairian whisper asked.

"His future is to be food for gors and maggots," the Dark Flame declared.

"No," the Clairian whisper asserted. *"I see a young heir choosing to forget the past and rising toward a greatness that has been offered him through the blood of his father, Hornlynn, and his mentor, Newcomb."*

A warm breeze caressed Lassiter's cheeks, and for a split instant, he was standing on the beach of the Isle of Lills with Newcomb by his side. It was in this state of wellbeing that the true whisper announced, *"Lassiter, future King of Allsbruth. Rise and fight!"*

With renewed convictions, Lassiter pressed through the deluge of accusations being unleashed upon him by the Dark Flame. The Cauldron continued hurling insults and innuendos at him with hurricane force. But with each step of his will, Lassiter's courage grew stronger.

Lassiter found himself in a dreamworld stretching his fingertips toward a shimmering veil that glistened and hummed like a magnanimous waterfall. But the vapors of the Dark Flame clawed at his imaginary hand like lions upon a helpless fawn. Despite the searing agony, despite the seeming impossibility of hope, Lassiter gritted his teeth, and with all his might, lunged toward the silver veil.

*"Death begets life!"*the whisper of Claire hailed.

Soaring like a bird, Lassiter was in a land of exquisite beauty: the grasses pulsed with life, the blue sky radiated warmth, and the mountains echoed eternal strength. High upon a granite summit, he saw a castle. Flags of white and red silk flapped in the wind as he zoomed over its walls. Carried by the wind, and unable to control his flight, he found himself flying toward an entrance into Marsien Vur's great hall. There, his flight slowed, and he floated before an enigmatic king whose black attire was regal yet subdued.

The king reached into Lassiter's pocket and removed the invitation, threw it high overhead where it exploded into balls of light that rocketed through the king. And with eyes that blazed like blue suns, the king said to him, "Long live the King of Allsbruth!"

While the words still echoed, he shot out of Marsien Vur with such speed that all he could comprehend were blurs of lights and colors. His mind began to clear, and the swirling hues faded into blackness. With a sudden gasp, he awoke.

Draemel and DeMorley stared at him, slack-jawed.

"Did you hear that voice?" Lassiter asked.

"I believe all of Allsbruth and Ebon heard!" Draemel answered, obviously spooked by the ordeal. "But tell me, what happened? You were in a daze and didn't answer us when we called. It was as if you were in a trance."

Lassiter, still spellbound by the ordeal, ignored the question and instead, asked one of his own.

"Could an army defeat the Gor King and his gors?"

Draemel lifted an eyebrow.

"Where did *that* question come from," he asked, taken aback by Lassiter's changed countenance.

Lassiter looked squarely into Draemel's face.

"I don't understand why Newcomb had to die. Nor do I have faith in the stories of Claire like he did; perhaps I will never have such insights.

Nevertheless, I cannot sit back and do nothing, especially if I'm to be king."

"Well," Draemel replied, masking his expression of respect at the boy's new resolve, "to answer your question, one would need an army of incredible strength. I too doubt Claire's tales and have little faith in anything beyond myself. But what I have seen in the last few days has convinced me of this: to win this war will take powers beyond what a sword or a lance can deliver."

"Then train me. I desire to lead such an army as King of Allsbruth. I desire to destroy Ebon's regime of darkness."

Skeptical that Lassiter's convictions could have swung in such a radically new direction, Draemel looked him over with the eyes of a seasoned warrior.

"So you're ready to leave your life as a minstrel in order to fulfill this...vision you've just had?"

"Yes."

Draemel's eyes squinted and his brow furrowed.

How is this possible? he pondered. *Lassiter possesses an inner strength that, only moments ago, was lacking. The young man who was ready to abdicate his throne is now ready to fulfill his destiny as king? Could this boy, whose father I knew so well, be the turning point for Allsbruth's future?*

"To lead such an army," Draemel continued, still not convinced of his allegiance, "you must be the greatest warrior-king Allsbruth has ever known." Draemel leaned close to him and asked in a hushed voice: "Do you remember what I asked you back in the tavern?"

Lassiter nodded.

"You asked if I had the courage to hear the truth."

Draemel gave a solemn nod.

"And so I ask again, do you have such courage?"

Even in the eerie red moonlight, Draemel could see a wry smile cross the boy's face. Draemel liked what he saw. Nevertheless, he continued to test the boy's mettle.

"It will take incredible sacrifice to become this king."

Lassiter yanked off his minstrel hat and threw it into the woods. He stared at Draemel with eyes full of fire.

"Then train me," he demanded.

"You will need more than passion and words drenched with emotion."

Lassiter pulled at his colorful coat and the buttons snapped, popping off into the dirt at his feet. He threw the garment into the night's shadows.

"You will suffer much," Draemel added.

"I have *already* suffered much," Lassiter shouted. "With Newcomb's death, I have died within! What more do I have to fear?"

"Fear this: That we may fail."

Lassiter did not flinch, nor did his hardened eyes soften or his rising chest falter. Draemel asked one more question to make sure Lassiter was speaking from the heart and not from the emotions of his loss. He grabbed Lassiter's undershirt and pulled him almost out of his saddle.

"Once we begin this journey, there is no turning back; no avenue for retreat. Do you understand?"

"Yes," Lassiter answered as he pushed himself clear of Draemel's grip. "Now bless me so I may become king."

Shocked at the request, Draemel's eyes widened.

"I can't bless you. I'm a man who has done unspeakable acts."

"Newcomb taught me the stories of Allsbruth as well as the stories of Claire. I cannot be king until I have been blessed."

Draemel sighed, and with great reluctance, unsheathed Newcomb's dagger from his leather waist strap. Resting the blade flat upon Lassiter's left shoulder, he recited words from a blessing given him many, many summers ago when he left Hoitt to fight in the Dark War.

"From this day forth, you shall commit your heart, your courage and your mind to fighting for the King of Claire. For life only comes from the Only. And by the power of the Only..."

He paused, the last phrase towering before him like a mighty oak, as strong as the day when he first heard it in his youth. Life had dealt him many a bad blow, and he denied the tenet's existence, adopting his own oaths and promises instead. Now, against impossible odds and amidst dire circumstances, the promise stood before him once more. Despite his fixed philosophies, he had no choice but to acknowledge it.

"...death begets life!"

Draemel studied Lassiter's face in the light of the Martyr's Moon and marveled at the boy's resemblance to his father. As his mind made the connection, so did his heart, and the walls Draemel had built around his losses in order to control his emotions started to crack. In a paternal voice -one he had not used since his days nurturing Farron - he concluded:

"Long live the King of Allsbruth."

His tender delivery surprised both DeMorley and Lassiter and they flashed each other confused looks.

Draemel quickly regained control over his emotions, and as his horse pranced about, shouted out in his familiar hardened tone: "Come. It's time you learn how to become a warrior-king."

Draemel led them once more through the shadows and crimson light, only this time they marched with purpose as a bounty hunter, a minstrel, and a boy willing to pay the price to be the King of Allsbruth.

Chapter 44

Thunder and Lightning

Despite the hope the Martyr's Moon gave Brairtok, he was greatly troubled. As much as he tried to deny the truth, he knew that his enemy's tactic had worked. Kundle's story had soared to the summit of Netniath to be pulled within by the unsuspecting Dark Flame. Surely by now the Cauldron had examined Kundle's tale and discovered the massacre at Thornnblen as well as the names behind such a disgrace: Manno Vox and the Only.

So why haven't I been summoned by the Cauldron?

The question pinged about Brairtok's thoughts day and night, night and day. His anguish became so great that he decided to end the matter once and for all.

Brairtok set out for Netniath.

He knew it was a risky move on his part, but he hoped that the Cauldron would interpret his assertiveness as an act of honor and devotion.

As he walked through Kise toward Netniath, he noted that the streets were deserted save for a soldier manning his post or a citizen scurrying from one business to another. A glance skyward confirmed his suspicions about the city's ominous mood: storm clouds. Puffy gray-black billows churned and rolled low, making the morning sky dark and foreboding. Thunder boomed and echoed off the fortress walls as if giant boulders rumbled down a deep gorge during a slow-motion avalanche. Lightning flashed inside the clouds like the snorts from a fire-breathing dragon, yet there was no wind or rain. Brairtok, like all the citizens of Kise, recognized that these unnatural clouds were a result of the Cauldron's wrath.

He shuddered at the thought of facing the Cauldron when it was this enraged, but he preferred facing his punishment - if any was forthcoming - instead of fretting about it constantly.

Up the winding road he trudged, his determined gait leading him up to Netniath's main entrance. With every step, he contemplated what he would expect from the Dark Flame.

Imprisonment? Torture? Death?

One thing he knew for certain: he must choose his words carefully. Very carefully.

Guards manned either side of Netniath's massive steel doors, and when Brairtok approached they saluted him before opening the doors.

Brairtok returned their salute, marched in with head held high and made his way down the dark hall to the chamber.

When he reached the chamber's ice-covered doors his bravado failed him, and he stopped to gather his nerve. A whisper, like shards of ice grating together, called to him.

"Brairtok. How nice of you to come. We've been expecting you. Please, come in."

He drew in a deep breath, opened the frigid door, and walked in.

Before he had time to bow in humility, the Council confronted him about the report.

"Death at Thornnblen," they hissed.

"Glory given to the Only."

"Manno Vox the victor."

Brairtok swallowed hard but maintained his level gaze.

"I have already arranged for Commander Kundle's execution," he interjected. "In retaliation, I'm sending more men..."

A crack of thunder outside the hall silenced his tongue. The Council continued to list the crimes against the Oracles that were discovered in Kundle's account.

"Stories and tales," the Council accused.

"Whispers of hope."

"Dreams of glory."

Brairtok slammed his right fist to his chest in a salute.

"Ebon will not submit to the whims of the Only. I swear to avenge this day."

Brairtok sensed an invisible presence press toward him, like ghouls rising for a nightly prowl. He knew it was the Cauldron's power, yet such knowledge did little to settle his nerves. He held his tongue, drew in a deep breath and prepared for the worst.

"Your armies will face the nations united by a king," the whisper grated.

"That can't be," Brairtok said in his defense while making sure his tone was respectful. "I severed the royal line."

"The king's name is Lassiter."

"King Culdean did not have any sons. This *Lassiter* has no claim to the throne."

Brairtok gasped at hearing his own voice challenge the Cauldron. He knew he had said too much and clamped his mouth shut.

The Cauldron cast its drone upon Brairtok and he strained against the monotone's might. Beads of sweat pooled on his forehead and trickled down into his curly beard. His dark eyes remained fixed on the Council's shrouded heads, not wanting to blink or show any sign of fear or retaliation. The Cauldron pressed its invisible presence closer to the warlord of Ebon, goading him to cower beneath its power. Like an icicle being slowly forced into his ear, the Cauldron's shard-like whisper continued its accusation.

"Lassiter is the grandson of King Culdean. With the death of his mother, he became the rightful heir to the throne of Allsbruth."

"A young boy is powerless against my might," Brairtok snarled as he continued to strain against the drone.

"Your might?" the whisper cooed.

Brairtok realized his mistake and violently shook his head. Droplets of sweat flew through the air.

"No. Not *my* might, but *yours.* Only the Cauldron can overcome the deception of the impotent one."

The Cauldron lifted its drone away from Brairtok, but before he could catch his balance or his breath, the Cauldron whipped cold winds upon him.

"You're correct, Brairtok. It is by our might that you prevail. Never forget; your power is not your own."

Brairtok held up his arms to shield himself from the windy blasts.

"I'll not forget," he shouted into the gale. *"Never."*

The storm winds died down to a strong, icy breeze. Satisfied Brairtok had learned his lesson, the Cauldron explained its plan.

"My Gor King sniffed this news about Lassiter while hunting the Gilden Plains. And amidst such finding, he made an additional discovery: yet another storyteller survived the Dark War."

Brairtok swallowed hard, realizing he had failed to massacre them all during the Dark War.

"But I do not blame you," the whisper answered as chill winds blew the warmthless flames about the room. *"I blame the impotent one. He is cunning and conniving; I should have suspected as much."*

Thunder cracked within the hall. Even the stoic Council shuddered with trepidation.

"And yet," the whisper added, *"I do not fear such stories. After all, do they not reveal our enemy's quest to rely on the weak and helpless? Have I not amassed an army capable of defeating any and all who should rise to fight? Does not my Gor King indicate that the Oracle is coming to pass, and that we shall crush all 'when gors have a king?'"*

A tremendous thunderclap shook Netniath. The Council humbly bowed their heads before the Cauldron's greatness while Brairtok dropped submissively to one knee.

He hoped that whatever his punishment would be that it would be swift.

Witnessing their faithful obedience, the winds subsided and the whisper floated back into the Dark Flame. Within the black embers, it spoke to Brairtok.

"Brairtok, I am patient and merciful. Am I not?"

Brairtok nodded his head.

"Therefore, I shall overlook these...setbacks and will allow you to continue to serve me."

Brairtok's eyes widened, stunned that he would be blessed and not cursed. He wanted to sing a song of praise or shout a vow of allegiance as a thanksgiving offering, but thought better of it. The Cauldron expected action, not mere lip service.

The Cauldron explained its plan of attack.

"It is time to call forth the beasts of the Dark Flame. Their strength and power will make the followers of Claire cower before my greatness."

Brairtok blinked, unable to comprehend who or what these creatures were. The Cauldron perceived his thoughts and explained.

"Unbeknownst to the Only, I too have been secretly creating warriors for such a time as this."

The Council and Brairtok stared with rapt attention into the Dark Flames, awaiting more disclosure.

"Demoliths. Warriors and phantoms birthed from my vapors. Man-dragons."

Brairtok's eyes danced with delight at the thought of such creatures.

"Gather five thousand of your best warriors upon the parade grounds of Kise. There, you will witness my greatness as you behold them evolving before your very eyes, becoming powerful creatures capable of doing my bidding."

"It shall be done," Brairtok replied in earnest.

"There is more. Even as we speak, a brood the likes of which no mortal has witnessed, is hatching. Kodars: Colossal beasts that tower over sevritts with scales thicker than your best armor. You will build platforms to attach to their backs. In this way, the kodars can transport your troops into battle. With demoliths ruling the skies, kodars transporting warriors, and cavalry leading the charge, your army will be unstoppable."

Brairtok bowed, letting his silence adorn the Dark Flame with his adoration.

"Now go. Have your chosen men assembled by tomorrow morning."

Brairtok snapped his heels together.

"Death begets death," he trumpeted.

With that, he turned on his heel and marched out the dark hall, marveling at how quickly his fortune had changed. Only moments ago, he expected to be struck dead by the Dark Flame. Instead, he not only was given the opportunity to atone for his failures, but would be able to do so with powerful creatures.

He imagined what the demoliths - the man-dragons - looked like, becoming almost giddy as he pictured the heinous horde flying alongside vul jens and wreaking havoc on their enemy. He chuckled to himself as he pictured his archers perched atop a kodar and firing down into a citadel's courtyard. He would be unstoppable. Life immortal was attainable after all.

Exiting Netniath, he scanned the dark storm clouds overhead, no longer dreading their import.

Long live the Cauldron, he praised.

Lights flashed madly within the clouds.

Long live Brairtok.

Thunder boomed across Kise.

Chapter 45

Sojourn to Min Brock

Quinn and Areall gathered what they deemed necessary for their journey: blankets, extra clothing, a kitchen knife, dried meats and fruits. Quinn rested his hand upon his chair by the fire.

"In an odd way," he reflected, "I'll miss this."

Areall watched him run his hand gently across the chair's back, caressing it like it was his mistress.

"But I," she replied, her tone firm yet encouraging, "do not miss the man that used to sit there."

He gave her a loving smile and continued gathering some odds and ends.

Areall walked to the ladder and looked up into Elabea's room, hoping to see her face pop into view, her freckles and smile announcing the beginning to another day. But there was just blackness, and Areall could feel it covering her as if she were being buried alive.

She thought about Elabea constantly, but when she tried to share her concerns or thoughts with Quinn, he became distant and quiet. At first, she thought he was disinterested in hearing how she felt, or perhaps that he had lost hope that Elabea was alive. Then she realized he blamed himself for her departure. Now, instead of reminding him daily of her heartache, she kept her thoughts to herself, or shared them with Daryess.

In fact, she and Daryess had become even closer friends since their children disappeared. For just like Areall, Daryess worried about Galadin and when she shared such concerns with Gundin, his face clouded over with anger. Daryess also surmised that his anger was not directed at her, but at the fact that for the time being, there was nothing Gundin could do to change their circumstances.

Areall returned her thoughts to the moment and lowered her gaze from Elabea's room. Overwhelmed by her feelings of loss for her child and now for her home, Areall suddenly felt light-headed and short of breath. Quinn, sensing the change in her spirit, walked over and squeezed her shoulders.

"We'll see her again," he whispered into her ear.

She nodded, wiped her eyes and attempted a weak smile. Quinn pressed something into her palm.

A quick glance at the fabric made her gasp.

"Where did you get this," she asked, her voice full of emotion.

"It was hidden behind the logs on the hearth."

Tears rolled down her cheeks as Areall thumbed the soft cloth and embroidery.

"Elabea told me she didn't like sewing. She said she hated it. So why would she work on this in secret?"

"As a gift for you. See?"

He pointed to the black embroidered letters that spelled her name.

Areall traced them with her finger.

"But she can't read...or spell so—"

"She asked me to help," Quinn answered, emotions swelling into his throat.

Areall flung herself into Quinn's arms, and together they wept. They clutched each other to find the strength to not only leave Hetherlinn, but to believe Elabea was still alive.

Quinn and Areall joined Gundin and Daryess by the communal fire. The two couples studied the faces of those who chose to remain in Hetherlinn amidst Ebon's bounty. Quinn clasped Areall's hand and addressed their neighbors one last time.

"Should you have a change of heart, journey to Min Brock. You'll find us there."

"Make haste then," Mithe hissed with a wag of her finger. "Return to your failure, your shame like a dog to its vomit. You're no longer wanted here. We've already forgotten your names."

Although Daryess had to gently restrain Gundin from retaliating, Quinn remained level-headed and replied with earnest: "Then I will ask the Only to protect all of you."

"Protection," a man scoffed after drawing in a leisurely puff of his pipe. "You fools are the ones who need protection."

Quinn simply nodded. Although he did not know when or how, he sensed that Brairtok's army would destroy Hetherlinn, swiftly and ruthlessly.

The two couples turned and walked down the road and out of their village. They walked in silence, each dealing with a myriad of thoughts and feelings that weighed more than their packs.

When they were out of earshot of Hetherlinn, Gundin whispered to Quinn: "You never told me we were journeying to Min Brock."

Quinn flashed him a smile.

"Would it have mattered?"

Gundin pulled back and his face wrinkled as he pondered the question.

"No. I suppose not. Either way, we had to leave."

"Besides," Quinn added as he draped his arm across Gundin's broad shoulder. "The whisper from Claire has been leading our hearts back to Min Brock long before this day."

"But why? Surely it has crumbled to the ground. Besides, its name casts shame upon our names."

"I feel the same way, and yet, every morning Min Brock's shadow sits at my door like a black dragon. I tried to kill it with wildeberry drink, but it only grew in power over my life. I was without hope until Il-Lilliad brought the tulip. With its scent, courage returned, hope flickered and I began to believe the dragon could be slain. So we journey to Min Brock, to not only battle the forces of the Cauldron, but also this dark nemesis within us both."

"Didn't you just hear me," Gundin huffed, "by now, the fortress is a mound of rubble."

"Probably."

"Probably?" Gundin chided. "And yet still you lead us there?"

"Every person has a Min Brock; a moment of weakness or a fit of passion or a selfish act that stains their life with blackness. Some will overcome such despair, while others forever bask in deep shadows of gloom. For us, Min Brock must rise from its grave to show our people the strength of the Only."

"Our people?" Gundin repeated with a shake of his head. "*Our people* just rejected our offer to join us. They chose to remain in Hetherlinn."

"I know. But there are other villages throughout the lands."

"And what if they were also *blessed* by Brairtok and want nothing to do with war?"

Quinn did not answer, for he too had wondered the same thing. They let the conversation lag and continued down the road until Quinn heard something behind them.

He stopped.

"Did you hear that?" Quinn asked as the women huddled beside their husbands for safety.

"Yes. Voices. Moving this way."

Daggers were drawn and they shooed the women into the safety of the woods. Standing side by side, with daggers poised to strike, they prepared themselves for whatever was coming down the road.

From around the bend walked an old man and a boy. The boy skipped along carrying a box covered with a cloth, while the old man smiled and conversed merrily with the boy.

Quinn and Gundin sheathed their weapons and sighed in relief. Areall and Daryess emerged from the dense coppice. Areall squinted her eyes to study them. Recognizing them, her eyes widened.

"Your name is Bruun," she stated when the newcomers were close enough to hear, "and this is your son, Phinnton. You live in cottage Number 14."

The newcomers nodded. Although known by name and cottage, they had lived like hermits in Hetherlinn, as if they were invisible.

"We *lived* in cottage Number 14," the man corrected. "My muscles are old and my legs not as swift as in the Dark War," Bruun stated. "But I still have the heart of a warrior. Now we live where you live."

"You realize that joining us may cost you your life," Quinn asked.

Bruun chuckled.

"My life has been ebbing away ever since my wife died, some summers ago, and I know I am nearing my end too. Joining you is my last hope to make the name of Bruun great."

"Well said," Gundin trumpeted. He admired a man who longed to battle for his namesake. "But this will require strength of hands, mind and heart to secure victory."

Bruun's smile faded and his wrinkled face took on a more serious and determined expression.

"I won't sit inside my cottage and wait to die. I must try to do something."

"But what of your son?" Daryess asked. "What is his decision?"

All eyes turned to Phinnton. He was eight summers of age and lanky. Judging by how the boy fidgeted about, even with the box in his hands, Daryess could tell he was full of life and energy.

"What's in your box," Quinn asked.

Phinnton offered it up to him, and Quinn lifted the edge of the cloth to sneak a peek. He saw the edge of a wooden box, the type they used in Hetherlinn for gathering vegetables from the field, and staring back at him was rich topsoil.

Quinn dropped the cloth's corner and knelt to one knee to look into Phinnton's face.

"I don't want to hurt your feelings," Quinn said in a gentle voice, "but bringing planting soil to remind you of Hetherlinn is rather silly."

"Silly?" Phinnton countered with the defiance of a young warrior. "But you didn't see *this.*"

He threw off the cloth.

Rising boldly from the middle of the box, surrounded by a mound of black earth, was the red tulip.

As the adults stared in awe at the flower, Phinnton told his tale.

"Early in the morning, before sunrise, I'd go to my window and see you," he said, looking up at Quinn. "I'd watch you kneel over the tulip for the longest of time. Late one night, while all of Hetherlinn slept, I went and knelt down as I had seen you do and I breathed in the flower's aroma. That's when I heard it."

"Heard what?" the wives asked in unison.

Phinnton studied their faces before answering.

"A whisper."

Gundin huffed.

"That's ridiculous. How could a young boy..."

"Are you certain," Quinn interrupted with an elbow jab to Gundin's side. "After all, late at night, the scary sounds from the woods can play tricks on you."

Phinnton scowled at Quinn.

"I wasn't scared. And I wasn't hearing things, if that's what you mean."

"No," Quinn reassured, "I didn't mean to imply that at all."

But the others knew that he had.

Phinnton drew in a deep breath and continued.

"When you told the village that you heard the whisper of the Only, I got excited. I think that is what I heard too."

"Perhaps," Quinn replied as he took in Phinnton's sparkling eyes. "But there is another whisper that masks itself as that of the Only. Do you remember what the whisper you heard said to you?"

Phinnton looked to his father for courage. Bruun smiled and gave an approving nod.

"It said, *My delight!*"

Quinn smiled and patted his head.

"Yes, Phinnton. I'm convinced. You heard the King of Claire."

Phinnton's face lit with excitement.

"Then my decision is made. I want to join you and fight!"

"Fight?" Gundin chuckled, "you lack muscle like me!" He proudly patted his midsection.

"Those aren't muscles," Quinn teased, "that's fat."

Gundin's face clouded.

"I'm not *fat*. This is muscle. Solid. See? Listen...." He thumped harder to convince Quinn of his strength.

Turning his attention back to the boy, Quinn said, "Since you bear the tulip from Claire, I think it only wise that you lead the way."

Phinnton beamed and his father gave him a proud pat on the shoulder. Eager to lead the way, the boy and his father headed on down the road.

Gundin shook his head as he watched Bruun and Phinnton walk down the road.

"Does the Only expect us to rebuild Min Brock with just a skinny boy and an old man?"

"It seems that way for now," Quinn teased.

Gundin snapped his head toward Quinn.

"I'm serious."

Quinn's eyes focused squarely on Gundin's.

"All I know for certain is this: I sense an awakening all around us. It's not something I can see with my eyes, but something I feel in my marrow. It's like when you feel a storm coming when there's not a cloud in the sky."

Gundin shook his head.

"We need steel, weapons, men and horses to battle our enemy, not fancy words."

"Very well, then let us not forget my brother's quest. I know Linwith well and he will not fail us. There's also Il-Lilliad's mission to the Onderling. Perhaps he is on his way with an army even as we speak."

Gundin pulled away from Quinn's gaze.

"You're right," he said, his voice more somber than before. "And yet, so much could go wrong."

"I know," Quinn acknowledged as he took Areall's hand. She smiled up into his face. "We all know," he added with a kiss to her forehead.

"Let's also not forget our children," Daryess said as she wrapped her arm around Gundin's large frame. "They're alone and facing worse odds than us."

Gundin squeezed her tight.

"So my hope," Quinn said to Gundin, "is this: hidden from view, beyond the borders of nations and Oracles, men's hearts are being shepherded back to the stories of old, back to the days when Allsbruth was a proud nation, back to the days when Min Brock stood tall and proud."

"Yes," Gundin boomed, longing for the days of glory to return, "tall and proud."

"Besides," Quinn added with a smile as they began to follow Bruun and Phinnton. "If the Only can use a fat man like you, can't he use a skinny boy like Phinnton?"

Gundin's face reddened.

"This is not fat. This is *all* muscle!"

Quinn and Areall covered their mouths to contain their laughter.

Chapter 46

The Battle at DioBaith

After the Battle of Thornnblen, Romlin and Ela Claire were exhausted. While Romlin led the way on Bar-Treb, Ela Claire dozed on and off on Previn's back. They followed the shoreline of the Gilden Sea southward. After several days, the beach gave way to rugged mountains that butted up against the sea, so they headed inland to find an easier route.

Previn glided low overhead which gave Romlin the opportunity to converse with Ela Claire.

"What do you suppose is on the Isle of Rythe?" he asked as he maneuvered Bar-Treb around some large boulders near a thicket.

"The Only told me that it houses treasure from Claire stolen by Brairtok," she replied.

"How much treasure?"

"He didn't say. Does it really matter?"

"It does if it's part of our reward," he shouted up to her.

Ela Claire shook her head and ordered Previn to fly closer to Romlin.

"You're never satisfied, are you," she chided as they swooped through the trees.

He chuckled.

"Warriors never rest, and they are never satisfied. I'm just being who I was born to be."

"Then I guess storytellers hunger and thirst for other things."

"Like what," he asked, genuinely interested.

"Well, when I read, listen to or tell a story, my heart feels like it will *burst* out of my chest. I can't wait to tell more."

"So who's the one not satisfied now," he said with his impish grin.

She smiled. "I suppose we're the same and yet, very different."

Their conversation lagged and they focused on the beauty of the passageway they were traversing. The forest was alive with the scent of pine and rich earth. Rocks, jutting out of the ground like giant fingertips from forgotten tombs, were covered with aromatic green and brown moss. The higher they ascended, the taller the rocks became.

"Do you ever wonder what they're doing," she asked as Previn swooped around some tall pines.

"Who," Romlin asked, annoyed that he couldn't follow her conversation that jumped from thought to thought like a frog across lilies on a pond.

"Our families. My father. Your father."

"Oh...them," Romlin muttered.

"Don't you care?"

"Not really," he clipped.

"Why not?"

Ela Claire was stunned he did not think or feel the same way she did.

"Because *this* is what we've always wanted to do," he answered with a sweep of his arm about the beautiful landscape. "This is what we were born to be! Have you already forgotten that we dreamed such dreams in the oak? Now look at us. You're a powerful storyteller and I'm a great warrior. Do you really want to go back to the dull routine of Hetherlinn?"

"I suppose..."

"Why must there always be a *suppose* or a *but* when I talk with you?" he challenged gruffly.

"Please don't get angry."

"I'm not angry!"

"Then why are you shouting?"

Her voice quivered as his curt tone reminded her of the times her father, when drunk, would yell.

Romlin huffed, but he regained control over his emotions and addressed her in a more subdued tone.

"I'm *not* angry at you," he said with a glance at her face that he intended to convey tenderness.

Still hurt by his outburst, Ela Claire looked away. Romlin continued to try to explain his point of view.

"I simply get frustrated when we talk. I don't carry words like you do. They fly off your tongue and swirl all about as if alive, touching everything and everyone around you. I've even witnessed them destroy a whole company of Ebonite cavalry. I carry sword and brawn," he flexed his arm muscle and held it up for her to examine. "They do my talking."

Convinced his explanation was enough to satisfy her curiosity, which of course it was not, he turned his attention to the terrain they traversed.

"Look." He pointed up ahead of them. "We're nearing the top of the ridge."

Ela Claire spotted the crest and ordered Previn to higher altitude. She caught a glimpse of water through the branches.

"There's a river just beyond the summit," she called down to him.

Reaching the apex, Romlin took in the view.

"We're at the headwaters for the River Arrgient," he shouted up to her.

White water rushed over round, moss covered rocks, creating small waterfalls that cascaded into the deeper waters. Despite the river's dark brown color, it was clear and cast a dark hue upon the rocks and pebbles beneath its surface.

Previn landed and Ela Claire dismounted while Romlin slid off Bar-Treb. As the animals went to a swirling pool for a drink, Romlin joined Ela Claire and together, they pondered the powerful river.

"Look at the boulders," she said, pointing to the glistening tops protruding from the water like giant turtle shells. "They're close enough that if you wanted to cross, you could do so by jumping from rock to rock. But if you slip..."

Her mind imagined the horror of such a misfortunate tumble. For despite its beauty and grandeur, the River Arrgient's power would be too strong for anyone to survive. Tossing aside the horrible thought of drowning, she knelt and scooped up a handful of water.

"It's so cold," she marveled as she sipped from her cupped hands. "And sweet," she added.

Romlin knelt beside her and drank his fill.

"Look at that," he exclaimed, pointing upstream.

Ela Claire followed his line of sight. On the opposite bank was a giant tower of rock that leaned out over the river.

"That must be DioBaith," Romlin said as he rose to admire the tower. "I remember seeing it on the map."

He was so excited to explore the monolith that he jogged away from Ela Claire without so much as a *good-bye* or *come with me*. He headed upstream toward another set of rocks that led across the frothing river.

Ela Claire stared after him, fuming, but when he slowed down and stared at the rocks protruding out of the river, her feelings changed to dread.

"What does he think he's doing?" she muttered to herself as she stood back up. Growing up together in Hetherlinn, she had learned to read his body movements to learn exactly what he was thinking. And right now, watching him studying the rocks, the water and the rapids, she did not like what she thought he was thinking.

"Romlin," she shouted over the roaring rapids, "please don't try to cross."

She once more imagined the horror of what it would be like to fall into the swirling waters.

He waved her off and jumped to the closest partially submerged boulder.

"Be careful," she scolded.

"Relax," he fired back with arms outstretched to help maintain his balance. "I know what I'm doing."

With another lunge, he landed on the next rock and immediately launched himself to the third. Again he paused, teetering like a tot learning to walk, but without further hesitation, jumped and landed on the opposite bank.

Grinning ear-to-ear, he held up his arms triumphantly and gave her his battle roar.

"Must you make everything so dangerous," she huffed to herself.

He bounded to DioBaith, found some handholds, and began to climb.

Ela Claire walked upstream and watched his ascent with growing foreboding.

"Do be careful," she mothered as she folded her arms across her breasts.

He gave her another battle cry and skirted to the backside of the monolith.

"Romlin," she called when he disappeared from view.

She cupped her hands to her mouth. "*Romlin.*"

Movement at the tower's summit caught her attention. She shielded her eyes and saw him jumping up and down atop DioBaith's flat top.

"I am *Romlin*," he bellowed. His voice echoed above the white water as he drew his sword and thrust it high into the air with much bravado. "I'm a great warrior for the Only."

"And you could fall and be a *dead* warrior," she chastised with hands on her hips.

"Behold," he shouted down at her and with a thrust of his sword. "There is my storyteller. Oh, how she worries about things she should not."

Romlin continued his theatrics, and although she still worried about him falling, she could not help but giggle at his antics.

Previn and Bar-Treb looked up from where they were drinking to watch Romlin clowning about. As he slashed the air, fighting imaginary foes, large shadows crossed over DioBaith. Instinctively, Previn scanned the sky. But instead of seeing clouds, the sight that greeted his eyes turned his blood to ice.

"Vul jens," he breathed to Bar-Treb. "Hundreds. We're under attack."

The stallion answered with a loud whinny as he tried to alert Romlin to the danger. Previn swooped across the ground toward Ela Claire, who had also noticed the shadows. She shielded her eyes for a better look.

"Those aren't clouds," Previn said as he landed beside her. "That's an army of vul jens. Climb on. We must fly out of this trap."

Ela Claire knew first hand the deadly power vul jens possessed, and lost no time climbing onto Previn's back. Once airborne she let her gaze wonder toward Romlin. He had stopped his tomfoolery and was also staring into the sky.

As Previn flew up out of the forest, hundreds of Vul jens shot past them, their hideous cawing drowning out the sound of the booming rapids.

"Romlin," Ela Claire screamed in desperation. "There are too many. You can't fight them. Hurry down!"

Romlin scampered to the edge of the monolith when a vul jen swooped down and blocked his escape. The dreamhunter cocked its bony head to the side and studied Romlin.

"So *you* are Romlin," the vul jen's cold, monotone grated on Romlin's ears. "I must confess I am extremely disappointed. Based upon Kundle's shameful report, I imagined you to be...*stronger.*"

"I'm strong enough," Romlin fired back as his grip tightened about his sword's hilt.

"That remains to be seen," the dreamhunter spat.

Romlin put his fingers in his mouth and whistled. Bar-Treb galloped to the river's edge and boxed the air in anticipation of his master's next command.

"What's this," the Vul jen asked as he stared down at Bar-Treb prancing along the river bank. "The weakling is hailing his warhorse. Is it to fight or to flee?"

"Tell a story," Romlin shouted to Ela Claire as she flew past on Previn.

"Watch closely, Romlin the Frail," the vul jen taunted. "We will destroy her before your very eyes."

The dreamhunter cawed a command, and half of the vul jen horde took wind to attack Ela Claire. The remainder roosted about DioBaith and eyed Romlin as if he were a tasty morsel.

"That will never happen," Romlin countered.

His sword had begun to glow, evidence that his companion was telling a story. Recalling his battle at Thornnblen, and how his sword's wave of light had destroyed so many, he swung his weapon toward the perched vul jens. When the magical band of light hit, the vul jens raised their wings and the wave rolled harmlessly over them. The vul jen hopped toward Romlin.

"The Cauldron has learned of your sword's trickery and prepared us for such an attack. As the Oracles declare, *Greater is the Dark Flame within than the fire without!*"

A collective cackle arose from the surrounding dreamhunters.

"And now, foolish boy-man, I deliver a tale especially woven for you by the Dark Flame: today you die."

The assembled horde of vul jens hissed with the power of a cavalry charge. Their power hit Romlin, forcing him backwards. He stumbled backwards, and desperately tried to catch his balance.

"Death begets death," the vul jen screeched.

Romlin screamed as he toppled off DioBaith.

Ela Claire heard his panicked cry and stopped her story. She opened her eyes just in time to witness Romlin falling, with sword still clutched in hand and limbs flaying wildly. He somehow managed to miss the boulders that dotted the river and splashed into its churning, frigid waters.

Despite the massing vul jens, Ela Claire scanned the rapids for any sign of Romlin. At last, beneath the river's clear brown waters she spotted his blurred appearance. He had released his sword and was clawing the water trying to reach the surface. Swirling rip-tides and whirlpools battered him, clutching at him and trying to suck him down into the depths.

"He's trapped," Ela Claire cried as tears welled in her eyes. "The river won't let go of him,"

Bar-Treb galloped along the bank, following his master's submerged body, neighing and pawing the ground, but he too was unable to help.

"Previn, dive," Ela Claire ordered. "Save him."

"We can't," he answered as he dove to avoid the talons of an attacking vul jen. "The vul jens will destroy you if we descend."

"But you are the only one who can rescue him," she pleaded as her tears fell.

She clasped a hand over her mouth as she watched Romlin's plight. He continued to kick and claw to save his life, but the river's current was too strong. It pulled him deeper until his blurred form completely disappeared into the cold, dark void.

"*No*," she screamed.

The vul jens shrieked with joy at his demise, and drew strength from Ela Claire's heartache. The vul jen leader left its perch on DioBaith and ascended up to Ela Claire.

"It's time for you to join him, you homely child."

Ten vul jens raced for her with talons ready to tear her apart.

"Hold on tight," Previn ordered Ela Claire.

Previn gained speed, banked, and snatched four of the vul jens with his talons. He crushed them and dropped their lifeless bodies into the raging river. Despite the aerial combat, Ela Claire kept her eyes riveted on the river. She continued to call out Romlin's name and strained to see if the water had granted him mercy.

"Ela Claire," Previn called above vul jens raucous caws. "Tell a story. Quickly."

"But Romlin..."

"Is lost! As we will be if you don't tell a story. Now."

A vul jen attacked them head on. Previn waited until the last possible moment, shifted course and caught the creature with his beak. He shook his head violently, snapped the vul jen's back and then hurled him into two approaching vul jens. Dazed, they fell into the white waters where they were sucked below and not seen again.

"There are too many," Previn shouted to Ela Claire as he corkscrewed through the air swarming with vul jens. "*Tell a story.*"

Through a cascade of tears, she pulled her gaze away from the River Arrgient, closed her eyes, and began her tale. But her heart was too troubled. All she could think about was Romlin, the brown water and death that loomed.

The King of Claire sensed her agony and whispered to her.

"*Do not despair.*"

"Romlin's in trouble..."

"*Listen to your song!*"

She heard the refrains of her waltz and despite her concern for Romlin's life, it filled her with hope. As her heart began to settle, a story of such wonder filled her that she felt as if she were flying without Previn's help. Maybe, she reasoned, Romlin would be spared if she could tell a tale.

It's my only hope.

Multi-colored lights exploded out of her as if she were a living rainbow. Sparking and shooting in every direction like flaming arrows, they disintegrated any vul jen caught in their path. Soon, the sky was filled with trails of black smoke as vul jen after vul gen spiraled down in flaming death.

The outburst of Ela Claire's powers compelled the surviving vul jens to retreat. As the horde flew away, they cawed in victory at the success of their mission.

Romlin was destroyed.

Ela Claire, sensing their retreat, released the story and opened her eyes. With the skies safe once more, she focused her attention on the raging brown and white froth of the river.

"Dive," she ordered Previn.

The great bird tucked his wings and swooped down to the rapids. There, he glided as low and as slow as possible to allow Ela Claire to search for Romlin. Bar-Treb galloped along the bank and searched as well.

Ela Claire scoured the churning eddies, the rocky shoreline and even the embankment. Romlin was nowhere to be seen.

Her heart sank.

But I told a story, she reasoned to herself.

She was about to order Previn back around for another pass, when something up ahead in the river's bend caught her eye.

"Over there," she stammered, barely daring to believe her eyes. "I think I see him lying beside those rocks."

Previn also saw the form and raced toward the spot, but when they were close enough, they both could tell it was only a partially submerged log.

"Turn around," she snapped.

Hope sank under the weight of her despair.

Previn banked sharply and flew back upstream toward DioBaith. They continued to explore every crevice, cascade and nook of the river, and did so until the sun hung just above the horizon. Their heroic efforts were futile. Romlin was gone.

"Set me down. I want off," Ela Claire demanded. There was fire in her voice.

"These are dangerous times."

"I know he's here, I know it. Now let me *off.*"

Ela Claire's tone brooked no argument, so Previn descended. Before his talons touched ground, she jumped off and darted for the river.

"Romlin," she called as she ran along the bank. "Please answer me. Romlin! *Romlin!*"

Previn, worried the vul jens would return, flew overhead to keep watch.

"Romlin, please. Don't leave me." Tears burned her eyes. "You promised at Thornnblen. Remember? You promised you would always be here for me. You *promised.*"

Up and down the river she ran, calling his name, searching every pool and churning rapid.

Previn, convinced the sky and woods were safe, landed beside Bar-Treb.

"Have you found his scent," the great bird asked the warhorse as they watched Ela Claire's desperate search.

"Not on this side of the river," the Bar-Treb answered. "Surely you've discovered it on the other side."

Previn blinked quickly and looked into Bar-Treb's face. They both realized the truth that Ela Claire was unable to accept.

Romlin was gone.

Undaunted, Ela Claire continued to hunt for her best friend, for her love, all the while calling for the King of Claire to assist. She waded out into the cold pools. She peered beneath darkened cliffs. She felt beneath underwater crags.

At sunset, exhausted and overcome with grief, Ela Claire dragged herself from the river and dropped to her knees. Burying her face in her hands, she wailed.

Previn, who longed to comfort her, glided over to her and draped a wing over her. But when Ela Claire felt the brush of his feathers, her anger exploded.

"Leave me alone," she roared as she shot to her feet and sprinted back to the river.

Previn caught her scent. Her inner tale told him she was about to do something rash.

"Ela Claire," Previn hailed. "Come back. Night is upon us."

She ignored his plea and ran like a deer. Memories of the times she raced Romlin drew tears from her eyes. Once at the river's edge, she jumped across the rocks Romlin had crossed earlier. Gone were her fears. Gone were her apprehensions. All she could think about was Romlin.

Safe on the opposite bank, she bolted for DioBaith and without hesitation climbed the towering rock.

"No," Previn pleaded to her as he took flight. His usually calm voice was clouded with fear as he suspected what she was about to do. "Don't do it."

"Fly away," she boomed as she continued to claw her way up DioBaith. "I want to be alone."

"I will not obey you," he replied as he circled the monolith. "Not with our enemy nearby."

"Why didn't you save him," she asked with another push up the rock.

"I couldn't," Previn fired back.

He thought about snagging her with his talons and pulling her to safety but feared he would miss and send her to her death.

"You said all would be lost if I did not tell a story. I *told* a story. So why is he gone?"

"If you hadn't told your story, you would be dead, too."

She stopped her ascent and stared at Previn.

"Is that supposed to make me feel better?"

She shook her head in disgust and scampered farther up the slippery slope.

"No, my storyteller," Previn answered, trying to keep his voice calm despite his rising fears that she would dive off DioBaith to end her life. "It is simply to help you understand."

"Understand," she fired back as she stretched her hand to grab the summit's edge. "Here is what I don't understand: I asked the King of Claire to help, so why didn't he rescue him?"

Previn circled the tower and pondered her question. It was as dark as the night and was a valid query, one that bothered him as well.

"I don't know," he finally answered.

"For that matter," she asked as she strained to push herself up onto DioBaith's top. "Where was Manno Vox?"

"Climb down and we'll discuss such things."

She stood atop the apex. Dim moonlight covered DioBaith and made her white dress glow against the blackening sky. She stared in the direction of Claire.

"Stories and tales won't ease the pain of my heart."

She waited for a whisper or a sign, but when nothing happened, she walked to the edge closest to the river. When her toes dangled over the side, she heard a whisper.

"I tried to warn you. I tried to spare you such pain and anguish from the King of Claire. You should have jumped off the cliff as I had advised instead of entering Clair. But alas, you're a stubborn girl and had to find out yourself. Tsk, tsk, tsk. So here you are, once more with your toes dangling over the edge of a cliff and facing the same dilemma: is life worth living?"

She peered down at the River Arrgient far below. It was even more sinister looking at night. Rapids glistened and twisted in the bluish light like a massive serpent.

"As before, I offer you life. Jump!" the Cauldron whispered. *"Romlin awaits. Even now he's stretching his arms out for you. Can you not see him? Forever you two will reign. Forever you will be with him. Forever you will be free from the pain of this world.*

Forever..."

"Ela Claire," Previn shouted as he swooped closer to her should she jump. "Remember your time in Marsien Vur. Remember your waltz. For that matter, remember Romlin. Would he want you to end your life like this?"

Overcome with emotions, her eyes filled with tears and the river took on a mystical appearance. Far off in the distance, she heard the soft refrains of her waltz.

Although her hope and faith in the King of Claire were dashed, she knew Previn was right: Romlin would not want her to jump.

She stepped away from the ledge.

The dark whisper snickered.

"So be it. Live your life of pain while I drink my fill from your misery."

With that parting shot, it flittered away.

Ela Claire sprawled out upon the top of DioBaith. Her body racked with sobs, her back heaving as she mourned, her moans rising high above the sounds of the River Arrgient. She pictured her times with Romlin as they climbed the oak, when he protected her from Mithe or when he bemoaned her countless questions. Recollections of their journey to Claire burst like lightning in her darkened heart. She could see him hopping up and down on the draigg, and the time he was held upside down by the ivy of Marsien Vur. With each vignette, it felt like barbed arrows pierced her over and over.

Finally, she allowed herself to feel the loss she dreaded facing. When she realized she would never be able to tell him she loved him, or that she dreamed of marrying him and living beside their meadow, she wept bitter tears.

Previn landed beside her and once again unfolded a wing to shelter her. She felt his feathers brush her cheek, but instead of pushing him away as she had previously, she wrapped her arms around one of his legs. She pulled her knees up to her chest and rocked to and fro, her wails muffled by his feathers.

"I'll always be by your side," Previn reassured her despite the swirling questions in his mind. "No matter what you decide to do as a storyteller, I will always be here."

Had she been able to look into Previn's eyes, she would have seen a rare phenomenon.

Tears glistening like silver in the moonlight.

Chapter 47

Gems of Discovery

Linwith's flight with the Worms of Bal-Malin to Tristan was swift. He was thrilled that the skies were void of their enemy, and when he landed with his worms, he was delighted to find that bartering for Tristan weapons was quick and profitable. In fact, Linwith enjoyed the respect he was given by the Tristanites because he was master of such ferocious beasts. Men, who would not bow before anyone, humbled themselves before Linwith. Swordsmiths and merchants did not haggle over his prices. Some even gave him extra weapons for free.

While he loaded the weapons into the worms' carriers, he caught the eye of passing high-born ladies who batted eyelashes at him or flashed flirtatious smiles.

Linwith's confidence soared.

With his arsenal secured inside the carriers, Linwith climbed into the sapphire worm's saddle and donned his helmet. As the worms ascended into the sky, he waved to the children racing below to keep pace. They returned his wave, and as the worms' flight increased, stopped to watch them disappear into the sky.

Once they were high enough, Linwith leveled off his flight and placed his gloved thumb over the sapphire gem. *"We must deliver these to my brother, Quinn,"* Linwith said in the silent tongue to the Worm King. *"I wish I knew where he was."*

"Then it is time for a lesson," the Worm King answered in Linwith's mind. *"Prepare to place your thumb over the mandarin gem. Focus on your brother and your brother only, and then touch the jewel."*

Linwith focused his thoughts on Quinn and pressed his thumb onto the mandarin gem.

An orange hue saturated his imagination, but instead of seeing what was directly in front of the mandarin worm, Linwith beheld scenes of another place and time: Quinn stood alone in a great field. Looming in the background of the mandarin shadows was a dark building.

Startled by the ordeal, Linwith yanked his thumb off the jewel. Immediately the vision was gone.

He covered the blue gem and asked, *"What was that?"*

"My brother's gift is the ability to see into the future."

"So I beheld Quinn's destiny?"

"No, just a small portion of time."

"With this power, will I be able to see the outcome of the war?"

"No; the visions are not as encompassing as that. You can only see one person's future at a time. And in so doing, you will not see the exact outcome or the exact interpretation; just shadows and whispers of tomorrow's events. This will become clearer the more you practice. Now, try one more time but this time, cover my jewel as well. In that way, I can instruct you at the same time."

Linwith centered his thoughts on Quinn and touched the mandarin jewel. Once more, he was transported into the vision. Without raising his thumb off the orange gem, he lowered another finger upon the sapphire gem.

"Tell me," the Worm King asked his master, *"what do you see?"*

"Same as before: Quinn alone in a field with a large building or structure behind him, but the images are blurry and the field is too vague. It could be anywhere."

"True. But this is the future albeit a sliver of time. You need to know your brother's thoughts."

"How?"

"Continue to cover the mandarin and sapphire gems. Focus on Quinn, then touch the golden jewel."

Linwith complied, and was encased in blackness where neither sound nor sight could penetrate. The Worm King continued to instruct the Worm Master.

"Do not be afraid. Such darkness is normal. Now listen, but not with your ears. Use your heart."

Confused by the Worm King's instructions, Linwith nonetheless concentrated as instructed.

"Nothing. I don't hear a thing."

"Patience. Focus. Again, not with your ears but with your heart. Can't you hear him? I can, and he is not even my brother."

Linwith struggled to make the transition from auditory sense to the inner sense of his emotions. Suddenly, as if hearing the tolls of a great bell, words exploded deep within him, and with each peal came an exposed mandarin scene of the meadow.

War...hope...fight...Min Brock...Elabea...Areall...

As quickly as they came, they sounded no more. Linwith removed his fingers from the gold and mandarin jewels.

"The words," Linwith asked the Worm King, his thumb still upon the sapphire. *"These were from my brother?"*

"Yes. Can you interpret?"

"The vision must have been the Gilden Plains. And based upon the words, the dark building must be Min Brock."

"I concur."

Linwith took in his location. *"We're over the Gilden Sea and the sun is on our backs, so we're flying west."*

Turning in his saddle, he studied the southern sky. A sliver of land could be seen on the far horizon. *"That must be the Addoli Ridge and beyond that the Gilden Plains. And somewhere over the ridge is Min Brock."*

"What is your desire?" the Worm King asked.

"I sense we're to go find my brother. We must head toward Min Brock."

With that, all seven worms gently banked to alter their flight, staying in perfect formation. Once headed toward the Gilden Plains, Linwith covered the horn with the palm of his right hand.

"Assemble in single-file formation. I want to fly stealthily and stay alert should we encounter our enemy."

The six worms assembled behind the tail of the Worm King, and with wings perfectly synchronized, soared as one high above the Gilden Sea.

Linwith studied his jeweled saddlehorn. Specifically, he eyed the ruby, emerald, amber, silver and sapphire gems and curious as to each worm's powers, he pressed his thumb down upon the sapphire stone.

"So what do the others do?" he asked the Worm King.

"Ruby hurls balls of fire. Emerald emits a cloud of poisonous gas. Silver can become invisible. Amber can shrink in size, and I..."

The worm hesitated in telling Linwith his gift, not because he did not trust him with such powers, but because he realized that their wait to use such weaponry - of five hundred summers - was over.

"With the light of my tail, I can encase an area and freeze it in time."

Linwith was giddy with the information, and as he began to fathom the powers he wielded as the Worm Master, he felt light-headed. No wonder Rittmar had been so persistent upon him reaching the island of Bal-Malin. He commanded an aerial fleet that could dominate the skies...perhaps even the land.

As they swept closer to the mainland, Linwith yearned to experiment with each worm and see for himself how each used its power. Yet he knew that now was not the time.

First things first. Quinn needs my help, and these weapons.

The thought made him smile. When was the last time Quinn had needed him?

Never, he concluded.

Linwith sensed he was about to enter a new era in his life, one in which he would have equal notoriety with his brother. He liked the feeling, and noted at the same time that it was not a feeling of superiority. It simply felt good.

Really good.

He sat tall in his saddle and leaned into the wind that whistled inside his helmet.

Chapter 48

Birth of the Demoliths

A fine mist concealed Netniath and Vorak in a cold, ominous veil. Clouds hovered low like phantoms gazing at the military parade grounds below.

Constructed from massive black rock, each slab of the parade grounds was polished until it glistened like a mirror. One slab was large enough to hold four warhorses, and when laid side by side and end-to-end, the assembled area could hold the entire Ebonite army and cavalry.

Torch stands composed of strands of twisting copper were scattered about. Taller than a warrior on horseback, the torches were capped by black, metal pots at the copper's zenith, where eternal flames burned day and night.

Thousands of Ebonite warriors, hand-picked by Brairtok, stood at parade rest. The torchlight danced on their dark armor and reflected off the mirror-like black slabs. They stood, silent and motionless, awaiting Brairtok's arrival.

Click-a-clock-a-click-a-clock-a...

The warriors' eyes peered into the mist. Brairtok and his attachés emerged from the fog on horseback, the sharp reports of their warhorses' hooves reverberated across the parade ground.

With adjutants on either side, he inspected their columns then rode to the front of the formation. He arched his back and stared at his finest warriors.

"My glorious ones," he trumpeted. "You have been selected from all my warriors for greatness. The Cauldron wishes to bestow glory upon you. You shall become demoliths: *man-dragons.* Flight will be yours, and strength beyond your imagining."

Before the echo from his last words faded, a dark cloud descended from Netniath. It cast an unnerving, foreboding darkness over the warriors, despite their reputation for bravery. When it was closer, they realized it was not a cloud but thousands of vul jens.

"Shut your eyes," Brairtok instructed. "Let the dreamhunters carry you to your destiny."

Thousands of eyelids closed in unison.

The vul jens' talons tapped out an ominous rhythm as they hopped to their selected host.

"Warriors of Ebon," the whisper from the Cauldron announced. *"My vul jens will bring you glory, power and might. Now, fall to your knees. Let them fly within your dreams."*

With eyes shut, the men knelt to the black slabs and the Cauldron whispered an Oracle.

"Warriors dark of dragon birth, shadows fly o'er hearth and vale,
Decimate stories of royal worth, relish Dark Flame's eternal tale."

The vul jens let out a cacophonous cry.

Netniath rumbled.

The drone became so loud that Brairtok covered his ears, all the while laughing with joy in anticipation of his men's transformation.

Each vul jen dissolved into dark-purple mist and hovered before their warrior's anxious face.

"Soldiers of Ebon, breathe deeply their mist. Breathe long their dreams."

The warriors obeyed and the dreamhunters entered the warriors.

Agonizing screams filled the air. Torsos expanded as if being puffed up with air. Armor and leather stretched to fit the expanding bodies. Some dropped facedown on the parade ground. Others writhed about on their knees like madmen.

Large, dark green reptilian scales formed upon faces. Some retained patches of human flesh, though most were completely covered with scales.

Necks expanded and became as thick as small trees, then creaked and stretched, rising well above the warriors' collar lines. Eye sockets sank and yellow eyes peered out from the cave-like cavities. Limbs morphed into a dichotomous combination of lizard and human attributes. Gone was their jaunty Ebonite beards and shoulder-length hair. Now, only a few black strands grew in odd patches.

The warriors' screams changed to hisses and barks as legs expanded, rippling with powerful muscles. When they stood, they towered over Brairtok.

Faces contorted as long snouts emerged from noses and jaws. Long, black tongues flickered in the orange torchlight.

Long tails grew from the men's lower backs and extended down to the ground. From out of their backs grew long, thin bones that arched upward like the fingers of an old man. Dark green flesh formed over the bones and stretched taut to form featherless wings that rose above their heads and fell to their calves.

As each warrior transformed, he swarmed into the misty sky to join his brothers in a perfect formation. When the transformation was complete thousands of wings beat a silent cadence, dark tongues flickered and yellow eyes stared unblinkingly as they awaited a command.

"Demoliths of Ebon," Brairtok shouted. "Send forth your general."

One demolith descended from the formation.

"What glory do you request, Master Brairtok?" His voice resonated as if rising from a subterranean cave and felt just as dark and cold.

"Fly to Allsbruth," Brairtok commanded. "Descend upon Hetherlinn. Destroy everything. Destroy everyone."

The general bowed and ascended to join the ranks of the demoliths. As they banked and headed for Allsbruth, Brairtok shouted an addendum.

"Be certain to destroy the great oak. Burn it to the ground. Burn it. Burn it *all.*"

Chapter 49

Farewell to Arms

Yellow sunbeams graced the crest of DioBaith and fell across Ela Claire as she lay asleep beneath Previn's wing. The morning light shone on her eyes and she stirred. As she awakened, Ela Claire hoped Romlin's death had only been a nightmare, perhaps even conjured by the vul jens or the Cauldron. Surely Romlin was nearby tending a fire, brewing some morning tea.

She sniffed the cool morning breeze, but it did not carry the familiar scent of burning wood. Instead, the damp air reminded her of the river, and Romlin sinking down into its frigid brown depths.

She shuddered and threw aside the gruesome memory.

She pushed herself to her feet. Previn backed away. She tiptoed toward the edge, afraid to peer down at the river, afraid to learn the truth. Yet she needed to know the answer.

At the cliff's edge, she trained her eyes downward. Mist shrouded the river. Within, she caught the blurry image of the mighty waters rushing over rocks and gushing through gorge. Movement beside the bank caught her attention.

Romlin, she gasped as she strained into the fog to see who it was.

When she recognized the shape, her heart sank. It was only Bar-Treb who clawed the riverbank as if to conjure Romlin from his murky tomb.

Her hope died.

Without taking her eyes off the river, she shouted an order over her shoulder to Previn.

"Take me to Bar-Treb."

Previn ached for his storyteller and wished he could rescue her from such anguish, yet as powerful as he was, he knew he was incapable of providing such deliverance. He lowered himself, and once she was safely on his back, he glided down and landed near the stallion. Ela Claire hopped off, gathered in Bar-Treb's reins, and gently stroked his neck.

"Bar-Treb," she said in a quivering voice. "Romlin's gone."

It was one thing to think of such tragedy as reality, but when she heard her own voice say what her heart desperately hoped was not true, her eyes watered. She gasped, as if in want of air, and her wails rose above the noise of the rapids.

Bar-Treb nudged her with his snout, hoping to consol her. He had searched the river all night long, sniffing for Romlin's scent and hoping to find him sprawled out along the bank. The night had revealed nothing.

He too had held out hope that the morning would shed new results. But now, as her tears washed down his neck, he too accepted the worst.

Angered by this truth, Bar-Treb stepped away from her and tossed his head into the air and whinnied. Ela Claire held the reins tight. It was all she could do to restrain him.

His hooves pounded the ground.

"This isn't your fault," she declared as she strained against the reins.

He shook his head and snorted, desperately trying to talk to her, but knowing that on this side of the veil, his voice was mute.

"We all feel the same way," Previn chimed in. "There was nothing more any of us could have done."

Bar-Treb stopped prancing and lowered his head to hers. She gazed into his black eyes, and although she knew animals did not cry, she thought she saw them watering with tears. She pressed her forehead against his and Previn draped a wing over them both.

The trio huddled and mourned Romlin's loss in silence.

Finally, Ela Claire lifted her head and made her way to the saddle where Romlin's shield was tethered. As she stared at the shield, she could feel her arm rising, and as if in a dream she watched her fingers stretch toward it. They stopped short of touching it, and quivered. Gathering her courage, she pressed them forward.

Flesh touched cold metal.

She thought she heard Romlin's voice...smelled his scent...caught his gaze...

Tears flowed as she untied the shield from the saddle. It fell to the ground with a soft thud. She grabbed it with both hands and dragged it to the river's edge. Though cumbersome, it was not heavy.

"You've robbed me of my only friend," she shouted at the river. "I hate you!" She strained and lifted the massive shield up on its edge. "You took his life, now take all he possessed."

She pushed it with all her strength.

The shield splashed into the water and spun wildly down the river like a metal man-of-war. It plummeted over a waterfall where it disappeared into the depths, and did not resurface.

"Go, find him," she sobbed after the shield. "May you forever rest by your master's side. Guard him within this cruel grave. Carry him back to the gardens of Marsien Vur. Tell him...tell him to wait for me."

She wiped away the tears that stained her face and returned to Bar-Treb.

"You must return to Claire," she ordered Bar-Treb. "Shout the tale of Romlin, the son of Gundin, the greatest warrior Allsbruth has ever known."

Bar-Treb shook his head and snorted.

"If you won't go, then who will tell his story to everyone in Claire," she asked him.

The stallion meandered over to her. He nudged her in an effort to express his one true desire: to escort them on their journey and to seek revenge for Romlin's death.

"No," she said in a firm voice. "You must return."

Bar-Treb stared intensely into her eyes. She could see the anger pulsing within and knew vengeance was the driving force. She pulled away from his passionate stare.

"My mind's made up," she said with her back to him, unwilling to look into his eyes and see the anguish he too carried.

Bar-Treb rose upon his back legs and boxed the air with his front hooves. Nostrils flared and he released a loud neigh in honor of his fallen master. He dropped to the ground and galloped off toward Claire.

Ela Claire watched as Bar-Treb disappeared into the woods. His hooves beat out a mournful cadence. When he was lost to sight she turned her attention to the River Arrgient. She hoped against hope that Romlin would emerge from a pool, or his laughter would echo down from DioBaith.

"Don't despair," Previn reassured. "There is a reason for his..."

"Reason?" she seethed as she spun around to glare at the harrier. "That word makes no sense to me anymore. There is no reason in life. There is only pain."

"Remember the stories of Claire. They bring liberty to anguish and create hope beyond despair and..."

Anger boiled up Ela Claire's face, staining it crimson.

"We gave up *everything* to journey to Claire," she shouted. "The Only did *nothing* to help Romlin. We were to have more adventures together. We were to serve the King of Claire in this *war of whispers*. We were to marry and..."

As she realized her heart's greatest dream would never come to pass, tears gushed from her eyes.

"We were too..."

She looked back at the raging waterway. Again, she hoped he would emerge from the froth and foam shouting something silly like he always did, or ascend DioBaith to stand larger than life. But the River Arrgient delivered no such a dream.

"We were..."

She wiped her eyes and turned her attention back to Previn.

"I want to go home," she wept.

"Don't you remember the Only's words to you at Marsien Vur?" Previn said. "You can never return home."

She shook her head in defiance.

"I'm through listening with the ears of a child. I'm through guarding my heart and hoping in the impossible. I just want to walk in my meadow and sit beneath my oak. That's all I want, Previn, to sit beneath my oak."

"But you have been entrusted with the gift and calling of a storyteller."

She swallowed hard and looked into his keen eyes.

"I don't believe such things are possible. Not anymore."

Previn's eyes blinked rapidly.

"Please don't surrender your heart, Ela Claire. *Please.*"

"But I already have," she sighed. Softer still, "I already have."

Previn recalled when he was her rusk and how vibrant and alive her dreams had been. She seemed so much older now, weighed down by the loss of Romlin and the death of so many dreams. He knew the Cauldron was winning the fight for her, pushing and dragging her down into a black hole of hopelessness. The situation was grave. Time was running out.

"I'm your guardian," he replied. "I sacrificed my life as a rusk in order to secure your travels to Claire. And now, as your harrier, I cannot allow you to do such a thing. There is simply too much at stake."

Ela Claire raised her swollen eyes to his.

"Either take me home or I'll go myself."

"I'm not trying to hurt you further," the great bird interjected. "But to journey back to Hetherlinn and your oak will only bring you deeper pain."

"How do you know?"

"Because the Only would not have told you as much if it were not for your well-being."

She huffed.

"And what about Romlin's well-being?"

Previn stood speechless.

"Good bye, Previn."

She spun away.

Previn watched her walk toward the river to follow its course to Allsbruth's border. Confused by Ela Claire's reaction and alarmed about what he should do, he rose upon the wind to seek an answer. He dug his wings into the wind and pulled himself high above DioBaith and the River Arrgient. When he reached the crest of his climb, he leveled out and called to Claire.

"My King," he hailed, "My Only. Even I don't understand this tragedy. What was the purpose in Romlin's death?"

The whisper spoke. *"The purpose is mine and a great purpose it will be."*

"But Ela Claire is succumbing to the Cauldron's whisper and is journeying back to Hetherlinn."

"Yes, I saw this long before she even climbed her oak."

"Then I must force her back to Claire so she can..."

"You must do no such thing."

"Then her future holds even more heartache."

"The future is not for you to see, Previn, but this much I will tell you. Although the Cauldron's attack was meant to destroy, I will orchestrate it into the grandest of tales. Her heartache will be her tulip, and if she allows it to blossom, she will become the great storyteller she longs to be. Only by standing on the edge of a grave can she discover life, but even in this, only when she returns her heart to me."

Previn gazed down at the River Arrgient. At his great height, the twisting waters glistened in the sunlight like a brown ribbon. He caught a glimpse of Ela Claire walking along the shoreline.

"So I'm to do nothing," Previn asked, frustrated that he was not allowed a longer glimpse into her story to come.

"No, Previn, you are to oblige her wish and carry her on the wind to Hetherlinn."

"But my King," Previn said as he watched her disappear from site. "You told her she could never return home."

"As you've already surmised, Previn, it was not to punish or control her, but to protect her. Now that she has set her mind on returning, you must assist her. Guard her with your life. Be her champion. Be her guardian during her dark hours and during the lulls from the storm. Comfort her when she mourns. Offer her hope when she sips from the Cauldron's dark waters. Sing her song to her so she will learn that her waltz is forever playing in Marsien Vur. And how rich a song it is! I wish she could hear it now, but at this time, she is unable and unwilling."

"One more question, if you please," Previn asked, more afraid of the answer than he was the request. "Will she dance to her waltz again?"

"Previn, you know that when she journeys back to Claire she will forever dance with me."

"With all due respect, my King, I meant in this world, not in Claire."

"As did I. Now go. I shall not abandon her in her darkest hour and neither shall you."

Previn pulled in his wings and dove straight down for the river. As the wind whistled past him, he used his keen sight to spy her location. Pulling out of the dive, he glided above the treetops and followed her scent. When she walked into an area thin of trees, he swooped down and landed just in front of her.

She pushed on by without so much as a word or a glance his way.

Previn called after her.

"I've come to carry you to Hetherlinn."

She stopped and turned, with arms crossed beneath her breasts.

"How do I know that you won't trick me and carry me against my will to Claire?"

"The Only himself has ordered me to carry you to Hetherlinn and that is what I will do."

She scowled at him.

"I thought he said I couldn't go home?"

"No, what he actually said is you could never go home because.."

She held up a hand to silence him.

"It doesn't matter. But tell me this: what does Previn wish to do?"

The great harrier blinked in rapid succession and answered her as he always had: from an honest heart.

"I wish the Cauldron was destroyed. I wish I could have saved Romlin. I wish I could make your heart dance again to the waltz of Marsien Vur...forever."

"And will you?"

Previn shook his head.

"I can no more force your heart to change than I can see how your story will end."

Convinced Previn was bound to an oath he had secretly made to the King of Claire, Ela Claire approached, albeit timidly.

She grabbed a hold of his plumage and climbed upon his back.

"No tricks."

"None," he answered. "I promise."

"Then fulfill your vow to the Only. Take me back to Hetherlinn, to my oak where I can live with my memories. Take me away from this land of death."

True to his word, Previn rose into the cool air, banked and carried the love of his heart toward Allsbruth.

Chapter 50

A Lesson in War

Lassiter was curled up near the fire, fast asleep. Draemel strolled up to him and nudged him in the side with his boot.

"Get up," he ordered.

Lassiter rolled over and tried to get comfortable in a new position.

Draemel gave him another swift kick with considerably more force.

Lassiter grumbled as he sat up and massaged his sore ribs.

"Hey, that hurt."

"It was supposed to."

Lassiter rubbed sleep from his eyes.

"Give me just a few more moments..."

"We need as much time as possible to train and strengthen your muscles. Even now, your enemy is using every available moment to train so they can kill *you*. You can sleep when the war is over...or when you're dead."

Convinced Lassiter would not fall back asleep, Draemel walked to his tethered horse and pulled out an assortment of items from his saddlebags.

Lassiter stumbled away from the fire stretching and yawning. He tripped over DeMorley's sleeping frame, and as he regained his balance, he glanced up at the sky and realized just how early it was.

"It's only sunrise," he shouted at Draemel. "I could have slept longer."

"Welcome to the school of war, your majesty," Draemel answered with a bit of mockery in his voice. "Comfort, sleep and self-pity are to be left behind. They serve no purpose in battle. You must sharpen not only your fighting skills but your mind and your resolve as well. I have witnessed many a skirmish where a few men of stout heart were able to turn aside an army of greater size and strength."

"But what about him?" Lassiter pointed back at the snoring DeMorley. "Why is *he* allowed to sleep?"

"Oh, I have something special for our minstrel friend. He needs all the rest he can get,"

With that, Draemel turned and walked over to a fallen tree. There he knelt and ceremoniously placed the items from his saddlebag on top. Curiosity brought Lassiter to his side where he stared at them.

"I will teach you to master all of these," Draemel declared. Pointing to one, he said, "This is a dagger."

"I *know* it's a dagger and I *know* how to use it," Lassiter said flippantly.

Draemel gave him a sideways look.

"As a boy, cutting up an apple, perhaps. As a man using it to take another's life, no."

Draemel continued with his introductions.

"This is my sling and metal balls."

"A sling? Children play with..."

Draemel grabbed Lassiter by his tunic.

"I am not as patient a teacher as Newcomb. Do you wish to learn to become a warrior-king, or return to Blomseth and be a minstrel?"

"Warrior-king," Lassiter replied in earnest.

"As I was saying," Draemel continued as he released his hold on Lassiter, "when used properly, this is more accurate and lethal than a crossbow. Which brings us to..."

"Your crossbow," Lassiter answered.

"Yes, and I will also teach you the art of the long bow."

"But we don't have a long bow, so how..."

"Next, is the battle ax," Draemel interrupted, ignoring his question. "The sight of which will often send your enemy running for their life."

Lassiter nodded. The weapon's wicked, curved, metal edge sent a shiver down his spine.

"This, of course, is a short sword."

"Newcomb taught me how to handle a sword."

Draemel's eyebrow rose.

"Really?"

"Yes," Lassiter said, though respectfully, without bravado.

"Very well," Draemel said, tossing him the blade. "Give me a demonstration of your education."

Retrieving the dagger, Draemel said, "Begin."

He held the dagger loosely by his side while his feet were spread apart. He took no defensive stance, and was not ready to lunge or spring away.

"But you only have a dagger and you stand unprepared for my attack."

"So you say," Draemel answered as he studied the boy. "I said, begin!"

Lassiter snickered, shook his head and brought his sword back. He began swirling the blade about in the air.

Impressive, Draemel thought, though his face remained stoic. *So Newcomb's taught you the classical approach. But such education, although brilliant, is worthless on the battlefield. The days of gentleman combat are no more; it is time to learn the improvisational method.*

Lassiter, not wishing to harm his teacher, half-heartedly swung his weapon. Draemel easily dodged the blade and with a swift kick to the boy's bottom, sent him sprawling.

"What are you *doing?*" Lassiter huffed as he spat dirt from his mouth.

"That, your majesty," Draemel replied with a mock bow, "was something you will never be given in battle: mercy."

Lassiter stood and wiped the dirt off his face and tunic.

"Again," Draemel ordered.

Angered, Lassiter charged with his sword drawn back high over his head. Draemel knelt, picked up a stone and threw it, hitting Lassiter squarely in the forehead. Lassiter dropped to the ground.

"Ouch!" he said as he felt the wound. Warm blood oozed onto his fingers. "You could have killed me."

Draemel merely glared at Lassiter and dangled his dagger by his side.

"Again," he said.

Lassiter stood and threw his sword end-over-end at the bounty hunter. Draemel calmly raised his dagger and deflected the sword, sending it point first into a nearby tree.

"Bold," Draemel commented as he walked to the impaled sword quivering back and forth. "Yet very foolish," he said as he sheathed his dagger. "Because now *you* are without a weapon."

Draemel put his boot on the tree and with both hands on the weapon's hilt, yanked it free. Facing Lassiter with a snarl, he shouted, "Again!"

"But I'm defenseless."

"Is that what you'll say to the Ebonites?" Draemel replied as he marched toward him. "Do you think they will care? King or no king, Ebonites never take prisoners." Draemel slowly raised the sword. "Overcome the problem."

"But I don't have a weapon," Lassiter shouted as he backed away.

Draemel quickened his pace.

Lassiter froze.

Draemel swung the blade. At the last possible moment, he turned the edge away and struck Lassiter's flanks with the blade's flat side.

"Ah," Lassiter screamed as he fell to the ground and grabbed the back of his legs. Draemel, unmoved by the boy's pain, quickly prepared to strike again.

"Fight, Lassiter."

"With what?" the boy shouted up from the dirt.

"Find your strength."

Lassiter frantically looked around for a weapon. From the corner of his eyes, he could see Draemel preparing to swing. Lassiter reacted. Grabbing up a handful of dirt, he rolled over and threw it into Draemel's face.

"Excellent," Draemel managed between coughs. Once he cleared his eyes, he began his approach once more. "But I'm still out for blood."

Lassiter glanced over at the log of weapons. It was a risky move but what other option did he have? He hopped up and raced to the log. There, he grabbed the sling, popped the metal ball inside and spun it over his head. Draemel stopped and cocked his eyebrow.

"The sling is an interesting choice of weapons, your majesty. And you handle it with, dare I say, confidence."

"Please stop," Lassiter ordered. "I don't want to hurt you."

"Hurt me?" Draemel sneered and shook his head. "Doubtful."

Draemel raised his blade and continued his approach.

"I'm not joking," Lassiter warned as he increased his whirling sling's speed. "Stop."

DeMorley, awakened by the hubbub, sat up.

"What are you two doing," he asked while rubbing his eyes of sleep.

"I'm giving the king his first lesson," Draemel fired without taking his eyes off Lassiter's sling.

"This is my last warning," Lassiter shouted at Draemel. "I mean it."

A wry smile pursed Draemel's lips. With no warning, he charged.

Lassiter gave the sling one last rotation then released the metal ball. Draemel froze. The sphere's speed and accuracy were greater than he had anticipated. Instinct took over and he ducked just as the ball zipped past his head.

Thwack!

Draemel studied the orb embedded in the tree trunk, then looked back at Lassiter. The boy's eyes were wild with fear and adrenaline, and his chest heaved with each breath.

"You nearly killed me," Draemel muttered in a low voice.

"I gave you plenty of warning," Lassiter pointed out, fear giving way to anger.

Draemel flashed Lassiter a rare smile.

"You nearly killed me," he praised. "You *surprised* me and I underestimated your skills."

He strode over to Lassiter and swatted him on the back hard enough to knock him off balance. Lassiter stood dumbfounded and confused.

"So tell me," Draemel inquired, "was that a lucky shot or was that skill?"

The boy blew out a deep breath and regained a bit of his youthful bravado.

"Skill," he answered.

Draemel cocked his eyebrow.

"Tell me more, future King of Allsbruth."

"Well, life on the Isle of Lills was often boring, so I'd entertain myself at the beach with a sling Newcomb made for me. I'd try and hit seagulls with the round stones I gathered near our cottage."

"And how did you fair?"

"I eventually learned to hit them in flight."

"You could hit seagulls...while they were *flying?*"

Lassiter nodded, pleased that his days playing on the Isle of Lills were proving to be of value.

"To think," Draemel said with a faint smile, "I nearly had my head removed by Lassiter, the great hunter of gulls."

He gave Lassiter another approving swat before heading toward his horse. Lassiter smiled and noticed that in that brief interchange, Draemel's granite-like countenance had softened, revealing another dimension to his personality that had been dormant. He liked the change.

DeMorley still sat on the ground and continued to stare at them both with mouth agape.

"Seagulls? Slings? Lessons? What is going on here?"

"Yes, Master DeMorley. Seagulls, slings and lessons," Draemel answered while mounting. "A warrior must use all that life has taught him. That is his true arsenal. Now come, it is time for us to go."

"Go?" A bamboozled look painted DeMorley's face.

"Lassiter, retrieve my steel ball from the tree. DeMorley, gather up my weapons. We're moving this school to a new location."

As they went about their duties, Draemel studied the surrounding woods. The sun was higher and cast long shadows across the forest floor.

"Where are we going?" Lassiter asked as he swung his leg over his saddle.

"It's not proper that the future King of Allsbruth does not bear a sword," he answered. "DeMorley shall get you one."

"And how am I to do *that?*" DeMorley chortled while gathering in his horse's reins.

"By sheer cunning, my dear little minstrel," Draemel replied in his normal, ice-cold tone of voice. "By sheer cunning."

Chapter 51

Dark Cloud, Blue Sky

A vivid blue sky greeted Hetherlinn with another perfect day. Since receiving the blessing from Ebon, the villagers merged their old traditions with new ones. The women still gathered by the communal fire, but instead of mending old garments, they now fashioned new clothes for their families with the magnificent fabrics of Ebon. Laughter and gossip buzzed as quickly as their needles pulling thread.

The men, on the other hand, stood aloof and puffed on morning pipes, admiring their cottages. Murmurs of respect buzzed among the inhabitants of the village as they praised each other's work, whether it be as a seamstress or as a builder. Yet envy was an unseen canker. Each villager secretly wondered what to do next to outdo the other.

It began in the early stages of the remodeling when one family decided to add a front porch to their cottage. Not wanting to be outdone, every other family added a bigger or more ornate front porch. When one applied colorful stains to their home, other families did the same, choosing different shades in hopes of winning the battle of colors.

As fast as one added a unique feature, the others would emulate and embellish the creation: Gray slate replaced thatched roofs; flower boxes graced windows; additional rooms were constructed, not because they were needed, but simply because they could.

As their homes improved, the sight of Quinn's and Gundin's old cottages - Number 17 and Number 7 - became eyesores. One night, the mob lit torches and the homes were reduced to ash.

"A fitting end for the traitors of Min Brock," they hailed.

For widows like Mithe - who were unable to do manual labor in order to remodel - the villagers rallied to beautify their cottages. At the heart of their passion was not mercy, but pride, for they simply did not want their newly decorated homes to be sullied from sitting beside dilapidated cottages.

Soon, the children began to stir. Like a herd of boars, they raced past the countless playthings strewn about in the dust and began clawing into a new barrel. They dug, fought, pushed and whined, each wanting to be the first to get the biggest and best toy for the day.

Clutching their new prizes to their chests, they scampered away to play alone. When they became bored, usually within a few moments, they hurled the plaything to the ground and ran to snatch a new one.

Fathers stood oblivious to their children's wastrel antics. Rings of smoke billowing from their pipes as they pondered the next project that would make them appear more prosperous and important than their neighbors. Mothers also turned a deaf ear to their children's behavior, choosing instead to gossip about topics of little consequence.

Each day was identical to the one before. Until the day that Mithe, by sheer coincidence, happened to glance skyward.

"That's odd," she muttered to herself as she finished a stitch. "A storm cloud shrouded by a clear blue sky."

But the laughter and jovial conversation lured her attention from the sky back to the delight of the cloth. Time passed, and the old woman felt uneasy in her spirit. She glanced northward again; something about it caught her attention. Rising to her feet, she stared at the anomaly.

The other women followed Mithe's gaze and spotted the phenomenon. The men, catching the sudden silence from their womenfolk, continued to smoke but peered in the direction they were looking. Even the children stopped fighting long enough to gaze up at the sky. The whole village, numb with comfort, gazed silent and unsuspecting at the shade sweeping their way.

"That cloud," Mithe mused aloud, as if awakening from a dream. "It has form and shape unlike any cloud I've ever seen."

"The cloud is funny," a child shouted up from the dust. "It has wings."

Pipes fell from opened mouths as the men stared in disbelief.

"That's no cloud," one man commented. "It's a flock of flying creatures. But they don't resemble any bird I've ever seen. I wonder what they are?"

As the horde dove closer to the village, the corporate sense of nonchalant well-being was pierced by an odd quiver of foreboding.

"Perhaps they've flown from Ebon to bring us more blessings," one man proposed.

But old Mithe dropped her cloth as a chill ran up her spine.

"Ebon has already blessed us," she murmured. "Whatever this is, it is no blessing."

She hobbled away from the communal fire and called desperately for her granddaughter. Hearing the urgency in her grandmother's voice, the child ran swiftly to her side.

"Listen to me and do *exactly* what I tell you," Mithe instructed as she gazed into the girl's frightened eyes. "Gather the children and head for Min Brock. Go through the woods and stay off of the road. Do not stop for anything. Do you understand?"

"But what of you," the girl asked.

Mithe looked skyward. The dragon-like silhouettes were growing in size. Some had already landed in the meadow beside the ancient, massive oak.

"Leave," she ordered as she pushed the girl on her way. "Now. *Hurry!*"

Tears streamed down the girl's face, but she ran as she was commanded. Mithe hobbled back to the fire.

"Quick," she ordered her friends. "To your homes. Bar the doors shut. Stoke up the fires so they cannot enter through your chimneys."

Mithe hurried off to her home. She glanced back at her neighbors, who sat unmoved by her plea. Some even mocked her fear and paranoia.

She turned away and entered her cottage. She pulled the bar down over her door, then limped to her windows and pulled the shutters tight. She scuttled to the fireplace and fanned the coals until flames leapt into the chimney. After piling wood onto the fire, she pulled up a chair and sat, awaiting the inevitable.

The inevitable was not long in coming.

Loud thumps on her tiled roof made Mithe jump. Scratching claws, like nails on slate, set her teeth on edge and sent shivers down her back. From outside, she heard the agonizing screams of those who had foolishly remained by the fire.

Mithe shook with fear and tossed another log on her fire. The scraping sounds got louder and louder. Her breaths came in short bursts.

Wood cracked overhead.

Mithe pulled her shawl close and raised fear-filled eyes toward the rafters. Monsters with faces half-reptile, half-man, stared down through the small hole they had created. Mithe toppled to the floor in shock. She stared, as if in a daze, at the creatures from a nightmare who clawed at the hole, trying to make it big enough for them to enter.

"Please...forgive me," she pleaded. "Have mercy."

The Demoliths stopped their clawing for a moment, as they glared down at her with yellow, reptilian eyes.

"Forgiveness and mercy are gifts we don't bear," one sneered.

But Mithe was not addressing them. She hoped her plea would flash like lightning to Claire and retrieve the stories of her youth that once flowed so luxuriously through her veins. She knew she did not deserve such liberation, yet she yearned for the impossible.

Debris from the roof crashed all around her.

A whisper, like the song of a lark in a spring meadow, enveloped her as death fell from the rafters.

Chapter 52

A King's Sword

Draemel pulled back on the reins and turned to check on DeMorley. The minstrel's shoulders slumped and his head bounced to the cadence of his horse's plodding gait.

"DeMorley," Draemel barked, "Spur that animal. Make haste."

DeMorley lifted his head and glared.

"As I've told you before, I'm tired of being your live bait. Why should I hurry just so you can use me like a piece of meat to snare a fox?"

"You flatter yourself," Draemel snarled. "You're more like dung attracting flies."

DeMorley rolled his eyes and mumbled something crass about Draemel's mother. Up ahead, Lassiter noticed a clearing and pointed it out to Draemel.

"Be alert," Draemel advised him quietly.

DeMorley pulled up beside Lassiter.

"You know what to do," Draemel said.

"And if I don't?" he retorted.

Draemel flashed him a disconcerting look that sent any thought of rebellion retreating from DeMorley's mind like a beaten hound.

"Tell me something," DeMorley asked. "Are you from Tristan?"

"No, I'm from Ingloid. Why?"

"No reason. I was just curious."

With a disgruntled huff, DeMorley spurred his horse and lumbered into the clearing. He dismounted, pulled his lute from around his back and began strumming the chords to a song. The minstrel meandered about the small meadow singing an improvised song with great gusto, using the Tristan dialect. Lassiter, who was well versed in a number of foreign tongues, chuckled.

"What's so funny," Draemel asked.

Lassiter tried to stop laughing, but every time he did, DeMorley's next verse made him hoot even harder.

"Tell me," Draemel thundered as his face became as red as his hair.

"He's singing," Lassiter blurted between giggles, "about *you.* It's a clever song comparing a dumb ox and a dung beetle."

"Dung beetle," Draemel roared as he scowled at DeMorley. But the minstrel, who knew that there was nothing Draemel could do to stop him, continued to sing at the top of his voice.

"So what happens next," Lassiter asked in an attempt to get Draemel's mind off of the song.

Draemel focused his attention on Lassiter. He looked deeply into the boy's eyes, as if trying to impart a great truth to a young warrior.

"We wait for the Ebonites to take the bait. But there's no sense in letting the time go to waste. This is as good a time as any for a lesson."

"Shall we spar again?"

"Yes, but not with steel. With our minds."

Lassiter looked confused.

"To be victorious, you must know your enemy; you must know him better than yourself. Tell me, what is the Ebonites' weakness?"

Lassiter's mouth twisted in knots as he thought about an answer.

"I suppose...that the armor on their backside is not very strong."

"And why is this?"

"Because Ebonite warriors always attack head on and never retreat or surrender."

"Good. What else."

"What else?" Lassiter chuckled. "They don't have any other weaknesses. That's why they rule all the nations."

"Think," Draemel asked as he tapped his index finger to his forehead. "Every warrior, even one from Ebon, has more than one weakness."

"Well," Lassiter let out an derisive snort, "let me think. Of course. They tower over most men. They have the best armor and the strongest horses of any nation. Oh, and they are are empowered by the Cauldron. All great weaknesses, to be sure."

Draemel's brown-granite eyes smothered Lassiter's cynical smile.

"This is not some boyish lesson on the Isle of Lills with a sweetmeat as a reward for a correct answer. This is a lesson in life. Learn it, and you will rule well. Miss it, and you will perish, and your nation with you."

"Very well," Lassiter huffed as he turned his attention to the dancing DeMorley. "Do you want to hear my honest answer?"

"Yes."

Lassiter snapped his head back around to Draemel.

"Then here it is: they have no other weaknesses. They can't be defeated."

Draemel cocked his eyebrow as if to salute the boy's honesty.

"Good," he replied, though his manner never changed. "Now you're ready to learn."

Lassiter's mouth fell open.

"Didn't you hear what I just said? I said, they *can't* be defeated."

"No, what you really said is that you believe *you* can't defeat them."

"I did not. I said..."

"Listen to your inner voice. What do you feel right now? What do you *truly* believe?"

Lassiter fumed for a moment, but he did as he was told and examined his convictions.

I have too many doubts and fears. The fact that I'm to be Allsbruth's next king seems like a fantasy. No, it is an unattainable goal...impossible! But even if it were possible, what troubles me most is this: am I worthy to bear such a title?

Lassiter's shoulders drooped.

Draemel noted his body language, and as he pondered how to encourage him, a whisper floated to his ear.

"Tell him the story."

Unaccustomed to hearing a whisper from Claire, Draemel looked around for the source, afraid that an enemy has somehow managed to slip up on them. But the woods and meadow were empty, save for the capering DeMorley.

"Tell the tale you know well," the whisper added. *"It's time Lassiter hears."*

Draemel drew in a deep breath. Despite his reservation about the origin of the whisper, he knew it spoke true. He felt that the tale of Hornlynn might be exactly what was needed to ignite the boy's zeal.

"Lassiter, I would like to tell you a...story." The potent word hung in the air for a moment, and resonated with power. "It pertains to your father."

"Look," Lassiter said with more heat in his voice than he intended, "like I've already told you, Newcomb wasn't..."

"I'm not talking about Newcomb," Draemel interrupted.

He stared into Lassiter's eyes. In that brief interchange, he saw the resemblance: Lassiter had his father's eyes. And he recognized the potential greatness within the boy.

"I'm talking about the man I fought beside during the Dark War. I'm talking about Hornlynn. Your *real* father."

Lassiter's mouth dropped open in disbelief.

"Your father was a brave man; the likes of which I'd never seen before, nor am likely to see again."

Lassiter blinked his eyes rapidly as he tried to digest Draemel's story. He shook his head, not in skepticism, but because he was overwhelmed by the countless questions exploding in his mind.

"When did you fight with him?"

"Those tales are for another time. For now, this is what I want you to learn. The strength of any warrior is in his passion and his resolve. These are his greatest weapons. Not his steel, nor his arrows. Your father carried such courage and determination that he could make other men brave, just by riding beside them."

Draemel refocused on Lassiter's eyes and delivered his next words as if passing a torch to one traveling in darkness.

"You remind me of him."

Something stirred within Lassiter. Emotions he never knew he possessed came to life and dominated not only his thoughts but his passions as well. Confidence corralled his fears and doubts, as well as the lingering shame he felt over Newcomb's death. Hope gave him a sense that perhaps his father, the man Draemel just said he was like, was not only watching over him at this very moment, but was perhaps even proud of what he saw.

Lassiter's shoulders righted and his back stiffened. Draemel liked the change; a faint smile pulled at his lips.

"Now," Draemel stated as he shifted his weight in his saddle. "I shall ask you again: What is another weakness of your enemy?"

Lassiter thought long and hard, desperately wanting to find the answer, wondering what his father would have said.

"I suppose it's not what they do, but perhaps how they think."

"Go on."

"Well," he said, connecting his thoughts aloud as they arose "they never retreat."

"Yes. But why is that a weakness?"

"Well, because..."

Lassiter let his imagination wander as he pondered the question. He had so many questions to ask Draemel about his father, and it took all his will to not pester him with a single one. He forced his thoughts back to the present and the question at hand.

"Ebonites don't retreat because they are accustomed to victory. They are over-confident, or perhaps a better term would be, prideful, in a bad way. If we exploit their pride, we might gain an advantage."

Draemel's eyes sparkled with excitement. Lassiter was not only going to be a fierce combatant with steel, but would prove to be a worthy adversary in intellect and strategy.

"Excellent," he said with an approving nod. "So we'll spark their confidence into over-confidence to the point that pride will not let them fight rationally. And when they take this bait..."

Draemel studied Lassiter's face before delivering his final thought.

"...you will destroy them."

Lassiter did not flinch, nor did he whine about a mission that only moments before he had declared impossible. Amazed at Lassiter's new-found inner strength, Draemel simply stared at him in awe.

Lassiter, who wondered why he was gawking at him in such a manner, fidgeted in his saddle.

"What's wrong?" he finally asked Draemel.

Draemel did not reply. Instead, his joyous expression faded and he donned his mask of stoicism. With the snap of his reins on his horse, he led them deeper into the woods until DeMorley's song became a faint melody.

"Listen," Draemel ordered Lassiter.

Lassiter leaned forward in his saddle and strained to hear whatever Draemel heard.

He shook his head. "I only hear DeMorley..."

"Listen beyond his song. It is a low, rhythmic sound."

Lassiter's eyes widened as his ears caught the sound.

"Ebonite war drums."

Draemel's eyes, recently warmed by memories of Hornlynn, returned to cold granite.

"It's time we get your majesty a sword."

The drums became louder. Lassiter bobbed his head about, trying to get a good glimpse through the trees to the clearing's distant edge. In the distance a column of Ebonite foot soldiers emerged from the foliage, drummers marching alongside to maintain the pace with their steady *thud, thud, thud.*

"There are too many," Lassiter gasped beneath his breath.

Draemel sat high in his saddle, unmoved. If the number of Ebonite warriors troubled him, it didn't show. He kept his eyes focused on the Ebonites as he reached into a saddlebag and pulled out some items. Without a glance at Lassiter, he held them out for him to take.

Lassiter stared at the sling and spiked metal ball. He glanced at the column of warriors entering the clearing. He swallowed down his anxiety and then took the sling and orb.

"Stay here," Draemel instructed. "I'll move across the way."

"But there must be over fifty warriors," Lassiter whispered, apprehension and doubt joined his bile and rose into his mouth.

"Actually," Draemel said as a line of horsemen emerged into view, "if you count their cavalry, it looks to be closer to one hundred. Remember: their confidence is their weakness. Watch and learn."

DeMorley never heard the drums. He was too busy composing new verses to his *Draemel the Lonely Dung Beetle* song. When he modulated for the grand finale, and he stopped twirling about, he saw the horde of warriors advancing toward him.

His song died, as did his comedic spirit.

"DeMorley," Draemel whisper-shouted from his new position in the shadow of the thicket. "Be ready."

DeMorley remained frozen in place, not out of courage or any willingness to comply with Draemel's order. He was simply too scared to move.

The Ebonite drum cadence stopped, as did the column of warriors. Spying the minstrel, a command was shouted and a brisk cadence began from the drums. Two warhorses peeled away from the column and thundered toward the defenseless DeMorley.

"Steady," Draemel reassured him.

DeMorley snapped out of his daze and raced to his horse who pranced about, skittish after catching the scent of the Ebonite warhorses. DeMorley grabbed the reins, steadied the animal and quickly mounted.

"Not yet, DeMorley," Draemel called to him through cupped hands.

"Not yet," the minstrel squealed over his shoulder once he found his voice. "I'm the one unarmed and in their path, not *you.*"

"Let them get closer, then lead them through the woods."

The two Ebonite warriors loomed. Thundering hooves drowned out the drums. Draemel glanced back at Lassiter and mouthed, "Be brave. Fight with your mind first."

Lassiter nodded. The sling hung by his side. He could feel the heaviness of the steel ball tucked within. His muscles were ready to start the sling's orbit.

Draemel turned his attention back to DeMorley.

"Now!" he ordered.

The minstrel spurred his horse, but in his anxiousness to flee, he headed straight for the approaching warriors. The Ebonites drew their swords.

"What's the fool doing," Draemel muttered to himself. He raised his crossbow and was about to fire when DeMorley, regaining control of his emotions and his horse, turned about and retreated toward the woods.

"Shoot them," DeMorley squealed like a girl at the top of his lungs. "What are you waiting for? *Shoot them.*"

Lassiter twirled his sling.

"Wait," Draemel ordered Lassiter. "Stay calm. You have only one shot."

DeMorley entered the woods and quickly found the trail. The Ebonites were close behind.

"*Draemel,*" DeMorley screeched as he glanced over his shoulder at the warriors. "For the love of the Only, shoot, shoot, *shoot.*"

Lassiter spun the sling faster as DeMorley approached his hiding place.

"Let DeMorley pass then fire," Draemel instructed Lassiter.

"But..."

Draemel locked eyes with Lassiter. Cold and dangerous as the steel ball in his sling, Lassiter noted they were focused on only one thing: the demise of their enemies. Lassiter felt revived. Strength rushed through him like a flash flood in a dry riverbed.

"Shooooot!" DeMorley shrieked as he spurred his horse to a greater pace.

With the sling whirling overhead, and his eyes focused on the two warriors, Lassiter spoke quietly a hunting blessing that Newcomb had taught him many summers before.

"Guide my shot, make it straight and true. May I drink the pure waters from the victor's cup. May this day bring glory to the King of Claire, where death begets life."

DeMorley flew past.

Lassiter spurred his horse out of the shadows and blocked the warrior's path. Startled by the ambush, one Ebonite veered into the woods. Lassiter released his sling.

After zooming past Lassiter, DeMorley looked back over his shoulder and saw one warrior still in pursuit. When DeMorley faced forward, he encountered a tree limb looming over the path. He instinctively raised his arms to protect himself, and was snagged by the branch. Yanked out of his saddle, he clung to the limb dazed and baffled how he had ended up in such a precarious predicament.

The Ebonite pulled back on the reins and stopped. DeMorley heard the snort of the warhorse and began kicking his legs to try and pull himself up into the tree and out of the Ebonite's reach.

"What have we here," the warrior taunted. "A skinny minstrel dangling from a tree, like a doe waiting to be gutted. Before I draw first blood, perhaps we should have some sport."

DeMorley was about to drop to the forest floor and take his chances running when he heard another horse approach. He strained for a look, but was unable to see the two riders.

The warrior assumed the gate was that of the other errant companion, and kept his eyes centered on DeMorley. Over his shoulder, he joked, "So, which one of us will be blessed with first blood?"

The warhorse stopped beside the warrior, and from the corner of his eye he sensed something was wrong. He snapped his head around and was startled to see a young boy. His left hand held the reins while his right arm, hidden from view, dangled by his side apparently wounded. The Ebonite snarled as he recognized Lassiter from the recent ambush.

"Who *are* you?"

"I'm Lassiter, future King of Allsbruth."

The warrior looked him up and down then burst out laughing.

"You?" he said between chuckles. "A *king?*"

The Ebonite stopped laughing and an evil expression, the likes of which Lassiter had never seen before, covered his face.

"Yes, well, perhaps you are. Greetings, future King of Allsbruth," the warrior mocked. "I bear a message from the Cauldron of Kise: Death begets death!"

The Ebonite raised his sword to strike.

"And I bring you a message from Claire," Lassiter countered. "Long live the Only!"

Lassiter swung his right arm up. In his grip was an Ebonite sword which he thrust into the Ebonite's unprotected side. The warrior's eyes filled with horror as he realized the dishonor of not only being slain by a boy, but with an Ebonite blade. Black eyes rolled back revealing only the whites, as he fell from his saddle.

Draemel emerged from the shadows with his crossbow resting on his hip. He rode past Lassiter without a word and rescued the stranded minstrel from his predicament. Once DeMorley was secure back in the saddle of his horse, he cast his glance about.

"There were two Ebonite warriors chasing me," DeMorley peeped. "Where's the other one?"

"No need to fret," Draemel answered. "He's lying dead back down the path."

DeMorley sighed in relief.

"I'm glad you're such a good shot you can hit a man on a horse at full gallop," he said to Draemel.

"I didn't kill him. Lassiter did, with my sling."

DeMorley's eyes jumped from Draemel to Lassiter. Gone were the eyes of the boy from the Isle of Lills. Staring back at him was the warrior-king of Allsbruth.

"But now is not the time for celebration," Draemel declared. "When these two don't return, they'll send more to find out what's happened."

"So, what do we do," DeMorley asked.

"That's up to our king," Draemel answered with a nod to Lassiter.

Lassiter's eyes danced as he met Draemel's stare. The big man's eyes were still icy, hardened by years of hunting men for a few gilns. But deep within, he saw a glint of light, like a beacon glowing from atop a distant citadel. While gazing into that flickering light, Lassiter reflected on his life with Newcomb, and recalled the stories about his father.

"We ride to the nearest village," Lassiter announced.

"Thank goodness," DeMorley sighed. "I could use a stiff drink. For a moment, I thought you were going to do something rash, like go to war."

Lassiter gave the minstrel a disconcerting glance.

"I'm afraid you misunderstand, master DeMorley. We ride to the next village to recruit men into our army. And from there, we ride to the next village and then the next."

DeMorley's relieved expression fell while a rare smile raced across Draemel's face.

Without another word, Lassiter galloped ahead with Draemel and DeMorley close behind.

Chapter 53

Pyre of Pain

Ela Claire clung to Previn's neck, and every now and then took in her surroundings to make sure he was flying toward Allsbruth. Satisfied that he was staying on course, she hunkered down into his feathers and let her thoughts wander to Romlin. She was past the point of weeping. Her grief had settled into a steady, excruciating pain of the soul that throbbed throughout her entire being.

As the winds grew colder, and her homeland drew nearer, Ela Claire's emotions rolled like a stormy sea. She relived that fateful day at DioBaith over and over, trying to discover what she could have done differently that might have kept Romlin alive. She wondered why Manno Vox didn't help and worse, why the King of Claire had not intervened.

All of her examinations led her back to that frosty morning when she first discovered the parchment stuck in her door. She cursed ever touching it, and for the first time since leaving home, began to believe what her mother had told her about it.

"Its beauty is its deception."

Ela Claire was so consumed with her own self-abasement that she failed to notice the drone. The further they got from Claire, the stronger it became. Its lulling oppressiveness fell heavy upon her doubts and pains, stirring them like cold winds on dying embers. Prowling within its midst was the Cauldron's whisper.

"Was Romlin's death your fault because you didn't tell a story quick enough," it snickered. *"Why didn't you attempt a rescue before battling the vul jens? Tsk, tsk, tsk."*

The accusations doused her with even more self-loathing, and she began to question the delight she experienced dining and dancing in Marsien Vur. She pushed all joy and passion far from her thoughts, convinced she was unworthy of such emotions.

The Cauldron delighted in her choice and disappeared within the drone to seek a more challenging subject.

Ela Claire raised her eyes to check their flight and spotted a plume of smoke on the horizon.

"What's burning," she asked Previn.

"It appears to be the remnants from a battle," he answered, though it was not the complete truth. His keen senses had spied the smoke long before. Previn knew that it rose from a battlefield. What he neglected to tell her was that the battle took place in Hetherlinn.

"Remember," he added, hoping her desire to go home would wane and he could set course for a new direction and save her from more heartache, "the King of Claire told you that you could never go home."

"I remember," she snapped, "but my trust in his words has ebbed away. Romlin is dead, and my heart is wounded to the point of death. I simply long for home."

"His edict was not to punish you. It is to *protect* you."

"Protect me?" she erupted with swift furry. "Where was his protection when Romlin fell to his death. Where was his warning when the vul jens appeared out of nowhere? My trust in his *protection* has faded."

Previn continued toward the smoke that rose aimlessly into the brilliant sky. How he wished he could fly her away against her will and save her from what he knew must await them in Hetherlinn. But he had made a promise, not only to the King of Claire, but to Ela Claire as well. He would be faithful to his duty.

Ela Claire sat up in alarm.

"Previn," she exclaimed in anguish, "I recognize where we are now. That fire is from Hetherlinn. The whole village been set ablaze."

"Yes," he replied. "I know."

"You know?" she fired at him. "Then why didn't you *tell* me?"

Previn's heart sank.

"To spare you more pain. I hoped you would choose a different path and that you would be spared this."

He glided down to her village and circled above the trees to let her gaze upon the utter destruction. Hetherlinn was a heap of charcoal, puffs of smoke rising from the ash like steam from a lava bed.

"Set me down," she ordered Previn.

"It's too dangerous. Besides, can you not see? No one is there. They have all left, or been..."

"Take me down!"

Previn hesitated. A memory flashed of when he was her rusk and met her for the very first time. Her innocence was captivating as was her heart that embraced dreams of the impossible. But now, she was growing more like her father after his defeat at Min Brock, choosing despair as a life-long partner.

"Now," she barked.

Previn landed in the center of the village where the communal fire once burned. It was nothing but cold, black ash.

She leapt off and took in the destruction. The scent of charred wood was everywhere, the acrid smoke gagged her and seared her lungs. The drone took on an ominous weight, heavy and thick, smothering her like heat on a hot summer day.

"Where is my cottage," she whimpered to no one in particular as she spun about to find it. "Have I been away so long that I don't remember?"

As if recalling a forgotten dream, she pictured how Hetherlinn used to be before she and Galadin left.

"Mother! Father!" she cried as she ran to the charred remains of her home. She picked up a long, piece of burnt wood. Blowing off the ash, she revealed the black stains of a cottage number.

"Seventeen," she exclaimed. "My home!"

She used the charred plank as a shovel and began the heart-wrenching task of searching for her parents' remains. Ash was turned releasing clouds of smoke that brushed against her cheeks like a phantom caress. Her heart raced as if fleeing for her life, and an acidic taste covered her tongue.

"Oh please," she cried out. "Let them not be here."

Her tears sprinkled the cinders.

"Please..." she begged as she continued to dig and scrape away the debris.

Soot and ash fell like tarnished snowflakes on her white dress. Previn, unable to watch her painful ordeal, turned his head away, and chose instead to keep vigil against another attack.

Ela Claire, unable to find her parents' remains, exclaimed, "Perhaps they were at Romlin's home."

She ran over to the remains of cottage Number 7. She used the same plank to dig into the ash. As she flipped cinders out of the way, she thought she heard a human voice. She stopped and listened. Someone *was* moaning and it sounded like it came from another mound of ash and debris.

Ela Claire raced to the source and began pulling off the rubble. She froze. An arm covered with gray cinders chilled her to the core. The fingers wiggled accompanied by another moan.

Ela Claire snapped her gaze to where Previn sat.

"Someone's alive," she shouted. "Come and help me."

She worked to lift the debris off of the survivor, but gently, fearing her labor might cause additional harm to one who had already suffered unspeakable horror. She knelt and called out encouragement.

"Don't worry. We're here to help."

Previn joined her, and together they unearthed a battered woman, pulled her from the wreckage then gently laid her upon the ground. She was covered with so much soot and ash that they were unable to recognize her. Ela Claire knelt beside her and dabbed the woman's dust-covered face with the hem of her dress. Her eyes opened. Despite her mask of burned flesh and ash, Ela Claire recognized her gaze and backed away in horror.

"Elabea," Mithe muttered through blackened and blistered lips. "You're alive."

Strands of thanksgiving rose from the old woman's once bitter heart.

Ela Claire, despite the myriad of emotions she felt toward the woman, moved closer and lifted Mithe's head upon her lap. The widow looked longingly into her eyes.

"The children of Hetherlinn," she gasped. "I sent them into the woods before the creatures arrived. Are they safe?"

Ela Claire, not sure what to say, looked to Previn for advice.

"I did not see any children while we flew," Previn answered, "but perhaps they fled in a different direction. We have not checked the surrounding area yet. Let us assume the best."

Mithe closed her eyes and nodded her head. Her dry tongue licked scorched lips in an attempt to moisten them, but she merely smeared the soot.

"They called themselves *demoliths*," she whispered. "Man-dragons. Creations of the Cauldron...horrid beasts...so much destruction. So much pain."

"But where is everyone else," Ela Claire asked as she glanced about the smoking remains of the other cottages.

"Their *eyes!*" Mithe continued as her eyes widened with fear as she recalled the attack, "Yellow, like the sun...a great fire burning within...suffocating heat all around me. Cottages exploded into flame. Friends," she paused and closed her eyes as she relived the ordeal, her frail old body racked with a coughing fit. "All reduced to ash."

Ela Claire gasped in horror and covered her mouth with her hand.

Did my parents suffer such a fate?

Before she could inquire, Mithe continued.

"They told me I was to live and suffer for the Cauldron's delight, but the Only had a different plan. I can *see* that now. He has answered my appeal for mercy and forgiveness."

Ela Claire glanced back at the smoldering remains of cottage Number 17. Her throat clogged with her emotions and she could feel tears ready to burst from her eyes.

"Mithe...my parents? Are they dead?"

"No," Mithe whispered.

Ela Claire's face filled with hope as she gazed down into Mithe's face.

"They left for Min Brock long before the attack," she wheezed. "Listen to me, please. Life is departing me swiftly."

Mithe raised her scorched hand and touched Ela Claire's face, her blackened fingers cold upon her cheek.

"Daughter of Quinn, will you grant me two requests?"

"I will try my best," Ela Claire said with a weak smile.

"For most of your life I set out to harm you. I blamed you for the loss of my menfolk at Min Brock. Now that death approaches, I see things much differently. You were never to blame, and I wish I could take back all my hateful words. Could you ever forgive a bitter old woman like me?"

Ela Claire paused to think. It was not an easy request to grant. Mithe had indeed tortured her with words, and even found pleasure in causing such pain. Now, she asked for the impossible: forgiveness.

Ela Claire had dreamed of inflicting revenge on Mithe and even fantasized about her suffering a horrible death. And yet, now that she had the opportunity for such vengeance, her feelings were different; in part because of Romlin's death, and in part because Ela Claire herself had suffered so much. She was no longer an innocent child. She was a woman who was aware of the pain of loss.

Although she still had misgivings about her time with the King of Claire and his unbelievable stories, she thought she could still hear the faint refrains from her waltz. She knew what she must do.

Ela Claire focused on Mithe's forlorn, pleading eyes.

"I...forgive you."

Mithe's features relaxed and a deep peace, as if sunlight traversed a dark divide, covered her face.

"Bless you, daughter of Quinn," she whispered.

"What else do you wish?"

With what little strength she had left, Mithe clasped Ela Claire's face gently between her burnt hands.

"Be the storyteller you were invited to become."

Ela Claire shuddered. Offering her forgiveness was easier than promising to trust the stories from Claire. Sensing her inner turmoil, Mithe continued.

"Child, let my life of despair and bitterness be a warning to you. Return to the stories. Embrace them with your heart. Make haste or you will wander Allsbruth consumed with anger and become...like *me.*"

"I'll try," Ela Claire answered, still unable to recommit to a life as a storyteller.

Relieved that she had at least promised as much, Mithe released her tenuous grip on life, and breathed her last. Ela Claire gently rested her head upon the ground.

Ela Claire rose and remembered her oak. She turned toward her beloved meadow. The sight made her knees buckle and she crumpled to the ground.

"No," she moaned. "*No.*"

She regained her feet and bolted for the trail that led to the meadow.

"Ela Claire, wait," Previn warned.

She ignored his pleas. Previn launched himself into the air and soared over the treetops to follow her frenzied pace.

When she sprinted down the slope to the stream, a cool breeze greeted her from the shadows.

"*How far must you run,*" a whisper asked, "*to find the border where guilt and pain haunts you no more?*"

Ela Claire increased her speed.

"*I see,*" the Cauldron chided, "*you believe Romlin's death is your fault.*"

She leapt over the stream.

"*Good, good!*" the whisper praised. "*Such truth is freeing, is it not? After all, you chose to tell a story while your friend - or dare I say, the one you dreamed of marrying - was drowning.*"

Ela Claire tried to outrun the wails that filled the woods and reverberated in her ears.

"*There is a way for you to be truly free,*" the whisper invited. "*Become my storyteller, and I will ease your pain...forever.*"

Ebon's cool breeze delivered to her the scent of burnt grass.

"*Breathe deeply. Smell the remains of the one last thing you so dearly loved. And yet, why was it burned? Was it not you who chose to take the invitation and journey to Claire? And what has been your reward...your treasure? I shall tell you: trickery and death by the hands of the Only.*"

She emerged into the meadow and stopped.

"This can't be," she moaned to herself.

Her once vibrant field of grass and wildeberry was black from fire. Her eyes jumped to the knoll.

"My oak."

She charged toward her sanctuary. Her feet pounded a painful cadence on the charred field.

"*Yes, run Ela Claire. Run to where your dreams began. Where are your imaginings today? Where are the promises of Claire now?*"

The oak lay on its side, its great trunk hacked to pieces in order to topple it. It too had been set afire. Black and white ash covered it from top to bottom. She placed her hand on its charred surface; it was still warm from the blaze. The oak's magnificent limbs, the ones that once held her like the arms of a father, spilled out onto the burnt meadow, crushed, broken and black.

Previn landed nearby.

"Who would do something so evil," she asked him as her tears dotted the black trunk. "Everything I have cherished and everyone I have loved, even hated, have been taken from me. Why, Previn, why? What have I done to deserve this?"

"All that has happened is the work of Ebon and the Cauldron, not the King of..."

"Does that response satisfy the question that haunts you, daughter of Quinn? Are you not deserving of a better answer from the one who calls you his...delight?"

"Previn," she said, "the Cauldron is correct: there is great unrest within me. So tell me, why did the Only allow these tragedies to happen? Why didn't he stop them?"

For a long moment, Previn sat silent. Finally, he answered.

"I'm not given such insights, but there is always a reason for the stories of pain."

"There is your answer!" the whisper hailed. *"The ruler of Claire has manipulated you in order to get all that he desires."*

"Stories of pain," she fired back at Previn. "I'm sick of the tales from Claire."

"But they are true tales."

She spun around to look Previn in the eyes.

"His stories are the ones that have turned upon *me,*" she said with a jab of her finger to her chest. "They bewitched me into thinking I would be someone of importance. Instead, they have led me down a trail of broken dreams."

"Yes, broken dreams, lies and deceit. Come to the woods, child of Hetherlinn. My stories promise you glory and joy; purpose and passion."

She shook her head at Previn and then marched toward the dark thicket.

"Ela Claire," Previn shouted as he flew to protect her. "Don't listen to the whisper of the Cauldron. Believe me: the stories from Claire are true."

"True? This is what is true: Claire produces pain. Come. Closer. I will destroy your pain...forever."

"Leave me alone," she shouted up at Previn. "I don't want anything to do with you, the Only or the stories from Claire. I simply want the pain to end."

Ebon's cool breeze caressed and refreshed her as she turned from the stories of Claire and moved toward the Cauldron's tales.

"But...but that is impossible," Previn rebutted. "You're a storyteller."

"Not anymore," she fired as she stomped onward. "I choose to be...Elabea!"

"Yes! Forsake your new name. It was such a weak title and has delivered nothing but misery. Return to your old name and I shall make you a great storyteller for the Cauldron."

Previn landed to stop her advance.

"The Cauldron only desires to destroy you. Have you already forgotten what it did to Hetherlinn?"

She stopped and glowered at him.

"I'm already destroyed, Previn. If I'd left the invitation alone, all would be well and everyone I love would still be *alive.*"

With that, she pushed past and continued toward the woods. Previn took to the wind. The drone flooded Ela Claire with anguish, shame and guilt.

"Ela Claire," Previn shouted down to her in a last ditch attempt to alter her course and thinking. "You're the Only's delight."

"If I'm his delight, then why did he ignore my cries for help when Romlin fell into the River Arrgient?"

"*I will always listen...*"

She continued. "He hid within the shadows of Marsien Vur while demoliths destroyed Hetherlinn."

"*And he is hiding even still...*"

"He watched as my meadow and my oak were decimated."

"*Are you not deserving of so much more?*"

"He may still delight in me, but I do not delight in him."

"*Ýesss!*"

She stopped by the edge of the dark woods. Previn circled overhead and called to her, but the drone and the winds of Ebon drowned out his warnings.

"*Enter my forest and find sanctuary, for there is another who longs to hold you close.*"

She saw a familiar silhouette. A hand reached toward her from the shadows.

"Romlin?" she asked with a heavy heart. "Is that *really* you?"

Previn swooped by to warn her of the dangers around her, but she ignored him.

"Come," Romlin pleaded. "Peace is but a step away. Clasp my hand, Elabea, and I'll lead you from this land of pain."

As she reached for his fingers, she blinked, and in that brief moment, saw a pair of yellow eyes and felt a great heat. Instinctively, she pulled back, but whatever was there was gone.

"Romlin?" she called out as she scanned the thicket for him. "Are you still there?"

"Yes, Elabea, I'm still here. Join me in the cool of the woods. Forever we can journey the lands as we dreamed of from the oak's branches. Haven't the stories of Claire harmed you enough? Are you not deserving of love...peace...joy?"

She stepped closer.

The hand extended out to her again.

As they were about to touch, a warm breeze crossed her face and the shock made her once again retract her hand.

"Elabea," Romlin's voice called out. "You must fight the winds of Claire and hurry to my side before it is too late."

Before she could step in any direction, a windstorm broke out around her. Trees bowed and groaned against the storm's ferocity. Ash from her oak swirled into the air and grew in size to become a spiraling cloud. Howling like a banshee, it skipped across the black grass in a dance macabre.

In the midst of the howling winds, she heard the sound of a waltz. It entered the fray and grew in volume until it overwhelmed all other sounds.

"Did you dance to this in Marsien Vur?" Romlin's voice asked. "Ignore it, Elabea, and hurry to my side, become my bride, and we shall dance forever to our song. Listen..."

The Cauldron's winds perfectly imitated her waltz and captured its melancholic harmonies and stirring melody. As it pulsed along, it began to change. Odd meters of five and seven catapulted her into a dreamy, haunted soundscape. The tempo lost control and the volume grew to a fevered pitch. Yet, Ela Claire found herself accepting this variation of her waltz, willing to embrace an imitation in order to find a semblance of the life she once knew.

"Romlin," she moaned as she stretched her fingers through the storm toward his.

Fingertips were about to touch when something grabbed her. She screamed. Yanked from her feet, she found herself flying high into the air.

"I'm sorry," Previn shouted down to her. "I had to grab you in order to rescue you."

"But I don't *want* to be rescued," she shouted at him as she squirmed to free herself from his talons. "I want be with Romlin."

"That was *not* Romlin."

"Yes it was. I heard his voice."

"Look below and see for yourself."

Emerging from the shadows of the thicket were hundreds of demoliths.

"The Cauldron tricked you," Previn continued. "It emulated Romlin's voice, his flesh and even imitated your waltz."

Yellow eyes glared upward at her. A wave of heat washed over her.

"Don't look at their eyes," Previn ordered. "Turn away."

She turned her gaze toward the horizon and the heat immediately subsided.

The demoliths flew in pursuit, but the twisting cloud of oak ash settled itself between them and the retreating bird. Its whirling winds buffeting the beasts out of the air. Defeated, the demoliths had no choice but to break off their attack.

Relieved, Previn focused on the flight ahead of them. He quickly realized that carrying her in his talons was too dangerous, so he devised a plan to secure her on his back.

"Prepare yourself," he shouted down to her.

"Prepare myself for wha...?!"

With no further warning, Previn released her. Ela Claire fell, screaming and kicking through the air. Previn dove, then soared under her and caught her upon his back. She clutched his feathers for dear life.

"Why did you do *that,*" she chastised.

"It was the only way to get you safely on my back."

"You could have *landed.*"

"True, but then you wouldn't have discovered the truth."

"What truth?"

"Your thoughts may have led you toward death, but the truth is, your heart longs to live. That's why you screamed when you fell."

"You tricked me," she accused.

"That, my dear Ela Claire, is impossible," Previn replied. "How could I possibly trick a storyteller."

Her mood darkened once more as she reflected on her sorrow. Trapped on his back, she settled herself into his feathers and brooded.

"I know you don't believe," Previn tried to console her, "but a day is coming when the King of Claire will avenge this season. He will transform your fields of death into gardens lush with wonder."

"I doubt it," she moaned as she nestled into his thick, white feathers, and found comfort in their softness. Then, in a quiet, sad voice she added, "Maybe."

"*Maybe* is a good place to start," Previn said. "Maybe one day you will reclaim your name and your title as storyteller. Maybe one day, you will once again feast upon the stories of Claire with an insatiable appetite."

"It feels as if that day is like summer forever lost within winter's chill," she answered with a petulant pout.

"Come what may, I'll never leave you. You will forever be my delight."

"I don't understand the meaning of that word anymore. I simply want to go far away from Allsbruth and Claire, and do nothing but sleep."

Previn glided toward the ground.

"*Now* what are you doing," she asked as she sat up to take in their flight.

"I'm your servant," he replied as he soared just above the treetops. "As your servant, I find great joy in fulfilling your requests. You wish to sleep far from Allsbruth and Claire, so I am respecting your wish."

Previn dipped within the forest and soared through the shade of its branches, swooping around trees. But he refused to disclose their destination. Using his wings to slow his speed, he came to rest in a cool glen surrounded by thick woods and tall cliffs. Ela Claire studied the area. A dark thicket caught her attention.

"These woods look familiar."

"They should. Beyond that grove of pines is Il-Lilliad's cave."

Sliding off his back, she dragged herself toward the cave. Previn watched her retreat. She dragged her feet as if they were too heavy to lift. Her head hung low and her back hunched over as if she were an old woman. And as she slid between the branches and disappeared toward her cave of solitude, Previn made a vow.

I'll allow you as much time as necessary during this winter of your soul. Come what may, I'll stay beside you through your darkest of days and coldest of nights. I will supply you with sustenance and I will guard this cave from the Cauldron's hordes.

This, I promise.

And through it all, perhaps we both will learn how to live within such heartache and emerge with hearts of spring.

Chapter 54

Rain of Steel

"Stay with the others and keep watch," Quinn whispered into Gundin's ear. "I need to scout ahead."

Gundin eyed their group. Areall and Daryess were deep in conversation, no doubt about Elabea and Galadin or the fate of their friends back in Hetherlinn. Leading the way were Phinnton and Bruun. The boy carried the box with pride, and even Gundin was impressed that the boy was able to carry such a load in spite of his thin stature.

Their journey to Min Brock had been uneventful, something both Quinn and Gundin were thankful for. Nevertheless, the men sensed danger in the woods with every step they took. Quinn proceeded with caution, not out of fear, but as a leader wanting the best for those in his trust. Gundin, however, longed for a good fight.

"That I will," Gundin replied with a scowl, "but if you encounter Ebonites, you'd better summon me. I will not be Phinnton's nursemaid while you enjoy combat."

"You know I will," Quinn answered with a smile, clapping his comrade on the shoulder. "But tell me," he began as his eyes danced with mischief, "will you be able to run fast enough to catch up with me?"

Quinn swatted Gundin's rotund midsection.

"Yes, I will, and *this,*" he answered with a pat on his gut, "is solid muscle. You just say the word, friend," Gundin pushed his index finger into Quinn's chest, "and I'll be there."

The men gripped forearms, then Quinn jogged off.

Although Quinn was without a map, he was familiar enough with the terrain from his tenure during the Dark War. If his memory was correct, they should be nearing the Gilden Plains, but he had to be certain. The last thing he needed to do, other than stumble into a trap, was to get lost.

He pressed on through the copse noting that the woods began to thin and the terrain started to level off. Up ahead, he caught a glimpse of a field.

The Gilden Plains, he concluded as he made his way to its edge.

Waist high grass, golden brown from the winter, stretched as far as he could see. It swayed in the breeze like waves upon a yellow and mandarin sea. Small thickets of scrub were scattered about while rogue trees, smaller in size than those of Allsbruth, dotted the plain.

The Gilden Plains stretched westward and skirted the Mountains of Kline that were but a purple line on the distant horizon. Eastward, Quinn knew the plain flowed like a regal robe to Tristan and Ingloid.

He peered north across the sunbathed grasses to a mountain range that ran parallel to the Gilden Sea.

The Addoli Ridge, he reflected as memories from the Dark War flashed before him.

He remembered how strategic the Addoli Ridge had been during the war, specifically during the Ebonite siege of Min Brock. Like the Gilden Plains, the ridge was mostly grass and shrub brush with only a few stunted trees growing here and there. The Ebonites had scaled its heights and gained the advantage of seeing everything that moved upon the plains.

Since the Addoli Ridge was not far from Min Brock, they had the perfect vantage point to watch Min Brock like a bird of prey high above a hare's den.

Quinn's memory flashed with images of that fateful day. Ebon's cavalry lined the Addoli Ridge; an endless black line of death. He shuddered at the memory as feelings of shame and guilt for his cowardice that day swept through him.

Quinn shook off the memory, which was more like a nightmare, and cleared his mind of the disgrace. He chose instead to focus on his morning visits to the tulip and its sweetness and how he sensed a newness stirring within his bones. He longed for redemption. He vowed that this time, with brawn, blood and brain, he would fight for Min Brock and for those he loved, or he would die trying.

Quinn took in the ridge again, but did so with the new vision given him by the tulip.

Perhaps this time around, he reasoned, the Addoli Ridge would be their asset in the ensuing war. The ridge ran a great distance east to west, and was a buffer against the rages of the Gilden Sea whose cold waters were a constant reminder that storms could arise even in the warmest of summers.

More than a vantage point for war, the Addoli Ridge was a geographic anomaly of breathtaking beauty. One of the most beautiful spectacles Quinn beheld during the war was when the waning sunlight cast long shadows across the ridgeline. It danced with color and life.

Quinn drew in a deep breath. The cool air, rich with the scent of dried grass, revived his battered soul. Despite the possibility of his foes prowling all about, the plain and ridge gave him great peace and comfort.

"Maybe, he mused, *there is hope for me - for us - after all."*

Lost in such thoughts, he was unaware of an approaching group until he heard the swish of grass from directly behind him. He snapped out of his daze and spun around, ready to fight.

Gundin held up his hands before him to ward off any blows. The big warrior from Hetherlinn plodded up to Quinn's side and draped his arm over his comrade's shoulder.

"How many summers have passed since we've seen the Gilden Plains," Gundin asked, his voice betraying the same deep anguish as he remembered his role at Min Brock.

"A lifetime," Quinn replied introspectively as their wives, Phinnton and Bruun circled around them.

"It's in worse condition than I imagined," Gundin added.

Quinn gave him a puzzled look.

"The Gilden Plains look the same to me."

"I'm not talking about the plains. I'm talking about *that.*"

Gundin pointed northeast to a solitary mountain far off in the distance. It rose from the plain like a giant anthill. A dilapidated citadel sat on its apex.

"Min Brock," Quinn muttered beneath his breath. He shivered, but not because of the cool breeze.

Even though Min Brock was far away, they could see that its walls and famed seven towers had been eaten away by the winds and rains of the plains. Large birds, made small by the distance, circled the abandoned fortress as if it were a carcass rotting in the sun.

Gundin blew out a breath and shook his head.

"How will we ever defend...*that*?"

"We will work diligently to repair it and make it stronger than before," Quinn answered with dogged determination. "In many ways, the tulip was preparing us for this mission back in Hetherlinn."

Gundin flashed him a look of utter confusion. Quinn explained himself.

"We were like Min Brock. Broken, defeated, death swirling about us...and yet, a tulip, revived our passions and gave us hope to battle the impossible. I don't know the specifics yet. All I know is that we're to journey to Min Brock with the hope...no, with the confidence, that it will one day rise to rule the plains."

Gundin snickered.

"With you, me and *what* army?" he roared. "Our wives and Bruun can't be of much help. And Phinnton," Gundin scowled at the boy who was deep in thought and stared at the Addoli Ridge. "The boy can barely carry that box let alone a shovel."

Quinn's eyes narrowed.

"Phinnton has an inner strength greater than his muscles. Gundin, what has gotten into you? We can't live without hope."

"Hope," Gundin huffed as he returned his gaze to Quinn. "Your hope is more like the dreams and stories of a young girl's imagination."

Quinn's face flared red with anger at Gundin's insinuation and reminder of Elabea. His hands balled into fists, and his knuckles turned white as he envisioned her alone battling their enemy. At the core of his feelings was the notion that this was his fault and that he needed to right the situation. He was about to give Gundin a piece of his mind when Phinnton came up beside the two men with the tulip box cradled in his arms.

"Is this the Gilden Plains," the boy asked.

"Yes," Quinn answered as his anger at Gundin subsided.

"It's just as I imagined," he chirped. "Only it's even more beautiful."

Quinn knelt to talk to the boy face-to-face.

"Yes, it is beautiful. But it is a dangerous place as well. Many a battle from the Dark War was fought here. Long ago, these grasses were stained with the blood of men...good men."

Phinnton nodded and then turned his attention to the distant castle.

"Is that Min Brock," he asked.

Quinn nodded.

"For a youngster," he said with a smile, "you certainly are well versed in the geography of the lands."

"My mother and father taught me," he answered. "It looks run down. Will it be able to protect us?"

Quinn rested his hand on the boy's shoulder.

"It will be our new home," he said, "When the seven towers are reconstructed, we will be able to see far and wide across the Gilden Plains. Neither friend nor foe will be able to approach without our knowing about it."

"But it is far away," Phinnton noted as he shuffled the box to relieve his strained muscles.

"We'll be there soon enough, but we definitely want to be off the plains by evening."

Phinnton heard the urgency in Quinn's voice and snapped his head around to gaze into his face.

"Why?"

Gundin, who had watched the entire exchange, snorted and answered the boy.

"Because that's when the lions of the plain hunt. They're so big that they tower over an Ebonite warhorse."

"Lions," the boy gulped. He spun his head about in search of the predators. "Where are they now?"

"Asleep," Quinn answered while giving Gundin a reprimanding look.

"In caves," Phinnton asked in a small voice as his eyes, unable to stop roaming the plains, wondered if the swaying grass was caused by the wind or by prowling lions.

Gundin opened his mouth to answer but Quinn's angry eyes made him hold his tongue.

"No," Quinn answered in a calm tone. "They sleep beneath the trees. Perhaps over there," Quinn pointed to a lone tree on the horizon. "Or beneath those," he turned Phinnton's attention toward a thicket a good distance off.

Bruun walked up and placed his hand upon his son's shoulders.

"Now is the time to be brave," he encouraged.

Phinnton nodded his head and gripped the box as if it would protect him should a large cat lunge.

"I have the tulip and the stories from the Only to give me strength."

"Stories?" Gundin scoffed. "That's *impossible.* You cannot read and the stories were banned before you were born, so where would you have heard stories?"

Phinnton looked at his father for permission to explain. Bruun nodded.

"My mother taught me," the boy answered.

Areall, moved by Phinnton's memory of his mother, knelt beside him.

"I believe you," she gently replied, "but you see, the very utterance of a word from one of the Only's stories would have been discovered by the Cauldron. Death would have found you, and us, long before this day."

Undeterred by her explanation, Phinnton continued.

"While everyone else was at the morning fire, my mother would tell me the stories."

"Child," Gundin scolded with hands planted on his hips. "Are you *that* ignorant? Did you *not* hear what Areall said? This is impossible. The Cauldron would have heard and killed you by now."

"Perhaps I can explain," Bruun interjected. "Phinnton's mother, Korvik, wove these tales with her native tongue."

The adults gave him a puzzled look.

Bruun explained.

"My wife was Ebonite by birth."

Daryess nodded as she joined Bruun's side.

"That explains many things," she said more to the group than to Bruun. "I only met her a few times, after all, you all lived like hermits, but I'll never forget her eyes and how dark and beautiful they were."

Bruun smiled as memories of Korvik sparked in his imagination. With a sigh, no doubt from missing her greatly, Bruun continued his story about Phinnton's childhood.

"Despite the Dark War, Korvik was always loyal to the King of Claire and turned her back on the Oracles and the Cauldron. Shunned by her family, and knowing her life was at risk, she fled Ebon and made her way to Tellendale, not too far from the Ebonite border, and found work in a tavern.

"Many summers later, I met her while I was out selling my goods. I know what you're thinking, that a taverness is not bride material, but I could sense she was different. Men in the tavern grappled over her, but she firmly resisted their attention. I, on the other hand, saw her inner strength as well as her outer beauty. I stayed in the tavern until the last drunk had staggered out, and then I asked her about her tale.

"I'll never forget how graceful she was as she approached my table. Her feet slid - no, floated - across the planks; her body swayed in time as if she danced to her own music; her dark eyes burned with fire and passion. She sat across the table from me. Our conversation came naturally, and lasted well into the evening. Needless to say, our courtship was swift and before first-frost covered the ground, we were married.

"Several summers later, Phinnton was born. When he was old enough for stories, Korvik knew the risk of telling him a tale from Claire, but she did not want him to grow up shackled by the Cauldron's Oracles. So she experimented.

When Phinnton was three summers of age, we slipped away from Hetherlinn and camped near the distant marker. There, she told him a short story mixed with Allsbruthian and Ebonite words. Her hope was that this would confuse the Cauldron from detecting our whereabouts. We waited for several days; every twig snap or gust of wind filled us with dread, but nothing ever came of it. Convinced we would not jeopardize anyone, we returned to Hetherlinn."

Bruun paused. A smile creased his face as he reflected on his love for Korvik.

"Perhaps you found us odd, living as hermits like we did, but we did so to protect you all as well as Phinnton. Korvik was the bravest person I've ever known."

"You *both* are very brave," Quinn added as he stood back up and pulled Areall close.

"Or very foolish," Gundin added under his breath.

Daryess elbowed her husband in the ribs.

Bruun's eyes narrowed and he glared at Gundin.

"As an Ebonite, Korvik knew that if the Cauldron succeeded in snuffing out the tales of Claire, all would be lost. She could not leave Phinnton without such hope. She was anything but *foolish.*"

Gundin took in Bruun's expression. Despite the man's age, Gundin saw fire in his eyes and reasoned that in his youth, Bruun was a formidable fighter. Gundin liked what he saw and gave an apologetic nod.

"I meant no disrespect to you or your goodwife," he recanted. "Please, forgive my words, and continue."

Bruun nodded, then let his gaze wander to the Gilden Plains.

"When Phinnton was five summers of age, Korvik became ill. I tried to convince her to stop telling him tales because I was convinced the Cauldron's fumes or the drone was somehow making her ill despite our secrecy. She refused; her love for Phinnton and the King of Claire were too great. So I promised to stay by her side, to do whatever I could to help, but it was painful to watch her waste away. It wasn't long until she was too weak to leave the bed. True to my word, I stayed by her side until she drew her last breath."

Bruun's emotions clouded his vision. Areall and Daryess placed reassuring hands on his shoulder.

"I remember that day," Daryess chimed in a soft voice. "I saw you and Phinnton leave in a wagon well before sunrise. All this time I thought you were taking produce to barter. Now, I realize you were sneaking away to bury your wife."

Tears welled up in the women's eyes as they felt his anguish and loss. Daryess covered her mouth with her hand.

"Why didn't you tell us," she sobbed. "We were your neighbors. We would have wanted to help."

Bruun gave her a pain-filled, yet sympathetic look.

"It was best for all if we stayed aloof. After all, she was Ebonite. How would the others, especially Mithe, respond to Phinnton after witnessing an Ebonite burial ceremony? For that matter, how would *you* have reacted, knowing a child with Ebonite blood lived in your midst? So I fabricated the story that a night patrol had carted her off and let others embellish the tale."

Daryess was at a loss for words. She turned her attention to Phinnton.

"I suppose you're right, Bruun. We would have behaved horribly. But now that Galadin and Elabea are gone...I see life much differently."

"It seems to me," Quinn cut in, "that it's time for young Phinnton to tell us one of these stories."

Phinnton flashed them a concerned look.

"But the Cauldron will hear if I speak in Allsbruthian."

Bruun's story had softened Gundin's gruffness, and he found himself admiring the family's tale.

"Phinnton, it makes no difference now," Gundin declared. "Soon, all of Ebon will be warring against us. Even now, our own children are battling forces meant for us, all because of our fear of the Oracles. So tell us a tale. I could use a good story before crossing this lion-infested wasteland."

Phinnton nodded and closed his eyes.

"Bluest of skies o'er Gilden's Plain,
Witness fair children fleeing Ebon's night,
Hark! Humble men, your steel doth rain!
Death begets life when mercy's champions fight."

Gundin's brow furrowed with confusion.

"That's not a story," he huffed as his tough demeanor quickly returned and trounced his sentimental feelings for the boy. "That's a riddle. How can there be blue skies at night? And how could it rain steel?"

Quinn, also thought the tale was of no use, but did not say so. Instead he ruffled Phinnton's hair.

"Well said, young Phinnton. Well said."

Something beneath the boy's scalp caught his attention, and Quinn used his fingers to part the lad's hair. There, as plain as day, was a purple birthmark. The blood drained from Quinn's face as he looked to Bruun for an explanation.

"Now you know the real reason we kept Phinnton isolated," Bruun confessed. "He's to be a storyteller."

The others gasped and looked at the boy with awe.

Phinnton, lost in thought as he tried to unravel the mystery to the tale he just told, was oblivious to their attention. He simply stared at the plains.

"My mother told me bedtime stories about the Gilden Plains. She even said that one day I'd get to see it for myself, and that my stories would help many, many people."

Before anyone could reply, they all noted movement on a distant knoll to the north.

"Ebonites," Phinnton asked.

Quinn shook his head. "No, they're too small; too conspicuous. From this distance, they almost look like..."

"Children," the women chimed.

"Perhaps from Hetherlinn," Daryess noted.

"Perhaps," Quinn agreed, "but where are their parents?"

Phinnton took a step away from the adults and looked up at the blue sky then out at the throng of children.

"My story," he said. "Mother told me that it was an old tale, and yet, here it is unfolding before our eyes. See the blue sky… and the children?"

"Foolery," Gundin bellowed. "I don't see *Ebon's night*, and I'm still bamboozled at how *rain* could be *steel*."

"Bruun," Quinn said with his eyes glued on the children crossing the plain. "Lead the others to Min Brock. Gundin and I will escort the children to the gates before the lions devour them. Avoid the trees. Make haste."

"I want to go with you," Phinnton pleaded. "I want to see how my story comes to pass."

"Not this time," Quinn replied. "You're the bearer of the tulip. I need you to help protect the others. Can you do that for me?'

Phinnton nodded.

Bruun led them away while Quinn and Gundin marched toward the children on the bluff.

Gundin called to the children and both men waved their arms in an attempt to get the children's attention. Oblivious to their efforts, the children continued walking single-file.

The two men quickened their pace and continued to call and wave. Eventually, one of the little ones heard them and pointed the men out to the others. Quinn and Gundin waved and all the children waved back.

When they were close enough, Gundin recognized the children as indeed being from Hetherlinn.

"The older girl is Mithe's granddaughter," Gundin noted.

"You're right," Quinn answered. "I recognize some of the others, too. Since they're without their parents, I have to assume the worst."

When they reached the crest, the children ran and gathered about the men. Emotions that had been bottled up since the demolith attack in Hetherlinn burst free. Some of the children began to cry and others whimpered, while a few of the older ones remained sullen and quiet.

"Children, listen to me," Quinn said as he did his best to console them. "Gundin and I are going to help you get to Min Brock. We'll be safe there. See," he said as he pointed out the castle. "It's not too far away, but we'll need to stay together and you'll have to do exactly what we tell you. Does everyone understand?"

All heads nodded.

From the corner of his eye, Quinn noticed that Gundin had his back to Min Brock and stared across the plain. Quinn turned to see what had captured his attention.

On the far horizon was a haze of dust. Above it was a small, black cloud.

"It's been many a summer," Gundin said beneath his breath so as to not alarm the children, "but I'd recognize that dust cloud anywhere."

"Ebonite cavalry, Quinn half-whispered. "But what do you make of the lone, dark cloud?"

Gundin shrugged.

"Perhaps a storm cloud from the Gilden Sea."

"Whatever it is," Quinn said, "they're both moving this way and fast." He glanced back in the direction of Min Brock and looked for Bruun. His eyes swept this way and that, and just as he was about to fear the worst, he spotted Bruun and Phinnton's head bobbing along just above the tall grass. Areall and Daryess followed close behind. Relieved they were all well past the trees and closer to Min Brock, Quinn pondered Phinnton's story.

"What was the other part of the boy's story," he asked Gundin.

"Some nonsense about Ebonite nights," Gundin spat.

Quinn returned his gaze to the approaching enemy.

"Look, Phinnton's story *is* unfolding before our very eyes. With that black cloud shadowing them, the Ebonites approach like the darkness of night."

"If you say so, but it's still light out, and it still doesn't explain any rain of steel."

By this time, the children had also noticed the horizon. When they spotted the black cloud, they became hysterical with fright. Even the older children, who tried to calm the others down, were unable to keep their eyes off the ominous cloud.

Quinn pulled Mithe's granddaughter aside.

"What has these children so spooked," he asked her.

She bit her lip, glanced up at the cloud and then back at Quinn.

"It looks like the same cloud that came to Hetherlinn." Horror filled her eyes as she relived the ordeal. "Man-dragons. Hideous creatures...they landed in the meadow, the trees, the rooftops...." She paused and drew in a deep breath before continuing. "Grandmother made me take the children and run to Min Brock." Tears rolled down her cheeks. "Even when we were far away, we could hear them scream."

Her face wrinkled with anguish and she buried her face in Quinn's tunic. Quinn pulled her close and held her as she wept. Gundin, who had overheard the conversation, waved his arms to settle the children down.

"Children, listen to me," he bellowed.

His strong voice snapped them out of their panic, and although some still whimpered, they gave Gundin their undivided attention.

"Quinn and I will stay here and hold them off while you run to Min Brock. No matter what, don't look back and don't stop. Now hurry!"

He gave one of the older boys a push, and the group scampered off toward the lone citadel.

Quinn opened his arms and released Mithe's granddaughter, who ran to catch up to the others.

"Nice speech," Quinn said. "Now tell me how two defenseless men will fight a cavalry and these flying monsters?"

Gundin puffed out his chest and his eyes narrowed.

"I don't know."

They turned their attention to the enemy.

"But this much I do know," Gundin added. "If we don't detain them even a little, then no one has a chance of surviving. No one."

Quinn nodded in agreement and an idea, albeit risky, came to mind.

"The lions," he offered as he turned to face the Addoli Ridge.

Gundin's eyes narrowed.

"What do you have in mind?"

"Do you see the grove of trees near the base of the ridge," Quinn said as he pointed to the copse. "Certainly there's a pride sleeping in the shade. With the wind blowing our scent in that direction, we'll lead the Ebonites to the lions."

"So, you're great plan is to run *toward* the lions."

Quinn looked Gundin in the eyes.

"Well, when you put it like that, it does sound silly," Quinn quipped. "Actually, we may have to run *through* the lions to wake them up enough so they will attack the cavalry."

"And what if they decide to kill us instead?"

Quinn shrugged.

"I'm open to suggestions."

Gundin checked on the advancement of the Ebonites. The cloud was still a good ways off, but even from such a distance, they could see the outline of wings and the man-dragons' terrifying features. They now understood why the children were so frightened.

"Well, they're too close now to try and figure anything else out," Gundin said with a heavy sigh. "Let's just hope that today, the lions choose to fight for Allsbruth."

They turned and raced down the knoll toward the trees. The waist-high grass slowed their pace, and after a lengthy sprint, both men were near exhaustion.

"We'll never make it," Gundin gasped as sweat beaded on his forehead.

"We have to," Quinn fired through clinched teeth.

They pushed themselves harder. Limbs pumped. Lungs sucking in hot air. Quinn glanced over his shoulder.

"They've taken the bait," he wheezed. "The cavalry and even the man-dragons are following us and not the children."

The men focused on the stand of trees, and hoped the lions were there, and not in the grass surrounding them.

"The lions could be hiding anywhere," Gundin huffed as he gasped for air.

Shrieks came from overhead.

"The man-dragons," Quinn noted. "Keep going!"

Quick strides brought them closer to the grove. Sweat rolled off their faces as their legs sliced through the tall grass. Snorts and clinking armor announced the cavalry's arrival.

"We're almost there," Quinn encouraged between gasps of air.

An Ebonite command sounded from behind them.

Quinn and Gundin, desperate to reach the trees before the cavalry crushed them to death, pumped their arms, urging each other on.

Up ahead and in between the swaying grass, they saw what looked like a ball of dark brown grass rise up from the ground. Gundin and Quinn flashed each other a concerned look. During the Dark War, they had seen the lions from their high vantage point of Min Brock. They could tell they were large animals, and if their rumbles and roars were any indicators, they knew they were ferocious killers as well. Now, they were charging like madmen straight into the heart of the pride.

Quinn clinched his teeth while Gundin shouted the battle cry of Allsbruth.

More puffs of brown lifted from the ground.

A deep rumble washed over Quinn and Gundin and even cut through the cavalry's clamor and the man-dragons' shrieks. The sound grew in volume and unearthed Quinn and Gundin's deepest fears. Between shafts of swaying grass, they caught the first real glimpse of the predators.

Yellow primal eyes glared at them. Next came the roar. It was deafening. From crouched positions, the lions launched themselves through the air. The attack was so swift, that Quinn and Gundin only had time to react by diving to the ground. As if in a dream, they watched the colossal predators sail over them with paws extended. The two comrades rolled onto their backs as the lions landed on the Ebonite cavalry.

Claws swiped deep gashes into Ebonite armor and flesh alike. Horses bucked. Riders fell. Razor-sharp teeth ripped open flesh. Roars and low-sounding guttural noises drowned out the warriors' screams and the warhorses' whinnies.

Gundin and Quinn rose to their knees, scanned the grasses to avoid any other lions and then darted away from the feeding frenzy.

The demoliths spied them in the open and dove to attack.

The duo, alerted by the demoliths' screeches, glanced up into the man-dragons' faces. Heat enveloped Quinn and Gundin; their faces felt sunburned. As the horde got closer the heat increased, as did the burning pain. The duo shielded their heads from the invisible fire and resigned themselves to their fate.

A sword, as if hurled from the sky by an angry god, drove tip first into the ground near where they stood. Stunned, Gundin and Quinn stared at the blade that still quivered from its impact. A javelin slammed point first into the ground behind them. Another sword slammed into the ground in front of them, then another and another.

Like rain the steel fell from the sky as countless swords, spears, battle axes, daggers and javelins struck the plain. Awestruck, Quinn and Gundin scanned the sky to find the source of the weapons. Seven dark silhouettes soared toward the diving demoliths.

"Dragons," Gundin exclaimed.

"The rain of steel," Quinn whispered, as he eyed the weapons scattered across the ground.

As one of the silhouettes soared above the demoliths, a flick of its talon opened a large metal carrier attached to his underside. Out tumbled a multitude of swords and spears that fell tip-first, striking the unwary demoliths as they flew. Some were killed instantly and crashed to the ground with a loud *thud.* Others were wounded and shrieked in pain as they spiraled down and landed in the grasses.

The surviving demoliths turned into the attack, but they were no match for the onslaught of the seven. A fireball that exploded out of the mouth of one of the shapes incinerated a host of the man-dragons. The few that remained beat a hasty retreat, but the dark shapes gave chase, and the fate of the demoliths was sealed.

An injured demolith wobbled to his feet and yanked out the spear jutting through his shoulder. Tossing it aside, he withdrew his blade and staggered toward Quinn and Gundin.

Gundin ran to a two-handed sword stuck in the ground, jerked it free, and faced the man-dragon. The demolith swung first but Gundin parried the attack. While their blades were pressed tight, the demolith glared into Gundin's eyes. Heat like a furnace blast burned Gundin's face. Gundin slammed his knee into the demolith's midsection, sending it toppling to the ground. With the heat wave gone, Gundin shook his head in an effort to alleviate the pain and readied himself for another attack.

The demolith recovered and pushed itself back to its feet. It swung its sword high overhead and charged. Gundin met the demolith's blow with a counter-thrust that caused sparks to fly as steel met steel.

The demolith trained his fiery gaze on Gundin, but Gundin turned his face away to avoid being blinded.

"No more," Gundin shouted between clinched teeth as he continued to press forward. "No more night raids. No more restrictions."

Gundin could smell his singed hair. Sweat rolled into his eyes and stung. He raised his arm, and using it like a shield, hid his face behind his shoulder as he advanced.

"No more Oracles. No more threats to our children."

Astonished by Gundin's persistence and ability to withstand pain, the demolith abandoned its fire-gaze and brought his blade back for the kill stroke. Gundin felt the heat die, lowered his shoulder and faced his attacker. When the demolith's sword came crashing toward him, Gundin heaved his weapon upward. The blow knocked the demolith's sword out of his grip; it sailed end-over-end and disappeared in the grass.

Disarmed, the man-dragon unleashed his invisible fire but this time Gundin was ready. He swung his double-handed sword and sliced the demolith's face, right across its eyes.

The demolith screamed and covered his bloodied face with his reptilian-fleshy hands.

"Where is my son," Gundin demanded as his chest heaved and his fingers tightened about the sword's hilt.

The demolith staggered backwards with hands clutching blind eyes. He flapped his wings in an attempt to fly, but his wounded shoulder only allowed him to hover and hop, hover and hop.

"Answer me," Gundin demanded. "Where is Galadin?"

The man-dragon lowered his hands. A bloody stripe marked where his eyes had been.

"You're not worth my breath," the man-dragon hissed.

Gundin brought his blade back over his head, and with a loud grunt, swung it down as hard as he could. The demolith cried out in pain as his good wing—severed by the blow—plopped to the ground.

"Last time," Gundin spat. "Where is my *son*."

A feral smile crossed the demolith's partially scaled face.

"Dead," he answered with a snicker. "Fish fodder. Whimpered for his mommy as he drowned."

Gundin's fury erupted.

His steel split the man-dragon in two.

Gundin heard footsteps approaching from behind. He spun around, sword ready to attack, and came face to face with Quinn. His comrade also carried a bloodied sword and a weary smile. Together, they took in the battlefield.

Bloodied Ebonite corpses and warhorses littered the brown grass. Demoliths, dead or mortally wounded, lay scattered about, easy prey for the lions of the plains. That thought raised a question in Gundin's mind.

"Where are the lions," he asked.

The men stood back-to-back with swords gripped in front of them should the predators attack. They peered into the swaying grasses and flickering shadows of the nearby thicket for any sign of the beasts' yellow eyes and dark manes that fluttered like brown fire.

"They're gone," came a metallic voice.

Gundin and Quinn turned to see who had spoken. Walking toward them, with a spring in his steps, was an odd looking man. He wore a silver helmet with large alabaster lenses and a long leather jacket that fell past his knees.

More frightening than this unexpected, and oddly-attired man, were the seven dragons resting on the ground nearby. Their glossy eyes watched this fellow's every move, but they could tell those eyes watched them as well. Quinn and Gundin remained perfectly still, so as not to provoke the creatures.

The stranger continued his approach and his explanation.

"We saw the pride wander off long before we landed."

His voice pinged about inside his helmet and colored it with a metallic echo.

Wary of the stranger's intent, Quinn and Gundin tightened their fingers around their swords. The seven dragons, sensing an attack from the duo, flicked their tales about in the tall grass, and within the black orbs of their eyes, the two men spotted what appeared to be yellow flames.

The stranger, who immediately sensed the tension, stopped his advance and started to pull at his helmet.

"Quinn, have I been gone so long that you don't recognize your own brother?"

"Linwith?" Gundin blurted in surprise as his sword arm swung down by his side.

Linwith!" Quinn trumpeted. Excited and surprised to see him, Quinn charged through the grass and grabbed his brother by the shoulders. His eyes ran up and over him. "So *you* were the pilot?"

He was astonished to think that his timid brother would have even attempted such a feat.

Linwith merely smiled.

Quinn's mind was full of questions.

"When...how did this...what are these...?" he stammered.

"It's complicated," Linwith said with a quick shrug.

Quinn chuckled and squeezed Linwith's shoulders, delighted to not only see his brother alive, but to see him come into his own.

"Well then," Quinn said as his eyes darted to the weapons sticking out of the ground and then to the worms, "one question at a time. How did you purchase all these weapons with just our produce? How did you know where to find us? Do these seven creatures obey your..."

"Quinn," Linwith interrupted, "There will be time to answer all your questions, and I long to tell you the stories of my adventure, but not at dusk out here on the plains. There are lions on the Gilden Plains, and they prowl at night. Or hadn't you heard?"

Gundin joined Quinn's side.

"You must at least tell us how you made the weapons fall like rain."

"They were stored within my worms' carriers. See?" he pointed to the worm's underbellies where a portion of the silver containers could be seen. "It took quite a bit of practice with my worms, but eventually, I learned not only how to unlatch them in flight, but how to hit my target."

"Worms? You call these magnificent creatures worms?" Gundin huffed as he took in the colossal animals. "Any fool can see they're dragons!"

The worms glared at Gundin and the fires within their indigo orbs glowed red. The Worm King's blue tail glowed and he took a few menacing steps toward the trio. His gaze was centered on Gundin.

"Is the *fat* one always this arrogant," he asked Linwith.

Gundin's eyes bulged.

"Talking dragons? How can this be? There is no such thing as a talking dragon."

"Gundin," Linwith whispered, "don't call him a *dragon*, and trying to argue with him will only..."

Gundin snorted.

"I'll call him a *dragon* if I want to call him a dragon, and he needs to know that this," Gundin patted his large belly, "is solid muscle."

The worm's sapphire tail twitched and flicked about in the tall grass while his black eyes pulsed with fiery light. Linwith, seeing his worm's hostility growing, quickly stepped between Gundin and his Worm King.

"Let me give you a fair warning," Linwith declared with more authority than Gundin had ever heard in his voice before. "These are the mighty Worms of Bal-Malin. They take great pride in their heritage, their cultural sophistication and in their ability to communicate with us. So in the future, refrain from calling them..."

Before Linwith could whisper *dragon*, the Worm King arched his long neck upward and let out a loud, short bark that echoed across the valley. This sparked his brothers who also blurted thunderous howls.

Gundin shuddered with fright, but did his best to hide the fact from Quinn and Linwith.

"Worms...indeed. They're nothing but sky-mules."

"Well," Quinn said as he swatted Gundin's back "those sky-mules saved our lives."

"If you say so. It was obvious to all that our alliance with the lions was successful. In fact, we had everything under control."

"As you can see," Quinn said to Linwith with a twinkle in his eye, "Gundin hasn't changed much since your departure."

"I don't know about that," Linwith answered as he eyed Gundin's sour expression. "His lapses into senility seem to have dissipated and his size," Linwith lowered his eyes to Gundin's bulging mid-section, "appears to have doubled."

The brothers laughed as Gundin huffed and walked away.

"While you two chit chat like women," he flung over his shoulder, "I'll do something useful, like gather up these weapons."

As Gundin stomped off, Quinn studied Linwith. Beyond the odd attire that was obviously required for flying with his worms, Linwith looked different. Quinn noticed it when he marched across the field. His gait was sure-footed, confident and purposeful, as if he knew where his life was going and was eager to keep pace with it. His countenance almost glowed and he seemed taller. He walked with his back straight, shoulders pulled back and head held high. Even his voice resonated with fresh passion. He sounded new, alive.

"With your permission," Linwith said, snapping Quinn out of his introspection. "I'd like to fly to Waelryth."

"Why?"

"With my worms, we can block the entrance."

"How," Quinn asked, intrigued by such a tactic.

"Simple. The worms will gather huge rocks with their talons then hurl them into the cliffs. If we can start an avalanche, we can seal the entrance and buy some time to prepare for war."

Quinn's smile widened and he nodded in agreement.

"Yes, that's an excellent suggestion."

"Upon my return, we'll help rebuild Min Brock. As it is, it can scarcely stop the wind, let alone an assault by Ebon."

By this time, Gundin had gathered all the swords and spears he could safely carry, and returned to where Linwith and Quinn stood.

"Did you hear all of Linwith's ideas," Quinn asked Gundin as he draped a proud arm over his brother's shoulder. "He's come up with exceptional plans that involve his worms: sealing off Waelryth; helping us rebuild Min Brock. What would have taken us countless summers to do we can accomplish in no time at all."

"Barring any unforeseen incidents," Linwith added in a calm, confident voice, "although it will probably be more like weeks than days."

Gundin gave a simple nod, not to acknowledge the worms' powers, but because such expedient measures meant they would be better prepared for war. Gundin turned away from the worms and looked Linwith up and down.

"It seems you've thought of everything."

"Not everything," Linwith replied.

He knew Gundin well and sensed the man's jealousy at his new powers as Worm Master. Instead of showing off his worms' capabilities, which he feared would only humiliate Gundin, Linwith opted to encourage the man.

"We can't train men for combat, or man the towers and walls, or devise battle strategies. That, my friend, is your expertise."

Gundin scrunched his lips up, nibbled on Linwith's advice and nodded to his important role.

"But first," Linwith added, "I'll need your help in loading all the weapons back into the carriers. I'll then fly them to Min Brock and unload the carriers and weapons inside. After that, I'll leave immediately for Waelryth."

The men went to work, eager to secure their arsenal and depart from the lion infested grasses. Once the last spear was secured and all the hatches locked in place, Linwith started to don his helmet.

"May I offer you two a ride to Min Brock?"

Quinn and Gundin stared thunderstruck at each other.

Linwith stopped putting on his helmet and smirked.

"Don't tell me that the great Gundin and the mighty Quinn are afraid to fly?"

"Afraid?" Gundin roared. "I fear no man or no *thing*, and I especially don't fear..." he stared at the Worms of Bal-Malin and still refused to call them by their proper name, "whatever *these* creatures are. I simply desire to cross on foot...to reacquaint myself...with the lay of the land, as it were. Yes, that's the reason. Reconnaissance. For the sake of strategy."

Linwith chuckled to himself.

"Quinn, what about you?"

Quinn sized up the worms, pictured himself riding atop while they soared, and then gave a wag of his head.

"Brother, if I was meant to fly, I would have sprouted wings by now."

"Very well. But stay to this side of the Addoli Ridge. I spied more lions sleeping beneath the trees in that area. The last thing I need after rescuing you two, is to discover your carcasses beneath the paws of lions."

Linwith lowered his helmet and jogged to his worms. He grabbed the leather loop that dangled from his saddle and pulled himself up into the saddle of the Worm King.

Wings beat the air, stirring up dust clouds on the Gilden Plains. In unison, all seven worms took to the air and rose into the sky.

Linwith circled and gave them an enthusiastic wave. Quinn returned the good-bye, while Gundin planted his hands on his hips.

"Worms," Gundin huffed as he watched them fly toward Min Brock. "I don't see any difference. If you've seen one dragon, you've seen them all. I'm not sure I like the new Linwith: a bit arrogant, if you ask me. Saving us, *indeed.* He simply supplied us the means with which to destroy those man-dragons ourselves."

"Perhaps," Quinn replied as he admired his brother's flight and the worms marking the darkening sky with tails that glowed sapphire, emerald, ruby, pearl, amber, mandarin and gold. "But he did fulfill Phinnton's story, and had he not come when he did, we'd be dead."

"Nonsense," Gundin snapped. "We could have destroyed them. I'm confident of that."

"With what, your large muscles," Quinn joked as he poked Gundin in the belly.

"Yes, muscle," Gundin confirmed with a grimace and a pat on his tummy. "Solid muscle."

"Let's go," Quinn snickered as he headed toward Min Brock. "The sun is low and the lions grow hungry."

Gundin stared down at his midsection. "Quinn, this *is* muscle."

Quinn waved a rubbery hand as if to surrender to his banter.

"Did you hear me?" Gundin called as he ran to catch up.

With swords in hand, they marched toward the citadel that long ago had sealed their lives in shame. As they pressed through the tall grass, both sensed a stirring, a feeling that neither had felt since that fateful battle during the Dark War.

Hope.

GLOSSARY

Characters

Anessatia: Lassiter's mother; grand-daughter of King Culdean.

Areall: Elabea's mother; married to Quinn.

Brairtok: Lord/king of Ebon.

Bruun: Phinnton's father.

Council: Dark lords of the Cauldron; seers and overseers of Ebon's power.

Culdean: King Simeion's oldest son; heir to the throne.

Daryess: Galadin's mother; married to Gundin.

DeMorley: Minstrel who joins Newcomb and Lassiter to Claire.

Digri: Jolly, short chef of MerriNoon.

Draemel: Bounty hunter in pursuit of DeMorley.

Elabea: Journeys to Claire with Galadin.

Ela Claire: Elabae's new name as a storyteller; given to her by the King of Claire.

Farron: Draemel's son.

Friarlinn: King Simeion's youngest son; murders his brother to become king.

Galadin: Elabea's friend; superb huntsman; assists her on her trek to Claire. Becomes Romlin.

Gor King: Paradin after making an alliance with the Cauldron and a vul jen.

Gundin: Great warrior; father of Galadin; married to Daryess.

Hinnmith: Ebonite commander.

Hornlynn: Lassiter's father; married to Anessatia; died in the Dark War.

Il-Lilliad: One of the last storytellers; survived the March of Reeds massacre.

King Cameare: Sovereign of Sri Brune; Kinmin's father.

King of Claire: Enigmatic ruler of Claire; also known as the Only.

King Simeion: Once great king of Allsbruth.

Kinmin: Tiny, dark skinned SriBrunian; escorts Il-Lilliad to SriBrune.

Kundle: Ebonite Commander; defeated at Thornnblen.

Korvik: Phinnton's mother; Ebonite by birth.

Lassiter: Hornlynn and Anessatia's son; mentored by Newcomb.

Linwith: Quinn's older brother; See "Worm Master."

Manno Vox: One of the Only's mighty warriors.

Merriam: Draemel's wife; lives in Hoitt.

Mithe: Old widow of Hetherlinn.

Newcomb: Lassiter's mentor; storyteller.

Paradin: Draemel's partner.

Phinnton: Hetherlinn boy; mother sang about the *Singing Stones of Addoli*. Future storyteller.

Queen Riaa: queen of Sri Brune; Kinmin's mother.

Quinn: Great leader of Allsbruth; Elabea's father; married to Areall.

Romlin: Galadin's new name given to him by Manno Vox.

Rittmar: Bee-like creature; chancellor for the nation of Bal-Malin.

TyNorai: Chancellor of Aggellon; former storyteller of the Only.

Countries, Places & Cities

Addoli Ridge: Mountain separating the Gilden Sea from the Gilden Plains.

Aggellon: A timeless nation in the Onderling.

Allsbruth: Beautiful, tranquil land; home of Elabea/Galadin.

Bal-Malin: Island nation inhabited by insect-like creatures and worms.

Blomseth: village where Lassiter performs as a minstrel.

Caace: veil/portal from Sri Brune into the upper world.

Cauldron: Perpetual fires of Ebon; housed in the citadel of Netniath.

Cave of Freers: Lair of the four vul jens; located in mountains of Ebon.

Claire: Nation reportedly destroyed in the Dark War; home to storytellers.

Cor len Bluun: "Pools of tear" in Claire.

Correll: river that flows from Karajan into Sri Brune.

DioBaith: stone monolith beyond the veil; scene of Romlin's fall into the River Arrgient.

Ebon: Victors of the Dark War.

Ferra: Nation due east of Allsbruth; Torrens Bay is on its southern coast.

Gilden Plains: Enormous grassy plain; home to Min Brock.

Gilden Sea: Northern sea where the island of Bal-Malin is located.

Hetherlinn: Village in Allsbruth; home to Elabea and Galadin.

Hoitt: Fishing village in Ingloid; Draemel's home.

Ingloid: Nation east of the Gilden Plains.

Isle of Lills: Island in the Sea of Illsbruth; Lassiter was mentored by Newcomb.

Isle of Rythe: "Island of the cursed" off the east coast of Ebon; where Ela Claire is to journey to retrieve stolen treasures.

Karajan: cavernous lake that guards entrance into Sri Brune.

Kiarrey Glen: meadow in Claire where Romlin meets the King of Claire.

Kise: Capital city of Ebon; home to the Cauldron.

Marsien Vur: Fortress of the King of Claire.

MerriNoons: Digri's country; noted as excellent chefs.

Min Brock: Once great citadel of Allsbruth; turning point in the Dark War.

Netniath: Citadel for the Cauldron; located in the city of Kise.

Norrburn: village near the Gilden Sea; location Lassiter learns of the Martyr's Moon.

Onderling: Underground world; home to Aggellon and SriBrune.

Pillar of Addoli: Monolith beside the Addoli Ridge.

River Arrgient: Main tributary west of the Gilden Plains.

Torrens Bay: Southern port town of Ferra; exciting yet corrupt.

Thornnblen: beach where Ela Claire defeats Ebonites.

Tristan: Nation noted for mining ore and forging weapons.

Sea of Illsbruth: Southern sea; home to karshe and the Isle of Lills.

SriBrune: Kinmin's homeland; located within the Onderling.

Valley of Clouds: Near Waelryth; home to ryators.

Vorak: Brairtok's castle in Kise.

Waelryth: Passage created by the Cauldron to invade Allsbruth.

Worm Master: Linwith's new title; rules over the seven worms of Bal-Malin.

Creatures

Bangaleers: Crab-like creatures of Waelryth; latch upon their victim's face.

Bar-Treb: Romlin's steed from Claire.

Fea dracas: "Little dragons" that live in the hollow of trees.

Fingals: tiny, shiny creatures in the Onderling; noted for not being very intelligent creatures.

Dansel lors: large predators that live in Karajan.

Demoliths: *man-dragons* of Ebon. Created by vul jens entering the dreamworlds of Ebonite warriors.

Draiggs: round, flat creatures that guard Cor len Bluun.

Gors: Large, hairy scavengers.

Karshe: Silver-plated dragons in the Sea of Illsbruth.

Kodars: Massive Ebonite animals used to transport troops.

La-zeer: Predator from the Gilden Sea.

Previn: Ela Claire's harrier; formerly her rusk.

Rusk: Small animal that defends storytellers; very poisonous tail.

Ryators: Giant, translucent dragons that live in the Valley of Clouds.
Sevritt: Large, swift Ebonite tracker.
Vul jen: Large, dark, dreamstalker; favorite prey is storytellers.
Worms: Mysterious creatures that live on Bal-Malin.
Worm King: the sapphire worm from Bal-Malin.

www.ingramcontent.com/pod-product-compliance
Lightning Source LLC
Chambersburg PA
CBHW070043120726
47909CB00002B/276